# Behind

## Nicolette Rose

To Aunt Pat,
Thanks for believing
in me, and thanks
for your love.
~Nicolette ♡

*This book is dedicated to my sisters, especially my friend Jamie, who read my short story and encouraged me not only to publish this novel but also to follow my dreams and be the best woman I can be.*

The author has provided this e-book to you for your personal use only. You may not make this e-book publicly available in any way. **Copyright infringement is against the law. If you believe this copy infringes on the author's copyright, please notify the author at: authornrose@gmail.com.**

*Prologue – The Break Up*

Eric dodges the five-hundred dollar vase I throw at his head in hurt and anger.

"What is wrong with you, Madeline?!" He yells.

"What's wrong with me?! You break up with me out of nowhere and you're asking what's wrong with me!" I'm so mad that I can hardly breathe.

"Fuck you, Eric! Who is she? That blonde chick you say is your best friend?!" I yell.

"I'm not dating anyone else! I'm just telling you I can't juggle a relationship and this job at the same time."

"Bullshit!" I snatch up my purse and keys and run out of his townhouse. I hop into the car and speed off before I start to break down in tears. I pull into the Lenox Mall parking lot and sob into my steering wheel. This man did everything to make me think he was going to marry me and then he drops a bomb like this. I shouldn't be surprised. He had been spending less and less time with me. He hasn't even made love to me in a month. I thought he was just busy at work and he was probably screwing that blonde bitch the entire time. I frantically search for the pack of cigarettes I hid in my car just in case. I find the pack and anxiously light it up choking myself in the process.

"Ma'am? Is everything okay?" I hear a male voice say in my window. Damn, it's a cop.

"I'm...fine...I just need a moment" I tell him. He hesitates but finally walks off leaving me to my madness. I finish my cigarette and drive to the liquor store. I browse until I finally decide on a bottle of vodka.

"The hard stuff, huh? Tough day?" asks the cashier who usually sees me buying wine.

"You have no idea" I say. I speed towards my condo, grab my bottle and cigarettes so that I can rush to the elevator. I drop my things on the floor and pour a shot of vodka. I throw it back feeling the intense burn in my throat. I take one shot after another until I'm drunk and numb. Thank God he had the sense to break up with me on a Friday so I would have the weekend to process it. I mix myself a screwdriver and sit on my couch. I can't cry and I can't scream. All I can do is stare into space. I stumble onto my balcony to smoke and think about how my life seems to be crumbling.

Six months ago, we were a happy couple and then things changed. I thought he was starting to get bored with me. I tried different things…taking him out or exploring new things in bed but it didn't seem to help. I take a final puff before I realize that I'm drunk as hell and should go to bed. I stumble back into the house and manage to sloppily tie up my hair before I get into bed. I can't sleep for anything. I toss and turn wondering if Eric really did go behind my back with that girl…Leslie is her name and I always thought she was a little too flirtatious.

Well, forget him. I hope they have a happy life together. I'm tired of searching and I'm tired of being hurt. It always seems like I'm the headliner for someone else's happily ever after. It's okay, I don't need a man to validate me. I will just work my way up the ladder at my company and be as successful as I can. This relationship stuff is for the birds and impossible dreamers. I'll just focus on myself and forget about a finding a good man. After all, a relationship doesn't guarantee happiness…does it?

*A Risky Bid*

"Are you crazy?!" My dad exclaims looking over the paperwork I've given him.

"Dad, I know it's risky...but Ryan and I have the money..."

"The economy is shit right now! Why in the hell do you want to take on a failing company?"

"Because I know I can bring it back..." He sits back in his chair and drains the glass of scotch in his hand.

"This is incredibly stupid" he sighs, slamming the glass down on the table.

"Phil..."my mom takes his hand in hers.

"I'm telling the truth, Cynthia..."

"I know, but honey, if he wants to buy the company...let him. We know he doesn't get along with his bosses." She gives him the look that all mothers give their husbands when trying to defend the kids. My dad softens, never able to resist her.

"Do you really want to do this, son?" I nod.

"Then I will handle your bidding. I don't trust those two bit lawyers at Livingston." My grin is a mile wide.

"You don't know how much this means to me, Pops." He shakes his head.

"I still think you're stupid, but your mom is right. I know that you need to be your own boss. I'm sure Cooper and Harris will be sad to see you go if you win the bid."

"I suppose...but they trained me to take over for them one day. They know better than to assume I'd wait until they retired. My dad laughs loudly.

"You've got that right." My mom smiles and gets up to refill his glass.

"Do you want more, amore?" She asks me.

"Yes, thank you." She pours a generous amount of the amber liquid in my glass. Taking her place beside my father, she looks at me lovingly.

"Honey, maybe once you get this company, you'll think about your life in other areas?" I knew this was coming.

"Mom…"

"I'm just saying, bambino, you're thirty-five. Mama needs little grand bambinos." I scoff.

"You'd have to make him give up being bachelor of the year, baby." My dad pulls my mom close.

"I'll….see what I can do." A satisfied smile crosses her face. At least that'll make her happy…for now. Considering she was supporting my efforts to buy this company, I'll do my best to spare her feelings. I can't ever see myself falling in love much less having kids. Maybe she knows something I don't.

*Chapter 1 – When Will I Move On?*

"I have got to get out more," I sigh as I look at the mound of paperwork on my desk.

I never thought that at the age of 29, I would be a workaholic. Yet here I am, at the office on a Friday night, doing work that's not due for another month. Of course, if I went home, it would be nothing but another lonely night. I guess this is somewhat better. I am Madeline Davis, CFO of PharmaCO, and, if I may say so myself, I'm damn good at this job. At first glance, people might think that I may just be your average run of the mill Atlanta woman. Standing at no more than 5'2, armed with a pair of double "d" breasts and curves that speak to my heritage, I usually have no trouble getting noticed. However, with a CPA and MBA in International Business from one of the best universities in the state, I could easily tear an executive to shreds. Hired at 24, I quickly climbed up the ladder to receive the top promotion for my work with the responsibility of one of the most important company mergers in the medical technology industry.

"Madeline, if you don't need anything else, I'll be going now," chirps my assistant Lacy, pulling me out of my thoughts. She flips her long brown hair out of her face and retrieves her jacket from the nearby closet. Lacy has been by my side since the promotion and is a damn fine assistant. I couldn't ask for someone better to handle my affairs.

"Thanks Lacy, have a great weekend." I say leaning back in my leather office chair.

"Madeline, not that it's any of my business, but you don't have any plans tonight?" she asks timidly while fumbling for her keys.

"Please, when do I have time to go out? With this merger coming up, I'm buried in paperwork" I say, knowing damn well I finished that paperwork weeks ago. She scoffs.

"Madeline, you're a beautiful, sweet woman. I don't understand why you refuse to socialize. You're welcome to come out with my friends and me anytime you want. Do not stay late tonight; you are more than ahead on your work." Her voice lowers in a warning tone. Damn, she read my mind.

"I'll have to take you up on that sometime, Lacy. Thanks for staying late today."

"No problem, Madeline, anything for my favorite executive!" She declares with a warm smile.

"Good night, Lacy," I sigh.

"Good night, Madeline!" she speaks cheerfully as she turns to head out of my office.

Around eight, I decide it's time to call it quits. My eyes will never forgive me if I look at the computer any longer. I grab my purse and jacket, brush my hair back and head towards the elevator. As I make my way, I see John, the security guard walking around the office.

"Another late one, eh Ms. Davis?" he says with an infectious smile.

"Yes, John. Sometimes I wonder if I just need to live here." I chuckle. He laughs a hearty laugh and types the code into the elevator key pad for me.

"Have a great weekend, Ms. Davis," he tips his hat as the elevator closes. I give him a friendly wave and smile as he disappears behind the elevator doors.

I head to my blue BMW X3 and slide in the driver's seat. I look at the time and decide to swing by the liquor store to grab a bottle of wine. Suddenly, my phone rings, startling me. I press the button on my steering wheel that connects to my phone.

"Hello?" I answer.

"Hey, baby!" I hear a cheerful tone come from the speakers. It's Nathan, my best friend, obviously wanting me to accompany him in one of his bar hopping episodes.

"Hey, sweetie," I say with affection, "What's up?"

"Well, I was wondering if you wanted to come to Bailey's with me" he inquires with caution. I know I've been standing him up lately and suddenly feel guilty.

"What time?" I ask, "I'm just leaving the office."

"Can you be ready in an hour? I'll swing by and pick you up!" I can tell he's excited. Getting Madeline Davis to go out somewhere is like trying to pull a lion's teeth while he's awake.

"Sure," I say as I speed down I-85 towards my condo. I don't really want to go, but I can't face another night at home with a bottle of wine, sad love songs and lame pay-per-view movies.

I swipe my key card at the door which gives my identity to the pouty blonde sitting at the concierge desk.

"Greetings, Ms. Davis." She murmurs dryly.

"Good evening," I half ignore her. I warily step into the elevator and push the penthouse button. Once I arrive on the 25th floor, I unlock my door. Pricilla, my Golden Retriever, greets me with a barking, tail-wagging enthusiasm. I give her a loving pet and note that the maid service and dog walker have been there. Looking at my watch, I dash into the shower but not before I click a remote that controls my iPad. The sweet music of Frank Sinatra comes on as I turn on the warm water. My versatile taste in music and ability to enjoy different genres has always been my way into any social scene from college into my adult life. I linger in the steamy atmosphere, thankful for a moment of peace.

As Frank Sinatra sings about the second time around, I look through my closet and choose some dark wash jeans and a purple sweater that hangs off my shoulders. I browse through my hundred pairs of shoes for a pair of black stilettos and slide them effortlessly on my feet. As I'm putting the finishing touches of my makeup on, my phone rings again and I'm pretty sure it's Nathan. I give my hair one final brush and check myself in the mirror. I hop into the elevator and venture to the lobby just in time to see Nathan. His lean, muscular frame, dark brown eyes and tanned skin remind me of the reason why heads turn whenever he enters the scene. Wearing jeans, a tight white t-shirt and black leather jacket only accentuate his handsome features more. He'd totally be a ladies man…if he weren't gay.

"Girl, I haven't seen you in ages!" he yells as he embraces me.

"I know; I've been so busy. I'm sorry I've been a bad friend." I say while my eyes ask forgiveness.

"No worries, honey, I've actually been quite busy myself." Nathan works for one of the largest law firms in Atlanta and recently settled a huge lawsuit for the city employees.

"You look fabulous," he utters softly.

"So do you, dear," I whisper with a shy smile, "shall we go party?"

"Let's go! I can't wait to show you my new car!" he grabs my hand and leads me out of the lobby doors. Nathan has outdone himself. On the curb sits a brand new black Maserati. He looks like a schoolboy as he jumps to the passenger side to open my door.

"Nice!" I exclaim admiring the beautiful machine.

"I know," He grins.

Soon, we are speeding down the streets of midtown Atlanta. Everyone is out and about; I start to feel grateful that Nathan asked me to go out. I've almost forgotten how much fun it is to be in the Atlanta nightlife. We arrive at Bailey's which is a small nightclub that caters to the mid-twenties crowd. The valet runs enthusiastically to the car, eager to drive it, I imagine. He opens my door with a smile and takes the keys from Nathan who informs him we will be using designated driver services at the end of the night. The attendant nods with understanding and hands Nathan a blue ticket.

Once we are inside, I hear (and feel) the familiar thumping techno music beat; a few people are already braving the dance floor even though it's pretty early. I immediately decide that I need a drink and motion to Nathan, who has struck up a conversation with a very attractive guy who is dressed in a nicely tailored blue suit. I take my place at the bar and wave to the bartender.

"What'll it be, sweetie?" says a skinny, bearded bartender with a bright smile.

"Cabernet Sauvignon, and don't give me the cheap stuff," I laugh. He quickly and expertly opens a bottle of their best and pours it into the glass. I thank him, give him a good tip and find a place to sit near the bar. For the first time, I carefully observe the crowd around me. It seems to be a pretty good mix of people tonight, mostly local professionals in their mid-to-late twenties. Young girls in party dresses and handsome guys in an array of different attire begin to move onto the floor.

"Baby, you gotta get up and socialize" I hear Nathan's scolding voice as he sits beside me.

"I'm just getting a feel for the scene," I snap, annoyed, "we can't all be social butterflies like you."

"Whatever, you look fucking gorgeous and are sitting alone at the bar!" Nathan shakes his head.

"Just let me finish my wine and then we can mingle, okay?" I throw my hands up in defeat. Nathan smiles and orders a Long Island Iced Tea...his favorite poison. When he gets his drink, we head upstairs to a room that's a little quieter. Electronic jazz plays in the background as we find a place to sit.

"Sweetie, you know it's almost been a year since the break-up," Nathan says gently. I knew he was going to start this again. I didn't need a reminder. Ever since Eric broke up with me, I've been a big mess.

"It's time to get back out there," Nathan interrupts my thoughts.

"I'm trying, but it's tough. I work a ton and well....I just don't feel like putting myself out there to get hurt again." I tremble at the truth, and tears threaten to spill down my face.

"Don't let that asshole have your broken heart. He's had it long enough." Nathan gives my hand a reassuring squeeze. Deep down, I know he's right. Eric moved on ages ago, but I'm still here, pining over someone that doesn't want me.

"I'm going to try to move on," I promise, giving him a weak smile.

"Nathan! Madeline!" I hear the familiar loud voice of Wendy Chase. Wendy is an interesting character to say the least. She drinks like a fish and smokes like a chimney, but is also the head buyer for three national department stores. You have to admit the girl has great fashion sense which is evident from her form fitting red halter dress with matching stilettos. She runs to our table and embraces both of us. We talk for a while about mergers, the latest fashion and legal matters before a cute guy with platinum blonde hair scoops her up and gives her a kiss. A new boyfriend, I suppose. She reminds me a bit of Samantha from *Sex and the City*...body of a woman, and dating ego of a man. The guy...who seems to be much younger than us leads her away to dance, and I look at Nathan's hopeful eyes.

"Let's go dance!" I yell as we head to the dance floor with drink number four. The smooth techno beat pulses, and I let myself get lost in the music. Suddenly, I feel a hand on my arm. I twist around to see my ex standing there. Of all the clubs...Jesus Christ.

"Hey, Madeline," he says softly.

"Eric," I regard him icily as I turn to walk away but he grabs my arm.

"Can we talk?" he asks with caution, "I'll buy you a drink."

"I have a drink, Eric, and I really have nothing to say to you" I scoff, my face getting hot from anger at the thought of all the hurt I've endured from our break-up. I snatch my arm away and head outside where I see Wendy smoking her usual clove cigarettes.

"Mind if I bum one?" I ask, realizing my face is still hot from my anger at Eric.

"Sure, girl. I thought you quit?" She questions as she hands me the cigarette and a lighter.

"I did," I say as I take my first puff. The buzz of the heavily scented smoke surrounds me, and I start to relax again.

"So, what's been going on with you?" Wendy asks.

"Me? Work."

"Just work?" she scoffs.

"Just work."

"Girl, we have one year left in our twenties…you better spend that year enjoying yourself. After thirty it's all downhill." I laugh.

"I'd have to recover from my relationship first…"

"Hasn't it been a year?"

"Your point is?" I take an angry puff and cough lightly.

"My point is that while you're trying to heal from heartbreak, he's already in someone else's bed. You don't have to be in a relationship all the time. Date, have a fling, have some fun damn it!"

"Easier said than done, Wendy."

"Take it from me, the sooner you get a good one in your bed, the less worried you'll be about a relationship." She smashes her cigarette into a nearby ashtray.

"Whatever you say…" I sigh.

"Take my advice, girl. You won't regret it." She turns on her heel and heads back into the club.

At around midnight, I'm lightheaded from the wine and Nathan is drunk. Good thing we called a driver to take us home. As Nathan drunkenly flirts with our driver, I think back to my encounter with Eric. I'm so tired of him. I just want to get over this whole mess and he keeps wanting to talk. Talk about what? He already made it pretty clear that he didn't want to be in a relationship with me. I don't know what else there is to talk about.

As the driver pulls up to my condo, I give Nathan a kiss on the cheek before stepping out of the car. He grabs my hand and looks at me seriously.

"Are you going to be okay, baby?" I tell him I'll be fine and give him a smile as I close the door. I take a deep breath and scan my key card to get into the lobby of my building. A young, bored looking man with a short buzz cut sits at the desk and lightens up when he sees me.

"Evening, ma'am…"he says smoothly.

"Well, you're new…" I observe, my friendliness fueled by my drunken state.

"Just got the job…nice to see a pretty face tonight." I blush.

"Oh, you'll see a lot more…" I think of all the models and beautiful businesswomen that occupy our building. His grin grows wider.

"Looks like I have a lot to look forward to, then." I smile as I swipe my keycard at the doors leading to the elevator. My name pops up on the screen and he glances at it.

"Well, Ms. Davis, have a good one." He nods at me.

"You too…" I say as I make my way to the elevator.

Once I make it to my condo, I stumble in, which startles Pricilla. She whines, almost with concern which I find hilarious and ruffle her thick brown fur as I search for my cigarettes. Even though I am pretty drunk, I look in my fridge and pour the remnants of a bottle of wine from last weekend. I go to my balcony, allowing Pricilla to accompany me. She sits, watching intently as if the stars, moon and passing airplanes might pose a threat to me any minute. I light a cigarette and surf my phone, hoping to find out that someone on my social media news feed is awake and posting something interesting. Finished with my cigarette and glass of wine, I lock the door to my balcony and saunter to the bathroom, washing the night off my face. I change into a pair of pajama bottoms and an oversized t-shirt that boasts my alma mater. Once I make my way to the bedroom, I see that Pricilla has retreated to her bed beside mine.

"Yeah, that's a good idea" I tell her and climb into the bed.

My dreams are filled with fantasies of the perfect guy. It's been so long since I've felt the loving touch, warm kisses and searing thrusts of a man. Had I been younger, I'd think this was a sign that I needed to find a man to sleep with. Those younger days are over now, and I find myself longing for a man who sees the future in me. I hope to God that I find him soon.

Chapter 2 *A Night With Paris*

"Vince, I thought you would be interested in the article here." My partner, Ryan slides a folded copy of *The Wall Street Journal* to me. I observe an article featuring our CFO, Madeline Davis. She has pushed our first big merger ahead two months and it has gotten her noticed in the business world. There's a photo, presumably from her days as a potential candidate for job vacancies. She has a noticeable smile that seems optimistic and beautiful brown eyes.

"We're getting some pull from her talent. You oughta bring her here" Ryan suggests.

"I wouldn't want to take her away from home. She seems to be doing a good job from Atlanta" I respond, sliding the paper back to him.

"Lucas will be here in two weeks, maybe you should think about bringing her here to convince them." I take it into consideration.

"I'll think about it."

"All business aside, it's Friday. What do you say we hit the scene with Kendall tonight?" I laugh.

"Man, we're in our thirties, don't you think it's strange for us to party like we're in our twenties?"

"Not when you're rich..." he smiles, stroking his goatee. I shake my head.

"I'm not really into the club scene tonight..."

"Let's compromise." He brings out two VIP passes to a place called *The Lounge*. The pass reads *Grown and Sexy, for guests 25 and up*. I shrug.

"What time do you want to go?"

"Let's go now. It's getting late." I look at my watch and notice it's already midnight. Only crazy men like Ryan and myself would stay in the office this late. I glare at him as I shut down my computer, secretly cursing him for making me go out.

My driver, Lou, chauffeurs us to a place that has a long line wrapped around it. Dropping us off at the front, he tells me to call when we're ready to leave. I warn him to stay close by as we might not want to be here long.

We enter into the seductive atmosphere, heading straight for the VIP section. I see that Jack, my head security agent is already in place by the door.

"Mr. Marks…Mr. Lowe…" He greets us with a curt nod. Ryan immediately orders a couple bottles of Grey Goose and I settle on the couch surveying the scene. Our friend Kendall steps in and plops down beside me.

"You two work way too much" he shakes his head as he takes a swig of beer.

"Multimillion dollar company making its way to billion dollar. Takes long days and long nights."

"I still can't believe you two partnered up and bought a company" he says.

"Me either, man." He leans over to me.

"Hey, I saw a Nubian princess you might like…" I roll my eyes.

"Another one that ends up wanting a relationship? No thanks."

"Nah, man, she's cool. Might be a little dazzled by your money, but she told me she wasn't looking for a relationship."

"She told *you* that. She might tell me something different."

"Why don't we invite her up? Come on, man, I see that curiosity." I guess it couldn't hurt to meet her.

"Sure." I shrug. He gets on his walkie-talkie and tells one of the guys on the floor to send her up. As Ryan settles down on the couch with our two bottles and a plethora of mixers, a petite girl with chocolate skin and a fro of curls comes through the VIP entrance. Damn, she has some nice curves. Kendall smiles and gets up to approach her.

"This is my friend, Vincent Marks. Vincent, this is Paris Jackson." he gestures to me.

"He's the rich one?" she bites out in a harsh Brooklyn accent. I get up and shake her hand.

"There's more to me than money, Paris." She smiles, so I don't take offense to her blunt statement.

"Why don't you pour me a drink and we'll talk about your other...attributes" I laugh and gesture for her to sit on the couch next to Ryan who has thrown back a few shots.

"What's your pleasure?" I ask. She thinks for a second.

"You can add a splash of cranberry to that Goose." I expertly pour a generous amount of vodka and add just a bit of cranberry juice. I hand it to her and she thanks me before guzzling it down. I pour a drink for myself and sit next to her.

"So...you say there's more to you than money, impress me..." she sits her glass down. I lower my voice as Ryan and Kendall engage in their own conversation.

"I bet I could fuck your brains out." I expect her to be shocked, but she looks interested.

"Pour me another drink and I'll think about it." I give her a seductive look and pour her another drink. I hand it to her and she throws it back again.

"Damn, girl...you like your liquor" I observe.

"I like my men, too. Think we can get outta here?" her brown eyes sparkle with excitement.

"We sure can." I pull out my phone and dial Lou.

"Hey, think you can book the hotel for me?" I ask.

"Sure thing, boss. Suite or penthouse?" I look over at the ebony beauty as she pours herself another drink.

"Suite." The penthouse was reserved for when I wanted a woman to stay (without me of course) so that I could go back and fuck her again if I wanted. Tonight, I just wanted a hit and run.

"I'll book and come get you."

"Thanks, man." I hang up and gaze at her as she pauses to look at her glass.

"You sure?" I ask.

"I'm sure." She throws back her drink and winks at me.

"Oh, fuck!" she squeals as I hammer inside of her. I have her bent over the side of the bed so that I can see and slap that luscious ass. She grabs the comforter as I continue to pound with force. I grab her huge tits, loving the feeling of being with a curvy woman.

"Oh, sweet Jesus! Fuck me! Fuck me!" she screams as I drive harder and stroke her clit. I finally feel her come and she hollers loudly, shaking. She collapses on the bed, panting wildly. I continue my relentless rhythm until I pull out, snatching off the condom and releasing myself on her back. She looks back at me as I take a towel and wipe her off.

"Goddamn you're good..." she laughs. I smile at the familiar statement I've heard many times.

"You can stay here tonight and sober up..." I tell her. She laughs.

"Oh you're one of *those* guys." She shakes her head before getting up and sauntering to the bathroom.

"I expect you'll be gone when I get out of the shower?" She peeks her head out of the bathroom door as I put my clothes back on.

"You expected right, baby." She wraps herself in a towel and comes over to me.

"Enjoy it while it lasts, *baby*." She grabs my face and kisses me before heading back to the bathroom. I take the elevator to the lobby and step out into the humid New York air. Lou is waiting for me in the parking lot and I absently wonder what he must think of me taking all of these women to hotels, leaving them to fend for themselves. He gets out of the car to open my door.

"Where to?" He asks.

"Home…" I answer. He nods and drives me back to my apartment.

I take a long shower once I get home and decide that I need to stop letting Ryan sway me to go out. I'm getting too old to have one night stands, but she was just right. Enamored with my wealth but wise enough not to move it any further. She knew all I wanted to do was fuck and that bothered me in a sense. I don't want to be an asshole, but at the same time, I don't know if there will ever be a woman that will turn me monogamous. I lay in the bed, satisfied from the buzz of the alcohol and the sexual escapade. Maybe this will just be the way my life goes. Hell, I don't know what would change me.

## Chapter 3 *Coping*

I wake up with a pounding head, damn that wine. The clock reads six-thirty which is way too early to be up on a Saturday. I decide to make some coffee and order breakfast from the diner downstairs. As I sip from the steaming cup, I look at the sun stained sky through my floor to ceiling windows and sink into deep thought. My thoughts are interrupted as I notice that Pricilla has left her bed and is now standing by me. I nix the diner idea, down a cup of Greek yogurt and ibuprofen, change into my workout clothes and grab Pricilla's leash. Maybe a run will clear my head. Thirty minutes later, after a 3 mile run, I feel a little better. I decide to walk a little bit and watch the early morning Saturday crowd. Couples, families and groups of friends are walking down the sidewalk to catch the beautiful fall morning. Pricilla seems interested in the crowd, so we linger for a little longer. She makes a few new doggy friends and I smile gratefully at their owners for letting her play with their pups. Suddenly, my music is interrupted by a ringtone. I click my headphones to answer the call.

"Madeline, I'm sorry to call you on a Saturday, but since you finished the numbers for the merger so early, I was hoping we could have a lunch meeting to discuss it," my boss Joseph Dent speaks through my headphones.

"Sure!" I say cheerfully, secretly glad to have some work to do.

"How does one work for you?" He asks.

"One is fine, our usual place?" I inquire.

"Yes, ma'am, see you then" he says brightly.

Pricilla and I head back home. Once we are inside, I turn my iPad on again, and Jill Scott graces me with her voice. As I sink into the warm, soapy water in the tub, I think back to happier times. I was still getting on my feet as a young executive and he had just received a promotion as top marketing lead at his company. I thought we were on top of the world. Then my mind goes back to the dark place when I first noticed he lost interest. I remember how hurt and unwanted I felt when he no longer wanted to participate in our usual sexual games. Instead, he spent the night getting drunk with his friends and crashing into his place during the early hours. He wouldn't touch me.

Tears well up in my eyes and the hurt comes flooding back. Snapping myself out of my feelings, I jump out of the bathtub and try to decide what to wear. I finally pick out some light gray slacks and pale pink blouse complete with black flats. I pull my hair into a loose bun and dust a little makeup on before grabbing my papers.

"Would you like to try the house Pinot Grigio?" asks Joseph as I look over the paperwork.

"Sure," I say absently. I tell him how profits will measure up for the company we are working with.

"I am so impressed by your work, Madeline, you have the beauty and the brains." He gives me a scandalous grin. Ugh, he's being flirtatious knowing damn well he has a wife and three kids at home. I give him a half smile, showing my lack of enthusiasm at his attempt to butter me up.

"Well, if nothing else, I know how to do my job," I reply. We continue our meeting as usual and he sends the company CEO our findings.

"Alright Madeline, I know you'll want to enjoy the rest of your Saturday," Joseph says after we've done everything.

"Yes, well, it's not a problem to do a little work on the weekends. I always like to be ahead." I laugh and wave good-bye as the valet pulls my car to the curb. I hand him a tip and speed off. This time, I do stop at the liquor store and buy a couple of bottles of wine.

I get home and change into my favorite pink loungewear from Victoria's Secret. Pricilla follows me as I saunter into the kitchen to search for a corkscrew. I pour a tall glass of Riesling and sink on my black leather couch. Staring out of my windows at the beautiful sunset, the splashes of orange in the sky are reminders of pleasant summer evenings spent during my business trips. I step onto the balcony with my wine glass and light up my long skinny cigarette. Suddenly, the phone rings. I notice the familiar face of my mother show up on the screen. I answer hastily, knowing that she will freak out if I don't answer soon enough.

"Madeline, how are you my dear?" a soft familiar voice murmurs from the other end.

"I'm fine, Mom," I lie as I take another puff of my cigarette. She would kill me if she found out I started back smoking. I speak with her at length about the latest gossip in our hometown: who's getting married, who's pregnant, and who's sleeping with someone else's husband. An hour later, I tell my mother I love her and that I will be home for a visit soon. I step back inside my condo greeted by silence and a curious Pricilla. God, I hate weekends. At least during the week I can drown myself in work and not worry about being isolated. Trying to overcome my boredom, I get out a book and decide to catch up on some of my reading but quickly realize the last book I bought was a romance novel. Sighing in disgust, I close the book and toss it on the coffee table. As I refill my glass, the phone rings, making me jump and I answer it without glancing at the caller id.

"Madeline," Eric's voice comes through the phone.

"Well, I thought you would have erased my number by now," I snap.

"Madeline, don't be like that. You know I still care about you...I just couldn't handle a relationship and that job from hell..."

"Whatever!" I shout, "I know plenty of people who can handle job stress and a relationship. Why don't you just tell me you weren't attracted to me anymore and we can both move on with our lives!" shocked by my harsh tone, I huff to calm down.

"Madeline, I just want to make sure you're okay. I know you isolated yourself from everyone for a while and I felt guilty…"

"Look, Eric, you have nothing to worry about. Clear your conscience and go mess with those little hoes that hang out at the bar, goodnight." I hit the "end" button before he can produce a response. I slam the bottle of wine down as I pour another tall glass. You would think that a woman who has it all together at work would be fine at home as well. Instead, I am an emotional mess. I guess I wear the mask well.

It can't get any more pathetic than this. Pricilla, concerned, puts her paw on my leg reassuringly as if she can sense my loneliness. I give her an affectionate scratch on her head and she jumps on the couch with me, placing her head in my lap. Well, at least I have my dog.

The next morning, I awake to rain softly hitting the windows. I decide to linger in bed since I got up so early the day before. I hug my pillows, my body longing for the heat of a man. The big fluffy pillows seem to be all the affection I get nowadays besides Pricilla, who is pretty independent and doesn't give love very often. Sinking into my thoughts, I'm startled by my phone ringing. I look at the clock and answer reluctantly.

"Hey, sweetie. I know it's early but there is an awesome benefit for dyslexia…" my friend Tracie's voice says. I swear that woman works on more causes than a bored housewife. I guess being a nurse, she has a lot more compassion than some people. I tell her that I'll think about it and that we should get together soon. She murmurs in agreement and says she'll call me in a few days.

I pick up the phone to call the diner downstairs and order a veggie scramble with fruit. I'm surprised at how much better I feel after last night. Usually after a drunken, tear filled night, I feel like absolute crap. Maybe the grief is slowly leaving me.

Not wanting to destroy my love for music, I feel that it's time for a break and turn on my rarely used TV to see two correspondents arguing about politics which is not my forte. I switch quickly to an old episode of *Law and Order*. Once I get comfortable on the couch, my phone rings again and it's Joseph. It's strange that he's called me twice this weekend.

"Madeline, I know it's unusual for me to call on a Sunday, but I have some news for you."

"Oh?" I sit up with interest.

"Well, after looking over your initial proposals, Mr. Marks would like you to come to New York and work with the board at MedInc."

"Really? Why? I'm only an accountant." Even though I'm teeming with excitement, I don't want to let him know that I am.

"Um…only an accountant? You're the one who did these numbers, don't tell me you think so little of yourself."

"I don't, but I just do not understand why they would need me there."

"If I threw in the fact that you can stay for two weeks and take Lacy with you, would you try to pretend to be happy?" His frustration is evident.

"Okay, okay. You've convinced me. When are we going?" I ask.

"It'll just be you and Lacy. Have her book your flight for tomorrow. I'm counting on you to get this branch noticed, Madeline."

"You know better than that."

"Yes, I do. See you in two weeks." We hang up, and the knock on my door tells me breakfast is here, so I hurry to the door, pay the delivery guy and place my food on the breakfast bar. I then pick up the phone to call Lacy.

"Lacy, it's Madeline. I'm sorry to call on a Sunday but I need you to clear both of our schedules for the next two weeks. We're going to New York to help complete the merger," I say between bites of my veggie scramble.

"How exciting!" Lacy screams, "I've wanted to go to New York for so long now!" I can't help but to smile at her enthusiasm. I've wanted to see our main office in New York ever since I started working for the company. I can't wait to meet the mysterious Vincent Marks, the man who bought out our company a bit ago.

Lacy agrees to clear the schedule and make a late afternoon run to the office to retrieve some important documents and book our travel. I finish my breakfast and skip to my closet to pack. Making mental notes of what I might encounter, I pull out an array of leggings, sweaters, jeans and suits secretly praying that I will have some fun and get out of my rut while I'm in New York.

Lacy calls me back to tell me our flight will go out early the next afternoon. I decide to go ahead and perfect the merger contracts making sure I have all my ducks in a row. Around noon, everything seems to be in order. Citing that I don't have to leave my condo until the next afternoon, I decide to make myself a celebratory drink. Wine seems to be my go-to in times of sorrow, so I decide to change it up and break out the hard stuff to celebrate. The creative bug hits me (or rather I probably saw it somewhere) and I begin to mix a pitcher of vodka, pineapple juice and champagne. Pricilla follows me as I pour the drink into a martini glass and taste it, appreciating the sweetness. I take my glass to the living room and stop short to look at the mirror by the door noticing that I desperately need a refresh for my sew-in. Time to call Bruce…

"Hello!" a flamboyant voice on the other end answers.

"Bruce? It's Madeline."

"Maddie, baby! What can I do for you?"

"I'm going to New York tomorrow, you mind tightening up my sew-in today?"

"Yes, honey, when you want me to come?"

"Let's say around two?"

"One-thirty instead?" He asks.

"Sure."

"I'll be there!" I hang up and take a big gulp of my drink. Knowing how I am with hard liquor, I pledge to only have one more or else I'll be sleeping when Bruce does my hair. I take my drink and sit on the couch, scrolling through my guide until I see that some old episodes of *Sex and the City* are on. I sip my drink as I watch my old friends: Carrie, Miranda, Samantha and Charlotte go through their relationship turmoil. A couple of episodes later, I hear the intercom and get up.

"Ms. Davis, you have a Bruce here to see you?" the whiny voice drawls with a thick southern accent.

"Send him up." A few minutes later, I hear a light knock at my door and answer it.

"Maddie!" Bruce exclaims as he invites himself in armed with bags full of his tools.

"Bruce, thank you for coming on such short notice…"

"No problem, lady…I know you have to look good for those big, bad men in the office." I laugh and lead him to the kitchen. As he busies himself with my hair, I start to feel nervous about my upcoming trip. What will the CEO think of me? I'm so young; will he just dismiss what I have to say and declare that I have lack of experience? No, no, I can't think like that. I know my stuff, he'd be a fool not to follow my advice.

"Please tell me that you're going to go up there and have some fun" Bruce interrupts my thoughts. Jeez, even my hairstylist knows I have no life. I turn around and smile at him, a silent indicator that I will try my very best to get out of this damned slump.

After Bruce leaves me feeling like I've had a full spa treatment, I help myself to another drink and call Pricilla's dog sitter to let her know that I will be out of town for two weeks. She eagerly jumps at the opportunity for some extra pay and informs me that she will pick Pricilla up tomorrow afternoon.

Later that evening, I sink into a cucumber scented bath, reflecting on the weekend. I got drunk...one night with Nathan, the next night drowning in pity and now, celebrating my journey. I probably should find a better hobby. I contemplate taking up causes like Tracie or joining some type of organization. I've been lamenting over this man for way too long and pitying myself for being single is not helping. After a long bath in which I've planned my entry back into the real world, I do a final check of my suitcases and decide to call it a night. I shuffle around, trying to find a comfortable position before I sink into the first peaceful sleep I've had in a long time.

Around five, I wake up to a strange, rhythmic beeping on my work laptop. I get out of bed and turn on the computer which shows a message saying that my camera is active. I click a few buttons to turn it off and look at my computer quizzically. That's really strange, I only use my camera for video conferences and haven't used it this weekend. I shrug my shoulders and climb back into bed, hoping to get a few more hours of sleep.

The next morning, I get dressed in my best brown pantsuit, put diamond studs in my ears and brush my hair down my shoulders. I make sure everything is in order one final time before giving Pricilla a loving scratch on her head.

"You be good, okay?" I say as I roll my suitcase out of the condo and lock the door.

The new guy I saw Friday night is at the desk and smiles when he sees me.

"Good morning, do you need a cab?" He asks, eyeing my suitcase.

"No, thank you, the car is already here to pick me up. I'll be gone for two weeks. Keep an eye on things." I wink at him.

"Always" he says with a smile.

Chapter 4 *Craziness*

"Mr. Marks?" My assistant's voice rings out questioningly over the intercom.

"Yes, Alexis?" I answer.

"There is a Paris Jackson here to see you?" My brows furrow in curiosity. What is she doing here?

"Send her in…" I say cautiously. Paris walks in, dressed in a more professional manner than the short dress and come-fuck-me heels she wore Friday night. Her serious look indicates that something is wrong. God, I hope she's not about to lay something on me.

"Have a seat, Paris." I gesture to the chair. She sits down and those brown eyes burn into mine.

"Look, I don't stalk guys I have a one night stand with…just know that, but there is something strange going on." I take a deep breath bracing for something horrible.

"What is it?" I inquire.

"Some…woman has been harassing me…about you." Not this again! I never thought that a woman I had a short fling with would make everything miserable for the women after her. I sigh.

"What has she done?"

"It's not serious…phone calls, pictures…"

"Pictures of what?" I demand. She takes a stack of photos out and puts them on my desk. There, I see the pictures from the night I spent with her…in the club and the hotel.

"Did this woman tell you her name?" I ask. She shakes her head.

"I think I know who it is…don't worry, Paris, I'll take care of it."

"I came to you first, I figured some woman has the hots for you and was jealous that you spent Friday night fucking me." She grins. I like her crude humor.

"Well, that might be the case, but she has no right to bother you." She takes a breath and stands up.

"Look, Vincent, I know we agreed on a one night stand, but since your crush is stalking me, I figured you should know." I stare at her in curiosity.

"I'm a producer for Nightlife Records. If this chick gets too close, I have people who can handle her." I look up in surprise. I should have known she was acting, she seemed to be too familiar with VIP.

"A producer? Why the act of being impressed with rich men? You're around them all the time." She giggles.

"Kendall thought you might not go for it if you knew." I scoff, pissed off that he would assume that about me after more than ten years of friendship.

"You put on a good act...totally fooled me" I muse.

"Don't be offended, I usually prefer to be anonymous, but I knew who you were already. I don't understand sometimes how you keep yourself out of the public eye. You know how to keep the media at bay." I'm flattered that she even cared enough to do some research on me.

"I try to stay out of the spotlight as much as possible, but I have a feeling that it will change after next week."

"Why is that?"

"I have a big business deal coming up, and that's why it's especially important to me that the woman who is harassing you stays in her place." She nods.

"You have your people do what they will if she decides to be stupid about it, but I promise I'll talk to her."

"I figured you could handle it. You certainly handled me the other night." Her eyes narrow at me.

"You are a smooth talker..." I observe. She laughs.

"The best." She winks and leaves out of my office. Looking at the pictures, I start to get angry. I can't believe she's sinking this low. She should know by now that I'm not tied down to anyone. Sighing heavily and realizing that I have to meet with my CFO in a few hours, I pick up my phone.

"Vince..." the sultry voice on the other end answers.

"Look, I don't know how much clearer I can be with you about everything. It's over. Paris was a one night stand. Don't fucking stalk her because you're jealous. I'm sure you know that she has people that can wipe your ass out without a trace."

"Why did you go to her? You could have come to me!" she retorts. I scoff.

"Paris was a one night stand! And why am I answering to you anyway? We aren't together. Never have been, never will be." Her breathing becomes shallow.

"I can't believe you would say that after all we've been through..."

"We haven't been through shit. I fucked you several times, you got a free vacation. Get over it" I growl.

"Whatever, Vince. I know that you love me. I know that you will realize it."

"Just leave Paris alone damn it!" I grow frustrated.

"I'll leave the slut alone..."she concedes.

"Not any more of a slut than you..." she laughs at my accusation.

"Careful there."

"Look, you know I have a merger coming up. Don't cause trouble..." I say and she sighs in frustration.

"Someday, you will wake up..."she lowers her voice.

"I'm awake, *you* are the one who seems to be living in dreamland." I hang up, my temper flaring from the confrontation. Massaging the tense muscles in my neck, I take a deep breath and will myself to calm down. I need to be ready to meet Ms. Davis and I certainly don't want to be in a bad mood when she comes.

"Alexis..." I call on the intercom.

"Coffee?" she predicts when she hears the tension in my voice.

"Yeah" I respond as Ryan comes in my office.

"I can't believe I'm gonna miss out on meeting the CFO" he says.

"You gotta see what they need at the lab." I shrug. The whole reason Ryan and I bought this company was because he is the scientist and I am the businessman. When business went well, we were able to hire more people to work on the pharmaceutical technology; thus, giving Ryan more time to spend in the office.

"Well, we really need this merger to go down. MedInc has access to more research databases. We could really see a surge in profits." I nod as Alexis brings me coffee.

"Do you need anything Mr. Lowe?" she asks Ryan. He shakes his head and she breezes out, assuming we are having a private conversation.

"Ms. Davis' boss tells me that she is an excellent accountant, and is ready to prove her numbers" I tell him.

"How does it look?" He asks as he sits in the chair across from my desk.

"From her projection…over a 45% increase in profit." He straightens in surprise.

"45%! Talk about a multimillion dollar company!" He smiles.

"Let's not get ahead of ourselves. You know we will have to revise again when their quarterlies come in from their CFO."

"I'm sure she's probably in the ballpark. Have you ever read her accounting reports? Jeez, it's like right down to the penny!"

"She is talented at the numbers game, I'll give you that. Joseph tells me she's a bit of a work-a-holic though. The first week will be for her to take a break. I certainly can't afford for her to burn out any time soon."

"Good idea, man. Yeah, we'll need her for a few more years. Maybe we should hook her up with Kendall or Brandon…have them show her a good time." I shake my head.

"I said take a break, not get rammed by hypersexual men." Ryan laughs loudly.

"Pot calling the kettle…"

"Shut-up. Besides, she might be married or have a boyfriend."

"She's not married. No boyfriend either from the amount of hours she puts in at the office. Up until a month ago, she was swiping out at midnight." I glance at him in surprise.

"Really? So you've been doing some research on her?"

"Just checking her out a bit." I shake my head. I hadn't really bothered to do much research on her. I read her reports which were impeccably done, but mostly Joseph relayed everything from her to me. I thought that was strange as she was our company's accountant and I should be speaking with her personally. It almost seemed like he was keeping her from talking to me. Maybe he was afraid she would impress me too much. I look at Ryan.

"You ever think Joseph is trying to keep her away from us?" I inquire.

"Why would he do that?" I think to myself.

"I don't know, he seems a little possessive. Like he thinks I'll offer for her to come here."

"Why not? She is the only chief that works out of a branch besides Joseph, and we just gave him that position so that he would stop whining about us beating his bid when the company was sold."

"You're right about that…" Alexis taps on the door and I gesture for her to come in.

"Ms. Davis' flight left on time and she should be here in two and a half hours."

"Alright let Jillian and Lou know. Tell Jillian that I want her to meet Ms. Davis as she will be the security detail for her." Alexis nods and steps out of the office as Ryan gets up.

"Well, tell Ms. Davis I will meet her next time. I will see you in two weeks." I stand and shake his hand.

"Safe flight. Make sure you get back to me about the problem with the database." He nods and leaves out of the office.

Once I am left alone, I think about Ms. Davis and am kind of excited about meeting her. Female executives have always excited me; I have even fucked a few of them. I know of course, that I cannot do that with her. I need her to know that I take her seriously and that her work has moved us forward more quickly than I anticipated. We need this merger, and she will be the one that helps us get there.

## Chapter 5 *New York, New York and the Mysterious Mr. Marks*

Lacy and I sit patiently waiting for the plane to take off; the pilot has informed us that there are 7 planes ahead, so it will be awhile before take-off. Lacy speaks idly about her new boyfriend and how she really likes him. I half listen to her as I try to calm my nerves.

"So, what do you think?" asks Lacy, tearing me away from my thoughts.

"Huh? About what?" I look at her, confused.

"My new boyfriend is a teacher and has a single friend who recently moved to Atlanta. You two are about the same age. Would you want to go on a double date?" She repeats. I roll my eyes and sigh.

"Oh, Lacy, I don't think I'm quite ready," I pause, "but when we get back, he's invited to the company gala." I don't think I've ever seen Lacy's smile so big. It takes so little to make her happy.

Before we know it, we are taking off towards the Big Apple. I look out of the window at the puffy white clouds that surround our plane. I've always loved flying, it gives me a chance to let my mind wonder with no interruptions. Lacy is heavily invested in some book which, by the looks of it, is a trashy romance novel.

"What are you reading?" I ask.

"Oh, just some cheap book. It's kind of raunchy." She giggles looking at the picture of a heavily muscled man and a scantily clad woman on the front.

"Lacy? Do you think I'll ever get out of this slump?" I look at her genuinely.

"Of course, Madeline, but you have to will yourself to do it."

"It's hard" I sigh.

"Well, make it a priority while we're here. There's plenty to do in New York."

"I'll be busy."

"Not so busy that you can't go out and have some fun."

"You're right." Lacy gives me a caring smile and goes back to her book.

After a smooth flight into the city, Lacy and I head to the baggage claim. The company hired a driver and security for us since I possess secret information. We grab our bags and see a man and woman coming toward us. The man introduces himself as Lou, the driver. He's a tall, dark haired guy who looks like he might be from the military or something. The lady introduces herself as Jillian, our security detail. Jillian looks like an interesting character. She has radiant ebony skin and wears her hair braided down her back. The woman must work out twice a day! She has muscles that would easily qualify her for a body building contest. We shake both their hands and they lead Lacy and me out to a waiting black SUV.

Once we arrive at the company building, I can hardly contain my excitement but know I need to keep my professional stance. Jillian leads Lacy and I into the office. We encounter a huge lobby that is bustling with a diverse set of professionals. We approach the front desk and a friendly brunette greets us.

"Ms. Davis. I am Alexis Stanley, head executive assistant. Mr. Marks has been waiting for you. I'll let him know you're here," she says with a smile. After picking up the phone and informing her boss that I'm here, she leads us to the elevator where she presses a key code and selects the floor. I've heard a lot about Mr. Marks, our new CEO, but I have never seen him. I could have just Googled him, but honestly wanted to see him for the first time in person. He has been a mystery to our Atlanta office. I'm excited to get a sneak peek at the man who bought and saved our company.

The elevator dings, distracting me from my thoughts. As we step out, Alexis points Lacy to a desk equipped with a computer and all the office supplies she needs. Lacy cheerfully thanks her and mouths, "Good luck" to me. Alexis knocks on a mahogany door, and my mouth drops open as our CEO opens it.

Mr. Marks can't be any older than 35. He towers over me, probably a good 6'4 in height with muscles that would shame male models worldwide. His caramel skin gives him a healthy glow, his bald head shines in the light and he regards me with a set of deep hazel eyes. The gray suit and crisp white shirt he's wearing is perfectly tailored to his athletic build. Damn! I had always envisioned our CEO as an older married man, but he is definitely nothing like I imagined. My God, this man is fine!

"Ms. Davis, it's a pleasure to meet you!" he says with a glow in his eyes.

"Mr. Marks, the pleasure is all mine," I reply, my eyes scanning him. Lord, have mercy on me! I try to snap out of it.

"So, Ms. Davis. I was thinking I could let you get settled. You will be sharing my office; there will be a late lunch meeting at 4:00, but there's coffee and a few snacks in the staff kitchen for now. Please make yourself at home," He looks at me warmly. I swallow hard, not able to speak and quickly nod to make up for my awkward silence.

"If you'll excuse me, I must get some more coffee myself. My desk is at your disposal." He gives me one last smile before exiting the office. Holy shit that man is hot! I haven't felt like this since…well, since Eric and I started dating. Clearing my throat, I smooth my hair and put my things on Mr. Marks' desk. I look around his office and am amazed at his taste. Perhaps a wife or girlfriend helped him decorate. A black leather couch sits in the corner and sleek black bookcases filled with business books line the wall. As I open my briefcase, I notice a few pictures on his desk. One is a girl with wild curly hair and hazel eyes like Mr. Marks. The other is a dark skinned, bald man and an olive skinned lady with long black hair. Maybe this is his family? I shrug and get ready to start my work.

A few hours later I've removed my jacket, poured a huge mug of coffee and started working furiously at the computer. Mr. Marks has us on speakerphone with the CEO of MedInc. I am calculating the numbers as they talk.

"Mr. Lucas, the numbers that I have come up with correlate with those done by your CFO," I say confidently.

"Excellent, Ms. Davis. Our flight will land at 11:30AM on Sunday. We can start first thing Monday morning," says Mr. Lucas.

"Sounds great, I look forward to working with your company," I smile. Out of the corner of my eye, I notice Mr. Marks looking at me with a boyish grin. After he hangs up, I close my laptop, thankful that I won't have to deal with those numbers again until Sunday.

"Well, Ms. Davis, shall we go to lunch?" he asks with a glint in his eye.

"Of course! Would you like me to fetch Lacy?" I remind myself to tone down the enthusiasm.

"I was thinking it would just be me, you and Dina Andrews today." I almost roll my eyes. Dina Andrews is our Chief Communications Officer and I've heard a few unflattering things about her. This will be quite interesting, but I'd love to be anywhere this beautiful man is. He has me swooning like a high school girl.

"Okay, just let me grab my jacket." I reply with a smile. He heads out of the door and I shrug on my jacket, making sure that my hair and makeup are still okay.

We arrive at a high end Italian restaurant and are greeted by a bouncy platinum blond. This must be Dina. Well, the guys at the office weren't lying about her looks. She has to be at least a slender five-ten, with long blond hair, big breasts and pouty red lips. Her look is accentuated by a gray Prada dress that I contemplated buying for myself a few weeks ago. I almost feel awkward in her presence.

"Ms. Davis! There's been a lot of buzz about you around the office. I understand we have you to thank for this successful merger!" she gushes.

"Call me Madeline, please." I answer, "But what good is a company without a fabulous CCO?" I gush right back. Maybe that sounded a little too fake. I make up for it with a warm smile. Something doesn't seem right about this woman, but I can't tell what it is.

"Well, is it alright if I call you Madeline as well?" Mr. Marks chimes.

"Of course, Mr. Marks." I say.

"None of this Mr. Marks nonsense. Please call me Vincent." I think I'm going to faint. First names are usually reserved for the big boys up top. I can't help but to feel a sense of accomplishment. I give a huge smile to both Dina and…Vincent.

We sit at a table and the waiter brings out a great red wine. Merlot, I think. I order their pasta of the day, take a gulp of wine and start to relax for the first time since I met Vincent. Dina engages me in conversation about her years at NYU and asks me about my undergrad years at the University of Georgia. I tell her about the football, the partying and of course the grand education I received at the school of business. Vincent shares that he graduated from Harvard and moved up the ladder more quickly than he intended to. The man is intelligent and good looking.

We discuss the details of the merger, and what will be known to the public after the transition. Before I know it, it's five o'clock and Vincent tells me to relax and that business is over for the day. As Dina says her good-byes and climbs into a black sedan, Vincent gently grabs my hand.

"So, I was wondering if you might accompany me to a benefit dinner tonight?" he asks cautiously. My mind starts racing, but before any other part of my body can react, I quickly stutter that I would love to.

"Wonderful!" he smiles gratefully, "I've been meaning to find a date, but with all of the business our company has had, I've barely had time to think." I chuckle at the familiar excuse that I give all of my friends when they ask me why I haven't started dating again.

"I know what you mean. What time should I be ready?"

"My car will come get you around 8:00; will you have enough time to get ready? I know you ladies love to look your best." He smiles.

"I will. Thank you for the invitation. I'll see you tonight." Oh my. I feel compelled to call Nathan. I wave goodbye to Vincent and jump into the car with Jillian. I immediately get out my phone.

"Nathan Paul," I hear the familiar voice croon.

"Nathan! It's Madeline."

"Maddie! Please tell me you love New York."

"It's beautiful, but I have something to tell you." I suddenly realize I'm in the car with Jillian, "hold on one second, Nathan."

"Jillian will you drop me off here?" I notice we're only a block away from the hotel. Jillian nods and drops me off at the curb. She speaks into her earpiece and tells Main Security that I've just been dropped off.

"Thank you." I smile at her and she smiles back.

"Madeline!" exclaims Nathan, "What is it?"

"Well, first of all, my boss is one hot man. Secondly, I've been asked to accompany him at a benefit!" I realize how excited I am.

"Go get him girl!"

"Oh, Nathan, it's not like that. I'm his employee. I think he's being nice."

"Bullshit! You better tell me all about it when you get back. I'll be waiting. Gotta go! Love you!"

"I love you too, Nathan." I smile as I press "end" on my phone. I must find something delicious to wear. I pick up my phone and dial Lacy.

"Lacy, meet me downstairs in five."

"It looks absolutely gorgeous!" Lacy gushes as I walk out of the Neiman Marcus dressing room in a floor length red gown. I look in the mirror and have to admit to myself that I do look pretty damn good. Once the hair and makeup are done, I'll be quite a sight. I immediately decide to purchase the dress. The damage is a thousand dollars; I certainly don't mind it though, I'm sure Vincent will be quite dashing himself.

I sit in the hotel salon and tell the stylist I want a tasteful up-do. She immediately agrees and gets to work. It feels so good to really dress up and go somewhere. I remember Eric and I used to always frequent nice restaurants and parties. I always felt like a princess…until…no, no, no, I can't think about this now. One of the salon attendants brings me a glass of champagne and I sip it until I start to relax, succumbing to the luxury of being pampered.

I slip on my dress and matching strappy, red heels. Looking at myself in the mirror, I see the old Madeline. Happy go-lucky Madeline, who always wanted to look pretty and have fun before that bastard. Lacy comes to do my make-up and I sit patiently as she figures out eye shadow colors to compliment my dress. I would let the salon do my make-up, but Lacy does it so well, I can't resist getting her to do it. When she finishes, I look in the mirror. I look absolutely stunning. My phone rings and it's Vincent telling me that he's downstairs in the lobby. Oh my!

I wave good-bye to Lacy who looks genuinely happy for me. I step into the elevator and pledge that I will have a good time tonight. As I step out, I see Vincent. His mouth falls open as I greet him with a smile. For a minute, I think he's at a loss for words, but then again so am I. He looks absolutely gorgeous in his black tux, and that smile could stop World War III.

"Madeline, you clean up well!" he says with wonder.

"So do you…" I look him up and down.

"Well, shall we?" He holds out his hand and I take it cautiously as he leads me out to a limo parked outside the hotel. We ride in silence for a few minutes, but I notice he does not stop staring at me.

"What is it?" I finally ask.

"Oh, I'm just taking you in." I scoff.

"What's so special about me?"

"Need me to give you a quick rundown?" He chuckles. I can't help but to smile at his sense of humor.

"Now, there's a smile. Loosen up a bit…you seem to be all business."

"I usually am."

"Well, let's see if we can change that…at least for tonight." I laugh lightly.

"You and I have the same goal."

"Common goals are good, Ms. Davis." He takes my hand and kisses it gently which prompts me to blush furiously. I want to remain cautious, but those genuine eyes begin to tear down my walls.

"So, what's your story?" He asks.

"Which one?" I laugh.

"The one you want to share."

"There's not much to tell. Maybe when you get a few drinks in me, I'll share a little more." He laughs.

"Joseph did say you had a grand sense of humor."

"Joseph told you about me?"

"Of course. I know about everyone that works in your office." I scoff.

"There's so many of us…"

"Ms. Davis, I am not your traditional CEO, no one is nameless or faceless as far as I'm concerned." I chuckle softly.

"That's most definitely not traditional, Mr. Marks."

"I've always believed that a new generation businessman has to do what the foundational ones don't. It's the only way you'll make your mark in the world."

"I like that. Did you argue with your professors on that logic?" He laughs again.

"Actually I did. My views on running a business weren't very popular."

"Well, just because it's not popular doesn't mean it won't work. I happen to believe that you're going in the right direction."

"I certainly hope so. When I was bidding to buy the company, my dad told me I was a damned fool."

"I think most people would have thought that. We were a failing company, and in this economy, no one was investing like they usually were."

"Well, I knew there was plenty of work to do, but with such talented people in our offices, I didn't have to do much outside of basic restructuring." I nod.

"So, you're a risk taker…"

"In more ways than one." He gives me a wicked grin and I laugh. Well, at least he has a good sense of humor and a great mind for business.

"What does that mean?" I inquire.

"Oh I think you'll find that out as you get to know me." I blush again and he touches my cheek gently.

"Well, I'm glad you think I'm worthy of getting to know you." He laughs loudly.

"Oh, you're more than worthy. I can only hope you think I'm worthy of you."

"Nonsense…" I say nervously.

We continue to ride in silence as I'm utterly shocked by his tenderness. It feels strange to have this sort of attention again; although, I am certainly not complaining. The man is dashing with a personality to match his good looks. I don't mind spending time with him at all.

"So, what is the benefit for?" I ask, breaking the silence and shushing my inner thoughts.

"It's a fundraiser to build libraries in low income schools here." My eyes light up.

"That's a noble cause" I say with approval.

"I've been working with this foundation since I was in college. We used to come here in the summers and work with the summer school program."

"That's amazing, do you still work with the kids sometimes?" I ask.

"When I have the time, I always try to make it to a couple of the elementary schools. The kids say I'm a good guest reader." He smiles fondly. Can this man get any more amazing?

"I work with some of our local high schools" I say.

"Really? What is your line of work at the schools?"

"I help with the Future Business Leaders of America. I take them on field trips, show them the ways of a successful businessperson." He gives me another grin as the car comes to a stop at a nice hotel. I secretly pray that I have the time of my life tonight. He seems promising. I guess we'll see.

The hotel is absolutely gorgeous with low lighting and soft jazz playing in the background. I survey the scene, swooning at all of the lovely decorations. Vincent has been a true gentleman, introducing me to all of his high power acquaintances. I think I've died and gone to a high class version of heaven. As we move around the ballroom, Vincent points out a young couple. The woman is dressed in an elegant baby blue strapless gown and the incredibly handsome man in a gray tuxedo. His arm is tucked around her waist as if to warn others that she already belongs to him.

"That is Emily and Gustavo Cruz...recognize the last name?"

"I sure do, they own one of the biggest ad companies in New York" I smile.

"You've done your homework, they do most of our campaigns." He leads me over to the petite, black haired beauty and her equally attractive husband.

"Gus? Emily? I'd like you to meet the CFO of PharmaCO, Madeline Davis." He says as we approach them. Emily gives me a cosmetic smile and holds out her hand.

"Ms. Davis, we've heard and read so much about you" she says.

"Really?" My eyes light up in surprise.

"Actually, we are excited that you came to New York, we'd like you to consider doing a photo shoot for *Inc.* Magazine" Mr. Cruz eyes me.

"Oh, my..." I stutter.

"It would be great publicity for the company in the face of this great merger you helped command" Mrs. Cruz says.

"I'd love to! Just contact me when you're ready..." I smile.

"Let's have a meeting at the office next week. We'll be in touch." Gus shakes my hand firmly with a million dollar smile.

As we sit at the table for our delicious seafood meal, Vincent gives me a little more insight into his life. He grew up in Connecticut and his mother is the principal of an all-girls private school while his father is a business attorney. I light up at our commonality. My father was high school math teacher and my mother was on the legal team of our community college. He is absolutely a dream to talk to, and I start to feel a burning desire for this man.

"Would you like to dance?" he asks as a familiar slow jazz number plays.

"Yes, I would" I say shyly. He sweeps me onto the dance floor and I feel like I'm in some rendition of *Cinderella*. He smiles tenderly as he glides me across the dance floor. I secretly thank Tracie for dragging me to ballroom dancing lessons, as I dance just as smoothly. I look into his eyes and start to feel sad. This is way too good to be true. I've been swept off my feet before...look how that turned out. Vincent, stares in my eyes, sensing my sudden gloom.

"Madeline, is something wrong?" he asks with concern.

"Nothing, it's just that it's been a while since I've had such a wonderful time."

"Me too" he smiles at me with a sparkle in his eyes.

We clap as the song ends and I ask him if we may have a drink. He nods and summons a waiter. I order a glass of champagne and he orders scotch on the rocks. This man is my dream, but deep down I know that this could never go anywhere. He's my boss for Christ's sake. I look at him with admiration. He's a young, intelligent CEO of a growing company and handsome as hell, now that's an eligible bachelor! I try to calm down with another sip of champagne. Vincent gazes at me with strong eyes.

"Madeline, I know this is a little unconventional, but let me just say that I'm shocked you don't have a man following your every move."

I chuckle nervously, "Well, there was one, but we grew apart."

"I would never want to grow apart from you." I freeze.

"Vincent, you only just met me"

"I saw your smile in the Wall Street Journal and I've been dying to meet you."

"Did I disappoint?" I ask quietly.

"You exceeded my expectations." Wow. I'm stunned by his words; furthermore, it makes me cautious. I've heard similar words before and it ended up crashing and burning. Trying to get some focus back, I sit my champagne down.

"Vincent, you know it would be unethical to ever start something up…unless you're looking for a quiet one night stand" he looks shocked at my response.

"Do you have so little faith in men?"

"I have good reason."

"Really, now? Are you one of those women who says all men are dogs?" I stare at him, icily regarding his comment.

"Let's just say I've had my heart broken far more times than I've wanted, and don't want to end up like that again." He reaches up to caress my face.

"Madeline, I am a man who doesn't play games, I'm a bit too old for that." I have to laugh at his comment, and my desire rears its head once again. I notice that it's eleven and I probably need to get some sleep before heading to the office in the morning.

"We should probably go; I have an early morning tomorrow, but I would like you to see what the city has to offer." He says this like he's just read my mind.

"Oh, Vincent, we have so much work to do…"

"Are you kidding me? You've pushed this merger ahead two months! You deserve some time for yourself."

"I don't know what to say."

"I invited you to New York because your boss expressed his concern about you overworking yourself." I'm shocked and confused. He sees the look on my face and explains further.

"That's no bad reflection on you, but I wanted to give you a break, which is why I requested you for two weeks. Lucas and crew won't be here until Sunday. I want you to enjoy your time here." He says gently. I sit back in awe.

"Okay, I will agree on one condition: I am called in if there are any problems" I say cautiously. He smiles and nods his head in agreement then calls the car to pick us up.

On the ride home, Vincent rarely takes his eyes off me. Honestly, I was ready to slip out of that dress and give him everything he desired and more. However, I maintain my composure and give him a soft look, steadying my trembling breath. Before I know it, the moment takes over and he grabs me in a powerful, electric kiss. His hands never leave me, and he sighs which makes me melt. I finally surrender, giving in to the desire that has been haunting me since I first saw him.

We get so lost in each other that I barely notice we have arrived at my hotel. He looks at me with a lustful longing, but I figure that the kiss is enough for tonight. I give him another smile and sweet kiss goodnight. For a minute, I sense disappointment, but he regains his self-control and tells me goodnight. When I step out of the car, he grabs my hand.

"Madeline, you might have just been my godsend," he breathes. I'm shocked by his words. What life am I living in again?

"Thank you for a wonderful evening Vincent and remember the conditions of our arrangement." I say in my businesslike manner. I can't wait to call Nathan to tell him about my night.

"The pleasure was all mine, Madeline, and I'll remember." He eyes are smoldering with passion as Lou closes the door.

It takes all the strength I can muster to not run into the hotel giddy with laughter. This man, this beautiful man just kissed me more passionately than Eric did for the whole year of our relationship. As I try to steady myself, I look at my phone to see that there is a text message: *I really enjoyed our time tonight, Madeline. Until tomorrow. VM.* I am becoming undone.

In my dreamy state, I get on the elevator, hardly noticing the couple who can't seem to keep their hands off each other. Once I arrive on my floor, I practically float to my room. I'd absolutely love to date him, but I know that this could cause major drama at the Atlanta and New York office. I want to be hopeful, but something is keeping me from being too wishful.

I shed the beautiful gown and carefully hang it in a garment bag, inhaling the faint whiff of Vincent's cologne still left on it. It is exactly how a sexy, smart, generous man should smell. Trying to shake the hypnosis from tonight, I wash my face and change into a nightshirt. I know I won't be able to sleep for a minute, so I decide to check my emails and phone messages. There's a few emails from the secretary at MedInc, who was nice enough to send me her boss' travel itinerary. There's also a few from Lacy who has proofed my documents and sent them back for approval.

Once I get my technology fix, I decide to text Nathan: *Call me! I have so much to tell you!*
My phone pings almost immediately in response: *I better get all the juicy details. I'm finishing up at dinner with a client. I'll call you in the morning.*

I text back an "Okay" and put my phone on the nightstand. I can't wait to tell him about one of the best nights I've ever had.

Chapter 6 *Deep Thought*

"Mr. Marks?" Lou says interrupting my distant thoughts of the amazing woman we just dropped off.

"Yes, Lou?" I answer.

"Are you heading home, or are we going someplace else?" He knows me so well. Usually after an event, I'll have a drink at the hotel near my apartment.

"Not tonight, Lou. It's late and I think…I've had enough for tonight."

"Very well, sir." He smiles in the rearview mirror. I continue to think about Madeline: her smile, those delicious curves, that full ass…God, I could have taken her the moment she got into the car. The dress fit her just right, and I would have rightly torn it off her. My cock twitches as I think about holding her close. I talk myself down, not wanting Lou to see me get out of the car with a huge hard-on.

Once I get into my apartment, I loosen my tie and jump out of my clothes quickly, hating the confinement of this damn tux. I check my voicemail… and find another one from that asshole William. He keeps asking me if I'm sure Madeline's numbers are in order. That bastard doesn't know what he's competing with here, and he better watch it before he's out of a job. Shaking my head in annoyance, I grab a bottle of water from the fridge and head to my bedroom. I know it's late and I need to sleep, but that woman has bewitched me. Oh, the things I could do to her…I imagine pulling her up by her hair and fucking her from behind, that big ass against me. *Christ, man! Stop it!*

I try to sleep and it's just not happening. Teeming with frustration at my unstoppable arousal, I consider calling one of my stand by women to get rid of my annoying thoughts of her. For some odd reason, though, I don't want to. I'd rather have her, and I'm going to. She told me she had been hurt before. Whoever that bastard is should have his ass kicked. She's so goddamn amazing. Ok, this has got to stop. I don't do this, I don't think of women like this. While I appreciate the idea of monogamy, I never thought it was my thing. She has me thinking about it though. She lives in Atlanta, I could never…

I look at the alarm clock. Damnit, it's four, and I haven't slept a wink. My phone rings and I wonder who in the hell could be calling me this early.

"Yes?" I snap.

"I knew you would be up…" her voice rings out on the other end.

"What do you want?"

"I missed you…don't you want to come over?" I sigh heavily.

"You have no reason to miss me, we've been over this."

"Oh, Vincent…come on, now. You know you love to fuck me." Not particularly. I think back to the absent thrusts she swore were the best she's ever had. If that's the case, then she needs to re-evaluate her sex life.

"I'm going to make myself clear, again. There is nothing between us." She grows quiet.

"Vince, I felt it between us the last time we made love." I growl in frustration.

"We never made love, we fucked…" She gasps, obviously offended.

"You know that I have pictures…" Her tone grows dark.

"Right now, I don't give a fuck if you sell those to the tabloids. As much as I pay you, I'm insulted that you would do such a thing."

"You'll realize that I'm the best you ever had…" I laugh loudly.

"Lady, you've got me twisted… Don't blackmail me and flatter yourself by thinking I even remotely enjoyed fucking your bony ass." I hang up, done with this conversation. Well, I'm not sleeping now, I might as well get some time in at the gym.

I swipe my key card to get into the gym on the lower level of my building; between my sexual frustration and dealing with a crazy woman, I need a release. I hop on the treadmill, turn the TV to catch the opening bell, and start to run. As I run, I think about her again...Madeline. I can't get her off my mind and it's annoying. I have more than enough in my inventory to keep me satiated for the rest of my life. There is something different about her...she's intelligent, sweet, and one hell of a businesswoman. I actually enjoyed her company last night, loved the shine in her sweet brown eyes as we danced, and the kiss we shared that left my dick wanting more.

"Marks?" I hear the familiar voice next to me. Gusatvo Cruz hops on the treadmill beside mine. I slow down to a brisk walk.

"Gus" I regard my best friend.

"Great event last night..." he says, turning the TV to CNN.

"Yeah, I'm glad we were able to raise so much money."

"Let me ask you something..." he pauses and looks at me.

"Yes?"

"Stop your treadmill, man..." he orders. I reluctantly halt the treadmill and look over at his icy blue eyes.

"Madeline Davis...you like her?"

"Why would you even ask that?" I cut my eyes at him.

"I don't know, man...you looked different. Like you were dazzled by her." Damn him. Roommates for two years of college and he thinks he knows everything about me.

"She's...interesting."

"Interesting?"

"Okay, I haven't stopped thinking about her. Are you happy now?!" I snap. Gustavo looks amused at my response.

"Well, why aren't you doing anything about it?" I huff with frustration.

"You're the expert, what should I do?" My voice drips with sarcasm.

"You know goddamn well what you should do. Don't tell me you didn't learn from my experience." He was right. I remember when he first met Emily, that guy was walking around like a lovesick puppy until she stopped playing games and gave in.

"Yeah, well, you know me. I don't do relationships." Gus laughs loudly, drawing attention from the sparse crowd.

"Buddy, this girl has a hold on you. You gonna ignore it?" I roll my eyes.

"Well, are ya?"

"Goddamn it, I don't know man! She stays in Atlanta!" I exclaim with frustration.

"And…a branch of the company *you* own is in Atlanta. Try again with another lame excuse." I scoff.

"You're really pissing me off right now, man."

"And you're really pissing me off! You are not a gigolo, man! One day, you're gonna get old and fat, your dick will shrivel up and then what?"

"I'll take Viagra." Gus laughs again.

"What about the old and fat part?"

"I'll work out until I'm a hundred."

"Just give the girl a chance! At least she's not playing hard to get like Emily. Good God, that woman was almost the death of me!"

"She still is…" I chuckle.

"Come on, think about what I said. At the very least go talk to her for Christ's sake!"

"Damn it, Gus." I get off the treadmill and take a swig of water from the bottle in my hand. Gus laughs at my expense, knowing just how quickly he can make me mad when he's right. I look at the time on the scrolling news headlines noticing I spent a longer time here than I thought.

"I've got to go…"

"Lunch later?"

"Yeah, you bastard, we can go to lunch." I shove him and head to the elevators. That asshole, he thinks he knows me so damn well. I guess he really does…

After a hot shower, I wrap a towel around myself and head out of the bathroom. Just as I get dressed, I hear keys in the door. Undoubtedly, it's Mrs. Lovett, my housekeeper. She comes in like the usual ray of sunshine she is.

"Morning, Mr. Marks…" she sings but looks at me strangely.

"Good morning, Mrs. Lovett, what's wrong?"

"You look different."

"I do? Well, it's just a new suit…"

"No, no. Your face…I just can't put a finger on it." She looks at me pensively.

"I promise you there is nothing different about me."

"If you say so. What do you want for breakfast?"

"Just coffee, I'm running a little late." She nods and puts her things down.

I finish getting dressed, grab my briefcase and go to the kitchen. Mrs. Lovett, being the motherly type she is has packed me a breakfast of yogurt and fruit.

"Have a good day, Mr. Marks" she smiles. I pause and look at her.

"I won't need you for dinner tonight, Mrs. Lovett. I think I'm going to cook." She raises her eyebrows.

"Are you sure?" I nod.

"When you go grocery shopping, will you buy the ingredients for chicken enchiladas?" She gives me an even more surprised look.

"Of course." I thank her and leave out of the door. Wait, what the fuck am I doing? I'm actually considering cooking for this woman? This can't be happening.

I come into the office, which is busy as usual. Once I reach Alexis' desk, she looks at me warily.

"What's wrong?" I ask.

"Can you please call William? He's tying up the phone line!" she complains. I laugh.

"I'll take care of it, Alexis. Tell me what's on the agenda today." Annoyed and flustered by William's obvious verbal abuse, she takes out her iPad.

"Nothing pressing for the time being, Mr. Marks."

"Add lunch with Gustavo Cruz around 1:30. I'm…going to take a little time this morning outside of the office." She eyes me suspiciously.

"Very well. I'll take your calls." She grins. Maybe she knows something I don't.

"I owe you."

"Just doing my job" she waves me off.

I step into my office and wonder how I will do this. Maybe I just need to go to her hotel, fuck her brains out, and it will be done with. Yes, that's exactly what I will do. I open my desk drawer and rummage around, looking for a box of condoms. I only have one, and know I'll need more than that. I call my extremely personal assistant, Ralph. He's the only one that knows about my sexual endeavors besides Lou, and is responsible for booking hotel rooms and fielding calls from women who think they can get my heart along with my dick.

"Yes, Mr. Marks?" He answers.

"Ralph, I need condoms. Could you meet me at the Loews Hotel in oh, about thirty minutes?"

"Of course, should I book you a room, sir?"

"No, that's not necessary…she's already staying there."

"Anything else? Lube? Toys?" Good God this man reminds me of what a perverted bastard I am.

"No…just the condoms please."

"See you in half an hour" he says. I call William prepared to argue with him once again.

"Mr. Marks, I've been trying to reach you…" he answers annoyed.

"I do have a life William, you should try it sometime. What can I do for you?" He scoffs.

"Are you sure…this…this woman knows what she's talking about?"

"What is really your problem, William? The numbers or the person who is calculating them?"

"I'm just not confident in a woman accountant. You know, they get emotional and screw that shit up." Is he kidding me?

"Dude, you really need to get into the 21st century. I promise you her numbers are intact and they match yours for Christ sakes! Do you really think I wouldn't check her numbers?" He sighs, obviously this guy has some issues with women.

"If it makes you feel better, I'll recheck them myself" I lie, knowing damn well her numbers are good. Hell, we just went over them with Lucas. This guy could use a good lay…or something to kill the bug up his ass.

"It will. Thanks. See you Monday." I hang up frustrated.

Now, back to Madeline. She's smart, she's not going to accept my usual booty call lines. I need a good excuse without her demanding to come into the office. Suddenly, remembering my conversation with William, I know exactly what I will do. Just as I'm about to pick up the phone to call her, my phone rings.

"Yes?" I bark, irritated at the interruption.

"Who pissed in your cornflakes? You're a businessman, you can't answer the phone like that, muchacho." Gus says.

"Sorry, what do you want, Gus? I'm kind of busy right now."

"Alexis called me, I'm just confirming our lunch at 1:30." he honestly sounds like he's a bit hurt that I'm brushing him off.

"Yeah, that's fine...I'll see you then."

"Hey...what are you gonna do about that thing we talked about?" I close my eyes with aggravation. He's just going to keep throwing it in my face until I give him something.

"I'll talk to you at lunch." I growl. Maybe I do just need a good fuck; this irritability is getting to me. I need to do something quick.

"Are you sure you weren't a woman in your past life? Take a chill pill amigo! You owe me an hour." He hangs up and I take a deep breath before dialing Madeline's hotel.

## Chapter 7 *Only the Beginning*

"He kissed you?!" I hear Nathan's squeal through the phone as I detail the events of the night before.

"It was...the most magical kiss I've ever had." I stop suddenly and begin to be fearful again. There is no way I could date this man and reach my fullest potential at the company. Reality hits me hard.

"Maddie, don't over think it. If it's a fling, you get some dick that might keep you satisfied until you do find the one" Nathan's wildly inappropriate comment strikes a chord. Could I sleep with this man without falling madly in love with him? Would I have to work for a new company? Would it bring scandal when we're doing so well? I wouldn't want to contribute to the demise of the company that gave me my start in life.

"I'll keep you updated."

"Please do, and remember what I said!"

"I will. I love you."

"I love you too baby..." I press "end". Before I know it, I'm drifting back to sleep and have maddening dreams about Vincent. Oh boy, this is going to be a tough call. I dream of his touch, his kisses and his words of admiration towards me. I even start to think what must be under those wonderfully tailored suits. Could he pleasure me and take me to heights I've never known? The way he twirled me around the dance floor certainly indicates he has some moves. I can imagine him taking me, giving me multiple orgasms...Jesus, I get wet just thinking about it.

My desire burns even deeper now and I wake in a frenzy. What in hell am I going to do with this situation? I know Nathan would tell me to stop thinking so hard, but I can't help myself. I think of my night and wonder for a minute if it was all a dream.

I relax in the hot shower with soft music playing in the background on my iPad. I have so much to consider today; I hope that there are no emergencies at the office. As I step out of the shower, I look at myself in the mirror and start to realize that my body is in definite need of attention. Perhaps that's why I crave this man so much. Maybe it's nothing but simple, high school grade lust. Maybe it's time to find out...

I'm interrupted by my phone ringing and see that it's Vincent. I pause before answering so that I won't sound so eager.

"Madeline, would you mind if I stopped by your hotel to discuss some discrepancies in the numbers?" Discrepancies? I go into a panic.

"Sure, I'm in room 2112." I say nervously. I've never screwed up the numbers before, so I'm deathly anxious. I quickly slip into a pencil skirt paired with a flowing blouse and order a quick breakfast from room service.

As I'm quietly eating my fruit and sipping coffee, I hear a soft knock at the door. I get up to answer the door. There is Vincent, in all black dashed with a baby blue tie. I want to faint at the sight of those strong muscles, those beautiful eyes. Before I can say anything, he grabs me, holds me close and kisses me frantically. The kiss is thrilling and I feel currents of arousal surround my body as this beautiful man wraps his strong arms around me.

"I had to see you again, so I told you a little white lie. Is that okay?" he breathes.

"Yes." I say simply as I grab his tie and pull him into another kiss. God, I want this man so badly. He slowly moves his hands up and down my body and I melt at his touch. His breathing turns ragged as he begins to undo the buttons on my blouse.

"Is it alright for me to do this?" he asks in between kisses.

"Yes, please." Seems to be the only words that come to mind. He takes off my blouse and begins to unhook my lacy bra releasing my breasts.

"You are so…beautiful" he sighs as he cups my full breasts in his hand. I feel my nipples harden in response, and unbutton his shirt. We never seem to stop kissing each other. He finds the zipper to my skirt and unzips it quickly, making it fall to the floor and revealing my black lace panties. I secretly thank Victoria's Secret for the pleasing selection. He picks me up and lays me on the queen sized bed. His kisses send shivers all over my body. He suckles my nipple and I throw my head back in pleasure, humming with appreciation. He expertly caress spots my body hasn't felt in almost a year. I slowly brush every part of him with my fingertips, finally finding what I'm looking for, gently teasing the huge bulge between his legs.

"Mmm" he murmurs as he slips a finger inside of me. I moan as his tempo quickens. I feel so hot with desire; it would take the whole FDNY to cool me off. Finally, he kisses that sweet spot in between my legs, and before I know it, I'm acquainted with the skills of his tongue. I writhe and moan on the bed, loving the feeling. He continues his brutal assault as my cries go up an octave. His moans vibrating on my sensitive area turn me on even more. I grab his slick bald head to increase the pleasure. My body climbs higher and higher before I climax loudly, shouting his name as he moans in response. He climbs up and kisses me allowing me to taste the evidence of my arousal.

He looks at me for a second before he asks, "Do we need a condom?"

I nod weakly. I want to give this man everything he wants, everything he needs, and I need it as well. He produces a condom out of his pocket, rips the wrapper and glides it onto his thick, long erection. He climbs on top of me and slides in effortlessly, moaning sweetly as he fills me up. It feels…delightful, primal as if he were made just for me. He begins a slow movement inside of me and I wail loudly. He groans with the rhythm and covers my neck with hungry kisses. As he speeds up, I feel like I am going to explode again. His gaze never leaves mine as he slides in and out. I feel the climax building inside of me again and lose myself in his sensual tempo.

"Oh! Faster!" I yell loudly as his rhythm quickens more and more honoring my request. We're panting, needing, and wanting each other. I explode around him, crying out as I arch off the bed with an intense orgasm.

"God! Madeline!" he shouts as he finds his release, his body trembling violently. He stares into my eyes and kisses me with fervent passion. I have never known this type of desire before and it almost scares me. His intense look as we made love gives me a feeling I've never encountered.

"Madeline, do you know how amazing you are?" he says, panting as he lies down beside me.

"Smart, yes. Amazing, no" I reply. He shakes his head and kisses me once more.

"I wanted to do this to you last night." He says matter-of-factly. I knew he did. I wanted him to do that to me last night as well. This man has aroused feelings in me that I haven't had since the breakup. I feel tears in my eyes.

"What's wrong?" he asks with concern.

"I don't know how to handle this resurrection of feelings" I respond shakily.

"Just go with the flow, baby" he croons.

At that moment, I feel his erection poking me once more, and I know he's not done with me yet. He takes out yet another condom and tears the wrapper.

"Wait," I say, "let me." I slide the condom over his beautiful long cock. I then climb on top of him, feeling passion take over me. I slide down on him and begin to rock seductively.

"Oh, God, I don't know if I can take this" he says as I pick up the pace. I keep the rhythm going, loving the feeling of him inside me.

"Madeline" he growls softly. He matches my rhythm and grabs my ass. He holds me tightly as he groans in response to my hostile takeover. I feel myself climbing again and he finds that sweet spot in between my legs to massage as I continue.

"Oh, Vincent" I whimper, my body craving release. Suddenly, I feel as if I'm free falling. My orgasm is so intense that I clutch him tightly as I scream his name.

"Ah, Fuck!" he gasps at his release. He trembles and grabs my face to kiss me. The intensity makes me sob. I've never come so hard before.

"Madeline, what have you done to me?" he says as he holds me close. I wonder the same thing. What has he done to me? He wipes the tears from my eyes.

"We're going to have to keep this a secret" I whisper as I think of the upcoming merger.

"I will if that means I can keep you." He strokes my hair and I look up at him.

"You know nothing about me. This could be a simple case of infatuation."

"Why do you doubt it?" His voice reflects frustration.

"Because I've been here before" I look at him with seriousness.

"Give me a chance, Madeline. We can keep it a secret for now, okay?" I give him a glance with admiration and nod. Suddenly, he glances frantically at the clock.

"Shit, I've gotta go. Can you meet me for dinner tonight?" he asks giving me a hopeful look.

"I most certainly can."

He gets up to take a shower, and I lie in the bed feeling wracked with guilt. This man just took over the company. He's been too much of an asset to us for me to ruin it because I lust for him. After putting on a t-shirt and shorts, I saunter over to my iPad and turn on the relaxing sounds of Zero 7, and immediately feel the need for a drink. It's just now twelve-thirty, but I call room service and order two screwdrivers…with extra shots.

Vincent emerges from the shower, looking as gorgeous as ever with his fresh scrubbed skin. He glides across the floor and kisses me passionately.

"Can't wait to see you tonight." He grabs his briefcase and waves as he heads out of the door.

"Girrrrrrrrrl…" says Nathan when I tell him of the morning tryst over the phone as I guzzle down my screwdiver.

"I don't know what to do." As usual, sexual resentment has hit me.

"Go with the flow, like he said. This is not your first fuck buddy." I scoff.

"I feel like this is a cheap thrill for him. Take one of the most powerful females in the company." I hear Nathan's grin on the phone, "What?" I demand.

"Just have fun for now! You can think about the serious stuff later. You said yourself that he knew what he was doing, girl take all the orgasms you can get!"

"You're right, there's plenty of time to think about this. For now I'll just go with the flow."

"There you go! I love you and have fun for the next two weeks. Keep me posted!"

"I love you too." I sigh heavily. I can't get my mind off the intensity I felt this afternoon. Can I do this? I have so much to think about.

I am done with yet another revision of the merger agreement and look at the clock realizing that I've been in a work coma for longer than I expected. I email the documents to Lacy and hop in the shower while thinking about Vincent. His hands and kisses intoxicated me. I close my eyes thinking about how he made me come, my body squeezing his dick until he came. My skin begins to heat up and I take a deep breath, trying to calm myself so that I don't tackle him the minute I get there.

I choose a short, sexy black wrap dress that I always travel with just in case. As I'm putting on my earrings, I hear the ping that signals a text message. I pick up the phone to read it. *My car is outside waiting. V.* Wow, I didn't think he would send his car for me. I text him back, letting him know that I will be down momentarily.

When I get into the car, I notice he is not in the car as I anticipated. Lou slides into the driver's seat and heads into the lights of the city. In a matter of minutes, we arrive at an elegant apartment building. I gasp and can already feel the eagerness and arousal, the space between my legs aching for the feel of him. Lou punches a number at the gate in the parking deck and the gate opens. I shift in my seat, trying to quiet the throbbing between my legs. Lou opens the door for me and punches a code into the elevator.

"Have a good night, Ms. Davis" he says with a smile. I push back my thoughts as the elevator lands on the thirtieth floor. I hear the ping of my phone indicating a text message. *3320. V.* I take a deep breath and glide to the foyer. He…looks…so…hot, wearing jeans and a black button-up shirt that hugs his muscles. I can't help but to stare.

"Hi baby," he says in that sexy deep voice of his. He moves towards me and kisses me passionately before I can respond.

"Hi" I breathe, my voice flaming with fervor. Just as I consider jumping into his arms, I am distracted by a delicious aroma coming from the kitchen.

"You cook?" I ask with amusement.

"Do I cook? Ms. Davis, you have no idea" he says with a grin.

"You're so talented." I reply with awe.

"Me, talented? Nah." he laughs. He leads me to the kitchen where I recognize the sweet, spicy aroma of chicken enchiladas.

He pours us each a glass of Cabernet Sauvignon and raises his glass, "To the beginning of something beautiful". We talk over dinner, and laugh at the shenanigans of some of our top people. It feels great to be carefree, and Vincent is really wonderful to talk to. His eyes glimmer with interest as I tell him my dreams for the future.

"I think we need some music" he says as he clears our plates. After he places the dishes in the dishwasher, he grabs a remote and presses a button. A soulful ballad courtesy of Earth, Wind and Fire fills the room. This man never ceases to amaze me.

"Dance?" he asks, eyes glowing with fire.
I grab his hand and we float on the living room floor. We move in time to the music, and for the first time, I notice the gorgeous view of New York from his gigantic windows. This is my ultimate fantasy, and I have no idea if the affection I feel for him right now is real.

As the music fades, Vincent kisses me passionately. The kiss grows deeper and I sense his urgency. I kiss him back with the same determination. I have to have him now. I moan as I melt into his arms. He stops for a second and looks at me with a silent request. I look at him in agreement, my shaky breath indicating that I am ready. He takes my hand and leads me to the bedroom.

Vince slowly removes my dress and stares at my figure. He unhooks my bra, cupping my breasts as I unbutton his shirt and pull it off, admiring his rippling muscles. He grabs my hand, stopping me.

"Are you sure about this?" he asks with concern.

"I've never been so sure about anything in my life" I say, my desire taking over me. He growls at my answer and picks me up. He lays me on the bed and swiftly pulls off my panties. Kneeling over me, he places kisses all over my body. As he suckles my right nipple, I start to feel the tingling in my groin. He sucks harder; I want to push him away, but it feels so good. He keeps sucking, and I feel that oh-so-familiar burn inside. I twist, thinking I'm going crazy and detonate with a scream, my toes curling.

He pulls a condom from the nightstand drawer and rips the wrapper quickly. Before I know it, he slides it on and buries himself in me. This time, he pushes all of the way inside me, shocking my body so much that I let out a trembling moan. I see a different man; one burning with lust. He whispers my name as he pounds mercilessly inside me. I can't take it; tears start to well in my eyes as he speeds up. I surrender, holding on to him tightly as he continues moving.

"Come for me, Madeline. I want to feel you come for me" he orders .My body obeys, exploding from the inside out. I yell his name, the orgasm clenching so hard that it hurts. My body arches off the bed as if I'm levitating. He groans loudly and holds me tightly as he comes. The painful pulses continue inside of me until I am overcome and descent into darkness.

"Madeline? Are you okay?" Vincent says as he caresses my face. I come to, but am almost too weak to talk. No man has ever brought me to the point of passing out.

"I'm okay" I say quietly as tears fall out of my eyes. He holds me tight and kisses my forehead.

"Madeline, for the first time, I'm undone. I can't stop thinking about you."

"Vincent... Give me time, I've been hurt so badly before."

"I hope you don't think I would ever hurt you" he says, shocking me.

"Let's just see where this goes" I say.

"Good things come to those who wait, and I have been waiting for you" he kisses me.

"Just let me grasp this and I promise you, if it is what I think it is, I will concede."

"Promise?"

"Promise."

"Good, go to sleep" he says and wraps his arms around me. I don't mind following his command as my body is absolutely exhausted. It feels so good to have his arms around me and have someone next to me in the bed. Mine has felt so cold and lonely for the past year. I caress his hands and he pulls me closer obviously feeling grateful to have someone sharing a bed with him as well.

As I sleep, my mind begins to race with questions. What in hell am I going to do? I've spent two days with this man and he has a hold on me. No man has made me feel so wanted, or given me orgasms that bring me to tears. He has definitely put a spell on me and I will have to control myself around him. To quiet my mind, I resign that maybe I'm still suffering from school girl lust. This will surely pass. I have to convince myself of it before I fall in love and risk a broken heart again. I'll go back to Atlanta, he'll go back to his life and it will all be over with. For now, I'm just going to have fun.

During the night, Vincent wakes me up with his fiery kisses, ready to take me again. He definitely has some energy in him. I could so get used to this. He rolls me on my side and I hear the urgent slam of the nightstand drawer and the ripping of the wrapper. He slides into me, grabbing my waist and I moan at the feeling of him inside of me. He is so…big, stretching me to fit him.

"Vince…" I whisper in pleasure.

"Goddamn…you're so wet…" he moans, picking up the pace. He slides his fingers from my waist down to my clit, applying just enough pressure to arouse me even more.

"Oh! Vince!"

"That's right…damn girl…I love fucking you" he growls in my ear, tantalizing my neck with hot kisses. He keeps pounding until I am pierced by another hard orgasm. Everything inside of me squeezes him, and I scream his name loud enough for all of Manhattan to hear. I didn't think it was possible to come harder than I did before but I did.

"Fuck yes…Oh my God…you're coming so hard…"he moans before succumbing to his own hard, shuddering release. I turn around and seal our seductive session with a deep kiss and he pulls me close, leaving light kisses on my forehead.

Chapter 8 *More than Desire*

I look at Madeline sleeping peacefully in my arms, a strange sight for me. No woman has ever been in my apartment…with the exception of my mother, sister and Mrs. Lovett. I'm acting like a damned teenager…and yet, I don't see it as a bad thing. The sleeping beauty next to me has put me under a crazy hypnosis.

I was so damn sure that fucking her at the hotel would get rid of these feelings, but once it was done, I wanted more. I found myself blurting out the invitation to dinner before my mind could even think it. I said much more tonight than I wanted to, but I wanted to let her know my feelings. She dazes me like that. I could even…see myself doing this for a lifetime with her. Just her. My cock stirs, and I know I want her again.

I kiss her full, soft lips and she moans softly her eyes fluttering open.

"Again?" she asks, sleepily.

"Yes, again…" I say, my dick growing harder in anticipation. She laughs and runs her fingers around my arms. God, I love her touch. Letting my lust take over me, I roll her over and kiss her again. Reaching under my pillow, I bring out another condom and quickly tear it open. I slide the condom on my dick and sink into her. At least Ralph knows how to choose the bare skin condoms. Jesus, she feels good and wet, that pussy wanting me. I begin pounding into her, my animal instincts taking over. She lets out a yell that turns me even more. I kiss her neck, as I continue sliding in and out of her. She grows wetter each time and it makes me even harder.

"Oh! Vince!" She cries out as she comes, her body grabbing me, milking me. I want her to come again and slow down, willing myself to hold on until she does. She trembles as I keep pounding. Her legs lock and she screams again, her body bucking into me. She sobs my name loudly, and I'm finally unable to take it anymore. I finally come with a loud, cursing roar, pouring myself into her. We both shake, coming down from a high that neither one of us seem to have experience with. She sighs with obvious satisfaction and looks back at me.

"Well, I guess cooking and business aren't your only specialties..."she breathes and I laugh loudly.

"The lady is happy..I think I've done my job" I say, caressing her wild hair.

"Happy isn't the word for it..."

"Oh? I was that good, Ms. Davis?"

"Something like that." I pull the condom off, throwing it in the trashcan beside my bed before pulling her back into my arms. This feels so right, so normal. Why did I never try it? Maybe I just never had the desire to, or never met a woman who made me want to. Madeline Davis has certainly changed this man.

I look at the sweet, sleeping face and wonder why on earth some guy hasn't claimed this gem. What did that asshole do to her? Even though I've gotten her to open up some, I notice she still holds back. If she were to really let go, I know I can find my way into her heart. I can already see that whatever bumbling, small dicked bastards she's been with weren't fucking her right. If I had my way, her ass would be naked in my bed every night and she would never have to wonder what I feel for her.

As much as I try to sleep, I can't stop staring at her, thinking about making love to her. Reluctantly, I roll over. I need to stop staring at her. I hear her let out a small sound and she shifts, putting her arms around me. She needs someone to love her, someone to take care of her, and maybe I'll be that man.

I wake up at seven-thirty finally feeling rested. I see Sleeping Beauty has rolled over, her arms around one of my pillows. She probably needs the sleep. I was quite...energetic last night. I get up, taking care not to wake her. I need to be at the office and can't be as absent as I was yesterday. My rendezvous with Madeline and lunch with Gus ran longer than expected, but I was glad for the distraction.

I hear Mrs. Lovett coming into the apartment and go to the kitchen to talk to her. In the absence of my own mother, who still lives in Connecticut, she's always a welcome sight. When she sees me emerging from the bedroom, she smiles.

"Did you sleep late, Mr. Marks?" she asks in that thick British accent of hers.

"I did. It was essential for my survival today." I look back towards the bedroom.

"Listen, I have a...guest this morning." She stops cold and glares at me.

"A guest?" Her tone reeks of disbelief.

"Yes, her name is Madeline Davis. When she wakes up, please make her breakfast just in case I'm gone." A huge grin forms on her face.

"*Her* name? Mr. Marks, that's why you looked different." She beams.

"Huh?" I look at her with question.

"You're in love." Hmph. After two days? Doubtful. Extreme lust maybe.

"I don't know if it's that, Mrs. L. I just met her."

"I do. Don't worry, I'll take good care of her. Anything else on my list today?"

"Yes, I'll probably be at the office late, so if you could just leave dinner in the oven for me to heat up later, I'll be thankful." She nods.

"What do you want for dinner?"

"I trust you. Also, I have a shipment from the wine club coming in today. I've told them your signature is fine."

"Anything else?" I think about it for a minute.

"No. I think that's it besides the regular list…and…I'm sure the sheets need to be washed" I smile sheepishly at her. She stifles a giggle. Women.

"I'll get on it." She busies herself in the kitchen while I head for the shower.

I run the water and realize I can't get Madeline off my mind. I start to grow hard again, thinking about her squirming under me, crying my name as she comes, her pussy squeezing me until I come. Jesus Christ. I have got to clear my head or I'm going to be in trouble. I talk myself down mentally, thinking about the merger we have coming up. I make a few mental notes, and remind myself to meet with Alexis later to discuss some accommodations for Lucas and his crew. Ugh, and I have to deal with that awful asshole William. I sigh and decide to get out of the shower before my temper flares. Mad or horny, which one is worse?

As the water runs over me, I absently wonder if she'll wake up before I leave. I'd love to fuck her just one more time before leaving, or at least eat her. I'm getting hard again just thinking about it. I might have to wake her up and fuck her senseless. No woman has ever made me hard like this. I step out of the shower and my phone rings. The office number comes up on the caller ID and I wonder if something has happened.

"Alexis?" I answer.

"Mr. Marks, I'm sorry to call you at home…" she says.

"It's fine, what's going on?" She lowers her voice.

"It's Dina." Anxiety strikes me.

"What about Dina?"

"I don't know, Mr. Marks, she's acting really strange."

"What is she doing?"

"She's been hovering around your office all morning. I figured if she needed to see you, she'd call, but obviously, it's not the case."

"I'll be there shortly, Alexis. If she pulls anything, call Jack." She agrees and tells me that she'll see me in a bit. Great. Now I have to put up with this crazy bitch. Feeling irritated, I call Gus. I know he has people that can find out anything.

"What's up, Muchacho?" He answers.

"Gus, this isn't a social call..." I say.

"What's going on?" He asks in his businesslike manner.

"I need you to do some background on Dina Andrews."

"Your CCO? Why?"

"I don't know, she's been threatening me with blackmail and just acting crazy lately. I think she's up to something."

"I'll get Alistair to look into it, but I have to ask you...am I gonna find something that she has to blackmail you with?" I sigh heavily.

"Look...when I first bought the company...I slept with her a few times."

"Okay...anything else I should know about?" He doesn't sound surprised.

"She..." I pause, ashamed of what I did.

"Tell me, man. I don't want to have a heart attack at thirty-five."

"I took her on vacation...you know, as a thank you for helping with my transition. For a while, she was my right hand woman. I had to have someone who knew about everything before I got there."

"Did you take photos when you guys were..."

"Yeah, she did." He sighs.

"So, when I find this stuff and whatever else, what do you want me to do with it?"

"I need you to get rid of it."

"I'll have Alistair forward all the information. I can have it done by noon."

"I knew I could depend on you."

"Always, brother, you know that."

"I don't need this chick sinking my company."

"No doubt. So…are you gonna tell me what happened yesterday?"

"Gus!" I let out a frustrated groan.

"What you didn't think I would ask?"

"I'm…still figuring it out."

"Liar."

"Do we really have to talk about this now?" He chuckles.

"What?" I ask.

"She's there isn't she?" I swear this man has my apartment bugged.

"Yes, you nosy bastard she is. What about it?"

"Might be why the other chick is acting crazy."

"She wouldn't know!"

"Don't comfort yourself with that thought. This woman handles media campaigns. She can get someone to spy on you anytime."

"You think so?"

"I've been in public relations for ten years, yes, I think she could."

"What do I do?" I start to grow worried. There's no way I'm going to let this woman bring my company down because she feels romantic rejection from me.

"You let me see what my man can find out. Emily and I will do whatever we can to make sure you stay safe: professionally and personally."

"I know, Gus. Thanks, man. Let me know what you come up with."

"Take care, I got this." He hangs up and I feel better knowing I have him on my side.

Chapter 9 *Hard Decisions*

I awake suddenly to the sound of an echoing voice, and remind myself I'm in Vincent's apartment. He must be in the bathroom. I get up and open his drawer, looking for a t-shirt. I find one with our company logo and saunter into the kitchen to find some coffee. A petite woman with long brown hair is making a list while going through the pantry. I am embarrassed in my half-dressed state, but she gives me a welcoming, friendly smile.

"You must be Ms. Davis; I'm Mrs. Lovett, Mr. Marks' housekeeper" she says warmly. She has an accent...British maybe. Holy crap, how does she know about me?

"Would you like some breakfast? I can fix you anything."

"Coffee, Scrambled eggs and toast would be great. Thank you, Mrs. Lovett." I say with a smile.

"Getting acquainted with my number one ace, I see." I look up and see Vincent in a blue suit. His smile is infectious and he looks so fine. He moves over to kiss me, and I feel uncomfortable in the presence of Mrs. Lovett. She doesn't seem to mind. In fact, she almost seems relieved to see him showing affection towards me.

"I have to say, I like you in that t-shirt. Why don't you keep it?" he says, smiling even wider.

"Well, I'm always up for free stuff..." I pip. He shakes his head and laughs.

"What would you like for breakfast, Mr. Marks?" asks Ms. Lovett, interrupting my swooning thoughts.

"Just some coffee, thank you" Vincent says. He looks at me with admiration.

"What are your plans for the day, Madeline?"

"I'd like to have Lacy today if it's possible. I promised her I would take her sightseeing." I tell him.

"Whatever you want, baby" he says, "are you going to tell her about us?" I shake my head. Lacy doesn't need to know until it is absolutely necessary.

Vincent moves closer to me and whispers in my ear, "I want to have you one more time." He leads me to the bedroom telling Mrs. Lovett we'll be back.

My body is convulsing and I whimper quietly as Vincent finishes his assault between my legs. I am standing against the wall of his bedroom, amazed at the skills of his tongue. He flickers his tongue one more time on my sex and kisses my inner thigh.

"You are amazing" I breathe. He smiles at my compliment.

"I must confess…I've never felt this way about anyone before." I don't know what to say, and start to laugh nervously. He looks hurt at my response.

"Vincent, we've known each other for about a minute. Don't count your eggs before they hatch."

"When this merger is done…I'd like you to take over Joseph's position. I'm promoting him to Chief Business Development Officer." I begin to laugh again, this time I howl with laughter noticing the tears running down my cheeks. He looks confused.

"You want me, Madeline Davis to take over the Atlanta branch? Are you insane?" I shout a little loudly.

"I don't think I've ever been so sane in my life. I think that we would make a fantastic team…"

"Do you know how that would look?" I grimace.

"I am the CEO, the head boss, and the owner. What are they gonna do, fire me?" He has a valid point, but I'm not so sure how my co-workers would take it.

"If you can promise me that none of my co-workers will be treated any differently, and that everyone will have a fair shot at taking over Joseph's position, I will move up the ladder. You can't just give me a position. I need to interview like everyone else."

"You have no idea do you?" He looks at me, "Joseph is the one who wants you to be his successor and refused to consider anyone else. I was going to announce it Sunday and surprise you, but when I'm with you I get dazed..." I gasp at this news. Suddenly, all the signs come to me. Joseph was calling me on the weekends and putting me in charge of top projects even though I was a novice. He was grooming me to take over our branch of the company all along because he had counted on moving up.

"You've done great things for this company, Madeline. You deserve everything you get." I sigh with the weight of indecision falling on my shoulders.

Unexpectedly, we are interrupted by a timid Ms. Lovett through the door, "Breakfast is ready, Ms. Davis."

"We will talk about this later; I'm coming into the office." I sense his disappointment, but he stays silent.
After he leaves, I eat breakfast and talk to Mrs. Lovett. She is a kind, gentle woman and I can tell that she treats Vince like a son. Even though he only asked for coffee, she snuck yogurt and fruit into his bag before he left. Maybe that's why he never thought it necessary to have a significant other. He was already taken care of.

I get back to the hotel and realize how exhausted I am. Vince woke me twice last night, and made love to me until I wilted. Not only does this man overwhelm me with his looks, intelligence and lovemaking but also the proposition of a huge promotion. I have to seek advice from someone. I step out of the shower and dry myself off. I look at the alarm clock and realize I have time, so I pick up the phone to call Nathan.

"Madeline? What's wrong?" Nathan senses the worried tone in my voice.

"First, he tells me that he wants me to take over the branch, then tells me he never felt this way about anyone before." Nathan is silent for a minute.

"Maddie, maybe he is genuine."

"He has only known me for two days, Nathan!"

"Honey, you've gotta have more faith. Just because that asshole Eric didn't know how to treat you doesn't mean this man won't give you the world." Everything finally starts to hit me and I burst into tears.

"Maddie," Nathan says gently, "Don't be dumb if there is something sketchy going on, but please let this man love you if he's willing to. I can tell that you are falling for him too." His words resonate in my mind.

"You're absolutely right. I need to let myself be loved."

"Please do, and I have a feeling that this is the one. Love knows no time frame. Allow yourself to feel it."

"I love you, Nathan" I say sniffling.

"I love you too baby, please have fun and let yourself feel for him." I press "end" and look for something to wear to the office. I change into a black suit with a skirt that shows off my legs. I brush my hair out, put on makeup and head towards the elevator. Lou is waiting for me with the car. I smile and thank him for coming to pick me up.

Once I get to the office, everyone seems to be busy. I saunter towards Lacy, and she greets me with a big smile. "Madeline!" She exclaims and studies me carefully, "You're glowing! Did you get a facial on your time off?" I didn't realize she knew about Joseph's ploy to get me to relax.

She is entertained by my look, "Yes, Joseph told me that for the first few days you were to rest."

"Well, get your work done, lady. I'm treating you to lunch and then we're going shopping." I say. Lacy squeals and squeezes me in a tight hug. I tell her I'll be back after a brief meeting with...Mr. Marks. No one has to know that I'm on a first name basis with him. Right?

I approach the huge office door and knock softly.

"What?!" I hear Vincent snap. I open the door slowly. His face softens as he sees me.

"Close the door and lock it" he orders. I obey his command and shut the door, twisting the lock. He grabs me, pulls me to him and kisses me. I feel dizzy as his tongue invades my mouth. After hypnotizing me with his deep kiss, he caresses my cheek softly.

"Come here." He takes my hand, leading me over to the plush leather couch. He strokes my face with affection.

"Madeline, did you think about what I said?" He asks gently.

"I did and still want my other co-workers to have a chance. Just as a formality to make sure I'm the most qualified." He scoffs.

"Fine." He gets up and retrieves papers from his desk.

"These are their final quarterlies. Do you want to look through and see if the numbers will change?"

"Sure." I sit down next to him and look at the reports. I glance at him as I read, remembering how he was when I first came in.

"Why were you so angry when I knocked on the door?" I inquire.

"Ah, well, I tell ya. I like Lucas alright but his CFO is a bastard." His eyes darken. I roll mine. I'm familiar with that asshole, William. He always snapped at me when I called during the beginning of the merger.

"Is there a problem?"

"Yes..."he sighs.

"Well, what is it?"

"William seems to have a problem working with a woman."

"I figured he was agitated that I was a woman."

"I've been fighting with him all morning, but don't worry. You will wow him on Monday. The asshole won't even be able to speak in your presence." He smiles reassuringly.

"Screw him, I'm not worried. My numbers are in order."

Before I know it, he pulls me onto his lap. "Is the door still locked?" he asks seductively.

"It is," I breathe. We embrace and lose ourselves in a passionate kiss. He gently takes off my jacket and removes my camisole.

"Shhh.." he says, "we're gonna have to stay quiet." He unzips his pants and slides a condom onto his growing erection. He is always prepared. He slides my panties to the side and enters me. I want to cry out, but his kiss silences me. He moves me up and down on him, letting out a groan and moving me faster. I match his rhythm and whimper. He stares into my eyes and I watch him unravel beneath me. I start to feel that familiar climb. Our rhythm increases and my quiet cry rises higher and higher until I explode around him. His mouth covers mine and muffles my orgasmic scream. My body convulses continuously around him. He holds me tightly and comes, groaning with a jolt. He kisses me powerfully, his tongue massaging mine.

"Lacy is waiting." I whisper and gently slide off of him. He hisses as I remove him from me.

I put on my camisole and jacket while Vincent straightens himself up. I check the mirror and notice my hair looks a mess, so I take a brush out of my purse and put it back into place. Vincent comes over and puts his arms around my waist, kissing my neck.

I turn around and stroke his face one last time and leave out his office. Lacy sees me and packs her laptop bag excitedly. Maybe on the way home, I will tell her about Vince. I want to shout it from the rooftops but I know that we have to be careful. It pains me to keep him a secret. Nathan was right;

I have to allow myself to fall in love. Fuck what everyone else thinks. One day, everyone will know that this amazing man is mine.

Chapter 10 *Let Go*

"You want another?" I ask as Madeline finishes off her wine.

"Sure," she shrugs, "I *am* on vacation." I laugh at her humor and signal the bartender for another bottle. He comes over and opens a new bottle of Merlot, pouring a serving into each of our glasses.

"I guess we should have gotten dinner. I'm feeling a buzz" I observe. She giggles and touches my face.

"I'm actually not very hungry for food..." her eyes flirt with me.

"Oh? What are you hungry for?" I ask, knowing the answer.

"I think you know what whets my appetite" she says seductively. My cock awakens.

"Whoa...calm down there. Traffic is a nightmare right now, we can't get to my place."

"*You* calm down..." she teases the bulge between my legs and I catch her hand.

"Stop..." I warn. She smiles at my agitation and puts her hands up in playful defeat. I finally got her to let loose and I love it. I can't wait until she lets loose in the bedroom. I look deep into her eyes.

"What are you staring at, Mr. Marks?" she asks.

"Call me Vince."

"Vince, huh?"

"Yeah, a term of endearment. All my friends and family call me Vince."

"Oh! So I'm a friend?" Her eyes are sparkling dangerously.

"You're more than a friend." She scoffs and drains her glass.

"Don't drink too many of those, love. I need you to be awake later."

"I'm not an amateur at this." She laughs as my phone rings.

"Lou?" I answer.

"I'm here."

"Give us ten."

"I'll be waiting." I look over at Madeline.

"Let's chug this bottle...Lou's here." She smiles and pours herself another glass.

Once we get into my apartment, I grab her and put my lips to hers. She moans in surprise as I reach under her skirt and shred her panties.

"Vince..."she protests in between kisses. I pick her up and take her to the bed, finding the zipper to her skirt. I undress her, admiring her dangerous curves. I jump out of my clothes, eager to be inside her.

"You can't..."she moans as I bury my face between her legs. I devour her, taking her clit into my mouth and sucking on it. I apply pressure with my tongue and she twists on the bed moaning. Her breaths quicken as I lick harder, sticking my tongue inside her.

"Vince!" she calls out before she whimpers and gives in to her climax. I lock my arms around her legs, tasting the result of her release. I'm ready to make her come harder than she ever has before. I rise up and reach for a condom, eager to get it on me so that I can fuck her out of her mind. I look into her eyes with silent intention and thrust into her. She gasps, wrapping her legs around me and I start pounding.

"Vince...Vince..." she moans as I go faster.

"Let go, Madeline...let go..." I command. She digs her fingernails into my back as she hollers with her release. Her body squeezes my dick so hard that I almost lose control. I sink deeper, loving the feeling of her. She trembles and tears fall out of her eyes as I keep going, longing to feel her come again.

"Fuck..." I bite out through gritted teeth.

"Ah! God!" She comes again, almost driving me insane. I grab her face, kissing her deeply.

"Don't do this to me…"she cries in a whisper. I slow down and look into her eyes.

"What, baby?" I ask.

"Don't make me fall for you…don't hurt me…" she shivers as tears stream out of her eyes. I lean close to her ear.

"I'll make you fall for me…but I will never, ever hurt you" her breathing quickens.

"You can't promise that…" I pull her up into my lap.

"Yes, I can…and I'm going to show you." I start to drive into her and she moans loudly. She twists in my lap and I hold her down as I kiss her shoulder. She comes with a deafening scream, her fingers squeezing my thighs. My cock swells and I tighten my grip around her waist as I explode into her, cursing loudly.

Around one in the morning, she grows limp in my arms after an especially powerful climax claims both of us. She dissolves into sobs, gripping me tightly. I say nothing, pulling her close and pressing my lips to her forehead. A bit later, she finally quiets and looks at me, her eyes red with tears.

"You promise?" she whispers with a sniffle.

"I promise, baby." I kiss her gently and she touches my face.

"Come on, now. You need some sleep…" I start to pull away and she holds me tighter.

"No…stay." I let out a soft laugh.

"I've gotta take the condom off." She smiles and lets me go.

I awaken to my phone ringing and notice that it's light outside. Shit! I'm probably late. I gently unwrap Madeline from me and grab my phone as I dart into the bathroom.

"Hello?" I answer.

"Glad to see you're alive! Did you forget about our meeting today?" Gus' voice comes through the speaker.

"I'm sorry, Gus...I don't even have a good excuse." I kick myself. I never forget meetings.

"I'm not gonna rib you too much. This is the first time you've ever been off. What's going on, muchacho? That chick still bothering you?"

"No..."I sigh. He pauses for a second.

"It's her, isn't it? Madeline?" he asks. How can I lie to my best friend?

"I'm undone, man...she's cast a spell on me."

"You say it like it's a bad thing..."

"It is!" I groan in frustration.

"No, it's not...Vince, come on."

"I'm not focused...I'm absent...physically and mentally. I can't do this, not with the most important merger in our company's history on the line."

"Who said it was on the line? You told me yourself that she was a beast at calculating numbers, you haven't had to do much."

"I'm not...familiar with this."

"With what?"

"This! Thinking about her all day and night, fucking her for hours, holding her as she sleeps. I'm not that type of man!"

"Yes, you are, you just never found anyone that made you want to do those things. Don't you remember me, how I was? The crazy bullshit I used to do?" He knew better than to ask me that.

"Gus...when Ryan comes back...I think I want to move to Atlanta."

"Really, man?"

"I just...I can't stay away from her. Damnit I think I'm falling in love with her."

"Okay, slow down. First of all, you need to tell her this when you're not in between her legs."

"Jesus, Gus." I scold his bluntness.

"Hey, I don't sugarcoat shit. You know that." I sigh heavily and it literally pains me to say the next sentence.

"I'm listening. Tell me what to do."

After a long conversation with Gus and an equally long shower, I come into the bedroom to see Madeline sprawled on the bed. In the light of day, my bedroom looks a mess. Condom wrappers litter the floor, the sheets are rumpled and the comforter is on the floor. I shake my head and step into my closet to dress.

When I come out, Madeline is donned in a t-shirt and tossing the condom wrappers in the trash can. She smiles as we lock eyes.

"I thought I'd clean up a bit..."

"That's not your job."

"I really would prefer if Mrs. Lovett didn't see your bedroom floor decorated with condom wrappers." She laughs. I love her smile, her laugh. She's so genuine. Looking at my watch and knowing that I'm terribly late, I give her a quick kiss.

"Let's talk tonight, okay?" I give her an endearing look.

"Okay."

I sit at my desk focusing on my conversation with Lucas. After talking to Gus, I feel more stable with my new feelings and it has helped me get back on track.

"Marks, I've looked at the final numbers. Looks like we're both looking at profit increases of 40% or more."

"That seems to be the projection."

"So, with the merge, I'm almost certain that layoffs need to occur..."

"Not at all, Lucas. The projections were made with the assumption that all employees would keep their jobs."

"Still, I think I could use some restructuring on my end."

"Hear me out. I plan on promoting Madeline Davis. William can take the CFO position if he wants it. We don't have to do any layoffs, but we can rearrange."

"I'm…actually stunned at your intelligence, Marks. You're so young." I laugh.

"Remember who I used to work for?"

"Yes, they taught you well."

"We'll talk about all of that when you get here. Our first meeting will be at eight-thirty Monday morning."

"Sounds like a plan. I'm looking forward to working with you and hearing all of your ideas."

"Same here, Lucas."

"Take care and have a good weekend."

"You too." I hang up.

I start to plan how to sell a transfer to the Atlanta branch to everyone. I need to be in Atlanta with her, and I will make that happen.

Later that evening, I decide to tell Madeline of my plans.

"Madeline…" I sit next to her as she leans back on the couch.

"Yes?" she turns towards me.

"I want to talk to you about something."

"What is it?"

"I…want to transfer to Atlanta." Her eyes grow wide in disbelief.

"You want to do what?"

"You heard me. How would you feel about that?"

"Me? I'd feel great about it. The rest of the company…I don't know."

"Leave them to me. I want to know how you feel." She sighs.

"I don't want you to pick up and leave New York for me. What if things don't work out?"

"They will..."

"You are wildly optimistic. I wish I had as much faith as you."

"Hear me out, I'm simply going to switch places with Joseph. He will move here, I'll move there. Nothing will change except your promotion and his."

"If I get the position." I roll my eyes.

"If you get the position." I repeat without enthusiasm.

"Don't pick up and move right away, stretch it out over a few months. That way, we will all have time to adjust and have time to get to know each other" she suggests.

"Deal." I smile at her before giving her a kiss to seal it.

Chapter 11 *Confessions and Confrontations*

On Friday morning, I lie in my bed at the hotel and look over at Vince (as he asked me to call him Wednesday night) sleeping beside me. I feel like most of my time has been with him. I have finally started to let loose and am feeling completely relaxed with our relationship. Vince stirs and blinks open his eyes.

"Morning" he smiles at me.

"Morning" I say as I lean over to kiss him, caressing his solid six pack. He grabs my hand and kisses it tenderly.

"I'm going to order breakfast, what do you want?" I ask beaming.

"Spinach and mushroom omelet, wheat toast, fruit and coffee. Your antics at night have me starving in the morning." He's right; we have been pretty...active lately. Wednesday night we didn't even eat dinner. We went to his apartment and made love several times. Heat runs through my body as I think about how many times he took me to heaven that night.

"How about you order the food, and I run us a bath?" he looks at me lustfully, interrupting my thoughts.

"Sounds great." I say with a silly grin.

The warm water in the huge tub feels so good. I sit in between Vincent's legs with a post-coital glow from our earlier quickie. Just as the water begins to get cold, I hear a knock on the door.

"Oh, the food's here." I say as I hop out of the tub, dry myself off and pull on a fluffy robe. The attendant rolls a cart with our food. I hand him a tip and smile graciously. Vince emerges with a robe that matches mine. We sit at the table by the window and eat our breakfast. He is engaged in the Wall Street Journal and I in some new paperwork from our company merger.

"So, I'm sleeping alone tonight?" He asks bringing up my plans to go out with Lacy.

"Well, I don't know if you'll be sleeping alone, but you'll have to find some activity to do while I'm out." I tease.

"Just don't get into any trouble." He says with a grin, "save that for me later."

"Naughty boy" I narrow my eyes at him.

"After you finish your breakfast, I'll show you just how naughty I can be."

The muscles in my stomach clench at his voice. I give him a fabulous smile and finish my breakfast....

A few moments later, we are lost in each other again. I find myself yelling his name over and over as I climax in his arms. He cries out louder than I've ever heard him, and holds me even tighter as he trembles. I whimper as my body continues to vibrate around him.

"Oh, God...Madeline..." he's still shaking and squeezes me harder, "what... the fuck are you doing to me?" he shudders, almost in a sob.

I hear his shaky breathing and hold him close to me. Our lovemaking is so intense. I think back to Wednesday when I cried for an hour after our last time making love that night. This romance is arousing unknown feelings in me. I look into his eyes and I see tears streaming down his face.

"Vince..." I wipe his tears.

"I...don't know how to handle this sometimes." He says weakly.

"I don't either. Wednesday..." my voice trails off as I remember the heavy weight of emotion I felt as I sobbed through my climaxes.

"Wednesday was the first time you really let go. I just couldn't stop making love to you."

"I remember..."

"Please stay tonight and Saturday with me." He requests.

"Okay, I'll pack a bag and leave it in the car" I smile.

"I can't wait."

"Me either" I pull him towards me for a kiss.

"I've gotta get to the office. Relax today, baby. I've been keeping you busy all week…in more ways than one."

I giggle, "I didn't mind it at all." He gets up and heads to the shower while I lay back on the bed. For the first time since I've been in New York, I turn on the plasma screen TV noticing that I haven't touched it since I got here.

After Vince leaves, I linger in bed and watch an old episode of *The Golden Girls*. It feels so nice to just…relax. I plan on not seeing any more merger papers until the crew arrives Sunday. I haven't been this happy in a long time, and it feels so good.

I stay in bed until twelve and decide that I will go to lunch at the cute café on the corner. I can't wait to go out tonight. I look at my clothes and decide on a short pink dress with nude stilettos. I look in the mirror; Lacy was right, I am glowing. It must be that crazy Vince. I really hope things work out between us. I couldn't bear to have yet another failed relationship.

"I'm so excited!" Lacy exclaims as we hop out of the car. We are at a hot new club that Vince recommended. I see the line wrapped around the corner and frown.

"Madeline!" I hear a voice calling at the door. It's Dina. She looks dressed to kill in a bright red halter dress with black stiletto heels. I still don't trust her, but I know I have to be nice.

"Come on to the front!" She motions for us to come to the door.

"How are ya, Madeline?" She asks.

"I'm fine, thank you. This is Lacy, my assistant." They shake hands briefly.

"Come on in!" The club is crowded, but there seems to be enough space to hold the mass of bodies. Red seems to be the theme, and it has an aura that makes me a little dizzy.

"Drink?" asks Lacy.

"Sure! I think I'll do liquor tonight" I smile as we go to the bar. The bartender looks at a screen then up at us.

"Drinks are on Mr. Marks tonight, ladies" he says. Lacy puts away her wallet with excitement. I sigh, that man never ceases to amaze me. I'm starting to contemplate on whether or not I should tell Lacy about him. I don't think I should now, but I do want her to know before anyone else. Honestly, after a few cocktails who knows what might come out of my mouth?

A few hours and drinks later, we're on the dance floor moving to the beat of a new hip-hop song I haven't heard before. I let the music take over as I dance happily. Several guys approach me to dance, but I tell them no, it's girls' night tonight. After about an hour, I'm starting to feel my buzz fade from all of the activity. I tell Lacy that I'm going to rest for a little bit and she volunteers to come with me.

We saunter upstairs to a room that's a little quieter and has more of a lounge feel. I order two more drinks.

"So. What's Mr. Marks like?" asks Lacy, "He's hot!"

"Well, he's most definitely smart enough to run a company and sweet...most of the time." I grin.

"Do I sense a crush?" Lacy gasps.

"Well, he's someone to be admired."

"Does he have a girlfriend?"

"Sort of."

"How do you know?"

"I just...know"

Lacy gasps again, "You asked?"

"Not really" I say casually.

"What are you hiding from me, Madeline Davis?" She asks, her tone serious. How does know me so well?

"Okay, I wasn't going to tell you until later..." I look down.

"What?" Her eyes are piercing me.

"We've been seeing each other since the benefit."

"You've gotta be fucking kidding me!" Her face is showing every ounce of surprise.

"Nope, I'm pretty serious."

"Whoa! Well… I think you two fit together." She says quietly.

"You think so?"

"Well, come on! You're both powerful people, and obviously for something to escalate this quickly, you must surely feel something for him."

"It's a more powerful connection than it was with…Eric. When he makes love to me, I have the most intense orgasms ever. Eric never had that effect on me." I say slowly, his name leaving a bad taste in my mouth.

"That asshole never deserved a chance!" Lacy's eyes narrow with disgust. She must be thinking about how I was after the break-up. I had completely fallen apart, and my only saving grace was staying at the office until midnight so that I wouldn't have to face my pain at home. She stayed with me most of those nights which is why we're close now.

"You do seem much happier," she observes, snapping me out of my reverie.

"Do I?"

"Yes, I haven't seen you smile like this since you first started working at the company. I like it, Madeline."

"Honestly, Lacy, I do too."

"Well! This calls for a celebration! Let's get drunk!" Lacy exclaims.

"Let's!" I order another round of drinks and we quickly drain our glasses.

As we're having a fifth or sixth round, Lacy tells me that she has to go to the ladies' room. I nod and sip on my cosmopolitan, awaiting her return. Dina sits down on the other side of me with a strange look.

"So, I'm assuming you and Vince have gotten rather close…" she says.

"What do you mean?"

"Oh, come on! Working in his office, accompanying him to the benefit…there has to be something going on."

"I…honestly don't know what you're talking about. He's just been extending me courtesy to show my boss that he acknowledges the Atlanta office" I try my best to restrain the Davis temper I inherited from my dad and older brother. What concern is it of hers anyway?

"There's something going on between you two…"

"You're crazy."

"Oh, am I? We'll see…" She gets up in a huff. Lacy comes back just in time as Dina breezes past her.

"What did she say to you?"

"Nothing important, now come on, we're not drunk enough." I order another round of drinks.

A little later, both Lacy and I are drunk off our asses and it's the greatest feeling ever. Dina's remarks still stick with me, but I try to ignore them. That bitch can be bitter all she wants; Vince is mine. We finally leave the club around two and Lou drops Lacy off at the hotel. I make sure that she gets in safely; although, I never realized how well she could hold her liquor.

Lou and I make our trek towards Vince's apartment building and I will myself to sober up which doesn't work. I occupy my mind by looking at the city lights which makes me dizzy instead. I decide to close my eyes and wait for my arrival. Vince comes into my mind like lightening. I'm really starting to have some insane feelings for him, and it scares me. I already lost one year of my life recovering from heartbreak, I don't need another. It might actually do me in this time. I can't even bear to think about it. At first, I was willing to just let loose and have fun. Now, I don't know. What's going to happen between us? Does he feel the same way? It's one thing to hear a man affirm his feelings during times of intimacy, but quite another when there is no heat between us, and there is always heat between us. Dina's outburst didn't help things. What is her stake in this? What is Vince not telling me about that crazy bitch? Ugh. I'm too drunk to even think about this right now. I just want to see Vince, let him fuck me senseless and go to bed. Maybe that will quiet my mind if only just for a little while.

Chapter 12 *Demons*

I finish the amber liquid in my glass as Gus pours himself another.

"You want more?" he asks. I shake my head. I don't want to be too drunk when Madeline comes back. Emily comes out of the kitchen with a glass of wine and joins us in the living room.

"How's everything going, Vince?" she asks gently.

"Can't keep a secret can you?" I give Gus a fake scowl.

"Not from my wife." She giggles and I soften.

"I'm new at it, Emily. Still figuring it out."

"You'll learn. This one over here did." She shoves her husband.

"Yes, he did."

"So, mixing in a little business here, I've scheduled Madeline's photo shoot for Saturday. I figured that would give her time to finish up everything with the merger."

"I'm sure she'd like that. I'll give you her number." She nods.

"Well, all business aside, have you seen the tabloids?" My heart lurches in my chest at Gus' statement.

"No...should I be concerned?"

"Well, not you..." he laughs as he hands me the paper which reads *Cruz Baby Bump Watch*. I look over at Emily.

"Should we be on baby bump watch?" They both dissolve in laughter.

"Not yet..." Emily smiles.

"Are you guys...trying?" The thought is foreign to me. Gus and Emily seemed destined to conquer life with just the two of them. To even think about them having a kid...

"We're timing it, we want the baby to be born around our ninth wedding anniversary" Emily interrupts my thoughts.

"Has it really been that long?" I think back to Gus' marked nervousness on the day he proposed when I almost had to drag him to the hotel room he'd arranged for them.

"Doesn't seem like it." Gus smiles.

"I'm pretty sure you guys won't have any issues trying…"I joke as Emily blushes.

"Oh, come on Emily. I know you two the best. No need to be embarrassed." Gus shakes his head as my phone rings.

"Lou?" I answer.

"I've just dropped off Ms. Peters and we're headed your way."

"Great, thanks." I get up.

"She's back from the club. Thanks for dinner and drinks you two."

"Always…" Emily stands to kiss my cheek.

"Don't keep her up all night, man. You two have a merger to tackle on Monday" Gus teases.

"Mind your business." I say as I step out of their door.

I don't know what to expect when she gets here as I did tell Kendall I'd pay her tab, so I make sure to have a bottle of water and two aspirin waiting on the breakfast bar. Suddenly, the phone rings. Without looking at the screen, I answer.

"Vince…"a teary voice comes out on the other end. Shit it's *her*.

"What do you want?" I ask, my temper flaring.

"Why can't you just accept that you're in love with me?"

"Because I'm not, damnit. You need to move on."

"I'm not moving on without you."

"Are you drunk?"

"No…"

"Yes, you are. You do this every time you drink. Now, listen to me: we aren't together. All this time you spend contacting me and worrying about what I'm doing could be spent on finding someone for you."

"You are for me…"she sobs.

"This conversation is over. Get yourself together and go to bed."

"Just let me come over."

"No."

"Vince…"

"I said no!" I growl and hang up. I have no idea how I'm going to deal with this. I want a new start with Madeline and I'm not about to let this bitch ruin it. I start to think of a way I can nip this shit until my phone pings with a text message from Lou. *Coming in now.*

Chapter 13 *Real Romance Exposed*

My tipsy self stumbles out of the car around 3 AM. Lou looks amused as he watches me stagger to the elevator.

"Are you okay, Ms. Davis?"

"I'm fine. I just…I just need to find the elevator" I say trying not to slur my words. He helps me out by typing the code in the keypad and bids me good night. I step off the elevator when I am accosted by a young man with dirty blonde hair.

"Well, Ms. Davis."

"Who are you?" I ask, my senses alert.

"Charles James, New York Times. It seems like you and Mr. Marks have much more going on than a company merger." When he says this, I become stone cold sober.

"Let me tell you something Mr. James. I am not particularly fond of leeches like you. If you know what's good for you, leave me alone." I snap at him and walk away. I knock on Vince's door and he opens it immediately, his smile fading when he sees the frantic look on my face.

"What's wrong?"

"I was just harassed by some gossip columnist."

"Great." He sighs in frustration.

"I think we'll be alright for now, but we really have to be careful." He studies me.

"How many drinks did you have?" he asks.

"What does that matter? You worried about the tab?"

"Not at all, how many?"

"I don't know, I lost count after the fifth one." He hands me a bottle of water and two aspirin.

"You'll need that." I drink the water and take the pills, looking around worriedly.

"Are you okay?" he asks with concern.

"Ugh, I've been through this before. My ex broke up with me shortly after my promotion and reporters were relentless."

"Seriously?"

"Seriously. Worst time of my life. I can handle anything now."

"You never cease to amaze me, Madeline." He takes my hand and pulls me to him, kissing me. I let the kiss take over me. He picks me up and carries me to the bedroom...

The next morning I wake up feeling relaxed and rested, surprised that I don't have a massive hangover. I turn and look at Vince who has his arms wrapped around me and is sleeping soundly. I stroke his arms and he wakes with a smile.

"Good morning," I say returning his smile.

"Good morning. I'm glad you're up; let's shower and get dressed. I have a surprise for you." I wonder what it is.

After a refreshing and orgasmic shower, I slip on some jeans and a red sweater. I sashay into the kitchen and see Mrs. Lovett hard at work.

"Smells wonderful!" I say as I greet her.

"Pancakes, eggs and fruit. I hope you don't mind whole wheat pancakes. Mr. Marks is quite the health nut." She laughs fondly.

"Not at all!" I say. I look out of the corner of my eye and see Vince walk into the kitchen. Dressed in dark blue jeans and a long sleeved Harvard t-shirt, he looks more relaxed than when he is in his three piece suits.

"Thank you Mrs. L," he addresses Mrs. Lovett, "Hey, baby" he says to me and gives me a kiss.

His phone rings and he answers hastily, "Jillian? Is everything ready? Good. We'll be ready to leave in about twenty minutes." What does this guy have up his sleeve? After we finish our delicious breakfast, we take the elevator downstairs to the lobby. I see Jillian and the other guy; I think his name is Jack Lloyd. He's a buff, dark man with dreadlocks down to his back who looks like he's in the Secret Service with his black suit and sunglasses.

"Jack, this is Ms. Davis, our Chief Financial Officer" says Vince.

"Pleased to meet you, Ms. Davis. I'm at your service" he holds out his hand and I grasp it briefly.

"Madeline," says Vince, holding out his hand. I grab his hand and we walk out to the black SUV. Jack opens the door for me and I hop in. I'm tingling in anticipation. We pull up to Central Park; it's a gorgeous fall day even if it's a little chilly.

"Let's go for a walk." says Vince with a smile.
We walk through the park, and Vince tells me everything about himself and asks the same of me. We laugh about our antics in college and young post-college years. He fondly tells me more about his mother, father and sister. His sister is 21 and attends Ithaca University, but, he tells me that her life ambition is to be a model. He rolls his eyes at the notion, but when he shows me her picture, I can see why she has that ambition. She has a beautiful face framed by naturally curly hair and looks to be about 5'11 with a slender figure.
I tell him about the small town I grew up in, my friends and my parents. I share that I have two siblings, a sister who lives in Washington State and a brother, who lives in Tennessee and works in the Vanderbilt athletic department. I tell him about how, as the youngest, I was overprotected.

"So, I should be afraid of your brother?" he asks, amused.

"You should, he's been known to rough some boyfriends up occasionally." I say with a laugh.

"Well, I guess that means I should be on my best behavior."

"Yes, that is my recommendation." We suddenly come to the entrance of the park where Jack's SUV awaits.

"Now, we're going to destination number two" says Vincent. He seems to be excited and I can't imagine what's next.

We pull up in front of the Gucci store, and for a second, I think I'm dreaming.

"I thought we could do some shopping" he says. My mouth drops open in disbelief.

"Shopping?" I repeat.

"Come on," he says grabbing my hand.

"You really don't have to do this. I can afford Gucci on my own, you know." I say, cocking my head to the side.

"I want to buy things for you" he says, moving closer to me. I give up. After all, how often will anyone buy Gucci for me?

When we get inside, I learn that the staff has been informed that I'm shopping for an evening gown. My curiosity is piqued as the staff brings in a huge selection. I ultimately choose a black shaded silk gown. It's the most beautiful dress I've seen so far. It has long sheer puff sleeves with gold button cuffs. When we get ready to pay for the dress and matching shoes, I throw my arms around Vince.

"Thank you" I say, "for everything."

"It's not over yet" he says with mischief in his eyes. He gives the cashier his credit card before she can even tell him his total, but I know it's well over $10,000. The dress by itself was seven grand. I've always had expensive taste, but not that expensive. I start to protest, but take a deep breath. If he wants to buy things for me, I might as well let him.

We climb back into the SUV and head back towards my hotel. I'm puzzled, but decide to let myself enjoy all of his surprises. We stop at the hotel, and Vince grabs my hand leading me inside. We step on the elevator, but Vince doesn't push my floor. Instead, we go to the penthouse floor. My breath gets caught in my throat. What has he done?

Vince leads me into the huge penthouse suite that overlooks the city. The view is absolutely gorgeous. I'm in awe of everything he's done for me today. Realizing we're finally alone, I grab him and kiss him hard. He wraps his arms around me and squeezes me tight. I start to unbutton his jeans and fall swiftly to my knees, pulling his boxers down with me. I hastily take him in my mouth.

"Fuck! Madeline…" he moans with pleasure. I suck harder, taking all of him in my mouth and his breathing becomes shallow. I can tell he's close.

"Oh, no you don't," he says as he pulls me up to face him. He kisses me again and pulls my sweater over my head. He gently unclasps my bra and looks at me with undeniable intent. He jumps out of his jeans and boxers and picks me up to carry me towards the bedroom. He gently lays me down and removes my jeans. He plants hot kisses all over my body, making sure to give every spot attention. Finally, he reaches that sweet spot in between my legs and begins that delicious assault with his tongue.

"Oh, Vince," I whisper as his tempo quickens. He moans as he continues until I feel that familiar tingle below my waist. My cries go up an octave as I get closer and closer. I come loudly, shouting his name. He crawls up and brushes his lips against mine.

Turning me around, he enters me from behind, making me gasp. He groans as he begins his hot rhythm and pulls my hair.

"Harder…" I moan and he pounds into me letting out a loud groan. My body climbs, and know I'm close. He plants a tender kiss on my shoulder and slows down his relentless thrusts.

"Come for me…" he orders and my body obeys, sending me into spirals of pleasure. I cry out his name repeatedly as my body convulses under him.

"Madeline…Jesus!" he calls out as he finds his release and clutches me tightly.

"Wait here" he whispers as he eases out of me and heads out into the living area.

He reappears and scoops me up into his arms, carrying me into the bathroom. The huge garden tub is filled with a lavender scented bubble bath and rose petals. There are candles and wine sitting on a tray and Jill Scott is singing pleasantly in the background. He gently sits me down in the bathtub and sits behind me. The water is deliciously warm and Vince rubs the soapy water on my back. He kisses my shoulder gently.

"How do you like it?" He asks continuing to rub my shoulders.

"I love it, thank you" I reply. He kisses my neck and gives me a gentle bite. I inhale sharply at the sensation. He begins to stroke my breasts, paying special attention to my nipples. I moan in response and he increases the pressure, making my nipples stand at attention. He moves his fingers down and reaches that special spot, massaging it at a gentle tempo. I begin to writhe, making the water splash. He slips a finger inside me and I squeeze his legs. I feel him rise behind me. I turn around and straddle him, lowering myself onto him.

"Madeline…" he moans weakly. I start to move up and down as he holds my waist. I whimper and the room spins around as I increase my tempo.

"You feel so amazing" he moans in my ear.
I feel the indication beneath my waistline and my voice rises in anticipation. Vince growls loudly and I go faster.

"Yes, baby, that's it." he says. The orgasm comes powerfully, tightening everything below my waist. I hold onto him and scream, grasping him close to me. He lets go as well, shouting my name as I dig my fingernails in his back.
We lie in the bathtub for a while and reluctantly get out when the water starts to turn cold. I wrap him and myself in the big fluffy towel; melting in his embrace. He caresses my face and kisses me softly.

"I plan on coming to Atlanta in a week or so. Is that okay with you?" he says.

"I would love that" I say with a smile.

"I have one more surprise for you, baby. Your evening gown is on the bed." He says.

"Who put it there?" I ask, nervous that Jack heard us.

"Jillian. Don't worry, she's not judgmental" he laughs at my shocked look. Well, I guess there's no point in being embarrassed. She already knows I've spent the night at his place many times this week.

After we get dressed, Vince takes my hand and leads me to the elevator.

"Where are we going?" I ask curiously.

"You'll see." He flashes a gorgeous smile as we arrive in the lobby. Jack is waiting for us outside of the door, and I thank him graciously as he helps me into the car.
As we drive, I glance at Vince lovingly, he matches my look with that sexy grin.

"What?" He asks.

"Everything today has been so great, I could never repay you."

"Stop it. You deserved everything and more." He kisses me gently. The car makes a stop in front of an elegant restaurant. Hmm, I think this is one of those dinner clubs I read about.

"Shall we?" He takes my hand and leads me inside. The place is absolutely wonderful: a live jazz band is playing at the front and elegantly dressed tables surround an oak dance floor. We go to the maître d who is stylishly dressed in a black tuxedo.

"Reservation for Marks?" Vince smiles at him.

"Ah, yes, Mr. Marks. We have your table ready. Follow me, please" The man says in a soft French accent. We follow him to a table that sits on the edge of the dance floor. The band plays "Fly Me to the Moon", another one of my favorite Sinatra songs.

"Vince, I'm speechless" I sigh.

"I hope that's a good thing." He chuckles lightly. I touch his face gently and give him a deep kiss indicating that it is a wonderful thing. I truly am feeling something for this man; every day I fall deeper and deeper. The night nor the week could get any better than this. A sense of pure bliss surrounds me as we spend the night indulging in dinner, drinking perfectly mixed cocktails and dancing. By the end of the night, I look at the man who has changed my world in just a week and take his hand with a silent gratitude that only he can decipher.

The next morning, I wake up entangled in Vince's arms, still floating on cloud nine from the night before. After our delightful night at the dinner club, Vince brought me back to our penthouse suite and made love to me so many times, I lost count of how many times I came. It was a true fantasy that I will always harbor in my dreams.

"Good morning, beautiful..." he whispers softly, caressing the messy hair I forgot to tie up.

"Good morning..." I turn around to brand his lips with a soft kiss.

"Lucas will be here soon..." He says with thought. It's time to get out of fantasy land and actually begin working. There is a soft knock at the door and I look at Vince wondering if we were expecting company.

"The newspaper..." he informs me. I get up, tie a silk robe around my naked body and open the door to retrieve the paper. Vince gets up, not bothering to cover up his nakedness.

"Were you a nudist in your past life?" I tease as I have observed that he sees no need for clothes very often.

"Shut up..." He says as he walks towards the bathroom. I take a look at the room service menu and mark my choices.

"Hey Vince?" I yell towards the bathroom door.

"Yeah?"

"What do you want for breakfast?"

"Surprise me..." I scoff and mark an egg white omelet with wheat toast and coffee for him.

After putting the room service request on the door knob, I sit down with the thick Sunday paper and pull out the business section, knowing that's the first thing Vince will go for. I curiously open to page six for some celebrity gossip before I get into the seriousness of the merger and gasp at what I see. Well, our relationship is no longer a secret...everyone knows now. I look at the picture of me and Vince dancing at the dinner club along with a blurb that reads: *The up and coming business mogul, Vincent Marks is seen dancing with his company's CFO, Madeline Davis who is working with him on a merger between PharmaCO and MedInc. Could there be more "merging" going on than we think?* I slam down the paper in disgust.

"What's wrong, baby?" Vince asks coming out of the bathroom wrapped in a towel. I look up at him fearfully. "We've been exposed..." I hold up the newspaper and he walks over to me, taking it out of my hands. Studying it carefully, he shrugs.

"Are you okay with us being exposed, or do you want me to call someone to make him print a retraction?" Shocked, I drum my fingernails nervously on the table.

"I'd prefer not to be splashed all over the *New York Times* for fucking my boss..." I chime.

"Who said anything about fucking? For all they know, we celebrated our merger by having dinner and dancing."

"Vince...you know they probably followed us to the hotel." He huffs.

"What do you want me to do? I can make it disappear, or you can just own it."

"What do you mean, own it?"

"If you really intend to be with me, Madeline, then it shouldn't matter."

"It's not about whether I intend to be with you, Vince. It's whether or not people will still have faith in the integrity of our company." He gives me a half smile.

"Baby, do you think having a relationship will suddenly make my associates lose faith in me?"

"Not just any relationship, Vince. One with your executive…the one who controls your company's finances…you don't think that will be suspicious?" He lets out a hoarse laugh.

"What can I do to assure you everything will be alright?" I shrug, honestly not knowing what would make me feel better. He kisses the top of my head just as another knock comes to the door.

"Breakfast…" I say, tightening up my robe. He retreats to the bathroom to finish getting dressed and I open the door to receive our food.

Later that afternoon, I try to get my mind off the damning evidence of my relationship with Vince. I could see his point; however, I was still concerned about what my office would think about this. It'll only be a matter of time before I get a phone call from someone back home. Sure enough, my phone rings.

"Madeline, I want you to know what you're dealing with, here" Joseph says as soon as I answer.

"Joseph, I think I know very well what I'm dealing with, here." Everyone has their opinion, and it annoys me at times.

"Madeline, he's been a womanizer for years. If you don't believe me, Google him" he says. My world stops. Could this really have been a charade for him? While still on the phone, I pull my laptop out of its case and search Google. There's a few pictures, some with known models, others with equally beautiful women.

"Joseph, he dates, what's the big deal?"

"The big deal is that since he's taken over the company, he hasn't had one steady girlfriend" Joseph insists.

"That is hardly a ground for womanizing."

"All I'm saying is look at his interview a few months back. This has nothing to do with the company, Madeline. I know you can hold your own; that's why I have faith that you will take my place with ease. I don't want you to get hurt."

"And I won't." I hang up quickly, not wanting to discuss my love life with him.

I take a deep breath and watch Vincent's interview. He tells the reporter that there were just too many women in the world to get married and that monogamous relationships aren't for him. He even flirts with her and asks if she would like to go out for drinks later! He has a lot of explaining to do. I silently decide to confront him after we meet with Lucas tomorrow. It would do no good to get him stressed out before such an important meeting.

That evening, I pick at the food on my plate and Vince studies me carefully.

"What's on your mind?"

"Nothing…" I say quickly and drink my wine slowly.

"You're not talking to me anymore? There has to be something plaguing you."

"I'm just a little nervous about this meeting tomorrow, that's all." He lets out a frustrated groan and takes his plate to the kitchen. I follow him, hoping that I won't burst out with it. As I put my dish in the sink, Vince grabs my hand.

"I need you to tell me what's really wrong…"

"Vince…do you intend to stay with me, or am I just one of the many women you want to have your way with?"

"What the fuck are you talking about, Madeline?" I snatch my hand away from him.

"I'm talking about the interview you did three months ago!"

"Madeline..." He doesn't look surprised, I'm assuming he knew it would eventually come up.

"Is this your idea of a game?!" I suddenly grow angry.

"Madeline...just let me explain, damn it!"

"I spilled my heart and soul to you!" I yell.

"Now that's enough!" he roars, startling me, "shut up and listen to me!" I sit down on the bar stool, shocked at the tone of his voice. He sighs heavily, looking at me with regret for raising his voice.

"I obviously can't change the past, and I do admit that when I saw you in the newspaper, all I wanted to do was take you to bed. But...at the benefit, you floored me. I've never wanted to just...be in someone's presence as much as I want to be in yours. In all my years of sleeping with women, no one ever had access to my bedroom. You were the first woman to sleep at my house. I always took other women to hotels." There is a silent pause and I can hear my shaky breaths going in and out.

"Madeline, when I first kissed you, I felt a fire from you. This week has meant more to me than you'll ever know. I enjoyed planning stuff for us and buying you things...I...I'm fucking falling for you damnit! Haven't I shown you that?!" My eyes grow wide.

"What?" I don't think I hear him right.

"I'm falling for you," he breathes as if it hurt, "and I know you have fallen for me".

I take a deep breath and stare at him, "Yes, Vince, I have, and it scares the shit out of me."

"I know it does. You don't think it scares me? I'm not a man who easily expresses his feelings. I'm not even a man who falls in love." I tear up.

"How can I be sure that you won't long for those days again and leave me?" He moves over to me and tips up my chin.

"Nothing will ever make me leave you. If I feel this strongly about you after only a week, I know that it is real." He kisses me with such fiery passion that it makes me dizzy. He picks me up effortlessly, and I wrap my legs around his waist. Taking me into the bedroom, he quickly slides off my dress.

"God, I have to have you..."he says as he spreads my legs. I shiver in anticipation as he reveals his rigid cock and expertly unrolls a condom on it. He gently slides inside of me and I groan in pleasure. He holds my waist as he begins a slow rhythm.

"Faster baby..." I moan.

"No...I want you to feel all of this hard cock. Feel what you do to me..." He groans. My toes curl as I feel my body succumb to ecstasy.

"Ah! Vince!" I cry out as my body trembles. He looks in my eyes and kisses me deeply.

"Oh, God..." his body shakes as he keeps his slow, torturing rhythm.

"Vince! Vince! Oh my God!" I yell as I explode from the inside out. He cries out, obviously feeling my body squeezing him.

"Baby..."he moans as I feel him being pulled in by my convulsions. He breathes harshly as he grabs my wrists, his thrusts are hard and fast. Tears roll down my cheeks as we stare into each other's eyes, the intensity between us almost too much to handle. I start to feel a release brewing inside of me again and come so hard that it hurts. I scream his name, my fingernails digging into his shoulders.

"Jesus..." his body weakens as he desperately tries to keep his rhythm. He whimpers, letting me know that he's close.

"Fuck! Ah!" He sobs loudly as his body tenses up with his hard release. He collapses on top of me, panting wildly. I grab his face, kissing him hungrily. Whether I like it or not, he's right. I am falling for him…fast. Vince lays his head on my breasts, and I stroke his hot, slick head. We lay silently, both speechless from our intense lovemaking.

"You're going to be the death of me…" Vince breaks the silence.

"Why do you say that?" I ask with a laugh.

"I'm gonna fuck you just like this every single day." He kisses me again.

"So vulgar…"

"Yes, I am…" I giggle at his confession. He rolls over and pulls off the condom, tossing it in the trashcan beside the bed. I lean on my side and rest my head on my hands, looking at this perfect specimen. I almost feel like I did when I dated my first boyfriend in college, Edward. Of course, he had a different element about him that supplemented the hard body and delicious sex.

"I'm sorry…for earlier." I look at him genuinely.

"No need to apologize, you had every right to confront me about that. I don't ever want you to hold back. Yell at me, kick my ass, and make me behave." My mouth curves into a smile as I think about the ways I really could make him behave.

"You sure you want to tell me that?" I ask.

"Don't be afraid to be yourself. I'm excited to know what adventures you'll take me on next."

# Chapter 14 *Preparations*

"You're here early…" Alexis peeks her head into my office.

"Just trying to get ready for this meeting."

"The catering company will be here in a few minutes with breakfast. Lacy and I will set up the conference room." I nod.

"Did you print out all of the documents?"

"Yes, I did that yesterday." I look up.

"You came to work yesterday?" She shrugs.

"I figured there might be changes during the weekend, so I waited."

"What would I do without you?" I shake my head.

"I don't know…die?" she smiles and leaves out of my office. I come out just in time to see Lucas and his board get off the elevator.

"Marks!" He shakes my hand.

"Lucas. Welcome to New York. Breakfast will be available soon in the conference room, gentlemen." Alexis appears beside me immediately.

"I'm Alexis Stanley, head executive assistant. If you'll follow me, there's breakfast for you." She smiles and leads the gentlemen to the conference room. I follow them, trying to get a feel for their vibe. I drink coffee as the gentlemen indulge in a huge breakfast. I decided not to eat as I'm already nervous as hell. Madeline's assistant Lacy moves around quickly, making sure everyone has what they need. My phone vibrates and I see that Lou is calling.

"Lou?"

"I just picked her up, we should be there in about twenty minutes as traffic is kind of slow today."

"Very well. Be careful."

"Sure boss."

Lucas sits next to me with a plate piled high. I chuckle to myself at the man who is probably twice my size.

"How do you feel about today, Lucas?" I ask.

"Everyone seems to be optimistic."

"What about your guy, William?" Lucas laughs before taking a sip of orange juice.

"William is an asshole, simply put. He might give Ms. Davis a hard time, but I will try to cage him as best as I can."

"I can help with that."

"I hope that he will keep his mouth shut, honestly. He can't argue with the numbers."

"No, he can't. Madeline is extremely meticulous." He puts down his fork and looks at me.

"I saw you two in the paper. Not that it's any of my business, but what is going on with that?" It certainly was not his business, but I think back to what I told Madeline about owning it.

"No, it's not a fling, Lucas." He raises his eyebrows.

"Do you think that's a good idea?"

"I would have never thought so…but…what can I say? Shit happens." He laughs again.

"It does. Just be careful, Marks. I know you mentioned promoting her. I would at least consider others before going forward." Jeez. He sounds like Madeline.

"Madeline demanded that. I assume I'm blind to things like that. I've always thought business not emotions."

"Well, you have to consider everything. I've been in the business for years, and you always have those that get butt hurt over bullshit." I nod in agreement.

"I'll go through the necessary protocols to be safe. I promised Madeline that." Lucas regards me with approval and digs back into his breakfast. Alexis sits on the other side of me and passes me a book containing all of the documents.

"Thought you'd want to see it before I passed it out."

"Thanks, Alexis." I look through the book at the documents Madeline poured all of her blood, sweat and tears into. It was impeccable: the numbers, the colorful graphs, and the commentary. I shake my head in admiration.

"It's perfect. I can't even..." I'm speechless. Madeline is so modest about her talent. She deserves the promotion, the raise, and everything in the world. My feelings for her surge forward, and I fall even deeper. Taking a breath, I close the book and look at Lucas.

"You're going to be blown away, man."

"I have no doubt about that." He smiles. Alexis, speaking to someone through her wireless headset, gestures to me.

"Mr. Lowe for you." I look at my watch.

"I'll take it in my office." I excuse myself from the conference room and slip inside my office where the phone is blinking. I pick it up and hastily answer.

"I know what you are going to say..." I start.

"Are you out of your fucking mind?!" Ryan yells. I sigh.

"Ryan...what can I say?"

"Ten plus years of watching you jump from woman to woman and you do this? Please tell me that you are serious about her and not playing around." I take a deep breath.

"Ryan, I'm serious to the point that I'm making plans to transfer to the Atlanta office in a few months." The other end falls silent.

"Say something..." I demand.

"What in the hell did she do to you?" He asks softly, obviously shocked.

"I'm still trying to figure that out myself, Ryan."

"It's only been a week..."

"It's crazy, I know."

"It's insane! I never thought I'd see the day..."

"You and everyone else."

"I'm...I'm happy for you, man. I was getting worried about you. When Gus got married, I thought...maybe there was hope for you too." I'm surprised at his statement.

"I never knew you were worried about me."

"That night...at the club...you just went through the motions with that girl. I mean, come on, Vince. We've been friends for a long time. All of us can read each other."

"You're telling me..." I scoff.

"I'm serious, Vince. Do you think you're in love with her?"

"I don't know yet, but I am willing to find out."

"I know you have the merger meeting coming up soon, but when I get back, we'll talk. I want to help make your transition as smooth as possible."

"Thanks, Ryan. I will call you after the meeting to let you know how everything went."

"Sounds like a plan. Good luck, Vince."

"Hey, Ryan?" I call out before he hangs up.

"Yeah?"

"Thank-you, for understanding me, for caring."

"I always will." I hang up and Alexis steps into my office.

"Ms. Davis just arrived, we're ready to get started."

"I'll be there in just a moment." I sit back in my chair in a moment of reflection. I can't believe that everyone seems to be on board about this. I was almost expecting to fight everyone left and right about this relationship. Was it really that obvious that I was a promiscuous asshole? Ryan's voice haunted me when he confessed he had been worried. I push my thoughts away, knowing that I need to be present for this meeting. I get up and walk towards the conference room, ready to move to the next level.

Chapter 15 *The Merger*

Once I arrive at the office, Alexis greets me with a smile, my papers and a big cup of coffee. I smile at her graciously, thankful that she senses my nervousness. She leads me down a hallway into a vast meeting room full of "good ole boys" who are finishing a catered breakfast. Alexis and Lacy sit near the door with tablets to take notes. I am secretly thankful that I'm not the only woman in the room.

Lucas and his associates listen carefully as I compare and contrast earning potential for our companies if we merge. Lucas seems pleased, but William scowls at me. As I finish the presentation, I have to ask the dreaded question.

"Does anyone need clarifications?" I look around the room. Of course, William stands up. Bastard.

"How do we know these numbers are accurate?" His eyes count on me being embarrassed but are quickly disappointed as I give a rapid response.

"Well, seeing that you and I worked together on these numbers four months ago, six weeks ago and a few days ago, I think you would know they are" I retort. Lucas hides a laugh behind a fake cough as the rest of the men hide smiles behind their portfolios. William grows angry at the response.

"Woman, don't you get smart with me…"

"Whoa! Whoa! My name is Ms. Davis and you will address me as such" I try to keep my cool.

"William, you're being ridiculous now. Why don't you just have a seat?" Lucas stares him down.

"If we are going to merge with this company that is barely on its feet…"

"I beg your pardon, but we are not 'barely on our feet'. If you will make use of the presentation notes Mr. Marks' assistant gave you, you will see that our profit margins are much higher than yours, and I have personally monitored all earnings since I've become CFO."

"That doesn't mean shit."

"Why doesn't it? Please give me one good reason!" Now he's starting to piss me off.

"Because....CFO should be a man's job!" His eyes gleam with hatred.

"Now that's enough, William!" Vince stands up ready to pounce. William holds his hand up to Vince.

"I think I have a right to ask questions..."

"Within reason, William, but right now you are being an asshole" Lucas warns.

"William, I assure you that I spent many early mornings and late nights calculating both your company's numbers and ours. The fact that I'm a woman has nothing to do with how well I do my job, and if I may say so myself, you were the one who first screwed up the numbers because you wouldn't take my phone calls at first." I'm simmering, but still desperately trying to keep my cool.

"She's right about that, William" a young man on the other side of the table says. William looks defeated.

"William, why don't you do us all a favor and sit down? Ms. Davis has done a phenomenal job and I personally think that this merger would benefit all of us. You, my friend, need to learn to work with women. I don't want my company looking like a crew of misogynist pigs." Lucas' sharp gray eyes sparkle intensely. William huffs and sits down with an embarrassed look on his face.

"Well, then, do we have a deal, Lucas?" Vince asks.

"We have a deal, Vince." I heave a sigh of relief as murmurs of agreement follow. Lucas gets up and shakes my hand.

"I'm going to enjoy working with you, my dear. Please bear with William, he's just not a people person." His gaze asks forgiveness.

"I've dealt with worse..." I whisper and we both laugh.

After work that evening, we all sit in a beautiful restaurant that boasts a Bohemian theme. Bottles of the best champagne are ordered as the men speak loudly and happily about random issues. Vince scoots a little closer to me as a collective laugh erupts from our table.

"You killed it, baby, I'm so proud of you…" I smile with pride and look at William who is inhaling glass after glass of champagne.

"You think he'll ever warm up to me?" I giggle.

"I could give a rat's ass. You're here to stay, if he doesn't like it, he might have to find another job."

"Oh, I think I can charm him…"

"Like you charmed me?" He smiles and kisses the tip of my nose before we both rejoin the boisterous conversation.

After the men have had more than their fair share of champagne, Lucas pays the bill and leads his tipsy crew to the front where their limousine is waiting. Vince lingers at the table with me as I finish my final glass of champagne.

"There's relief all over your face…I didn't realize you were that nervous. You carry yourself well" He compliments me.

"Well, I was so unsure about what kind of an outburst William would have. This is the biggest move of my career; it was terrifying." He takes my hand.

"Calculated risks, baby." He smiles. Of course he knows about that, he bought the company when the only other person who wanted it was Joseph, my boss. Everyone else probably thought he was being stupid. I nod and finish my glass before grabbing my jacket.

"Well, ready to get out of here?" I ask as he stands.

"As ready as I'll ever be" he laughs and takes my hand, leading me out of the restaurant. As if on cue, Jack pulls the black SUV in front of us. He gets out, opening the door for us and we slide in. The ride to the hotel is relaxing, but a plaguing thought compels me to feel sad: it's almost over.

"Okay, Ms. Davis, I want you to look over towards the left..." the photographer commands. I look to the side with a serious look.

"Perfect!" He says as I see the flash out of the corner of my eye. Emily and Gus both take supervisory stances by the door of Vince's office as the photography crew scurries around me. After a few more photos of me by the window overlooking the city, by the bookcase and sitting on the desk, the photographer calls the session. Emily comes over to me with a wide smile.

"You looked great! The cover will be to die for!" I return her smile and thank her as I take down the neat, tightly wound bun sighing at the release.

"Are you looking forward to going home?" she asks as I place the bobby pins on Vince's desk.

"Yes and no, it's been great here." She smiles even wider.

"I bet it has been." I blush.

"Don't be shy...I've known Vince for years. I'm happy he found you."

"Really?"

"Maybe I'll tell you about it over drinks tonight." I look up in surprise.

"Tonight?"

"Yes, Gus and I are taking you and Vince on a double date."

"Sounds like a great way to go out with a bang." I didn't know that Emily and Vince had a history. I'll have to ask him about it later. For now, I'm ready to relax for a bit. I've been busy all week, going through merger contracts to make sure everything was right. The photo shoot sealed it for me; I am exhausted.

"I'll see you tonight, Emily..." I wave to her as I head out. Lou drives me to a little Mexican restaurant and I thank him as I jump out of the car. I'm sure Vince told him to drop me off here, so I'm prepared to meet him. I see Vince sitting with another guy and cock my head in curiosity. The guy is handsome, with mahogany skin, a bald head and goatee. I walk over to them and give both men a huge grin.

"Madeline...I'd like you to meet my partner, Ryan Lowe." Ryan stands up and shakes my hand firmly. I knew that he was a silent partner and it surprised me to see him.

"Nice to meet you, Madeline."

"Likewise." We both sit down.

"Don't look so stiff. This is not a business meeting" Vince says with laughter in his eyes.

"Oh?"

"No, I figured that you need to meet my friends, and this one here has had that title for a while." Ryan scoffs.

"Yeah, almost seventeen years of torture" he jokes.

"Oh shut-up." Vince slaps his back.

"But in all seriousness, I had to meet the girl that has made Vince lose his damn mind." I giggle.

"I don't think he's completely lost it" I say.

"I'm sitting right here." Vince glares at both of us.

"So, how did you guys meet?" I ask.

"In college. There are seven of us: all tall, dark, handsome and successful." I'm assuming that means two things: they are all minorities, rich and rich as hell. The rest is obvious and by looking at Ryan and Vince sitting side-by-side, it's not an exaggeration either.

"So...you're in a crew of seven hot guys, huh?" I look at Vince who rolls his eyes.

"That's in the eye of the beholder."

"So where does Emily come in?" I ask. The two exchange glances.

"Gus is one of us..."Ryan pips.

"And he's been married the longest, so she's kind of an honorary member." Vince rushes, nudging Ryan.

"There's something you want to tell me?" Vince sighs.

"I'll tell you the actual story later, for now, just know that Gus went through a very tough time and she was the reason he got out of his mess." Now my curiosity is piqued. I wonder what that situation looked like.

As we order drinks and talk, I realize I'm touched by Vince's gesture. Introducing a woman to your friends is a big step. My admiration for him grows, and I start to become wildly optimistic about us. Taking his hand under the table, I give him a silent assurance that if he's willing to try, I will too.

Chapter 16 *Don't Want to Say Goodbye*

"Mmm, this steak is delicious…"Emily hums in appreciation as she digs into her salad.

"You ruined it with lettuce" Gus teases. She throws her middle finger up at him.

"You two stop it." I grin at their ridiculous tiff.

"Don't worry, he'll make up for it later" Emily says in between bites. Madeline blushes and Emily instantly looks apologetic.

"I'm sorry, we're a little too open sometimes." She smiles at Madeline.

"No worries" Madeline laughs before taking a sip of a dangerous cocktail.

"So, Vince tells us that he's planning to visit Atlanta in a couple of weeks." Emily changes the subject.

"Yes, can't wait to show him the sights. He's never been before" Madeline responds.

"We've been once or twice. I'd love to expand business down there someday, but the competition is quite fierce" Gus eyes Madeline.

"I can imagine. Atlanta is a hotbed of businesses."

"Well, it'll be big news once you get this one in your office" Gus nudges me.

"Cut it out…"I scold. We see a random flash come out of the crowd of tables and chairs followed by a commotion. Emily rolls her eyes.

"Paparazzi…"she explains to Madeline who raises her eyebrows.

"Really?"

"Yeah, didn't you read? We're on baby bump watch!" Gus laughs loudly to which Emily raises her glass of wine.

"Oh my…"Madeline gasps.

"It's not true…"Emily confirms.

"I didn't think so…they always assume everyone is pregnant" Madeline says.

"And you better be ready to deal with that kind of thing, dear." Gustavo warns. Madeline looks at me.

"I've kept them at bay for the most part, but I'm sure a slip up will happen occasionally."

"Like in the Sunday paper?" Madeline pips with a smile. Gus and Emily laugh.

"That is only the beginning." Emily looks at her phone and shows it to Gus. Noticing our curious glares, she shows us a plethora of posts on social media. Within the fifteen minutes that we were sitting there, a gossip columnist had posted a picture of us having dinner. The caption reads *Advertising greats Gus and Emily Gustavo schmooze with the up and coming power couple Vincent Marks and Madeline Davis, CEO and CFO of PharmaCO.* The comments are revolting. Some asking why Emily has wine if she is supposed to be pregnant. Others shaming me for supposedly seducing my CFO while she was working on a business deal. A few shamed Madeline for screwing around with her boss. Madeline's expression twists as she reads along with me.

"Ignore the comments, people are cruel" Emily advises her. Madeline shakes her head.

"Everyone always makes assumptions. Even I am guilty of it. I feel sorry for celebrities now." She laughs as she drains her glass.

Later that night, Madeline lays in my arms for our final night together. I told her I would stay for a while but she needed her rest to travel tomorrow.

"I'm going to miss you..."she says softly. I stroke her cheek while running my other hand up and down her bare back.

"I'm going to miss you" I kiss her forehead and let her go, reaching to grab something off the floor.

"Turn around..." I tell her as she sits up. I drop the diamond necklace I bought for her around her neck.

"Vince!" she exclaims in disbelief.

"Just a little something to remember me by until you see me again." She touches the necklace before turning around to face me with tears in her eyes.

"You have…certainly changed my mind about some things."

"Like what?"

"Vince, I never thought I would ever be in this place again. I've been spending these past two weeks telling myself not to get my hopes up because I am so afraid of getting hurt."

"I know you are." I pull her onto my lap, and my cock stirs under her.

"Listen, I can't promise you that we will have the perfect relationship. I have my shit to work through and you still have to build trust with me. I get it, there is a lot of work to do. But what I can promise is that I am willing…more than willing to commit myself to making this relationship what it needs to be." She sniffles and I pull her mouth to mine, my urgent need evident as my cock is at full attention. She reaches beside me and hands me a condom. I lay her down gently and for a moment, admire her naked body. I know this is the last time I have to make love to her before she leaves and I want her to remember it until I get to Atlanta.

I slip the condom on my cock and hover over her, letting the tip tease her clit. She breathes heavily in anticipation, her shining brown eyes stare into mine. I slide into her with a shaky groan and she instinctively wraps her legs around me, her feet pushing me all the way in.

"Fuck!" I groan as I reach the end of her. She's so wet! I start to move slowly, wanting her to feel the length, the thickness of my cock.

"Vince…"she sighs, holding on to me. I kiss her deeply, my tongue massaging hers. She raises her hips to meet each push, which turns me on more. I slip a finger between the warm wet folds of skin below her waist and gently massage her clit.

"God…yes" she moans. I speed up, panting wildly.

"Vince….Vince…"she warns before she comes with a scream, the vibrations inside of her grab my dick, weakening me.

"Christ, girl…"I growl. I push through the pulsations and she trembles violently, moaning through her orgasm. I stop and look down at her.

"Can you take it?" I ask through shuddering breaths. Her eyes reflect fear, but she nods her head.

"Don't hurt me…"she pleads.

"I won't…" I begin driving into her, my cock stroking her g-spot. She whimpers softly and I keep going until her legs lock around me and she sobs my name loudly, arching off the bed. Tears roll down her cheeks and her body shakes.

"Good God…." I moan loudly as my dick is squeezed by her pussy. I keep going, craving release. A new feeling comes over me as I continue, and I start to worry if I will be able to handle my climax. I push one more time before I lose control and come with a roar.

"God! Fuck! Fuck!" I hear myself yelling as a painful stream comes from me. I hold her tightly as I keep coming, unable to control the moans coming from me.

"I…can't…"she whimpers before I feel her climax again. She cries my name over and over.

"Oh, Jesus…"I breathe out, holding her as she bucks into me, the spasms inside of her milking me. She still trembles and I hold her tightly against my chest, not wanting her to see the emotion on my face. I almost blurt out that I love her, but I can't yet. It will freak her the fuck out if I did. But I do…I love her. I can't deny it any longer, and with that realization, I start to cry. Every emotion I never felt for any woman but for her comes out of me in the form of hot tears and shaky sobs. Madeline strokes my head softly, not saying a word.

Around one, she falls asleep and I kiss her forehead tenderly, taking in her face one final time. Trying not to wake her, I get up and freeze when she turns around. She clings to the pillow I left behind and I breathe a sigh of relief. I slip into my clothes and text Lou to come get me. It is going to be a hard week without her.

Chapter 17 *Home Sweet Home*

I wake up alone for the first time since I spent that first night at Vince's apartment and hug my pillow to make up for his absence while touching the necklace he gave me last night. I sigh, New York has been a dream, but I miss Nathan and my baby Pricilla. Vince is planning to come to Atlanta next weekend and work at our office for the next two weeks. All of our days (and nights) of lovemaking have me in a daze. He's so virile and energetic, it drives me crazy.

My phone rings snapping me out of my remembrance. It's Jillian.

"Ms. Davis, I'll be there in ten minutes to take you to the airport. You will be flying on the company jet, compliments of Mr. Marks." Of course.

"Thank you Jillian; I'll be ready!" I make sure that everything is packed and that the chargers for my laptop and iPad are safely in my bag. I do one last sweep before I pull my hair up into an elegant ponytail and roll my suitcase to elevator.

"Ms. Davis, it's been a pleasure" says the desk attendant as he gives me back the company credit card. "Same here. Take care! I'm sure I'll be back soon." He smiles at my response. Jillian waits outside and takes my bags, hauling them in the back of the SUV with ease. I look at her earnestly.

"Jillian," I say softly, "Thank you for taking care of me." I pull out a jewelry box from Tiffany's. Inside is a 24K gold necklace with a charm of two swords crossing. Jillian's smile could light up a room.

"Thank you, Ms. Davis. It's been my pleasure" she pulls me into a brief hug. Boy, for someone that looks so tough, you would think she wouldn't show emotion. Apparently, I have that effect on people nowadays.

The drive to the airport is quick and uneventful. Lacy and I wave good-bye to our security detail as we step onto the sophisticated private jet. When we get on the plane, a stewardess greets us with a smile and indicates that lunch will be served as soon as we're in the air. Suddenly, my scalp prickles and I know he's behind me.

"I had to wish my girl a safe flight" says Vince as he kisses me passionately.

"Um, I'll give you guys some privacy," says Lacy as she saunters to the front of the plane with a huge smile on her face. I know I'm gonna hear it later.

"Take me one more time," I whisper, aware that there's a bedroom on the jet.

"Madeline, always hungry for more," he teases, "I think you've fucked me dry these past two weeks. Besides, I'll see you next weekend." I pout at his response and he softens.

"Don't pout, come back to the bedroom and we'll...talk" he smiles.

"Stephanie!" he calls to the stewardess who comes running.

"Tell Jonathan to delay the flight by about twenty minutes."

"Yes, sir," she says grinning at the both of us as he leads me towards the back of the plane.

"Vince!" I call out as I tremble around him.

"Shh!" He responds, finding his release as well.

"That was delicious, Mr. Marks..." I say, kissing him once more.

"I can't wait until I have you all of the time." He kisses me goodbye and heads off the plane, and I see Lacy's smirk follow him as he leaves. She gives me a sly look.

"So, that was a long talk" she teases.

"Oh hush!" I laugh at her.

Before I know it, we're thirty thousand feet in the air and Lacy and I are enjoying spinach and chicken Alfredo pasta with crisp sangria. Lacy and I laugh and talk about random topics to keep us occupied during the flight. In the midst of our laughter, Lacy pauses and studies me.

"Madeline, the Marks effect looks good on you. I love it!"

"I love it too, Lacy, and can't wait to get him to Atlanta."

"How do you think the people in the office will take it?" She eyes me seriously.

"Hard, I imagine. It will look suspicious that I got a promotion."

"Well, fuck them. You deserve everything you've earned and didn't have to sleep with anyone to do it. I dare anyone to say anything in my presence." I laugh at her declaration of overprotection.

"I'm serious. I've seen you work from morning until midnight despite the fact you were hurting, I've seen you defend yourself against ruthless assholes, do you need me to go on?" I shake my head.

"Despite that, Lacy, I'm just preparing myself for the backlash."

"You know I have your back no matter what."

"I know you do." I take her hand, grateful that I at least have one person on my side.

We land in Atlanta that afternoon and I give Lacy a hug and kiss on the cheek as I head to a waiting Limo. I have so much to think about and so little time to do it. I arrive at my condo and see that Pricilla's dog sitter has already dropped her off. She greets me eagerly at the door.

"Hey, baby girl! Oh, mommy missed you!" I ruffle her thick fur and she whines happily, jumping for joy. Suddenly, my phone rings. I eye it curiously, usually no one calls my landline except telemarketers. I run past Pricilla and answer it.

"Hello?" There's no answer.

"Hello?" I repeat. Nothing. Maybe it's a wrong number. I hang up and shrug pulling out my pack of cigarettes. Since I've been with Vince, I haven't had the urge, but for today I need it. I pour a glass of wine and go on the balcony. As I look over the lights of the city, I wonder what will really happen at work tomorrow. I guess I'll just have to face it and honestly, Vince is worth it all. I just hope that we will make it.

As I come inside, my phone rings yet again. I decide to let it go to voice mail. The automated voice prompts the caller to leave a message and I notice that whoever it is doesn't hang up. I quickly pick up the phone and ask who it is but once again hear the click. I look at the caller ID and notice that the number is blocked. This is really strange.

I pick up my phone and call Vince, still unnerved by the eerie phone call earlier.

"Madeline..." he answers.

"Hey...I miss you already."

"I missed you from the minute I got off that plane, baby..."

"I got a couple of strange phone calls today" I tell him.

"What do you mean by strange?"

"The person called and hung up, then called again."

"They didn't say anything?"

"Not a word." He sighs.

"Maybe it's just some pranksters."

"It's just really weird, Vince. Do you think someone with the company is upset about us?"

"Who would be upset?" He asks. I scan my head.

"Dina?" He laughs at my assumption.

"Dina is the least of our worries baby. Now, get some rest. I'll talk to you tomorrow."

He hangs up and I still can't shake the uneasy feeling but try to shrug it off. I have to go back to the office and am sure the gossips have probably already started spreading the news about Vince and me. I don't know how they will take it, but at least I know Lacy will shut them up. I hop in the shower and change into a t-shirt. After spending two weeks sleeping in absolutely nothing, it feels strange to be in clothes. I climb into my bed with Vince on my mind. It felt so good to have him next to me, waking me up every few hours because he couldn't get enough of me. I didn't even mind that I hadn't slept much on the trip. As my thoughts calm, my exhaustion finally catches up with me and I sigh into a deep, dreamless sleep.

The next morning, I get up early to psych myself up for work. Brimming with nervous energy, I decide to get a quick workout in. I put Pricilla's leash on her and we go for a three mile run. I finish just in time to see a beautiful sunrise come over the city's skyscrapers. I start to feel a little better and walk Pricilla back to my condo. As I remove her leash, she looks at me as if to thank me for taking her on a run. I giggle at her human-like personality and refill her bowls with food and water.

Once I shower and get dressed, I take a deep breath. I don't know why I'm so nervous, I think about what Vince said about owning it. If he had been anyone else besides my boss, I wouldn't worry at all. I've always been the one who wanted to project a good image of myself: a hard working woman who could independently make her way to the top. The people at my office know me as someone who takes her job seriously. What will they think now? That I went to New York, wooed the CEO and fucked my way to the leader of our branch? I sigh and give my baby one last pet on her head before leaving out of the safety of my condo.

Chapter 18 *Emotion*

"Son?" My dad answers, surprised that I'm calling so early in the morning.

"Dad, how are you?" I ask.

"What's wrong, Vince?"

"Why do you think something is wrong?"

"I hear it in your voice. Is everything okay?"

"I don't know…"

"Talk to me."

"I…met this woman and…" He sighs.

"And?"

"God, she's turned my life upside down!"

"Vince, really?" He sounds like he half expected me to be in trouble rather than in love.

"Yes…really."

"Who is she?"

"My CFO…"

"Doesn't your CFO work out of Atlanta?" he asks.

"Yes, she came here two weeks ago to help close the merge."

"What happened?"

"I fell for her…hard, Dad."

"Does she feel the same way about you?"

"I…honestly don't know…you're going to think I'm crazy, but I've fallen in love with her."

"Well, son, what are you gonna do about that? She lives in Atlanta."

"I'm transferring to the Atlanta office in a few months."

"Wow…I'm…speechless. And you've only known her for two weeks?"

"I know it's crazy, but it has to be love. I've never felt this way before. You know how I am…I don't take relationships seriously. But here I am…a fucking mess."

"Okay, the first thing you need to do is pull yourself together. That is a short time to know someone and think that you're in love…but…I think you should go for it. You've been screwing around since you were in college. If this girl can get you to settle down, then she is the one."

"You think so?"

"I know so. Get your shit together, handle your business and get down there to her." I feel so much better now that I've let it loose. It felt like a deep secret that I wanted to shout to the world, and I knew I couldn't.

"You think it will work?"

"You just have to make sure that she feels the same way, Vince. Make sure you know what it's going to take to keep her."

"I plan on doing all that and more."

"I have faith that you will. Let us know when you make your move."

"I will, Dad. Thank you for talking to me about this."

"Can I tell your mom?" He asks. I smile.

"Of course you can, just tell her not to get her hopes up yet."

"I'll remind her who we're dealing with here." He laughs.

"I'll talk to you soon."

"Love you, son. Good-bye."

I hang up and heave a big sigh of relief as Ryan comes into my office with some paperwork.

"What's up?" I ask him as he sits down.

"Just thought I'd show you the new access codes we received to the research database thanks to our merger." I nod and gesture for him to have a seat.

"So, you're planning on leaving for Atlanta Friday?" he asks.

"Yes, I'll be there for a week or so." He nods.

"Are you sure you're going to come back?" He asks quietly. I look up at him.

"Why wouldn't I?"

"Vince, you have done a one eighty the past two weeks, I don't think you're coming back to live here."

"That's ridiculous, I have to find a place…get to know the city."

"I'm just telling you what I see." I sigh and look through the paperwork that is giving us permission to access medical technology labs across the country and worldwide.

"This is impressive." He nods.

"It's gonna take us to the next level, man. The head technician squealed when I gave her the codes. I smile.

"We're on our way."

"That we are, Vince. I think Madeline deserves a bonus."

"I'm glad we agree on that" I say.

"I'm thinking fifty g's."

"I think that's fitting, another fifty once the new profits come out." He nods in agreement and I send an email to payroll.

"That'll be a nice surprise for her. I like her, Vince. She's sweet, smart and her looks aren't too bad either." I smile.

"Don't get any ideas, Ryan."

"Hey, man…I'm ready for you to settle down. I'll worry about me later." I shake my head.

"You're crazy."

"You're crazy" he repeats.

"Get outta here!" He laughs loudly at my irritation before getting up. As he opens the door, Alexis comes in.

"Mr. Marks, I booked your trip for you."

"Thank you, Alexis." She hands me a few papers from payroll that request my signature. As she starts to leave out, I stop her by calling her name.

"You've been quiet lately…"I observe.

"You've been busy lately…"she replies with a smile.

"I know you have an opinion about all of this."

"Mr. Marks, it's really none of my business."

"I want to know what you think." She sighs and sits down across from me.

"I saw the picture of you two dancing...on a website" she says slowly.

"And?"

"I've never seen you look the way you did as when you looked at her, Mr. Marks."

"Really?" I never really looked at the picture, but now I have to look at it.

"You looked happy, relaxed. You haven't looked that way since you started working here. There was a hope, an optimism in your eyes." I lean back and smile at her.

"I'm glad you are honest with me. Never forget that I always value your opinion. You believed in me, followed me when I bought this company."

"I had faith that you, Mr. Marks. I always have. When I started out, they advised you against hiring me because I was inexperienced. You said you knew I would be good at my job. You had faith in me, gave me a chance. I'll always be grateful for that."

"Same here, Alexis..." She gets up and starts to walk out but turns around.

"You're making the right decision..." She breezes out. I sure as hell hope she's right.

Chapter 19 *Trouble*

I walk into the office to a grand applause. My smile is a mile wide as I glide into the office. My accounting team has a bouquet of flowers waiting for me and there is a catered breakfast on the table. Joseph walks up to me and shakes my hand enthusiastically.

"Davis, you are a beast; I have complete confidence in you" he whispers in my ear. I smile at his compliment. Ashley Parris, head of HR for our company approaches me.

"Come to me after lunch and we'll do your contracts." I look at her quizzically.

"I thought Mr. Marks was interviewing other candidates?"

"Be serious, Madeline. No one was qualified to interview for that position. You deserve it." I scoff as she brushes a few strands of her blonde hair out of her face.

"Just take the goddamned position. You're way too modest for the amount of good work you've done here" she scolds.

"Okay, okay. I'll come see you after lunch." I concede in defeat.

"Good." She gives me a smile and goes to get herself another serving of orange juice. Still reeling from the news Ashley has just given me, I decide to videoconference with Vince.

"Well, well, well" he says as his grin appears on the screen.

"Good morning" I say with a smile.

"I sent your contract to Ms. Parris this morning."

"She told me…" I say reluctantly.

"Don't give me that look. No one wanted to interview for that position. You should've already known that. Everyone just assumed you would be the next to get a promotion." He takes a sip out of a travel coffee mug.

"It doesn't seem right…" I start.

"Why the hell not?! Madeline Davis, you just closed a merger two months ahead of time. Good God! Will you give yourself some credit?" I look down, knowing that everybody is probably frustrated at my modesty. I can't help it. I never had the confidence to accept when I'd done well.

"Okay, Vince. I'll sign the contract." His face relaxes.

"I expect to see it on my desk by close of business."

"So bossy…" I tease.

"That's right, and you have to do everything I say."

"I don't know about all that…" I laugh.

"You're a force, girl." He chuckles lightly.

"Well, that's why I'm good at what I do."

"I hear that. Alright, babe, I have a meeting with the board in a few minutes. I'll see your pretty face later." He smiles.

"Talk to you later…" I click on the screen and sigh.

"Maddie!" Nathan comes running to me like he hasn't seen me in years. He insisted that we meet for a Thursday night happy hour to catch up.

"I missed you!" I exclaim as I hug him tightly. We decide on the wine bar across the street from my office and order two bottles of wine.

Over our fourth glass of Chardonnay, I give Nathan the details of Mr. Vince Marks. He looks at me in awe as I go over our conversations, lovemaking and work relations.

"Madeline, be careful. You know some of those bastards you work with will try to wreck this, right?"

"Oh, yeah, I know" I say, thinking of Dina. I steer the conversation to him to ease my nervousness. He tells me about a new man he's met who is in educational law and policy. I nod my approval and we keep talking about our new loves and hopes for the coming days.

Later that evening, I walk into the lobby and get my key card out to swipe, but a chilly feeling surrounds me. I turn around and there she is…Dina Andrews.

"So, this is where the magnificent Madeline Davis lives" she says with a smirk.

"Sure is," I say sweetly, "would you like to come see my condo?"

"Vince is mine, you know" she says, sneering at me. I feel my face get hot with anger.

"Keep living in that fantasy, Dina." I start to walk away.

"Oh, it's not a fantasy," and she approaches me. My adrenaline begins surge. She hands me pictures and sure enough it is her and Vince...in bed, out on his yacht, and in the tropics. I take a deep breath and clench my teeth.

"Dina, I want none of your bullshit. He's with me now." I say calmly.

"He is NOT with you! Don't you see what he's doing? He's manipulating your naïve ass!" I've had enough and I find myself slapping her hard across the face.

"Bitch, I know how to handle myself, and if you have concocted some grand scheme, believe me, I have my ducks in a row. Watch your fucking back!"

"I know what you really are, Madeline."

"You know nothing about me" I laugh in her face.
I turn and leave her standing outside of the lobby feeling her icy stare follow me into the building. I see Jeff, a familiar concierge, at the desk.

"Call security" I snap.

"Yes, ma'am" he says as he reaches for his walkie-talkie to call for security.

I head upstairs and look in the mirror trying to calm down. Once I feel sane enough, I call Vince and tell him about my fiasco with Dina. I ask him about their connection. He pauses and tells me that he and Dina had an affair, but she thought it to be more serious than he did. As he starts to explain, I hear soft knocking at my door. I bite my lip and tell him that I need to go; however, I expect the full story when I call him back.

I see the concierge standing with a man that I presume is a police detective.

"Ms. Davis, I'm Detective Sommers" he says in a gruff voice, shaking my hand firmly.

"Come in, Detective Sommers" I gesture for him to follow me and point to a chair by the couch. Sitting opposite the occupied chair, I study him carefully. Detective Sommers is an older man with traces of gray in his copper hair; the poor guy looks like he desperately needs sleep, or at least, a good roll in the hay.

"Your security guard apprehended a woman known as Dina Andrews? Said she approached you outside the revolving doors." I nod.

"Did she threaten you, Ms. Davis?" he asks.

"No, but she followed me here and I have a feeling she's been following me since I was in New York."

"What is your history with her?"

"She is the CCO of our company."

"What company is that?"

"PharmaCo."

"I see. I'm assuming that since you said you were in New York that is her primary residence."

"As far as I know."

"Why would she follow you? What's in it for her?"

"She seems to be obsessed with my relationship."

"Your relationship with whom?"

"The guy I'm dating…Vincent Marks."

"And his primary residence is…"

"New York" I finish. He nods.

"Do you think this is a jealousy issue?"

"I don't know what her issue is, but I just don't want to come home and discover that she's found her way in."

"Understandable, we will charge her with harassment. I feel I should let you know that after we screened her, we found out she has a history." I'm intrigued.

Detective Sommers continues, "In fact, she's known for harassing women." Holy shit.

"Should I be afraid? Has she done bodily harm to any of those women?" I ask, the fear rising in my throat.

"Mostly vandalism and harassment, but I promise you she won't come near you again. Given her record, I recommend a protection order for your safety." I nod warily.

"Keep a close watch, ma'am. I would be aware of my surroundings at all times" he warns.

"I'll do that."

"Well, that's all for now. If she bothers you again, please don't hesitate to call. In the morning, I'll file a protective order on your behalf." he stands and hands me his business card.

"Thank you, detective" I say and show him the door. As I stroll back into my apartment, my intercom buzzes. Jeff, the concierge comes on to tell me I have a visitor.

"Who is it?" I ask.

"A man by the name of Eric Thomas" he says. As if my night wasn't bad enough already.

"Send him up" I sigh. It's time to nip this shit in the bud!

Eric appears at my door; I can immediately tell he's just as tipsy as I am.

"What do you want, Eric?" I ask, annoyed.

"Damn it, Madeline, I want to talk!" he says harshly startling me.

"What the fuck do you want to talk about, Eric!? Please enlighten me because if I remember correctly, you dumped me!"

"Madeline…" he says as he moves towards me. I take a step back.

"Madeline, I just need to know you're okay" he says.

"I'm fine, Eric" I snap and before I know it he sweeps me into a kiss. I grab his tie and twist it, bringing him to his knees.

"What the hell are you doing?! How dare you?!" My mask has come off; I am now the Dom. I used to be into BDSM, but when Eric and I broke up, my desire for it had dwindled. I guess Vince resurrected those feelings as well.

"I want you back..." He trembles, but does not look up at me. Hmm...at least he hasn't forgotten his place. I cock my head at him and secretly wonder if I should beat him with my riding crop and make him leave. However, I'm not for inflicting pain without pleasure, and he certainly won't get any pleasure from me.

"Let me guess, you saw a picture of me and Vincent Marks and got jealous."

"I did...but I also realized how much I missed you." He stands up.

"You didn't seem too concerned with me when you left my heart in pieces all over the floor! I'm done with you Eric! Lose my number, don't come by my house and move on with your life!" He looks shocked by my reaction.

"I didn't realize you hated me so much."

"Yes! I hate you! I hate you for making me feel like a worthless piece of shit! For leading me on like a lovesick puppy and leaving me out in the cold! For making me question what was wrong with me! Yeah! I hate you! You're lucky I don't beat the hell out of you. You know I can do it." I step back.

"I never thought you would feel that way, Madeline."

"Well then you must be the dumbest man on this earth. Fuck you! Goodnight!" At this point, Pricilla matches my mood and growls at Eric.

"Good-bye, Madeline" he says as he heads out of the door. I slam it behind him just in time to hear my cell phone ring. Hopefully, it's Vince.

"Hello?" I answer gruffly.

"Is everything okay, Madeline? I've emailed HR, Dina is now terminated."

"Vince, what exactly is your story with this chick?"

"Well, when I first took over the company, Dina was the one who introduced me to everything and…well, she was kind of forward so we started…sleeping together."

"Sleeping together? I saw the pictures, Vince. You took her on vacation."

"I did, as a thank you. She didn't mean as much to me as I meant to her. She told me she'd fallen in love with me, questioned why I never let her come to my house. I told her it wasn't like that and I thought we had an understanding. She got upset and threatened to expose everything about us. I had to shut her up which is why she is in charge of communications. Ever since then, she's been harassing any woman she thinks I'm with. I should have said something sooner…I'm sorry."

"Well, she's surely going to be angry that she got fired…"

"She needed to be. She's been leaking information for months. I even got the SEC to look into whether or not she was doing insider trading." I sit down, shocked.

"Is she…dangerous?"

"Honestly, Madeline, she's capable…"

"Capable of what?"

"I hate to say it, but she's smart as hell and has friends in the media. I truly don't know what she could do." I start to feel queasy.

"It will be fine…I'll make sure she doesn't come anywhere near you." I can't help feeling fearful. What if he can't protect me?

"Vince…I'm young, I'm just starting my career. This woman can end me, and you want me to trust you?"

"Yes, I want you to trust me, Madeline."

"Vince…I don't know if we are at that point in our relationship yet." He scoffs.

"So you trust me to fuck you left, right and sideways but can't trust me with this?" his tone is angry. Surely he must understand why I don't trust him since he lied about their relationship to begin with.

"Fucking and business are two separate entities…or at least it used to be" I say, matching his harsh tone.

"Madeline, if you don't want to trust me fine, but what else are you going to do? I'm the only one that knows how to deal with her blackmailing ass."

"When I came back, you said she was the least of our worries…now you say that she could be dangerous?"

"Look, I guess I didn't think things through with Dina, but I will fix it. You know better than anyone that I can fix even the bleakest situations. Look at my fucking company! You guys were a few months from closing your doors, and look at where you are now. If you don't want to trust me based on your heart, you should at least do it with your brain." He's right. The man saved our company from going under, of course he has the means to stop her. I huff, hating the fact that I'm wrong.

"You have to understand where my frustration comes from, Vince."

"I understand completely. But I want you to trust me."

"Vince, it's going to take me awhile, but you're right. Based on what I know about you and your business sense, I know that you can handle your own. Emotionally, it's hard for me to see that because half of me thinks you still see this as a game." He scoffs again.

"What is it going to take? How can I assure you that this is real for me? What do you need Madeline?"

Chapter 20 *Fixing the Past*

My phone rings after I hang up with Madeline.

"Hello?"

"Could I speak to a Mr. Vincent Marks?" A gruff voice asks.

"Speaking."

"Mr. Marks, I am Detective Sommers from the Atlanta Police Department. I understand that you are in a romantic relationship with Madeline Davis here in Atlanta?"

"I am."

"I'm sure she informed you of the incident with Dina Andrews?"

"She did." He pauses.

"Mr. Marks, are you still in communication with her?"

"She has been calling me ever since I broke it off with her." He sighs.

"Now, your private affairs are none of my business, Mr. Marks. But anytime someone crosses state lines with the intention to harm one of our citizens, it becomes my business."

"I understand, and intend to be forthcoming about everything."

"Mr. Marks, I need you to detail the last contact you had with Dina Andrews."

"I communicated with her through email about the details of the merger to release to the *Journal*."

"How about before that?"

"She called me Friday before the merger took place."

"What did she want?"

"She called me crying, begging me to come over."

"Did she mention Ms. Davis?"

"No. She didn't say anything about Madeline. Last I heard of her was an email from HR that she had taken leave for two weeks. I figured she was embarrassed about calling me."

"Mr. Marks, I have a protection order here for Ms. Davis. If you receive any contact from Dina Andrews, you are to call me immediately. Do you understand?" Jeez, he's acting like I have something to do with this.

"I will. I am coming to Atlanta tomorrow. You can reach me wherever Ms. Davis is. I'm not letting her out of my sight."

"Very well. You have my number. Call me if you can think of anything else."

"Of course." He hangs up. I did not like that conversation. I'm tired as hell right now, but know it damn sure sounded like he suspects I had something to do with this. I would never hurt Madeline. Hopefully, Dina is either behind bars, or on a plane back to New York with a guard. I had hoped that my trip to Atlanta would give me an escape from her crazy tactics, but I guess she's not letting go. I call my security advisor, Shane Watson. Shane is a retired FBI agent from the behavioral analysis unit. If anyone can get to her, I know it will be him.

"Marks?" he answers.

"Watson, I need you to keep tabs on Dina Andrews. I am emailing you her employee profile now. She's in jail in Atlanta for the time being, but I know they will probably let her out. Trace her every move. See if she will have an ankle bracelet for monitoring. Do whatever you can."

"Right. Would you like me to accompany you to Atlanta?"

"No, I want you to fly out tomorrow afternoon. I don't know if she's watching me or has someone following me. The worst thing would be if she discovered that you're involved."

"Once your jet gets back here, I'll be ready."

"You'll call once you're in Atlanta, and keep in touch with me if you find anything, understood?"

"Understood. I'm on it now." He hangs up. I sit in my office, staring out the window at the city before me. Damn

Dina! I wish she would just leave everything the hell alone! A part of me hoped she would see what Alexis saw when she looked at the picture of Madeline and me. I guess her demented mind refuses to see that. Maybe she needs a reminder. I call Dina's second in command, Leah.

"Hello?" a tired voice says.

"Leah?"

"Yes, Mr. Marks?" her voice becomes more alert.

"Until further notice, you are now acting CCO. I know you don't want it, but I need you to have it for a few weeks until I can hire someone."

"Okay, what do you need me to do?" I find it funny that she doesn't question what happened with Dina, but I can't worry about that now.

"I'm going to email you some pictures. I need it to be in every gossip rag, social media account, and blog. Release them strategically."

"Okay, I'll take on the duty for a couple of weeks, Mr. Marks. I'm on call."

"Thank you, Leah."

"No problem." I carefully select pictures taken during Madeline's two weeks and send them. I know that Leah can do the rest. Maybe that will quiet Dina for good.

## Chapter 21 *Secrets Revealed*

Vince's question resonates in my mind and heart. I don't know what it's going to take. A crystal ball, maybe. I tell him that I will think about it, and talk to him tomorrow. I get up, pour a glass of wine and stand on the balcony, looking at the beautiful view of Atlanta. Feeling the effects of the alcohol as well as adrenaline from my encounter with Dina and Eric, I call Joseph and tell him I'm taking half of the day off, I have things to do…

On Friday, I stand at the airport entrance, with my hair freshly done and a new outfit that accentuates my curves. I see Vince heading towards me. He stops for a second to make sure it's me, and a ridiculous grin lights up his face. He takes my hand and pulls me into a passionate kiss, obviously not caring who sees.

"I have something to share with you" I say, grabbing his hand.

As I speed up I-85, Vince looks at me lovingly and grabs my free hand to kiss it. I give him a smile, nervous that he won't be very affectionate when he realizes what kind of lifestyle I have. I mentally prepare myself…this could go either way.

As we come into my apartment I lead him to the couch where Pricilla looks on with interest. She allows him to scratch her head and puts her paw on his lap. He laughs as she rolls over for him to rub her belly. I've never seen her react that way to a guy. Even with Eric she would sometimes go in a corner by herself. I guess dogs really are a good judge of character. As Vince gets comfortable, I take a deep breath and look him in the eye.

"I…have something to tell you" I say hesitantly. His eyes grow wide, not knowing what to think.

"Well, what is it?"

"I've been hiding something from you."

"What does that mean?"

"I'm… involved in a pretty controversial lifestyle, and after my last relationship I hadn't really considered it. Now that we've met, I want to share it with you."

"Oh my God are you like a swinger or something?" He looks at me in horror.

"No, no, no. I am a Dom." I say slowly, letting it sink in.

"As in BDSM?"

"Yes." He pauses, absorbing the information.

"Holy shit, why didn't you say anything back in New York?"

"Because I thought it was over, but I guess you can say I've been awakened again. You did it." There is silence between us, but I can tell he's thinking.

"Madeline, I've never really been involved in something like that…"

"Well, if you give your consent to try, we could start slowly."

"How…um…involved are you?"

"I've been in the practice since I was in college. I dated a guy who was a Switch and he taught me how to be a Dom. I've been in the lifestyle ever since."

"It all makes sense now" he muses, "no wonder you are such an extraordinary executive; putting that asshole in his place at that meeting…"

"Well? What do you think? Is this something you could live with?"

"I…er…would have to see how I like it. I'm not a man who is used to being…dominated."

"Well, when you're ready, I'll show you." I look at him with seriousness.

"Show me now" he says. I can detect his nervousness.

"Are you absolutely sure?" I ask with doubt.

"Just…go easy on me."

I head to the bathroom to get ready. When I emerge, I'm wearing a black leather bustier, lacy black panties and thigh high black boots. My long hair extensions are pulled into a sleek ponytail. I approach Vince and look at him.

"The safe word is gold, and I will stop if you say it. If you just want me to let up a little, the word is silver" I tell him. I hear a shuddering breath escape from him, "You must address me as Madame, understand?"

"I understand."

"You understand, what?" I sneer.

"I understand...Madame."

I unbutton his shirt, leaving his tie on. I take off his belt and pants, leaving him in only his tie and boxers. I lead him to the bed and push him down. His eyes grow wide in anticipation.

"I'm going to restrain you now," I say, taking a red scarf out of my cleavage and tying his hands to the bedpost. He begins to tremble and I enjoy watching the growing evidence of his arousal in his boxers. I remove my panties, leaving on my bustier and I slowly climb on top of him, freeing his erection from his boxers. I take out a condom and slide it carefully on him. He groans as I lower myself down slowly. I grab his face and look into his eyes.

"Do you like it?" I ask as I begin a slow rhythm.

"Yes" he breathes.

"Yes, what?" I snap.

"Yes, Madame," he moans as I pick up the rhythm. I run my long fingernails down his chest and move faster. He cries out and pulls against the restraints.

"Uh-uh-uh, be a good boy and stay still" I warn.

"Oh, God that feels so good" he groans. He seems to get the hang of it. I go harder and faster, feeling that familiar tingle, and I explode around him with a scream. Vince writhes against the restraints again, crying out as he comes with force.

I collapse on top of him, running my fingertips on his chest. A few moments later, I untie him and stroke his face.

"Well?" I say.

"I have a feeling that was a really easy introduction" his hazel eyes burn into mine, "does it always have to be this way?"

"No, I can do both. We would just have to compromise."

"What…other things do you do?" he asks anxiously.

"I think the best question is what I don't do." Intrigued, he sits up.

"Okay…What don't you do?"

"I'm simplistic; I don't do all the crazy stuff…although I used to. Come here." I lead him to my…other closet. I unlock it and show him my variety of whips, belts handcuffs, blindfolds, masks, and my favorite…a riding crop with gold trim.

"You've used all of these?"

"Yes, but…we don't have to use anything you don't feel comfortable with." Vince exhales.

"This is a lot to take in…I had no idea…you seemed to like me taking control." He pouts and I have to laugh.

"Believe me, I was on my way to cleaning out this closet and never using this stuff again until I met you."

"I admit…I would have to get used to this, Madeline, but I'm willing to see what this is about." I look at him and breathe out a sigh of relief.

"I was convinced you would leave me if you knew about all of this" I say.

"That would be a stupid reason to leave, Madeline," he strokes my cheek. I take his hand and plant a kiss on his knuckles. Before I know it, he takes me…the regular way.

A few hours later, Vince and I walk into the office. I can see the stares from my co-workers, most in awe of Vince but some whispers indicate that not everyone is happy to see me with him. We approach Lacy's desk and he shakes her hand telling her he's glad to see her again.

Lacy gets up with a smile and gives me a long list of things I need to do before the weekend begins. I sigh, gone are the days of being grossly ahead in my work. I take a big folder of paperwork from her as Joseph greets Vince with a firm handshake and a smile.

"Vincent, welcome to our Atlanta office! Would you like a tour?" Joseph says.

"Certainly, Joe, lead the way." I wave them off as I head into my office. My phone pings a notification from social media and I look at it curiously. I've been tagged in a photo. Knowing that I haven't posted any, I open the app curiously. There is a picture of Vince and me, hand-in-hand at Central Park. The post reads: *Vincent Marks and his CFO, Madeline Davis are awfully close as they walk in Central Park*. I scoff, but at least they aren't saying the vicious stuff about us...yet. I close the app and begin working on a partnership proposal. A few minutes into my typing, Lacy buzzes me.

"You have a phone call."

"Who is it?"

"The person says they are with the Atlanta Police Department?"

"I'll take it." I answer the phone hastily.

"Ms. Davis, it's Detective Sommers. I thought I would tell you that Ms. Andrews has posted bail." My heart jumps in my throat and for a minute I swear I stop breathing.

"Your restraining order has come through and Ms. Andrews has been ordered to go back to New York. If she approaches you or the offices in any way, she'll be back in jail."

"Thank you, Detective" I say quietly. Before I can hang up, he stops me.

"My number is there for you, day or night. Do you hear me?"

"I understand." I hang up and lean back in my chair. I'm really nervous and don't know what this bitch might do. I take a deep breath and head to my closet which houses my gun. I don't usually carry it, but I feel I need to. I slip it in my desk drawer and continue typing my proposal.

At the end of the day, Lacy knocks at my door, startling me.

"Yes?" I say trying to maintain my composure.

"Madeline, I'm getting ready to leave. Do you need anything else?" I shake my head silently.

"Are you okay, Madeline? You seem tense" Lacy comments with a worried look on her face.

"I'm okay, Lacy, but do me a favor. Don't go anywhere alone this weekend, okay?"

"What's going on?"

"Just...take me at my word please. Say you won't."

"I won't, Madeline. I promise. Have a good weekend with Mr. Marks..." She hesitates as if she wants to say something, but wisely leaves the office. Vince pokes his head in my office.

"Ready to go?"

"Give me a few minutes and I'll be right out" He immediately frowns as I say this.

"What's wrong?"

"She's been let out." A stone hard look crosses his face as he immediately whips out his phone.

"Alexis, give me all of the security companies in Atlanta and quickly." I hear her faint voice through the phone.

"Great, call them, tell them I'll pay whatever they want; I need two executive protection specialists...preferably former military or law enforcement." I hear Alexis' response.

"Yes, I want them armed! Send them to the Atlanta office immediately" he hangs up.

"Vince, I'm not sure I like this."

"Stop, you know I wouldn't let anything happen to you. Besides, you'll be with me all weekend. She'll have to get through me to get to you." I ease up a little.

We wait for the security detail in Joseph's office. Joseph looks nervous and is pacing around the office. Shira, Joseph's secretary buzzes in and says that the EPS's are here.

"Send them in, Shira and then go home. Call my wife and tell her I'll be home soon."

"Yes sir."

Two suited guys walk in. One is a stocky man with olive skin and jet black hair. The other is a tall, muscular blonde guy.

"Mr. Marks, you requested executive protection services?" asks the blonde.

"Yes, I'm Mr. Marks; this is Ms. Davis and Mr. Dent. Ms. Davis and I need protection for an unspecified amount of time. Mr. Dent will need one to watch him and his family over the weekend. What are your credentials?"

"My name is Rob Greene, I retired from the marines a couple of years ago" says the blonde.

"I'm Luis Bianchi. I worked for the FBI for fifteen years before retiring" says the Italian.

"Okay, Mr. Bianchi, I would prefer you stay with Ms. Davis and I. Mr. Greene, please keep Mr. Dent and his family under a careful, watchful eye. He has three children."

"Mr. Marks, is there any person in particular that we are protecting you from?" asks Rob.

"Yes, I've printed out her picture for both of you. Her name is Dina Andrews. We learned that she posted bail and should be considered armed and dangerous." he hands them both her picture. I look at the whole process in disbelief. God, what have I gotten myself into?

"Sir, what are your orders should we apprehend this individual?" asks Luis.

"You are to call the APD immediately and keep her restrained. You have handcuffs, I presume?" asks Vince.

"Of course, and we are both armed" says Rob.

"Good, we're getting ready to leave now; I assume you're in separate cars?"

"Yes, sir, we are both in black Lexus SUVs, I would recommend that we also drive you to where you need to go."

"What about my car?" I ask.

"If you need to get your car home, I'll drive behind you" Luis says gently. I like him already.

"Okay, if that's all, let's get going. This office is getting empty" says Joseph. I can tell he's fairly irritated.
As I start to follow Vincent and the men out of the office, Joseph grabs my arm.

"Madeline," he hisses, "What the hell is going on here?!"

"Disgruntled ex-employee" I whisper back.

"From New York?!" he says in disbelief.

"Yes, the CCO."

"The CCO? That blonde chick? You've gotta be fucking kidding me!" he throws up his hands.

"Between you and me, she's not after you. She's after me" I say quietly.

"For what?" he lowers his voice.

"She and Vincent used to date and she's not happy that he's found someone else."

"Damn it, Madeline, this is what I'm talking about! I can't afford to have something happen to you. Please, please, stay close to your security guy. Don't go for a run alone or anything!"

"I won't, Joseph. Go home, enjoy your weekend. I'll see you Monday." I walk out of the office and smile at Vince who is frowning.

"Last minute business" I lie.

Luis walks in front of us as we get on the elevator.

"Vince, do you think this is necessary? Maybe she tucked her tail between her legs and went back to New York."

"I don't trust her, Madeline. I just don't. She knows too many shady people."

"Shady people?" I ask as we head towards the parking deck with Luis.

"Yeah, mob types. She tried to get me to do business with them. I may be half Italian but I prefer to have a legit business." Luis turns around and looks at us.

"Mob types like who?" He asks.

"Some guy named Luciano."

"Is that so? Is she related to him?"

"I wouldn't know, but she was adamant about it. I kept having to tell her no."

"Do you know of him, Luis?" I ask.

"Yeah, I know of the bastard. They're still trying to pin a couple of murders on him." I gasp.

"Murders?" Vince glances at Luis.

"Yeah, we just have to be careful, especially if she is related to him." I shake my head nervously and Luis looks over at me.

"Don't worry, Ms. Davis. Fifteen years in the FBI and no one I've protected has been hurt yet." It's assuring, but still scares the hell out of me.

"Thank you, Luis" Vince says. Luis walks us to my car and points to his, so that we know what type of vehicle he is in.

Once we get into the car, I hesitate before turning on the engine.

"Madeline...what's wrong?"

"Vince..." my irritation finally takes over.

"What is it?"

"Why didn't you tell me about this? I mean, don't you think I should be informed that you had a psycho for an ex?"

"She's not my ex..."

"Fuckbuddy, whatever she was!" I snap in frustration.

"Look, honestly...I thought I could handle her myself. Had I known that she was going to fly to Atlanta and harass you, I would've acted differently."

"Regardless, you should have told me. You knew what she did previously."

"I'm not going to fight with you about this. What's happened has happened, and I've told you this before about looking in the past." I huff, knowing that we have had that conversation. Not wanting to fight either, I decide to shut down the argument.

"From now on, you need to be open with me. I don't care how bad it is. If you truly want to move forward with this relationship, you'll stop hiding this kind of stuff from me. I'm not a child, and I'm not one of your fuck buddies. You want my trust? That is what it's going to take." He gives me a serious look.

"Okay, Madeline, from now on, I'll be open with you." Relieved, I start the engine.

Chapter 22 *Running Away*

We drive in silence to Madeline's condo. My nerves are frayed, and I can tell hers are too as she is gripping the steering wheel tightly.

"Madeline. Don't worry." I try to comfort her.

"I just have a bad feeling, Vince, especially after finding out about this Luciano guy" I grab her hand.

"I will protect you, Madeline, believe that." We pull into the parking deck and notice police outside of the entrance. Madeline's eyes grow wide; she halts the car in the valet lane and runs from the car. I follow, worried that something horrible has happened.

"Carina! What's wrong?" She asks the dark haired woman.

"Oh Dios mio, Senorita Davis, someone tried to hit me with a car!"

"What?!" Madeline's face reflects horror.

"Pricilla...she got hit, oh lo ciento! I tried to save her!" my heart squeezes in my chest as I see the dog lying on the pavement a few feet away. Madeline runs to her.

"Oh, Pricilla!" She sobs and falls to the ground. I can do nothing but run to her and put my arms around her.

"Easy, Madeline, easy" I say as she cries uncontrollably. The police officer looks at us with sympathy as Madeline pets the motionless ball of fur.

"Ma'am, Ms. Hernandez was able to get a partial on the tag number. Now, is there anyone you know that would have wanted to hurt your dog?" Madeline pulls away from me and stares at him.

"Yes," Madeline says through gritted teeth, "Dina Andrews."

"We already have a restraining order against her. Why did you folks let her out?!" I exclaim.

"Sir, I don't know anything about that case, who is the detective that handled it?"

"Sommers…" Madeline says quietly as the tears continue to fall down her cheeks.

The young officer immediately gets on his walkie talkie, "we need Detective Sommers at the Metropolitan Condominiums ASAP."

Detective Sommers arrives ten minutes later, and I'm trying to regain my composure. This bitch just killed her dog and for what? Pricilla has nothing to do with this. It is a cruel and evil person who will run down an animal in cold blood. I pace anxiously as Detective Sommers approaches Madeline cautiously.

"Ms. Davis, I'm sorry to tell you that Ms. Andrews has disengaged her GPS bracelet. We are assuming that she is still in the area. This is automatic ground for bail revocation. We have set up roadblocks around Atlanta; we will find her" he says.

"I've only been in Atlanta for twelve hours, and I don't think much of the police force here" I snap.

"Sir, we're doing everything possible. May I ask what your name is?"

"Vincent Marks" I growl.

"Of course, Mr. Marks. We spoke on the phone. The best thing to do is stay close to your security specialists. We will handle Ms. Andrews."

I scoff and walk over to Madeline. She is quiet and blank.

"Madeline, say something" I coax.

"I…want…her…found" Madeline looks to Detective Sommers, "find her, or I will kill her myself! That you can count on!" she shouts.

"Now, now, Ms. Davis, I'm sure it won't have to escalate like that. I have complete confidence in the men that are assigned to this case. We will find her. Now, please, get some rest and don't go anywhere alone."

"She won't be alone" I bark again, irritated. Sommers seems exasperated himself and goes to talk to Carina. Madeline follows him, realizing that she totally forgot the girl who almost got hit by the car.

"Carina, listen to me. This is not your fault" She says hugging the girl.

"Oh, senorita, I loved Pricilla so much. I'm so sorry!" she breaks down into sobs. Madeline motions for me to give her the purse laying on the ground. I hand it to her and she writes a check for a thousand dollars.

"Here's your pay for the rest of the month. Go home to your family. Call me if you notice anything strange around your house, okay?"

"Gracias, Madeline!" she hugs Madeline and cries more.

"Ms. Hernandez, would you like me to take you home?" asks the police officer.

"Yes, if you don't mind" she sniffles. Sommers gives him the okay and we wave them off.

"Ms. Davis, as always, please call me if you notice anything suspicious. If it's okay, I would like to secure your apartment first. Agent Bianchi has agreed to come with me." Madeline manages to squeak out an "okay" before he follows Luis into the building. She calls the dog's vet on the phone and asks if they can cremate Pricilla. I hug her tightly, not saying a word. Sommers and Luis come back down and approach us.

"Ms. Davis, your condo has been vandalized, is there any place else you two could stay for the night?"

"What?" I can't process everything at once.

"Nothing is missing, but your TVs and mirrors have been smashed; it also looks like they tried to break into a locked closet." Thank God she keeps that thing locked.

"I can get a suite at the Westin; can we at least go get our things?" She asks Detective Sommers.

"Yes, Ms. Davis, just have Agent Bianchi following closely. I'm headed to the station to get the progress on Ms. Andrews. I'll be up until we find her; don't hesitate to call." he gets into his car and drives off. Madeline picks up her phone.

"Lacy, I need a huge favor. Will you reserve a room under a fake name for me?" I hear Lacy's faint reply.

"No, everything is not okay!" Madeline begins to sob again. Lacy speaks frantically on the other end.

"She...she killed Pricilla!" I hear Madeline explain everything from Thursday night until the events of tonight. Lacy responds at length.

"That sounds like a good idea, Lacy, I'll see you soon." She looks up at me and Luis.

"Okay, look, we're going to Lacy's condo in Athens. It's about an hour drive from here. Can you handle that?" She addresses Luis.

"Yes, ma'am. I know Athens like the back of my hand" says Luis. We head upstairs to get our things. The place is a mess. There is broken glass everywhere and her two plasma screens are on the floor cracked. She quietly packs her things and I watch closely.

"Madeline, are you okay?" I finally ask.

"I'm fine, I just want her to be caught" she sighs.

Suddenly, we hear the intercom.

"There is a Lacy here to see you" says the female voice from the concierge desk.

"Send her up" Madeline says.

Lacy comes in and hugs Madeline tightly, "Oh, Madeline! This is awful!"

"It's okay, Lacy. Do me a favor and forward all of my calls to your condo in Athens. I don't know whether she has the ability to listen to my cell phone conversations or not."

"Done, here are the keys. Do you remember where it is?"

"Yeah, I remember."

"Be safe, Madeline. Oh! By the way, the liquor cabinet is full. Take what you want."

"Thanks Lacy." They embrace again and I grab our bags. Taking her hand, I lead her to the elevator.

Luis pulls his SUV to the curb, I open the door for her and she climbs in. Our ride to Athens is silent, and I feel a wave of guilt. Unbuckling her seatbelt, I pull her into my lap.

"I will protect you" I whisper. She lays her head on my shoulder and cries again.

Chapter 23 *Athens*

    We arrive in Athens and I tell Luis the gate code to get us into the parking deck. I unlock the door to Lacy's condo. It's a beautiful place with very expensive white leather furniture. Lacy's parents are definitely loaded. Sometimes, I wonder why she wasn't okay with just being a trust fund baby. I tell Luis that he can have the spare bedroom upstairs. He nods and takes his bags to find it. I look at Vince and kiss him passionately.

"What was that for?" he grins.

"Thank you for being here with me" I say.

"If this would have happened when I wasn't here, I would have been on the first plane down here."

"I know. Now, you've shown me your cooking skills, so I think it's time I show you mine" I try to change the subject.

    I look in the fridge which is fully stocked. I decide to make chicken and spinach penne. Vince finds the wine cooler and pours us two glasses of Cabernet Sauvignon. Luis comes downstairs and studies us both.

"The rooms upstairs are clear. I'll keep watch throughout the night" he says.

"Thank-you, Luis" we say in unison.

I finish the pasta and make sure I take a plate to Luis, who is on the balcony having a cigarette. He thanks me with his sincere brown eyes and takes the plate. I head back inside and see Vince spooning the pasta into two plates. He hands me a plate, and we eat silently for a few minutes.

"You'll have to teach me how to make this." He says, breaking the silence. I smile at him and clear the dishes while Vince refills our glasses. Luis is on the phone with his boss, giving the details of his whereabouts and the situation. I start to relax, but still can't shake the uneasy feeling from earlier. Vince hugs me from behind with the silent reminder that he'll protect me. He turns me around, kissing my lips softly.

"Do you want to do anything tonight, Madeline?"

"I think a quiet night at home will suffice" I tell him. I gulp down the wine and ask for another refill. Suddenly, the phone rings. I eye it cautiously before I answer.

"Davis" I say into the receiver.

"Ms. Davis this is Alexis, Mr. Marks' executive assistant. May I speak with him please?" she sounds nervous. Vince works fast, how did she even know the number here?

"Sure. Vince, it's Alexis" I hand him the phone.

"Alexis" he says with concern. I hear her frantically speaking through the phone.

"Okay, is there anywhere safe you can go for the weekend?" He pauses to hear her response.

"It's alright Alexis, I'll call Jillian immediately. She can accompany you to your parents' house in the Hamptons. Be careful and don't leave until she gets there" he hangs up and dials another number.

"Jillian," he says, "I need you to go to Alexis' apartment and escort her to the Hamptons. She has been receiving threats from a former co-worker." I gasp as he pauses for Jillian's answer.

"Just make sure you don't leave her side" he says and hangs up the phone.

"Okay, so it appears that Dina has someone harassing her other former co-workers."

"Oh my God, so who is she working with?"

"I don't know, but at this point, I don't trust anyone" he looks irritated. I put my head in my hands. How can this night get any worse? I certainly wish that she would just go home and take her loss. However, women like Dina never take losses with dignity. I've known a few that are like her. I look up and sip my wine carefully, trying not to tremble from fear. She killed my dog, what else will she do?

"Hey, don't worry, we'll catch her and whatever assholes she's working with" he seems to have read my mind.

I turn away and pour myself another glass of wine. This is so stressful! He comes over to me and hugs me tightly, sensing my worry.

"We'd better call Detective Sommers" I say quietly as I pick up the phone and dial his number. At this rate, I have it memorized.

"Sommers," says a gruff voice.

"Detective Sommers, this is Madeline Davis. Dina must have an accomplice. She has someone harassing employees in New York."

"You're kidding me. Any idea who her accomplice may be?"

"At this point we don't know. It could be anyone who works or worked for the company."

"Ms. Davis...how much do you trust Mr. Marks?" I gasp at his indication and lower my voice.

"I trust him completely. Why?" The thought is horrendous.

"They have a history. Just watch your back, and don't leave Luis' side" he says before he hangs up. I look at Vince. Could he be behind this? No, no that's silly!

"Madeline, are you okay?" he looks worried.

"I'm okay, pour me another glass will you? I've gotta talk to Luis" I go back out to the balcony where Luis is observing the drunken college students staggering in downtown Athens.

"Luis? We've learned that Dina has an accomplice" I say.

"Do you know who the accomplice may be? Anyone I should be looking for in particular?"

"No idea." At this point, I'm a nervous wreck. I need to relieve this stress. Maybe Vince will oblige me. I go back inside where I see Vince on the phone. I idly wonder who he is talking to.

"Good. Is everything secure? Tell Mrs. Lovett to go to her sister's house. Keep watch over the apartment. Thanks Jack." He hangs up and looks at me.

"I need you to do something for me" I say to him.

"Anything."

"I need a...release...I need to regain some control."

"What does that entail?"

"You have to trust me." He looks nervous but nods in agreement.

"Go to the bedroom and strip down" I command darkly. I head to the master bathroom and change into my ensemble. This time, my bustier, panties and high heeled boots are red. I take my precious riding crop out of my suitcase. He's not going to like it, but this is what I need. I enter the bedroom where I see Vince standing by the bed, completely naked. I look down at him.

"Do you remember the safe word?" I ask.

"Yes, Madame."

"What is it?"

"Gold."

"Good... now get down on your hands" he obeys and puts his hands down on the bed.

"Do you trust me?"

"Yes, I trust you."

"Yes, what?!"

"Yes, Madame." He actually looks scared. I start to relax as I feel like I'm gaining control again. I take out the riding crop and show it to him.

"This object could be considered painful" I say as I run the crop across his back, "but actually, it could bring a lot a pleasure." I slap him hard on his ass.

"Ah!" he groans.

"Maintain control..." I growl as I slap his backside again. He exhales sharply. Man, I've missed this. I run the crop down his back before I smack him several times. I can tell he's becoming aroused.

"Get up" I say and he stands up immediately. I'm still going pretty easy on him; I don't want to scare him away. I walk around him like a lioness stalking her prey. His breathing has become harsh. I grab his tie and kiss him passionately before pushing him on the bed. I kick off my boots and climb on top of him.

"Now, you're going to fuck me, fast and hard. Understand?"

"Yes, Madame." He looks relieved and rolls me over on my back.

"Undress me" I order. He obliges me and eagerly pulls off my underwear and bustier. He takes the condom I hand him and sinks into me showing no mercy. I throw him over so that I'm on top. I hold on to the bed post so that he can continue drive into me. The scene is so arousing that I climax quickly and loudly. He cries out in response to my orgasm but I put my hand over his mouth.

"Control yourself" Trying honor my command, he grows silent and continues thrusting into me until both of us explode together.

I see a figure coming at me with a gun. I reach for mine, but it is nowhere to be found. I hear the shot before I feel it pierce my stomach. The figure comes closer to me and I see Dina's evil face. She shoots me again, and I scream loudly at the pain.

"Madeline! Madeline! Wake up!" I hear Vince's voice.

"God, this situation has me fucked up!"

"Shhh, don't worry, I'm here" he says affectionately. I get out of bed and put on my silk robe heading towards the kitchen. Feeling incredibly thirsty, I reach into the fridge for some orange juice. I look on the balcony and see the amber glow of Luis' cigarette. I tighten my robe and head out to where he is. I try to think of how I can help.

"Luis, would you like some coffee?"

"Oh, that would be great, thank-you" he says with gratitude.

I step back inside and put the coffee grounds in the coffee maker. Vince emerges in basketball shorts that hang off his rock hard abs.

"Coffee at midnight?" he asks.

"For Luis" I say.

"You know, Madeline. I could get used to this new lifestyle you've acquainted me with..." he says quietly.

"Really, now?" I gaze into his eyes.

"I can't say that I would enjoy it with anyone else, but I love it when you take control."

"That's good to know" I give him a quick peck and finish the coffee for Luis. Vince walks back to the bedroom and I step onto the balcony.

"So Luis, what's your story?" I ask as I sit in the wicker chair beside him.

"Well, my family came here from Italy when I was twelve. Graduated high school, went to Georgia State and started training at the academy after I got my degree. I met my wife while I was in training."

"Your wife doesn't mind that you have to do assignments like this?"

"No ma'am, actually she works for one of your sister offices in Macon. I hardly see her during the week."

"Really? What is her position?" I ask.

"She's in the PR division; Rosalind Bianchi. Thanks to you and your successful merger, she was able to secure a promotion." I look at him suspiciously.

"So, was it a coincidence that you came to protect Mr. Marks and me?"

"No ma'am. We have you to thank for ensuring that my wife didn't lose her job during the merger. I wanted to repay the favor." I'm surprised.

---

"Do you have any children?"

"Yeah, four" he pulls out his wallet and shows me pictures of four beautiful children.

"Bella, Marco, Sofia, and Angel" he points out the kids with smiling faces in the picture. Marco looks like a carbon copy of Luis.

"They're beautiful..." I croon as he smiles with pride. I look deeply into his serious eyes.

"They came quickly" he laughs fondly.

"Luis, I trust you with my life. Mr. Marks trusts you with his. Please just make sure we get through this weekend."

"I wouldn't dream of letting anything happen to you, Ms. Davis. I know that you are the wheels driving the company. If you were to ever leave...those selfish bastards would have my wife's job within seconds." I'm touched by his statement and silently vow to give his wife a raise when I get back to the office.

"Well, I'll let you get back to your watch, Luis. Call us if you need anything. I'm also armed, so I can be pretty good backup if I need to be." He smiles.

"I'll remember that, Ms. Davis."

I go back into the bedroom where Vince is checking email on his phone. He looks at me with a grin.

"Welcome back, do you feel like having one last rendezvous before sleeping?"

"Yes, please" I say as I hop into the bed and let him take over me.

The phone rings and I look at the alarm clock. It's four thirty, who could be calling this late? I answer the phone with a weak "hello".

"Naughty girl Madeline" snarls a deep voice on the other line, I can't recognize it.

"Who is this?" I say, my senses alert.

"Don't worry about who I am; be more worried about what's going to happen to you and your little boyfriend. No security will keep me away from you, bitch!" The phone clicks and I hear a crash in the kitchen. I gasp.

"Vince! Vince! Wake up!" I whisper harshly.

"Madeline? What is it?" he asks sleepily, rubbing his eyes.

"Someone's in here!" I hiss. Another crash comes from the kitchen.

"Okay, calm down. I'm sure Luis already has the situation under control."

We both jump at another loud crash. Then we hear a bang at the bedroom door. I start to shake out of fear. Maybe this is the end...Vince jumps out of the bed and I notice he has a gun...a Glock if I'm not mistaken. Suddenly we hear a voice.

"It's Luis!" says a frantic voice through the bedroom door. Vince opens the door cautiously. Luis bursts into the bedroom and slams the door shut.

"Whoever came in here broke some stuff and left. The door is wrecked, we've gotta get it fixed now if you're going to stay here."

"Did you see anything?" asks Vince.

"No! I heard them, drew my gun and came inside. But they were already gone. I hate to do this, but maybe we should go to a hotel until morning."

"Give me your phone" I instruct Luis. He hands it to me then secures the bedroom door.

"Thank you for calling the Inn, may I help you?" a voice chimes.

"Hi, my name is Tiffany James; my husband, his brother and I just had a break in, and we need a place to stay for the night" I say sweetly, using a character from some novel I read.

"Mrs. James, you're in luck! We have two rooms with a queen bed in each. Should I book them for you?"

"Yes, we'll be there in thirty minutes."

"Excellent, Ms. James. Will that be cash or credit?" I forgot how raunchy this hotel was.

"Cash."

"I've got you booked, see you in thirty minutes!" I hang up.

Vince and I get our bags together. We all scurry through the living area, and I see the broken glass from the wine glasses we used earlier. I make sure I grab another bottle of wine before we leave. Luis speeds up to the curb and we hop in. While we make the short drive, I pull my hair up in a bun and hope no one sees me looking disheveled. At this point, I feel like an actress being harassed by a stalker.

Once we arrive at the hotel, I pay our bill with cash and collect the keys. When we get to our room, I take one of the cheap plastic cups, open the wine and take a huge gulp. Vince looks at me worriedly.

"Madeline, take it easy on the wine."

"I will not. This day has been a fucking rollercoaster. I need to get drunk, damn it."

"It's almost daylight. Do you really want to be drunk in the morning?"

"I don't give a shit." With that, Vince concedes and throws up his hands.

"What do you need?" he sighs with concern. I sigh; I don't know what I need anymore. He takes my hand and pulls me into his lap. He nuzzles my neck and caresses my shoulders. Suddenly, we hear a knock at the door.

"It's Luis" we hear from outside. I slide off Vince's lap and answer the door. Luis comes in; he's starting to look tired.

"Ms. Davis, I don't know who it is, but one of Ms. Andrews' accomplices lives in the Atlanta area."

"How do you know?"

"I just got off the phone with Detective Sommers. Ms. Andrews has been making consistent phone calls to a number in Atlanta since yesterday evening."

"Holy shit. They don't know who it is?!" I exclaim.

"The phone calls are going to a prepaid cell phone; we're trying to match the records, now. Ms. Davis, is there anyone in Atlanta that might be looking for revenge against you?"

"I honestly don't know, I come into contact with so many people..." suddenly my mind takes a dangerous turn. My God, could Eric be her accomplice?

"I have an ex...Eric Thomas. He came to my apartment when I first started getting harassed by Dina." I notice Vince's eyes burning into me.

"We will do a full surveillance on Mr. Thomas. Other than him, is there anyone else?"

"I can't think of anyone that I've pissed off that badly."

"If you can think of anyone, tell me immediately. I've alerted hotel security. No one is to come near your room without speaking with me first. Does anyone know we're here?"

"No, I haven't told anyone besides Lacy, of course."

"Very well," he sighs, "try to get some rest, Ms. Davis and Mr. Marks, we'll figure this all out in the morning.

"Thank you Luis, and please call me Madeline" I say.

"As you wish" Luis leaves, closing the door behind him. Vince is still looking at me.

"Why didn't you tell me your ex came by your apartment?" He asks.

"Really? We're gonna hash this out now? I honestly forgot, and told him off anyway. I never thought I would have to deal with this...with him." He studies me then wisely decides to let it go. I pour more wine and glug it down.

"Give me some," he says, "this has been a long night." I pour him a cup and we drink in silence. Suddenly, his phone rings. We both look at it anxiously. He looks at the number and seems to recognize it.

"Marks," he answers, "Alexis? Are you okay? What? Is Jillian…Oh my God, where is she?" His face falls. "Stay at the hospital, I'm calling extra security for you and Jillian both. No, no, no don't apologize; I'm just glad you're okay. I'll talk to you soon." He hangs up and immediately dials another. I can hear my heart beating rapidly.

"Jack, it's Vincent. Listen, I need you to go to the small community hospital near the Hamptons. Jillian and Alexis were run off the road by an unknown person. I need you to stay close. Take Dawson with you; be ready for any phone calls." he hangs up and collapses on the bed with his arm over his eyes. Saying nothing, I lay beside him. He heaves a big sigh.

"This bitch has gone too far; it's time to get my team mobilized. The police are not working for me" he says leaning over and taking a gulp of his wine. I look down and nod in agreement.

"Are Jillian and Alexis okay?"

"Jillian is in intensive care; her condition is questionable right now. Alexis has several bruised ribs and a concussion. She's pretty shaken up, but her parents are there with her."

"Poor Jillian," I say sadly, "you should call her family." He sighs and gives me an exhausted look.

"Will you call? I'm not very good at giving this kind of news."

"I will" I say as I take his phone and look for Jillian's emergency contact information. She has a sister named Breanna Fox who lives in upstate New York. I take a deep breath and dial the number as Vince pours us more wine.

"Ms. Fox? My name is Madeline Davis, CFO of Marks Enterprises. I'm so sorry to call you this early in the morning, but I'm afraid I have some bad news. Jillian has been in a car accident right outside of the Hamptons." Jillian's sister is frantic and asking me tons of questions. I try to explain as much as I can.

"She is not quite stable, and you should head to the hospital immediately. Cheshire Community Hospital. Please keep me updated, you can reach me at this number." She tells me that she will give me an update as soon as she gets to the hospital.

Vince looks at me and pulls me into an embrace. We don't say anything, but I begin to realize how fatigued I am. I get up, chug the rest of my wine and look at Vince.

As I'm chugging, Vince picks up his phone and calls someone named Shane Watson. My mind wanders as I vaguely hear him discuss tactical team measures. He describes Dina and acknowledges that she has an unknown accomplices. He pauses as Watson speaks and seems satisfied with what he says. He hangs up and looks at me.

"I'm tired," I say weakly. I look at my watch and realize that it is now six in the morning.

"Well, let's go to bed" Vince says. I crawl into his arms and he holds me tightly. I feel safe again and finally, exhaustion begins to take over my body.

"Madeline?" Vince asks.

"Yes?" I say sleepily.

"You trust me don't you?"

"Of course I do."

"I got a call from Sommers...he questioned me like he thinks I had something to do with it."

"Vince, you have nothing to worry about...I trust you." I give his arm a reassuring squeeze. I just want things to be normal again. Could Eric really be Dina's accomplice? It was weird that he came by my apartment that night. Could she have gotten to him? Made him believe that he could get me back? Surely he wouldn't be that phased by her, but then again, she is manipulative. I secretly hope that even though I expressed genuine hatred for him that he would respect me enough to fend off any plot to harm me. My thoughts swirl in my head, but my body reminds me that I haven't slept. As the thoughts settle, my eyes finally grow heavy and I drift into a restless sleep.

Chapter 24 *Making Plans*

I hear my phone vibrating on the nightstand and pick it up quickly, not wanting to wake Madeline.

"Hello?" I whisper as I put on my shirt and slide out to the balcony.

"I'm here." Watson's voice rings out.

"What have you found out?"

"The ex is a heavy drinker and partier, but I haven't seen any evidence that he's working with Dina. It's someone else."

"And?"

"Dina is slick, that's for sure. We can't find her anywhere, and how she was able to get that bracelet off is beyond me. She must know some real criminals."

"Watson, listen to me. The detective is suspecting me, I need you to find out whoever this accomplice is."

"I'm on it, boss."

"How soon can you get to Athens?"

"Already on my way, I should be there in about fifteen minutes."

"Perfect, I'm in room 310." I hang up and duck into the bathroom to make myself presentable. When I come out, I look at Madeline restlessly tossing and turning on the bed. I sit on the edge and stroke her sweat soaked hair. She sighs and becomes still. She doesn't deserve this. Dina can come at me but not Madeline. This has to stop.

I get up just in time to hear soft knocking on the door. I look through the peephole and see Luis standing with Watson. I guess he meant it when he said no visitors without him. I don't mind it, though. He is a damn fine security agent.

"Balcony" I whisper as we tiptoe out of the sliding door. I gently close it shut, and look at the two men.

"Watson, thank you for getting here so quickly. Was the jet okay?"

"It was fine, sir."

"So, what's the next step?" I ask him.

"I think it would be best to take Ms. Davis out of the state. I'm not liking the fact that Dina was able to disappear. Even Gus's guy can't find her and he can find anyone."

"She'll never go for that."

"Do you think it would be better if I suggest it?" Luis asks.

"Maybe. I'll feel her out first." Luis nods.

"I am still trying to figure out who the accomplice is. For the life of me I don't know anyone who would help her do this."

"Mr. Marks, you said she knows the Luciano family. It is very possible they are helping her, and they don't mind doing illegal activity. This situation could be incredibly dangerous. You cannot handle this on your own, no matter how many people you've got working under you. No offense Mr. Watson."

"None taken, and I do believe you're right, Agent Bianchi. Thirty years in the behavioral analysis unit and this is bizarre even for me." Luis sits down in the wicker chair.

"Let's look at the pattern of her behavior. Mr. Marks, do you mind going through everything with us from the beginning of your relationship with her?" Watson asks.

"Well…" suddenly, I'm embarrassed. My days of sleeping with women as a favorite pastime are catching up to me quickly.

"It is imperative that you be honest with me, Mr. Marks. Detective Sommers is already looking at you as a person of interest." I huff.

"Dina and I were never in an emotional relationship. A sexual one, yes, and I admit that I probably gave her mixed signals. I took her on vacation, and didn't really think about how she would interpret that."

"When did you break it off?" Watson asks.

"We got back from the Bahamas and she started being obsessive. She'd call me crying and blubbering about how she was in love with me, and I wrote her off. So, when I started dating other women, she would find out everything about them and harass them."

"Harass them how?"

"Phone calls, breaking into their homes, or following them wherever they went."

"Did you let Ms. Davis know this?" Luis looks at me and I lower my eyes.

"Not at first…and she still doesn't know everything."

"So, something had to have happened that made her snap" Watson observes.

"Madeline came to New York three weeks ago to help seal a merger." Luis leans forward.

"What happened when she visited?"

"I…fell for her. We went to a benefit, and the rest is history. We've been together ever since then."

"Did Dina threaten her while she was there?" Watson asks.

"Not to my knowledge, but she had to know something was up. Madeline and I spent a lot of time together and I got a little reckless. Before I knew it, we were on page six."

"What was your contact with her during that period?"

"Late night phone calls, most of which I ignored because I was too busy with Madeline. She started stalking my office. I told her to stop or she would be fired. She blackmailed me with pictures and videos, promising that she would release them to the media."

"Mr. Marks, with all due respect, you should have called me the minute she started acting like this. We could have nipped this in the bud" Watson says. Luis murmurs in agreement.

"How was I supposed to know she would go all the way to Atlanta to harass Madeline? I figured she would just keep coming at me."

"Well, the past is the past. Now we just need to figure out how to stop her. Agent Bianchi, do you still have friends in the force?" Watson looks at Luis.

"Of course, what do you need?"

"Whatever I can get. We need to match Dina's number to Atlanta and New York area codes to see who she called most often."

"I can get that in about an hour."

"Very well. Here's my card." He hands Luis his card.

"I'll try to convince Madeline to go to my house in LA. They can't possibly find us there."

"Let's look at her phone records first" Watson suggests.

"You're the expert." I plop down in the chair beside me. My phone vibrates in my pocket and I look at the caller ID. It's Jack.

"Jack?" I answer.

"Hey boss, I'm here at the hospital."

"How is Jillian?"

"They're not really saying anything to me personally, but I can get her sister to call ya."

"Very well, is Alexis okay?"

"Shaken up, but she's fine. She went with her parents about an hour ago. I asked if she wanted protection but her dad assured me he could do it himself." I chuckle remembering Alexis telling me that her dad collected guns.

"I'm sure he can. Don't let Jillian out of your sight. Ask her sister if you can watch her hospital room."

"I'll be here until she doesn't need me."

"Don't forget to ask her sister to call me."

"Yes, sir." I hang up and run my hands over my head, frustrated and exhausted.

"We'll get to the bottom of this, Mr. Marks. I'll work with Alistair, Gus and Agent Bianchi." Watson shoves his hands through his salt and pepper hair.

"Fine."

"For now, remain cautious and alert at all times. Until we find out who this person is, trust no one." I nod warily looking through the window at Madeline who is still sprawled out on the bed. She must be exhausted, and so am I. Never in my life did I think I would be in a situation like this. As Luis and Watson discuss plans for the next step, my mind wanders as I'm trying to figure out who this woman's accomplice can be. Usually the person is right under your nose. Could it be someone I looked over for Madeline's promotion? Not many people applied, and even those applicants were less qualified than her. Everyone who works at the company knows she's deserving. Damnit I wish I could figure it out.

Chapter 25 *Flight*

I wake up from a restless sleep and notice that I'm alone in the bed. I hear voices outside on the balcony and recognize Vince's voice. Looking out of the window, I see Luis and another man talking to Vince. The man looks to be in his forties with gray streaks in his jet black hair; I'm assuming that is Watson. I duck into the bathroom to shower and change clothes.

When I emerge from the shower, Vince is sitting on the bed checking his phone for emails. He smiles as he sees me come out.

"Jillian's sister called, she's stable now and they are going to move her to a hospital in Brooklyn as soon as she gets an okay from the doctor."

"That's good news" I breathe a sigh of relief.

"Madeline, I think maybe you need to take leave from work. We can go to my house in Los Angeles and work from the office there."

"Vince, I'm tired of running from her. I'm ready to settle this once and for all. She is not going to ruin my life."

"Madeline, I have my team on her. They will find her and the asshole who is helping her."

"I know. Let's compromise; if she's not caught by the time we leave Athens, I will go to L.A."

"I can deal with that. Well, Madeline, let's get our minds off this. Why don't you show me around your old stomping grounds?" says Vince. I nod and we call Luis. He's deserted his suit and is dressed casually in some jeans and a blue hoodie. A way to be less noticeable on a college campus, I guess.

We head downtown and I take Vince to a restaurant and bar that I used to frequent during my senior year. I order two of their best calzones and a few beers. Vince looks around the bar, amused.

"What?" I ask.

"I can just imagine you, a bright college student, having fun with your friends."

"Seems like it was so long ago, now."

"Ah, stop sounding old, I have about 10 years on ya." He is always exaggerating.

"In the past few days, I think I've aged twenty years" I say tiredly.

"Don't worry, Madeline, it'll be over soon," Vince squeezes my hand reassuringly. I give him a sad smile. I am so stressed out right now. I really want to go home and be with my parents. I heave a sigh and take a swig of my beer. He holds my gaze as if he wants to tell me something.

"What is it?" I ask, looking into his tired hazel eyes.

"I'm sorry. I'm sorry that you're in the middle of this, and that Dina made a target out of you. You don't deserve it. I'm sorry that I didn't tell you how crazy she acted when I broke it off with her. I guess I was just so excited about moving things forward that I didn't want to ruin it with my past. But I want you to know that I will fix this."

"I don't blame you, Vince. You don't have to apologize to me."

"Yes, I do. This is all my fault. I've been playing with women's emotions for years, and I'm just getting what was coming to me. But you...you've done nothing wrong." I am appreciative of his sincerity and squeeze his hand.

"Vince, even with all of this going on, I still wouldn't change a thing. You have been more to me than any man I've ever dated or thought I loved." I smile at him as he places a hand on my knee and caresses it. My body lights up at his touch and I take in a shaky breath. He has such a crazy effect on me, and I love it.

After lunch, I take Vince on a tour of the UGA campus. I look admirably at the beautiful landscape and secretly wish for the carefree days of studying, going out with friends and exploring the city of Athens. Vince seems to enjoy the campus and muses about his days at Harvard. Luis follows behind us but tries to be inconspicuous. Suddenly, I feel a headache coming on.

"I think I want to go lay down for a bit" I look at Vince.

"You okay?" he asks.

"I just feel a little dizzy, I probably have been drinking too much" I give a light laugh. Vince summons Luis and we head back to the hotel. I welcome the bed with open arms. Almost immediately, the headache goes away.

"I'm going to try to get some work done, do you mind if I work in here?"

"No, I don't mind" I whisper.

A few hours later I wake with my stomach grumbling. Vince sits at the table working on his laptop and looks at me.

"Are you okay?"

"Yes, I think I just needed the rest."

"We can't have you sick all weekend." I get out of the bed and head to the bathroom to splash cold water on my face. When I return, Vince has his laptop closed and is studying me.

"Madeline, my security team has been following your ex. There's no evidence that he's Dina's accomplice. I need you to think…is there anyone else that might have a grudge against you?" I shake my head, I honestly can't think of anyone who would want to hurt me.

"We'll assume that maybe she's working with someone she knows that doesn't know you. The NYPD and APD are still looking for her. I heave a big sigh and lay back on the bed. Vince joins me and takes me in his arms. Before I know it, he kisses me passionately, and I respond with a moan.

"I want you so bad right now" he breathes fervently.

"I can manage" I say as I pull him to me for another kiss. I pull his t-shirt over his head and he unbuttons my pants. Suddenly we hear a knock on the door.

"Ah, shit!" Vince growls, "Who is it?!" I'm a little entertained at his anger towards the interruption in our passionate minute.

"It's Luis, sir" says a timid voice behind the door.

"Just a minute!" Vince says as he pulls his shirt back over his head and I buckle my jeans with disappointment.

"Uh..sorry to interrupt" says Luis, hiding a sheepish grin. I'm assuming he knows he caught us in a moment.

"It's alright, Luis, what's going on?" asks Vince.

"We're getting close to finding the accomplice. We were able to get a GPS track on the prepaid cell phone. Idiot didn't have the mind to dispose of it. Meanwhile, if you don't mind, I'd recommend you two stay in tonight. I was thinking you could order takeout for dinner and I'll pick it up."

"Sure, that works for me. There's a great Chinese place called The Dragon. We can order from there and..." I trail off knowing I'll get a disapproving look, "if you don't mind Luis, I'd like a bottle of white wine." Sure enough, Vince stares me down but says nothing. I always vow not to drink and reach for another bottle as soon as I'm feeling better.

"Just tell me what you guys want and I'll get it for you" Luis says. We look at the takeout menu, decide on our orders, and send Luis on his way.

"Back in twenty" he says as he goes out of the door.

"I thought you weren't drinking anymore?" Vince asks, concerned.

"Cut me some slack until all of this is over with" I snap. Vince looks entertained by my foul mood and as much as I try to stay mad, I can't help but to smile after my outburst. Vince caresses my face and looks at me lovingly.

"After dinner, I think dessert is in order" he says menacingly. Everything below my waist clenches in desire; I like that idea very much.

When we finish eating and drinking our wine, Vince gives me that familiar look that tells me of his intentions. He pulls me into his lap and caresses my face before he kisses me passionately, yanking my t-shirt over my head. I unbuckle his belt and unbutton his jeans. Our lips never leave each other. Vince's kisses grow more urgent as his hands explore my body. He grabs my jeans and quickly takes them off. He lifts me up gently and places me on the bed while trailing soft kisses down my neck. I moan as my body lights up with longing. He stops, staring into my eyes, and without saying a word, he thrusts into me. I scream loudly and shake violently, not expecting him to go so deep. He groans with the rhythm while he looks me in the eyes with intensity. He kisses me deeply, rubbing his hands over my breasts, moaning with appreciation. When he finally pulls away from the passionate kiss, I come to the hasty realization that he didn't put on protection. I was so swept up in the moment that I didn't notice. Nothing like ruining it, but I have to ask.

"We don't have a condom?" I breathe heavily, panicking at the thought. Honestly, no man has ever had the pleasure of having sex with me without a condom. I was always super paranoid. I don't quite know how to feel about this, but at the same time, feeling all of him gives me a new sensation.

"I want to come inside of you…" he whispers as he slides in and out of me. I can do nothing but respond with a groan to the harsh rhythm.

"Tell me you won't leave me" he requests in my ear with a tremor in his voice.

"I won't ever leave you…" I gasp. He increases his rhythm and drives harder into me calling out my name; an intense amount of pleasure radiates through my body. He pushes himself deeper into me with every thrust, I start to feel that familiar climb and hold him tighter.

"Oh…..God…Vince!" I sob loudly as my body starts to convulse brutally with my release. My toes curl, my pelvis lifts off the bed and tears roll down my face. I dig my fingers into his back, crying out to God over and over as the vibrations continue inside me. Vince becomes unraveled; his breathing almost panicked, like he's afraid of the intensity if he lets go. He holds my arms, not wanting to stop his powerful thrusts inside of me. His body quakes and he cries my name as he comes so hard that the results of both of our releases run down my legs. He finishes with a groan, and stares down at me.

Looking deeply into my eyes, he wipes away my tears and whispers, "I love you, Madeline Davis." I look at him panting, trembling and vulnerable above me. I'm speechless at first, but I know that within me, I have the answer.

"I love you too, Vincent Marks" I murmur. He kisses me with such passion that it makes me dizzy. He collapses on top of me and I stroke his head lovingly until we both fall asleep.

I wake with a strange feeling; something just doesn't seem right. I fumble around sleepily and turn on the lamp. Vince sits in the chair next to the bed with a grim look on his face, his phone sitting in his lap.

"Vince, what's wrong?" I ask.

"Well, it appears that whoever Dina's accomplice works for the Atlanta branch of our company."

"What? Who is it?" I ask, baffled.

"All I know is that they are an employee. I need you to think, Madeline. Who would work with Dina?"

I shudder and whisper, "It could be anyone...someone who's angry about the recent changes."

"No one has said anything to you directly?" asks Vince. Jeez, he's starting to sound like Detective Sommers.

"No one has said anything to me. I would have told you if they did."

"Hear me now, Madeline. No arguments and no compromises. We are going to Los Angeles until both of them are caught."

"But…"

"Discussion over." I immediately know that his mind is made up. Suddenly, chills run up and down my spine.

"What has happened?"

Vince looks at me warily, "It's Lacy…"

"What happened to her?" I ask frantically.

"She's been kidnapped…"

"What?! When?!"

"Last night. Her boyfriend said that she went to use the restroom at the movie theater and never came back. Detective Sommers feels the need to bring in the FBI at this point. Dina is nowhere to be found." I freeze in fear. This is more than just jealousy over our relationship…what the hell is someone trying to do?

"Madeline, Dina and whatever accomplices she has are out to get me, and I want you as far away from this as possible. If something were to ever happen to you…I would never forgive myself" he looks at me lovingly and sits beside me on the bed.

"I'll go, Vince. I'll go." My mind is racing a hundred miles an hour. I just want Lacy to be alright and this mess to be over.

"My jet will be in Atlanta at eleven; get your stuff together." Vince kisses me briefly before getting up to pack his suitcase.

I slowly pack my things and think of Lacy. She must be so afraid! I didn't want her to be involved in this mess. I angrily throw my pants into the suitcase. Damn Dina! I'm so ready to find her myself.

"Baby, I know what you're thinking. It won't work. Let my team handle it."

"Why can't we just go find her ourselves?"

"And risk you getting hurt? Hell no! We just have to trust that everyone working on this case is doing their best to track her and whoever else she's working with."

"What if something happens to Lacy?"

"I promise you that we'll find her before anything will happen."

"You can't promise that! You told me yourself Dina knows sketchy people. They don't give a shit about Lacy!"

"Baby, you have got to calm down. Everything will be okay." I sure hope he's right. I could never live with myself if I knew that it was my fault that something happened to Lacy. She's been my rock, always there for me. I can't let her down, and I refuse to.

"Vince…Lacy and I have a very special bond. She was there for me when I was an emotional mess after Eric…you don't understand."

"What don't I understand? You don't think I'd kill for Ryan or Gus? Any of the others?" He glares at me, his hazel eyes blazing.

"I do, but…she just seems to keep getting away!"

"I understand how you feel, baby. But you going out and seeking your own revenge won't solve anything. You don't know who she's working with. It would be different if it was just her. I know you probably could kick her ass on your own." I'm amazed at his confidence in me. Then again, this girl from South Georgia has her vast knowledge of guns and good fist fights. Vince doesn't know that part of me yet, but he will eventually.

As Luis drives us to the airport, I look out the window sadly. Per Detective Sommers' orders, I had to tell my family and friends that I was going out of the country for a while. Meanwhile, I can't use my cell phone or open any of my work emails until the culprits are caught. I think about Lacy and pray that whoever took her won't hurt her.

"Madeline, are you okay?" asks Vince snapping my out of my thoughts.

"I'm fine. This is just a lot to take in, and I'm worried about Lacy."

"I have confidence in my team; I'm sure she'll be alright."

"What if they won't stop until they harm one of us?" I ask him.

"You have nothing to worry about, Madeline. I'm more than prepared to handle whatever they want to throw at me. My chief concern is you; I want you to be safe."

"I know, Vince and I appreciate that…and everything you've done."

"Only for you" he replies and kisses my knuckles. We arrive at the airport and head to the private airfield. Luis jumps out of the car to open our doors. I see the jet sitting on the runway and am instantly thankful to get away from all this nonsense. Suddenly, Luis' phone rings and he shuts the door while he answers it. He turns a shade of crimson as he listens to the voice on the other end. He looks at Vince and swings open the car door.

"I need both of you to get on that plane, now!"

"Wait, what's…?" I start.

"There's no time! Get your asses on that plane!" Vince grabs my hand and leads me out to where the jet is. As I look back, Luis has his gun drawn and some of the airport agents have joined him. We head up the stairs to the jet and Vince orders the stewardess to close the door quickly. I glance out of the plane's window to see that Luis and the agents have disappeared. Feeling ultimate stress and exhaustion, I collapse in one of the cushioned seats and close my eyes.

"Ms. Davis, buckle your seatbelt, please" the stewardess requests in a tender voice. Vince eyes me anxiously but doesn't say anything as he sits across from me. I idly watch the stewardess as she gets into her seat and locks her safety belt. She looks pretty young, with kinky natural hair and caramel skin but definitely seems to be professional. As the plane takes off, the city of Atlanta shrink before my eyes. When the safety light blinks off the stewardess approaches us.

"Can I get you anything Ms. Davis, Mr. Marks?"

"I'll have coffee" says Vince. The stewardess looks at me to hear my request.

"A mimosa" I tell her. At this rate, I'll be drunk until this fiasco is over.

"Aw hell, make my coffee Irish then if the lady's going to be drinking" Vince glances at me with a hint of a smile.

"Very well, coming right up. I'm Lucy, by the way. Let me know if you need anything else" the stewardess walks to the back of the plane.

An hour into the flight, Vince and I are discussing our plans for Los Angeles. Though no one is supposed to know where I'm working from, I still have a gazillion proposals to finish. Reluctantly, I agree to work from Vince's house. I've always liked working in the office, so this will definitely be a change for me. Vince also tells me that he's brought his family to Los Angeles for their safety. I wonder what his family is like and wish they were meeting me under more favorable circumstances; though, I'm curious to know if he even told them the whole situation.

A few hours later, Lucy comes to tell us that we are about to land and advises us to buckle our safety belts. I can see the city of Los Angeles looming before my eyes and can't help but to be a little excited. This will be my first time coming here, and hopefully Vince won't keep me locked in his house the entire time.

We get off the plane and a tall, older man with radiant ebony skin greets us. His eyes look familiar to me, but I can't quite put my finger on it.

"Dad, good to see you!" he says with a smile as they shake hands.

"Same here, son" the man replies. I realize it's Vince's father; that's why he looks so familiar!

"Dad, I want you to meet my girlfriend, Madeline Davis" Vince looks at me, "Madeline, this is my father, Phillip Marks."

"It's nice to finally meet you, Ms. Davis" Mr. Marks extends his hand.

"Likewise, Mr. Marks" I say, shaking his hand.

"No, no, none of this Mr. Marks business. Call me Phil, please" he smiles and I instantly see where Vince gets that gorgeous grin of his.

"And you can call me Madeline" I reply.

"Well kids, everyone's back at the house, so we can head back there." Phil says, leading us to a sleek black Mercedes. Vince gives me the front seat and I slide on the warm leather, thankful to be out of the chilly fall weather for a while. When we pull up to Vince's house, my mouth drops open. If I thought his apartment was nice, this place is glorious. It is sleek and modern with huge windows. I can't help but gasp as we go inside. It's absolutely gorgeous inside with beautiful furniture and all of the latest gadgets.

We are greeted by a petite, older woman with jet black, back length hair and deep olive skin. Her emerald eyes sparkle intensely but she looks pleasant. She sees me and pulls me into a huge hug.

"You must be Madeline! Oh my, I've heard so much about you! It's so great to finally meet you!"

"Madeline, this is my mother, Dr. Cynthia Marks" says Vince as he hugs his mother affectionately. She gives him a smooch on his cheek and he looks at her with embarrassment.

"Dr. Marks, it's a pleasure to meet you!" I say, matching her enthusiasm.

"Cynthia, please! I'm only Dr. Marks at the school" she says with a bright, warm smile.

"Where's Chloe, mom?" asks Vince.

"She's doing some work for school upstairs; she'll be down for lunch. Speaking of lunch, Sylvia says it'll be ready soon."

"Sylvia is my cook" Vince says to me, responding to my quizzical look.

"Alright, well, I'm going to get freshened up. Where do I go?" I ask him.

"The master bedroom is upstairs on the right. Make yourself at home." he kisses me and heads into the kitchen. I go upstairs to the master bedroom. He has a king sized bed and two huge walk-in closets. I walk into the bathroom and see a gigantic garden tub and separate shower. Looking in the mirror, I notice that I'm in desperate need of a facial and then some. Black circles are starting to form under my eyes and I look like hell. Taking a deep breath, I wash my face and brush my hair, making sure I look presentable.

When I come downstairs, I notice that someone else has joined the party. It most definitely has to be his sister, I recognize the smiling face, curly hair and slender figure. She seems even taller than in her picture, wearing skinny jeans with a partially opened button-down shirt on. Her jade eyes are framed with designer glasses.

"So this is the girlfriend?" she says with a smile.

"Her name's Madeline" says Vince with a disapproving frown.

"Oh, come on Vince. Stop being so serious! Nice to meet you Madeline, I'm Chloe Marks. You've been the talk of our household, recently!" I smile in embarrassment as I shake her hand.

"All good I hope!" I tell her.

"Trust me, you're in" she whispers to me and winks. I see that lunch has been set out on the dining table and take my place beside Vince. He smiles and kisses my check with affection. Out of the corner of my eye, I can see his mother beaming at us from the other side of the table. The conversation around the table is light and his family seems to be very close. They tease each other and seem genuinely happy. I don't believe I've seen Vince this relaxed since before all of this stuff started happening. I take a deep breath and wonder about Lacy. I need to know what the progress is.

"What's the news on Lacy?" I ask him when his family is distracted by Chloe's inappropriate joking.

"They have the situation under control; she's in one of the warehouses in an industrial park. They are just trying to find the right one. Don't worry, she'll be fine."

"What are you two whispering about? Kinky stuff?" asks Chloe playfully.

"Chloe!" all the Marks say in unison. This must be a regular occurrence. I hide a smile at the family scolding.

"Is it just me, or have you guys gotten way more uptight since I went to college?" Chloe says with a disappointed scowl on her face.

"Just cool it. We have a guest." says Phil eyeing her seriously. Vince has that same stare; he could never deny Phil as his father! Chloe simmers down at her father's glare and holds her hands up in defeat with a bright smile. She is something else, but I like her spirit.

Suddenly, Vince's phone rings. He excuses himself from the table to answer it. I hope that it's a call telling him that Lacy is safe. Cynthia calls out to Sylvia to clear the table.

"If you'll excuse me, I'm going to step out for a minute" I say. I head outside and pull out a pack of cigarettes. I haven't smoked in a while, but I just have to clear my head. I stand outside the door and light it up. I feel a light buzz from the first puff, and it's just what I need. I blow a thick plume of smoke, and look down the block noticing houses similar to Vince's. I could almost imagine us living here….well, if we make it through this mess.

As I take a couple more puffs submerging into deep thoughts, an eerie feeling surrounds me, but before I can do anything, I feel a blow to the back of my head that knocks me out.

I feel like I'm moving but keep going in and out of consciousness. I can't see anything, and I can't move. I'm fighting so hard to stay awake, but a pinch in my arm ensures that I stay knocked out.

I drift in and out for what seems to be forever. In my haze, I notice a masked figure beside me looking forward. I try hard to keep quiet; they are obviously trying to keep me sedated. I need to be awake to see where I am. I lie completely still, attempting to fool whoever it is sitting beside me. I hear a male voice in the front.

"Is she still out?" The heavily accented voice asks. I close my eyes pretending to be asleep.

"Yeah" the voice beside me says. I can't quite finger the accent. Sounds like Boston or perhaps New Jersey.

"Better go ahead and give her another shot."

"Right." I feel another pinch in my arm. I don't want to fall asleep. I fight to stay awake, but before I know it, I'm out like a light.

I wake yet again and see that we are stopped. I notice that the two guys are no longer in the van and attempt to move around, but they were smart enough to tie me up. I look around frantically, trying to find anything that could tip me off. It's dark and all I can see is a junky floor littered with soda cans, cigarette butts and fast food bags.

A few moments later, I hear voices coming towards the van. I shut my eyes, not wanting to get another injection. The two guys get into the van and I smell the aroma of greasy fast food. I feel a hand wrap a blindfold around my face.

"Wake her up, we gotta feed her…" the voice up front says. I feel myself being moved to the sitting position and try to act a little alert so that he knows I'm awake.

"If you try anything, I'll cut ya. Hear me?" The gruff voice says to me. I nod my head quickly and feel him untie my hands. A warm sandwich is placed in my hand and I eat it hungrily, not knowing when I will be able to eat again.

"I don't know why we gotta feed her." The voice next to me says.

"Because they want her alive you asshole" the voice in the front says. I finish my sandwich and feel a straw being shoved into my mouth. I sip and taste a strong soda that I'm not familiar with but gulp quickly, not knowing when he will take it away. Once I finish, he slides me back to the floor and gives me another poke in my arm. My eyelids grow heavy and I fall asleep once again.

I wake up once more and notice the blindfold has been taken off. The masked figure lays asleep on the other side of the van. Trying my best not to make a sound, I turn my head slowly to see what else I can observe. There's nothing that tells me who these two buffoons are nor where we are going.

"Yo!" The guy in the front yells back.

"What?" He growls obviously pissed at the interruption of his sleep.

"Give her another shot, we're almost there. She needs to be knocked out."

"You don't think another one will kill her?"

"Nah. Go ahead and do it. Don't need to hear any bitchin' when we get there."

Chapter 26 *Vanished*

I come down the stairs frustrated at the slow progress everyone seems to be making at finding Lacy. Maybe it'll calm me down to see my girl, but I notice that she's missing from the table.

"Mom, where's Madeline?" I gaze at my mother.

"Oh, she said she had to step out for a moment" she says with a smile. I heave a sigh and go outside the door. She's probably smoking, but hell, I can't judge. I'd probably light up too.

"Madeline!" I yell, but I look down and notice a smoking cigarette laying on the steps. Shit! Where is she?

"Madeline!" I call again. I frantically run down the stairs and go around to the back.

"Madeline!" I yell, exasperated. That bitch! They took her! I run inside the house yelling Madeline's name. My mother follows me, worried.

"Is everything okay, bambino?"

"No! Madeline is gone...they...they took her!" I don't even know where to start. I promised her I would protect her and now those assholes have taken her! How the hell did they get here so fast?

"Okay, calm down. Is there anywhere else she could have gone?" Mom asks.

"No! If anything she stepped outside to smoke. Her cigarette is still there! Goddamn them!" I holler. My mom's eyes grow wide with horror.

"Vince, honey, what is going on?"

"No time to explain. Tell Chloe she can't go anywhere outside this house!" I run upstairs to grab my phone and immediately dial Luis.

"Bianchi.." He answers.

"Luis! They took her! What the hell am I supposed to do?!"

"Who took her?!" he demands.

"Dina and whatever assholes she's working with!"

"Okay, I'll call Detective Sommers…you need to get to Atlanta. There's no doubt they will bring her back here." I take a glass vase off the nightstand and hurl it against the wall. It shatters into a million pieces and the flowers that were\ in it fall to the floor.

"Goddamnit, Luis! Nothing can happen to her! You don't understand! I can't lose her! I can't…" I start to hyperventilate.

"Mr. Marks…I know…believe me I know. We are going to bring her back, do you understand? If I have to go out there myself, nothing will happen to her."

"I'm on the first plane to Atlanta." I hang up and explain to my parents that I will be flying back to Atlanta to find Madeline.

"But…what if they hurt you?" My mother asks with tears in her eyes.

"They won't…"

"You don't know that!" Chloe declares tearfully. I take her face in my hands.

"Hey, you used to have more faith in your big brother than that…I've got to find her…she is the only woman that I've loved…the only one that I will love. I promise you I'll be fine." I kiss her forehead as she cries softly.

"Well, son …I say go get her. You know who to call if you have trouble." Dad says. An hour later, the FBI is searching my house for any clues about where Madeline may be. I tell them I'm going to Atlanta to find her.

"Sir that would not be advisable. Perhaps she may still be here in California?"

"I know where this bitch does the majority of her work and it has to be Atlanta."

"Sir…I meant no harm."

"You just better make fucking sure nothing happens to my family or I will be on your most wanted list, do you understand?!" I snarl. He quickly nods and goes to talk to his superior. I call Jack.

"Lloyd" he answers.

"Jack, I need you to be on the first flight to Atlanta. Tell Shay to give you a credit card and dare her to deny you. If she has a problem, tell her to call me."

"I'm on it, boss" he says.

Three hours later, I'm met at the airport by Detective Sommers and Luis. We stand outside to Luis' car and I demand that they tell me everything.

"There's no leads, Mr. Marks. There are too many warehouses in that area and we have to get warrants for all of them." Sommers says.

"You were supposed to be working on this!" I exclaim in exasperation.

"Mr. Marks..." Luis tries to smooth everything over.

"You don't understand! If this woman loses her life...it'll be the death of me too..." My heart twists in my chest and tears rise into my eyes. I'm showing emotion in ways I never thought possible.

"Mr. Marks, we're gonna put you up at a hotel right near the precinct." I throw open the door to Luis' car and look at Sommers.

"Whatever" I say as I slam the door.

When I get to the hotel, I turn on Madeline's cell phone hoping to get a lead, and a text message from Lacy pops up. *Madeline...I think I know who is helping Dina.* She was obviously close to cracking the case before they decided to take her. I order two vodka on the rocks from room service and pace my room. I scroll through her numbers and remind myself to call her parents, but see a name that sticks out to me more: Nathan. He's the best friend she always talks about. I dial the number cautiously.

"Madeline?" he answers frantically.

"No...this is Vincent Marks..."

"Is everything okay?" he asks nervously.

"Madeline has been kidnapped and I need your help…" I say quickly.

"Kidnapped! How?! Why?!"

"Just know we have to find her before it's too late."

"Where are you?" he asks.

"I'm at the W…"

"Can I meet you at the bar in about fifteen minutes?" he asks.

"Sure" I reply, thankful to have someone to drink with.

Twenty minutes later, I see a tall guy with short, brown hair dressed in a business suit walk through the revolving doors. He looks frantic; it has to be him. I approach him carefully.

"Nathan?" I ask.

"Yeah, I'm Nathan Paul." He shakes my hand.

"Vincent Marks, I'm sorry that we had to meet under these circumstances, Nathan."

"Tell me what happened. I haven't heard from Madeline since last weekend. I called and called!"

"Come on, you'll need a drink." I lead him to the bar and he orders an extra strong Long Island Iced Tea. I follow suit and order one as well. As soon as the bartender sets our drinks down, Nathan takes a huge gulp.

"So, um…I don't know if she's told you about me…" I start. He laughs.

"I know all about you, Vincent Marks. But what I'm concerned about is this whole kidnapping situation." He loosens his tie, agitated. Madeline was right, he seems like a hell of a lawyer.

"Well, basically, a psycho at my branch in New York started harassing her after she got back to Atlanta, and…I didn't realize how dangerous this woman was…" Nathan laughs in disbelief.

"A woman? A woman did this? What is this an ex-girlfriend of yours?"

"So to speak, but listen, I just found out someone here in Atlanta is an accomplice." Nathan pauses and stares me down.

"Someone that works with her?" I nod uneasily.

"I wasn't sure until yesterday."

"So, what is the next step?"

"The police are dragging their asses. I know that they had a lead when her assistant was kidnapped." Nathan drains his drink and slams down the glass, looking at me in frustration.

"You mean to tell me that these bastards have kidnapped both Madeline and her assistant?! What kind of people do you have working in your company, man?!"

"Look, I'm just as shocked as you. Like I said, I had no idea that Dina was like this."

"Can I get you another, sir?" The bartender approaches us.

"Damn right you can" Nathan says. He turns around and looks at me seriously.

"Look, man. I don't know you, but I do know this: Madeline is my heart and soul. I will stay on your ass until I know you are not involved in this shit. Do you understand?"

"If you have to do that so you will trust me then whatever. I just want Madeline back." His look softens as the bartender sets down his drink.

"What do I need to do?" he asks, the brutal attitude fading.

"I don't know yet. I don't know where to start…I'm just a businessman, I have no expertise in shit like this."

"Well, the first thing we are going to do is get her face in the media." He takes out his phone and dials a number.

"Yeah, David?" he says when the person on the other end answers.

"I need a favor..." the voice on the other end has a few choice words. Old boyfriend, I guess.

"Oh, shut the fuck up, we'll deal with that later. Maddie's been kidnapped, and I need you to get on your job." The voice turns frantic and Nathan begins to give details. When they are done, he hangs up and looks at me.

"Now we wait. That should get the police department on their ass."

"I'm so glad I found you." I hold out my hand.

"I'm glad you did, too." He shakes my hand and attacks his drink. I order another one and join him. What the hell? I might as well drink.

Three days later, I sit in my hotel room, drunk out of my mind as I see my love's face on the news as a missing person. Luckily, they are offering a reward for tips; I just hope someone cares enough to call. A phone call comes through my cell and I take a breath as I answer.

"Marks."

"Mr. Marks...the APD is considering calling off the search and minimizing it to recovery" Luis' voice rings out.

"But she is not dead!" I yell.

"Mr. Marks...we might have to do this alone...no one believes she's alive. It's been too many days."

"Well, that's exactly what we'll have to do!" I hang up and call a cab to take me to the Atlanta Police Department. As we speed down Peachtree Street, I call both Nathan and Luis and tell them to meet me there. They will not call off this search if I have anything to with it. We all storm into the precinct where we are stopped by a female police officer.

"Can I help you?" she asks with a tint of nasty attitude in her voice. This police department is really starting to piss me off.

"No. I need to see Sommers, now!" I demand.

"Sir, Detective Sommers is busy..."she glares at me.

"Look, ma'am, I'm going to give you about five seconds to get your ass back there to get Detective Sommers!" I rave.

"Vincent..." Nathan says fearfully.

"Shh!" I hold up my hand, silencing him.

"I...I'll get Detective Sommers" she skitters away like a scared deer. Detective Sommers storms out of his office.

"Mr. Marks, what is your problem?!"

"You want to call off the search!"

"Look...this is political...the mayor..."

"I don't give a shit about what the mayor says!"

"I don't either" says Luis.

"Neither do I!" Nathan declares.

"And I guarantee that this woman has a big brother and father who wouldn't give a shit about the mayor either...as well as people in my office who want nothing more but to see her brought back alive" I say matching Detective Sommers' sour look.

"Okay, Mr. Marks...I don't need a militia on my hands...I'll call the mayor..." He looks genuinely frightened at my anger.

"You do that..." I say. By this time the whole precinct is staring at me as Detective Sommers pulls out his phone.

"Sir," he says, "we cannot call off the search on Madeline Davis and Lacy Peters..." he pauses for a response.

"Because...her family and friends are threatening to continue searching themselves. Sir, if they do this...the suspects will not come out alive. Her boyfriend is ready to draw blood." He looks at me.

"Very well, Sir." He glances at his department as he hangs up.

"What the fuck are ya'll looking at?!" He yells. The cops can't get back to work fast enough. He looks at me.

"You ever thought about working for the FBI, perhaps the Secret Service?" He asks me shaking his head.

"No, I just love that woman more than life itself. It would be nothing for me to die if she was safe…"

"Damn, man…I hope you put a ring on that woman's finger" Luis says, glancing at me with surprise at my proclamation.

"Believe me, I will."

I sit in my hotel room, brimming with anxiety. No one has called and it's pissing me the fuck off. I'd rather take my Glock and find her my damn self. A knock on the door interrupts my thoughts. I open the door to see Jack who looks exhausted.

"Mr. Marks, a huge tip just came in…they're ready to move." He doesn't have to say anything more before turning to leave. I grab my jacket and follow him out.

A few minutes later, Nathan, Luis, Jack, Watson and I stand amongst several FBI and APD officers as they are briefed on the situation.

"We need to consider the danger of our suspects. They will be armed, you need to be sure you are on your toes. There are two victims: Madeline Davis and Lacy Peters. You are to find them quickly, don't let the suspects get a hold of them before you do, or we could end up having a hostage situation" Detective Sommers tells the group.

Luis goes up to Sommers and whispers something. He nods and Luis takes off his jacket while an officer equips him with a bulletproof vest. I guess he wants a piece of the action. Detective Sommers comes up to Nathan and me.

"Marks, you need to stay your ass in the car. Whatever happens, you do not need to get out do you hear me?"

"Jeez, you don't have to talk to me like I'm a child, Sommers" I growl.

"Do as I say for once, damn it!" He cuts his eyes at me.

"Fine…" I turn around and sit in Luis' car. Yeah, I told him that I wouldn't get out, but if they fuck it up, I'll go in there and kill that bitch myself. I adjust the gun holster inside my jacket.

"You seriously brought a gun?" Nathan gives me a crazy stare.

"Insurance…" I say, looking out the window as the officers go inside the warehouse.

"I just hope she's okay…" Nathan sniffles. Sighing heavily, I pull out a handkerchief and offer it to him as he begins to sob.

"I've got my own…" he snaps through his tears as he pulls one out of his pocket. Of course he does. Jack stands outside of the car, guarding it, with his hand near his sidearm. That guy is always on alert when it comes to me. I make a mental note to give him a raise.

"You know, Nathan, I never thanked you for everything" I look over at him with seriousness.

"You don't have to thank me, I would have done it regardless." He is hard to impress.

"You still don't trust me?" I ask.

"I guess I trust you, but you better control whatever other crazy exes you have out there because if this happens again, I will kill you." His tone darkens.

"Nathan, do you really think I'm going to let this happen again? Yes, Dina is a psycho bitch, but this is a rare thing, man." Nathan scoffs.

"I haven't slept since you called me. I constantly worried about what she's going through. I don't want her to ever experience this again." He sighs heavily and I decide to leave him alone. I know he loves her, and I can't blame him for feeling animosity towards me for this mess.

Time seems to stop as we see no movement outside apart from paramedics who are standing outside of their ambulances. Please God let her be safe.

Chapter 27 *Somebody Save Me*

I awaken with a massive headache and blurry vision. I try to move but I notice that I am bound by my wrists and ankles with duct tape. I try to scream but I've been gagged and stripped down to my underwear. I squeeze my eyes to focus, and look at my surroundings. It looks like a warehouse with drab walls and a musty smell; I realize that I'm lying on a dirty mattress and shiver at the shitty situation I'm in.

"Well, well, well, did you think you could run away from us that easily?" It's a man's voice, and it sounds really familiar. Suddenly, I'm pulled off the mattress and pushed against a wall. The air gets knocked out of my lungs as I hit the cold concrete. I scowl at the mysterious figure. He's wearing a mask, but I can see blue eyes gleaming through the holes. I recognize the mask. It is very much like the one worn by my first and only Master.

He walks up to me and caresses my face. I whip my head to the side to escape his touch but he grabs my chin and makes me face him.

"Go to hell, motherfucker!" I say, muffled by my gag.

"If you defy me; both you and your little secretary are dead, do you hear me?!" he says angrily. My breathing increases rapidly.

"I said, do you hear me?!" he shouts. I nod my head quickly in response.

"Now, I know you like to be the Dom…Madeline, but here, I am the fucking Master, do you understand?" he says menacingly. I nod slowly trying to hold back the frightened tears.

"You've been a very naughty girl, Madeline. Fucking your boss, but not the right one. I think I might have to punish you." His blue eyes narrow through his mask. I swallow hard, knowing where this is going. He brings out a thick black belt. Oh my God this is not happening. He turns me around and I feel him run the belt down my clammy skin. He strikes me, harder than one would if this was just play. I let out a muffled scream through my gag and the tears do start to fall. I can't help it; this is not how I enjoy BDSM, in a hostile environment with a total stranger.

He strikes me again, even harder and I collapse to my knees. He pulls my hair and yanks me back up to my feet.

"Jesus, you are one sick man" a female voice says. It's got to be Dina. I see her walk over towards us and eye me with disgust. I scowl back at her.

"What do you want?" I muffle through the gag. He pauses and snatches the gag from my face.

"What do I want?!" he roars, "I want you to be punished, you cunt."

"For what?! What have I done so bad to you that you felt the need to torture me and my co-workers!"

"All these years, I wanted you. If you would have responded to my advances, we could have been a great team together. But you had to go for that son of a bitch, Marks. He stole the company from me, but he won't take you" he sneers.

"I don't know what the hell you're talking about!" He smacks my face.

"Don't be stupid, Madeline." He removes his mask and it's none other than Joseph Dent, my boss. My eyes grow wide in horror and surprise.

"Joseph?" I gasp.

"You're doing all of this because I wouldn't sleep with you?!" I say angrily, "For Christ's sake, you're married!"

"No, no, you've got it all wrong. This would have never happened if you would have left Vincent Marks alone" says Joseph. I roll my eyes and he grabs my bra, pushing me down on the mattress. He leans over me and my fear reaches a new height. I never knew he could be this dangerous.

"I was so close to buying the company when that fucker Vincent outbid me. Not only that, you went to New York and fell in love with him. You two fucked everywhere in your suite. Enough was enough." How the hell does he know that? Has he been watching me?

"Then why did you kidnap Lacy, and hurt Vince's secretary? They have nothing to do with this. Why did you kill my dog?" I ask, trembling.

"Bitch, I killed your dog because I don't like you! I was supposed to be with Vince. Not you! And suddenly, everyone wanted to protect you; even Alexis and Jillian turned on me for you." Dina snarls.

"I didn't even know you were dating Vince!" I yell at her. She takes her high heeled shoe and hurls it at me which prompts me to duck just in the nick of time. Jesus Christ, these two are assholes.

"And Lacy, your bitch? She was giving just a little bit too much help to you. I had to eliminate her, and if you're a good girl maybe I'll let her live." Joseph says.

"H-how did you know about...me; about my lifestyle?" He chuckles at my question.

"Tell me, Madeline, are you blind or just naïve?" he asks. I give him no response.

"Don't you remember your Master?" I still look silently at him. What is he talking about?

"Your Master, Edward Dent?" Holy shit, why did I never notice? The name and the familiar features...although Edward is so much younger.

"Why do you think I was so eager to hire you when you came to work for the company? My brother recognized your name and recommended you."

"Eddie would never approve of what you're doing right now you cowardly dick! I will never be yours! I'd be his again first!" I shout at him. He slaps me in the face again, harder than he did before.

"Well bitch, since both you and the company were stolen from me, I'm going to take what's mine!" He puts the gag back on my mouth and strips off my bra and panties. I fight back, twisting and writhing. I try to scream as he attempts to kiss my neck, but the gag won't allow me. He straddles me and I attempt to buck him off me.

"Take that bitch down!" says Dina with evil tinting her voice.

I see Joseph unbutton his pants and my fear reaches a new high. I do not want this to happen. I use all the strength in my pelvis and lift my hips to throw him off me. In the process, I think I injure him.

"Ah! You bitch!" he growls and slaps me again. He then proceeds to turn me on my stomach, take the belt and hit me repeatedly. I sob into the gag as he beats me mercilessly. The pain is so horrible; I think I'm going to pass out. He then turns me around and tries to penetrate me again. I don't know how much longer I can fight but I cannot let this man win. He slaps me a few more times before I feel darkness come over me. I keep twisting and turning but my strength is wearing out.

My body starts to succumb to the pain, and my eyes begin to roll back in my head. I can't fight anymore, and tears begin to stream down my eyes. I start to think of my mom, dad, sister and brother. I hope that they know that everything I have worked so hard for will go to them, that they will never have to worry about money again. I pray Nathan knows that I love him and God willing, I'm gonna haunt his ass forever. I think about Vince, my sweet Vince, and hope he knows I love him.

Just as my eyes begin to close, I hear a crash and yelling voices. Joseph gets off the mattress and through my haze, I see him point a gun. Detective Sommers brings him down with a kick and punch along with a few choice words. I feel frozen to the mattress, my body hurting from the torture. Luis races to the mattress, and shakes me.

"Madeline…Madeline…stay with me!" He commands.

"I'm trying…" I say weakly, tears falling. He wraps a blanket around me and scoops me up in his arms.

"You're safe now….you're safe now…I've got you…" he says in a shaky sob as he walks me out of the warehouse, pressing his face against mine. I see the sun for the first time in God knows when and try to breathe in the chilly fresh air. Luis climbs into the back of an ambulance where two paramedics help him lay me down on the stretcher. Immediately, they begin working on me, taking my vital signs.

"Her blood pressure is low…"one of the technicians observes. I try to stay awake, but just as they put an oxygen mask on me, my body gives out and my eyes roll back in my head, submerging me into darkness.

# Chapter 28 *Please Wake Up*

I follow closely as they rush Madeline into the ER. A brunette nurse sees who is on the stretcher and grows frantic.

"Madeline? Madeline!" she starts to hyperventilate as she follows the rest of the crew into another room. I wonder who she is. She obviously knows Madeline.

"Sir? Sir?" A tall, male nurse pushes me back.

"You can't...you can't let her be without me." I breathe heavily.

"We're doing everything we can. When we get her stabilized you can see her." I can do nothing but obey his orders and nearly collapse as I stagger towards the waiting room. A pair of powerful arms grabs me to keep me from falling to the floor.

"Come on, boss." Jack holds me up and leads me to a nearby chair in the waiting room. Luis comes into the entrance and looks at me with tears in his eyes.

"Is she okay?" I shake my head.

"I don't know Luis..." I say quietly. He sits down beside me and puts his hand on my shoulder.

"I'm sure she'll be fine, she was conscious when I got to her, she only passed out in the ambulance." I nod slowly. The nurse I saw earlier comes out to the waiting room and locks eyes with me.

"What happened to her?" she demands with tears in her eyes. Luis gets up, obviously seeing I'm in no condition to answer.

"I'm sure you saw her face on the news..."She sniffles.

"I was so worried! What happened to her?! What did those bastards do to her?!" She holds on to a nearby desk,

"Ma'am, may I ask you who you are?" Jack stands beside Luis.

"I'm...Tracie Willis...Madeline and I have been friends since college." Luis takes her hand and sits her down.

"Tracie?" Nathan comes out of the restroom, his eyes red. She holds open her arms and he goes to her, embracing her with just as much strength as she does him.

"Her family…I need to call her family. I told them I would call as soon as we found her" I choke out as they both look at me.

"Who are you?" she asks me.

"I'm…."

"Maddie's boyfriend" Nathan finishes for me and Tracie raises her eyebrows and takes my hand.

"Do you want me to call?" I look at her and can't hold back any longer. The stress of the past two weeks rushes at me like a freight train and I start to sob quietly, putting my head in my hands. A warm set of arms surround me.

"Shhh…" I hear Tracie's voice in my ear as she hugs me. I fall apart, crying audibly and Tracie hugs me tighter, joining me with silent sobs of her own.

After my breakdown, I'm blank, not able to process anything. Out of the corner of my eye, I see a couple walk into the waiting room. It has to be Lacy's parents. I start to get up, but Luis stops me, indicating that he will handle it. Both of them look disheveled as if they've been up since they realized she was gone. Luis talks to them quietly. I don't even know what Lacy's condition is, I was so worried about Madeline that I forgot to ask.

After what seems to be forever, a doctor comes out of the double doors.

"Mr. Marks?" He asks gently. I stand up with Luis and Nathan. He walks over to us and smiles.

"I'm Dr. Nielson. Ms. Davis is fine. She's conked out, probably from being injected numerous times with a tranquilizer." Those bastards!

"There's no…permanent damage?" I manage to ask.

"I have to be honest with you, Mr. Marks. Her attackers did a number on her. Her only saving grace is that the kidnappers must have kept her hydrated and nourished. An empty stomach and those tranquilizers could have caused serious damage." I close my eyes in pain as my heart wrenches in my chest.

"Can I…see her?" I ask cautiously.

"As soon as we get her to a room, Mr. Marks." I nod with understanding.

"Ms. Peters…" I inquire, looking back at her parents.

"Ms. Peters is awake and ready to go home. She just needs a few saline IVs to keep her hydrated."

"I'm sure her parents will be happy to hear that." I point over to them.

"Let me go over some things and I'll come back to talk with you, okay?" he looks at me through a pair of glasses.

"Sure." I sit back down and Detective Sommers comes into the waiting room with coffee and food from the deli across the street.

"Marks, you look like hell. When was the last time you ate?" He asks me.

"California" I admit.

"You need to eat, damnit. You'll be no good when she wakes up if you haven't been taking care of yourself." I'm too tired to argue as he hands me a box with a sandwich, chips and a big chocolate chip cookie. I have no appetite, but with the way that everyone is looking at me, I know that I must look damn bad.

"Hey, I'll call Maddie's parents. Let us do some work now; you've done enough, Vincent" Nathan scolds. I can do nothing but agree.

"Tell her parents I'll put them up at the W" I say quietly.

"You need to get some rest as well" Luis coaxes.

"No, I'll stay here." I finally dig into the box, realizing how hungry I am.

Later that evening, Dr. Nielson leads me to Madeline's room. I stiffen in horror as I see her lying on the bed, attached to IVs.

"Just a little hydration for her and something to counteract the drugs she was given, Mr. Marks" he explains, seeing my anxiety.

I take my place beside her bed and take her hand in mine. Her face is lightly bruised and I notice welts on her arms. I sigh, wishing she would wake up. I need to see her eyes, hear her voice. I kiss her cheek lightly and stroke her tangled hair.

"I love you…"I whisper shakily, squeezing her hand.

The next morning, Tracie comes into the room, giving me a sad smile.

"I thought you might need some breakfast…"she says as she hands me a plate with a bagel and fruit along with a small bottle of orange juice.

"Thank-you."

"Her parents are at the W. They send their thanks for the arrangements." I nod as she goes over to Madeline, taking her vital signs.

"She's okay. Her blood pressure is normal. Why don't you get some rest?" I shake my head.

"I want someone to be here when she wakes up."

"Trust me, she'll be okay. Her parents will be here soon." I sigh, knowing she's right. I need a shower among other things.

A soft knock on the door indicates another visitor. I see an older woman who looks a lot like Madeline and a tough looking guy, probably her dad. I stand up as Madeline's mother runs to her bed.

"Oh, baby!" she strokes Madeline's hair, branding her forehead with kisses. Her dad looks at me before holding out his hand.

"Thank-you, Mr. Marks." I nod.

"I don't feel like I did enough—"

"She's alive, that's all that matters."

"I...probably need to go take care of some things." Madeline's mom looks at me.

"Yes, you look like you could use some sleep, son." She smiles warmly.

"I haven't slept much since she was taken" I admit.

"She's safe now and her parents are here. Go get some rest" Tracie commands. I nod in agreement and leave the room. Just as I turn my phone on, I see numerous texts and voicemails. Just as I start to scroll through the texts from my parents, Gus, Ryan and a few others, my phone rings.

"Hello?"

"Oh thank God you're okay!" Gus' voice rings out.

"I'm fine..."

"How's Madeline?"

"Still knocked out. They tranquilized her from California to Georgia." He sighs.

"Listen, man. Alistair found out that Dina and Joseph were in cahoots with some sketchy people." I grip the phone.

"Luciano?"

"Yeah. We were finally able to break into her phone. Man, you are fortunate, they were going to kill you."

"I figured as much."

"If anything would have happened to you...I would have killed them myself." Gus' voice trembles with emotion.

"I know, Gus. I'm fine, I just need some sleep."

"You want me and Emily to come down there?"

"No, man, I'll be okay once she wakes up."

"Call me if you need anything, Vince."

"I will, thanks for staying on things for me."

"Anytime."

I finally make it to the hotel and collapse onto the bed before falling into a deep sleep.

Chapter 29 *Finally Awake*

"Madeline? Madeline, come on baby please wake up" a distant voice echoes. I feel a warm hand brush my hair back. My eyes flutter open and my vision is blurry. My whole body is in extreme pain. I turn my head and see Vince with worry in his eyes. He's stroking my hair lovingly. I try to sit up, but the dizziness won't let me. I lay my head back on the pillow. Vince's eyes light up when he sees me struggling to move.

"Don't try to get up, baby. I'm so glad you're awake! You've been knocked out two days." he kisses me gently. All of the memories hit me like a rush of wind.

"Lacy...what happened to Lacy?" I say with anxiety.

"Lacy is fine, a little malnourished and dehydrated but fine. She's already been released from the hospital." I breathe a sigh of relief.

The nurse walks in, and I am so glad to see her familiar face. It's Tracie! She smiles, walks over to the bed and hugs me gently; although, it still hurts.

"I'm so glad you're up, Madeline!" she exclaims, "Let's get you checked out." She takes my blood pressure and temperature and asks me how I'm feeling.

"I feel like I've been run over by an eighteen wheeler" I sigh. The machine beeps and she unwraps the cuff from my arm.

"Well, your vitals are okay. I'll go get the doctor." She gives my hand a final squeeze before walking out of the room. "What happened?" I ask Vince.

"One minute, you were outside my house and the next minute you were gone. It took us five days to find you." I didn't realize I had been gone so long.

"The doctor says you were drugged. They drove you from California to Atlanta. Christ, what did they do to you?"

"Gave me a taste of my own medicine so to speak" I give him a small smile.

"Assholes. You didn't deserve this in any way." His eyes grow red with tears.

"I know, sweetie." I stroke his hand. We hear a soft knock on the door, and the doctor comes in. He's a nice looking guy, maybe around my age. Through his black rimmed glasses, he looks at me and Vince with a smile.

"I'm Dr. Nielson, Ms. Davis. Good to see you again, Mr. Marks. How are you feeling?" He places a gentle hand on my shoulder.

"Very, very sore" I respond.

"Well, Ms. Davis, you are most definitely a survivor. The pain you feel is most likely from multiple contusions to your back. Honestly, I haven't seen…anything like that before; however, they will heal with time. You suffered a pretty bad concussion, but we haven't seen any head trauma. It's just going to take time and rest to heal up. You can be discharged tomorrow if you feel comfortable."

"That would be great, doc, and thanks" I give him a grateful smile.

"Oh, and I'll get you something for that pain" he says on his way out of the door.

"Well, I guess now that you're up, I have to call Detective Sommers. He made it his personal business to find you after some…persuasion from me. They thought that Dina and Joseph had…" his voice trails off. I take his hand and stroke it with my thumb.

"But they didn't…Go ahead and call him, I'm not going anywhere. And…please tell Luis I'm okay."

As Vince leaves the room, Tracie comes back with a small cup and a pitcher of water. I gladly take the pills and guzzle the water down.

"I was so worried…your face was all over the news and I hadn't heard from you since you got back from New York." Tracie says as I sit my empty cup down.

"It's been insane, but I'm so glad you're here. I promise you, I will go to fund raisers with you until I run out of money" I laugh but grimace at the pain. She glances out of the door and lowers her voice.

"He's so very sweet. He's been here the whole time. I almost had a heart attack when they brought you in and got kind of hysterical, so he realized that you and I were friends. Keep this one okay? Gotta go. I'll check on you later." Tracie pats my shoulder and leaves out of the room as Vince comes in with Detective Sommers. He looks relieved to see me up.

"Goddamnit, I thought we lost you" he says with a sigh of reprieve.

"I'm not ready to leave this world yet. You knew I would fight."

"Well we've got both of them in custody, now."

"Will they be able to post bail?" I ask.

"Oh, hell no. Kidnapping, assault and attempted murder? They will stay right where they are. Listen, I'm sorry that I didn't take this Andrews case seriously at first…I feel responsible…"

"Don't…" I interrupt him, "You saved my life." He smiles at me…the first time I've ever seen him smile since I've known him.

"Well, you have Agent Bianchi to thank as well. He's the one who realized that you were being followed at the airport. He would not rest until we found you. Old FBI habits die hard I suppose" he says with a chuckle.

"I'll have to thank him too. Thanks for working so hard on this case."

"Ah, just doing my job, but I do have to conduct an interview and get your statement. When you get home and settled tomorrow, give me a call." He shakes Vince's hand and leaves my room.

"Do you need anything? What can I do for you?" Vince looks at me.

"Well, I'm kind of hungry. Do you feel like picking me up some hot and sour soup from The Sesame Kitchen?"

"Not at all. I'll be back soon. Your friend, Nathan is outside. I'll send him in to keep you company." Vince plants a soft kiss on my forehead and steps out of the door.
I can hear Nathan's running footsteps coming towards my room. He stops at the door and bursts into tears. Seeing him cry stirs every emotion inside of me.

"Oh, Maddie" he cries walking to my bed, "Oh my God, I didn't know what I was gonna do if I lost you!" He falls to the bed, sobbing. I grab his hand.

"It's okay, I'm here aren't I? Did you think I was really gonna leave you to your own madness?" I say, stroking his hair. He laughs through his tears.

"I haven't slept in a week. Vincent called me after finding my name in your phone and made sure to update me on all the progress. Then they were thinking about calling off the search...and I...I just lost it. I didn't want you to be out there alone with those creeps. I was so happy when they found you!" He kisses my cheek gently and squeezes my hand. I grab a tissue from the tray next to the bed and hand it to him while taking one for myself.

"I'm glad Vince found you. Glad that you looked for me. I knew that if anyone was worried, it would be you."

"Of course I was worried! You're my best friend. But it looks like I might be replaced" he says eyeing the door with a smile.

"You will always be my best friend, stop being silly. But he is nice isn't he?"

"The man is fucking awesome! You should have seen him. When they were gonna call off the search, he single-handedly put the police department in its place." I smile as I think of Vince and his unholy words wreaking havoc on the police department.

"He really does love you Madeline. I hope you know that."

"I do, Nathan."

"I told him he better treat you right or I would kick his ass" I laugh even though it hurts.

"I already know…"

After Nathan leaves, Vince returns with my food and I realize that I am insanely famished. I greedily dig in to my soup when he sits it down on my tray. I notice he brought me brown rice, too. I open it up as well and devour it. He looks at me for a minute, his eyes shining but sad. The shadows under his eyes and on his jaw tell me he hasn't been focused on much else this past week.

"What is it?" I ask between bites.

"I'm so happy to see you alive." His voice breaks, stabbing my heart with guilt.

"Nathan told me you took the APD by storm" I say, trying to lighten the conversation.

"When it got to the third day, they were thinking of changing the search from rescue to recovery. I wouldn't have it. Luis wouldn't have it. We both told them that we would create our own search party if they did that. Of course that set them off, the last thing they needed was a bunch of vigilantes in the city. So, on the fifth day, the police got a call from a teacher who worked at the school near the warehouse. She noticed that there was activity going on and thought it was some of the students sneaking over there to do drugs. We knew it was the lead we were looking for…"

I look up from my food, "and then what?"

"They told me to hang back because I was the target of this whole fiasco. So Nathan and I waited in Luis' car. It seemed like it took forever. I prayed, Nathan cried and I started to contemplate going in there myself. Then Luis came out with you; you were naked with bruises and welts all over you. I wanted to kill both Dina and Joseph."

"So you already knew Joseph was involved?"

"Oh yeah, I knew. Before we went to California, you got a text message from Lacy. But we turned off our phones, so you never opened it. I'm assuming she knew it was him. We checked your cell phone after you were gone and it popped up. That bastard will never see the light of day if I have anything to do with it."

As I finish the last bit of my soup and rice, in awe of what Vince told me, the pain starts to come back. I push the tray away and lay my head back on the pillow, glad to be away from all of the torture. I look at Vince.

"I've never...been abused like that. At one point it was like they were just trying to find new ways to injure me." His face twists in pain.

"I'm...sorry, I wish I could have been there...that they would have taken me instead..." I shush him.

"Joseph and Dina are both painfully bitter human beings. There wasn't anything you could have done."

"Had I found them, I would have killed them both. I just don't know why they did this." I think back to my time with my two torturers.

"Joseph and I were more connected than I ever thought" I say quietly.

"What do you mean?"

"My senior year of college, I dated a man named Edward Dent. He was my first master...my only master. He was the reason I became a Dom, and I had no idea that Joseph was his brother. He always mentioned an older brother that he wasn't very close to, but I never met Joseph then. When I was hired, he seemed almost too familiar with me, but I could never put my finger on why. I figured maybe he'd just talked to a lot of my references."

"So, Edward was responsible for you getting the job?" I nod.

"Edward and I were on good terms; our breakup was mutual. It was time to move on and he wanted to be a Dom again. I didn't want to be his sub and he understood. It doesn't surprise me that he probably told Joseph why I would be a good executive."

"Do you think Edward was involved in any way?"

"Absolutely not. In fact, Joseph told me himself that his intention was to take back what he thought was taken from him…me and the company. I'm pretty sure Edward would disagree that I was his brother's." Vince's look grows grim.

"That…bastard. I knew he was angry when I outbid him, but I offered him a generous package and everything. Did he…you know…try to…?"

"Oh yea, he tried. But he didn't succeed." The pain is starting to radiate throughout my body and I buzz for the nurse. Tracie brings me another round of painkillers.

"It's almost the end of my shift. I'm off tomorrow; if you need any help at home let me know" she says as she strides out of the door.

"You look tired. Do you wanna sleep for a while?" asks Vince.

"Only if you stay here."

"I'm not going anywhere."

A few hours later, I wake up feeling a little better. I glance out the window to see the moon shining in the small window. Vince is sound asleep in the chair beside my bed, and I know that this is probably the first time he has rested since this whole thing started happening. Just as I attempt to change positions without it killing me, the phone in my room rings. I look nervously at it, but remind myself that I no longer have to be afraid to answer the phone. I pick up the receiver. "Hello?"

"Madeline! It's so good to hear your voice!" It was Eddie, I'd know that smooth tone anywhere.

"Hi, Eddie." My voice chokes up to know he was concerned about me.

"I am so…so… sorry for my brother's actions. I never thought he would do something like this. I'm so angry at him, it has taken everything in me not to go put him out of his misery."

"I knew that you had nothing to do with it. Joseph just snapped."

"I need you to know that I never blew your cover. Even when he asked me about you, all I told him is that we went to college together. He ended up finding out that I dated you, and already knew about my lifestyle. Not to mention he went through my things which had some pictures of you."

"Eddie, don't blame yourself. I'm fine, Joseph is in jail where he belongs, and I sincerely hope he gets psychological help while he's in there."

"Maddie…." He sighs

"Eddie, I don't blame you for anything. You were my first, honey. I'll never forget that."

"It pisses me off that he used the lifestyle against you. No one should ever use it to hurt someone…I…I saw the reports…he beat you with a belt." I take a deep breath.

"And you know that I fought back, even bound and gagged. Remember the old days?" I smile at the thought of our escapades when I would not submit.

"I just had to call you; I didn't want you to think that I had put any ideas in his head. I always will care for you; you know that. If he would've have done any permanent damage to you, I would have killed him anyway."

"I know, Eddie. Don't worry about me; I will get over this. I really appreciate you calling."

"Will you please let me know how you are? I know you've got a new man in your life, but my family and I feel responsible for what's happened."

"Of course I will, but I assure you, I'm fine."

"Goodnight, Madeline."

"Goodnight, Eddie."

I hang up the phone, and Vince is sitting up in the chair gazing at me.

"Was that your Master?" he asks darkly.

"Ha! He's not my Master anymore, but I think he feels partly responsible for everything. He apologized."

"Would you ever go back to him? You know, because of your connection?"

"Oh, Christ no! He's married now, and besides, I think I have a new subject that I want to keep for a long time."

"Really? And who might that be?" He grins.

"Oh, just some guy I work with. He's the boss." I smile at him and he kisses me.

"I need you to hurry up and get better. I missed you so much when you were gone."

"You did?"

"Of course I did. I love you, Madeline. You know that don't you?"

"I know that, and I love you too."

Vince kisses me again, and I secretly wish I wasn't in the hospital confined by this pain. While we are caught in our moment of passion, there's a knock on the door. Vince gets up to open the door and Luis walks in. He looks tired and disheveled, but happy to see me. His eyes light up when notices I'm awake.

"I heard you were up, and I had to see it for myself" he says grabbing my hand.

"Luis, how can I ever thank you…for everything?" I ask. He shakes his head.

"No one with a heart as good as yours should ever have to suffer the way you did. I'm only sorry we didn't find you sooner." I feel tears in my eyes as I remember him running to the mattress to carry me out of the warehouse and his emotional assurance that I was okay. It's time to do something for him.

"Luis, let me ask you. Would it be better if your wife were to work for the Atlanta office?" He looks at me in disbelief.

"Well, y-yeah. Our house is in Dunwoody, it would be much closer than Macon."

"I tell you what, we need a new CCO. I looked at your wife's record and she has magnificent PR skills. If she's willing, the position is hers in the Atlanta office." I look at Vince and he nods in approval.

"Seriously?"

"Seriously."

"We will be forever grateful."

"No, I'll be forever grateful to you. I hope this helps your family grow closer." Luis squeezes my hand a final time.

"I know you need your rest, and I can't wait to tell my wife about her promotion. I'll check on you from time to time if that's okay."

"Actually, Luis. I was wondering if you would be interested in working for me permanently" interrupts Vince, "I don't know if you'd be interested in leaving the security company, but I need security detail in Atlanta. I would hate to move my staff in New York away from their families. I could double your salary."

"Wow, Mr. Marks. I don't even know what to say right now."

"If it hadn't been for you...they would have given up on finding Madeline. You stayed up with me while I searched endlessly for her. I have to repay you for that."

"I can't thank you two enough" Luis says looking at the both of us.

"Come by the office on Monday and we'll sort everything out." Vince shakes Luis' hand.

The next morning, Dr. Nielson comes to check on my progress. I'm feeling a lot better and the pain is slowly subsiding.

"Well, Ms. Davis, everything checks out. You're ready to go home." I breathe a sigh of relief. I can't wait to get home in my own bed. I guess it's true what they say, you never realize how much you have in life until it's gone. I only wish that through this ordeal, I still had Priscilla. Maybe Dina didn't see it as a big deal, which is frightening. I truly hope that she has time to think about the way she turned my life upside down, and all for the sake of a man who didn't even have feelings for her. I couldn't imagine being so demented that I seek to ruin someone else in the process. As for Joseph…he can rot in hell. Never did I think that my own boss would turn his back on me and go along with Dina. It will take me forever and a day to trust someone again.

Chapter 28 *Recovery*

I walk into the hospital room with a few shopping bags from Macy's and smile when I see Madeline sitting on the side of the bed. At least she's fully up today.

"What's all this?" She eyes the shopping bags with curiosity.

"I thought you might want some fresh clothes to go home in."

"How did you even know my size?"

"Nathan." She laughs at my answer. She pulls out some soft grey sweatpants marked with her alma mater's logo. In the other bag is a matching jacket.

"It's gotten a little colder outside since we've been gone. You might need something a little warmer than what was in your suitcase."

"Thank you, sweetie. Will you help me get dressed?"

"Of course. By the way, your parents are here, but I sent them to a hotel near your place. I figured we could have a little bit of privacy before you're bombarded by visitors." She gives me a smile.

I slowly take off the thin piece of material the hospital calls a gown and look at the bruises on her back. She winces as I run my fingers along the welts.

"Am I hurting you?"

"No, it's just sore. When I get home, I could use a nice hot bath."

"I'm sure that can be arranged." I slip the long sleeved t-shirt over her head and she holds on to me as she steps into the sweatpants, gasping in pain.

"Easy, sweetheart." I put the jacket on her. A dark haired nurse rolls a wheelchair into the room and I help her into the chair.

"Here are your discharge papers, Ms. Davis. There are three prescriptions in here. One is for pain and the other two are antibiotics."

"Antibiotics?" Madeline looks worried.

"Nothing serious, but since you were exposed to the elements for an unknown time, we just want to make sure you don't get any infections." she nods and Dr. Nielson steps into the room.

"So, Madeline, we just need you to rest for the next couple of weeks. I'll fill out your FMLA paperwork and fax it to your office."

"Thank you, Doctor." She smiles.

"I'm going to get the car, baby." I kiss her lips softly.

"Well, are you ready to blow this joint?" The nurse asks as I walk ahead of them.

"As ready as I'll ever be…" I hear Madeline answer.

I drive Madeline home, and help her out of the car.

Almost immediately, a cluster of journalists comes up to the car. Damn it! I make a frustrated noise and Madeline touches my arm.

"I knew it was coming. It's okay." I look over at her.

"Wait here okay?" I step out of the car.

"Mr. Marks! Mr. Marks! Is Madeline okay?" A young blonde reporter runs to me.

"You can ask her yourself…" I say as I go around to the passenger side and open the door. Madeline gives a small smile to the reporter as she steps down.

"Madeline, how are you?" The reporter asks gently as Madeline takes my hand.

"I'm a hell of a lot better than I was…"She pulls me towards the entrance of the lobby leaving the vultures behind.

The concierge's face lights up when she sees Madeline.

"Ms. Davis! We are so glad to see you are safe!" She beams.

"Thank you, Amy." Madeline smiles at her as she opens the door leading to the elevator lobby. After a quiet ride up, Madeline takes her keys and unlock the door.

"I called your cleaning lady, and had her spruce up the place for you. I also paid her extra to fill up your fridge and pick up plenty of your wine."

"Vince! You didn't have to..." I put a finger to her lips.

"Yes, I did." I lead her to the couch where she sits down seeming to embrace the comfort of her home.

"Your condo association made sure that your things were replaced after they found out you got kidnapped. See? Everyone was hoping you would come home alive." she holds her chest in surprise.

"You want me to run you a bath?" I ask.

"Please..."I run warm water in the bathtub, and come back to help her off the couch. I lead her to the bathroom where I get her out of her clothes and into the water.

"You want some time alone?" I ask.

"Not really..." she looks up at me.

"Well, I figured I'd make us dinner while you relax for a bit, your parents will be here soon."

"You don't have to cook...we can order something—"

"Nonsense! I think we all need a home cooked meal."

"Do you ever cease to amaze me?" She smiles at me. "I hope not." I caress her face. I did not realize how much I missed hearing her voice, seeing that genuine smile. I haven't had time to think since she's been awake. I've been too busy trying to make her life as normal as possible. Truthfully, I feel so guilty about what's happened. It tortures me that she went through so much because they wanted to hurt me. I'm going to show her my love in every way possible until the day I die.

"I'll be in the kitchen if you need me, baby." I take her hand in mine for one final moment, not able to get enough of her touch.

Chapter 29 *Healing*

"Well, go on, Chef Vince…I'll be out in a little bit." As he closes the door, I lean my head back and let the warm water surround me, finally feeling safe and at peace.

After my wonderful hot bath, I finally find it easier to move around. I get dressed, taking care to put a loose t-shirt on, as my back is still sore. I put on some pink plaid pajama pants, knowing my parents won't mind since I've been through so much. I slip into some flip-flops, and go to the kitchen where I see my love cooking. It smells delicious, and I finally realize how long it's been since I had food outside of my soup last night and bland oatmeal this morning.

"What are you cooking?" I ask as he puts a dish in the oven.

"Lasagna and garlic bread. I made a salad as well."

"Wow…" I muse. He shakes his head.

"Mom always believed I should learn how to cook, so she used to share her grandmother's recipes with me. I know them all by heart." I grin just as I hear the key turn in my lock.

"Madeline!" I hear my mom's voice. I get up from the barstool and all but run into the arms of my parents. My mother sobs as she holds me close. I don't even care about the pain radiating through my back as I hug them tighter.

"We were so worried…" my mom sobs as we try to pull ourselves together.

"I was too…" I take her hand as Vince comes into the living room. My mom gestures for him to come to us and she pulls him into our hug.

"This man has been so amazing…" she kisses his cheek.

"Just wanted her back home, Mrs. Davis…" Vince says, with emotion on his face.

"And you got her back!" My mom hugs us again. My dad kisses the top of my head. He's a man of few words, but I know that he is relieved to see my face.

"I'm sorry that you had to meet Vince like this" I tell them.

"He's been great" my dad shakes Vince's hand.

"Well, I hope you guys are hungry, I made a little something…" Vince smiles at my parents.

"A little? Is that what we're calling it?" I laugh.

"Yeah, just a little." He heads to the kitchen.

An hour later, Vince is dazzling my parents with his hearty Italian food, funny jokes and political banter. Once the plates are cleared and my parents start to grow tired, I hug them good-bye.

"Come see me tomorrow?" I ask.

"Of course! We'll be here until you don't need us anymore" my mom says. I watch them disappear down the hallway and close the door, locking it.

"Wine?" Vince brings me a glass of red wine.

"Yes, thank you." I take the red poison willingly. I probably shouldn't since I'm on pain meds, but what could it hurt? We sit on the couch and I look over at the wonderful, amazing man I've found.

"What?" he asks with a shy smile.

"You wowed my parents."

"Nah. I just did what had to be done." I plant a gentle kiss on his lips.

"Thank you for everything…"

"Madeline, I love you, I will always do anything for you."

"I know that, Vince." I caress his face.

"Drink your wine, there's too much mush going on here."

"Oh, shut up!" I smack him playfully. Suddenly my phone rings, and I pick it up off the coffee table and answer it.

"Hello?"

"Ms. Davis, would this be a good time for me to drop by? I'm in the area…" Detective Sommers says.

"Sure, come on over." I hang up.

"Sommers?" Vince asks.

"Yeah." Vince drains his glass and gets up for a refill. As if on cue, I get a phone call from the concierge desk.

"Detective Sommers is here to see you Ms. Davis." A deep male voice says.

"Send him up." Just as Vince walks in, I hear a knock on the door.

"I've got it…" Vince opens the door for Detective Sommers who finally looks like he's had some rest, a haircut and maybe a romp in the sheets with his wife. I smile at him.

"Good Evening!"

"Evening, Madeline. This won't take up too much of your time, I don't want to interrupt your reunion" he says, almost cheerily.

"Have a seat" Vince points to the couch and Sommers sits next to me.

"I just need a statement from you, Madeline. Can you recount to me everything that happened?" I take a sip of my wine, trying to calm myself.

"Well, we finished lunch with Vince's family in Los Angeles and I went outside…"

"Why did you go outside?" I sigh.

"I needed a cigarette." He nods.

"While you were outside, did you see anyone?" I shake my head.

"I just felt a hard hit to the back of my head."

"What is the next thing you remember?"

"I was in the back of some van, and there were two guys."

"Did you see their faces?"

"No, they were masked." He looks uncomfortable.

"Who were they?" I ask, feeling nervous.

"Madeline, are you familiar with the Luciano family?" I glance at Vince who looks confused.

"Luis told me a little about them...why?"

"The two guys who transported you are identified as John and Giovanni Luciano." My eyes grow wide.

"What?"

"Yes, apparently Dina has some connections with the crime family, but since she won't roll over on them, we had to pull the footage from the warehouse cameras and that's who it looks like."

"Should I still be afraid?"

"No, you said yourself you didn't see their faces. You're not a danger to them." I give him a look of relief but deep down a rising fear makes its way through me.

After Detective Sommers leaves out of the door, I start to feel exhausted and Vince senses it.

"Ready to go to bed?" he asks. I nod and pull myself off the couch.

As Vince retreats the bathroom to take care of himself for the night, I slide into the soft sheets and sigh at the comfort surrounding me.

"Baby..." Vince comes out of the bathroom wearing nothing but a pair of pajama bottoms that so deliciously hang off his solid abs.

"Hey..." I whisper as he comes over to me, kissing me deeply.

"I've missed you so much" his voice breaks.

"Vince, I've taken you on an emotional rollercoaster in the past few weeks. Talk to me." He slides into the bed and holds me close.

"Baby, I have been to hell and back...but I would do it all over again just to have you here with me." He sighs and I know he's tired. Who knows what he went through while I was gone? I wrap my arms around him, looking deeply into his somber hazel eyes.

"You have been so wonderful to me, Vince. Just know that I appreciate everything that you've done, and I love you." He plants a delicate kiss on my forehead.

"I don't want to rush you into anything, Madeline. I'd rather just hold you in my arms tonight." I sink deeper into his embrace and exhaustion captures us as we drift off to sleep.

I wake up to an empty bed the next morning, but feel so much better. I wonder where Vince is, and my internal question is answered by his voice. He has to be on the phone; I've kept him from work for so long, I don't blame him.

Feeling a chill in the air, I throw on my terrycloth robe which Vince has hung on my bedpost. Heat runs through my body as I remember having him handcuffed there, completely under my control. I shake my head, thinking that I will probably never experience it again. Joseph completely turned me off to it; I don't even want to see a belt, gag, or mask for a very long time.

"Yes, I don't know how long I'll be here. If they need to see my face, we can videoconference" Vince says in his authoritative tone as he sits on the couch with his laptop surrounded by papers. I tiptoe behind the couch into the kitchen. Since he's been so great to me, the least I can do is cook him some breakfast.

"Well, we don't have to restructure. Just post the job opening, I'm sure we'll get some desirable candidates. For now, we'll just have to spread out the responsibility." He must be talking about the position that Joseph was supposed to take.

I take bowls and a skillet out of the cabinets, taking care not to interrupt what seems to be an important conversation. Looking into the refrigerator, I almost scream as it is full. He was not kidding! I take out the butter, eggs, onions, peppers, cheese and milk. Vince finishes his conversation, and joins me in the kitchen, wrapping his strong arms around my waist, kissing the top of my head.

"How are you feeling, love?" he asks.

"Much better today...I figured I'd service you for once..." I reach into the refrigerator, pulling out a bottle of orange juice before turning around to meet his kiss.

"No need to worry about that, baby...I love doing things for you."

"Nonsense! This relationship is equal..." I tease as I turn around, busying myself with the omelets. Vince huffs and pulls me back to him kissing me with such passion that he lifts me off the floor. I feel dizzy and speechless when he finally lets me go.

"Well..." I clear my throat and turn my attention back to breakfast. Out of the corner of my eye I see Vince smiling at my flustered state.

As we eat breakfast, I ask Vince when he plans to go back to New York. He looks at me through those endearing eyes.

"What would you think if I didn't?" I drop my fork in surprise.

"You're....seriously considering that?"

"I've thought about it, but wouldn't do it unless you were okay with it."

"Where would you live?"

"I'll hire a realtor, but if you don't mind having a roommate for a little..." I stare at him, perplexed by his suggestion.

"I...would have to think about that."

"It's definitely something I would like you to think about. Until then, I can always get my suite back..."

"Oh, no, don't do that. I like having you here, Vince. It's just...moving in is a big step. Give me a day or two to think it over..." He grabs my hand.

"Take all the time you need." Suddenly, I have an idea.

"Finish your breakfast, why don't I run us a bath? It's time for you to…relax." I touch his cheek. He gives me that smile I love so much and finishes his omelet.

A few minutes later, Vince and I sit in warm, soapy water, relishing in each other's company. Vince kisses my shoulder lightly, but pauses to see my reaction. I look back at him with trepidation.

"I don't want to push any boundaries, Madeline" he says. I shake my head.

"Be gentle with me…" He answers with a searing, hungry kiss to my neck.

"Not here" I rub his legs and feel evidence of his arousal. He stands up, giving me a view of all his naked glory, his huge erection jutting from his body. Taking my hand, he helps me out of the tub and grabs a towel to wrap around us, making sure I feel his lust. He kisses me deeply, running his fingers through my hair. He wraps his arms around my waist pulling me closer.

"Jesus…I've missed you so much…" he says, rubbing his hard cock against my clit. I start to shiver and Vince pulls back.

"Are you sure, Madeline?" He whispers.

"I'm sure…take me to bed." I gently stroke him and he moans, growing harder. His breathing becomes uneven, his hands trembling. He takes the towel from around us, leads me to the bedroom, and gently lays me on the bed. He trails light kisses down my neck, breasts and my stomach. The hot kisses awaken my body. I let out shaky breaths as he takes his time pleasuring me with his lips. He looks into my eyes, hovering over me before he slides inside. I gasp as he slowly fills me, realizing how much my body has longed for him. Vince groans, obviously loving the feeling as well.

He takes my legs and raises them to his shoulders, locking his arms around them. He starts a slow rhythm, panting with every thrust. I whimper, and Vince slows down.

"Please...don't stop" I moan. He speeds up, allowing the intensity of our passion wash over him.

"Vince..." I whisper, my legs trembling.

"That's it, baby..." he growls, speeding up more and more. My body finally gives in to him and I come violently, my body arching off the bed. Vince's body tenses and he groans loudly as my body embraces him. He drops my legs to his waist and I wrap them around him as he buries himself in me.

"Oh! Vince!" I cry out loudly as he speeds up his thrusts. He's lost in me now, and I in him. I reach up and put my arms around his neck. He kisses me deeply, maintaining his control.

"Madeline..." he warns, his body trembling. I know he's close, his hazel eyes burning with fervor.

"Christ!" He groans as I feel the hot thickness of his release. He collapses, panting, holding me close. After a few silent minutes, he recovers and grabs me up, gently flipping my body around. He trails his fingers down my back before sliding into me again.

"God!" I moan. My arms shake and I start to feel a release coming quickly.

"Vince!" I holler as I come again. I collapse on the bed unable to hold myself up any longer. Vince pulls me up into his lap and rocks me. I start to feel weak.

"Vince..." my body shakes, I don't know if I can handle it.

"One more time...baby..." his trembling voice begs as he drives into me.

"Please..." I beg as my body explodes again and I wail loudly. He cries out and clutches my waist as my body clamps down around him. He holds me tightly as I writhe on his lap.

"Jesus Christ..."he moans weakly and shakes violently as I feel his hot seed burst into me. He holds me even tighter as his body jolts with the continuous flood coming from him, and I feel his hot tears fall on my back.

"Are you okay, sweetie?" I ask as he continues to sob laying his head on my shoulder.

"I thought I lost you…" he whispers, and I start to feel a wave of guilt. This man was tortured while I was gone and I can't even get over myself enough to let him move here. As I caress his hands, I tell myself to get over it and let him love me.

"You didn't and you won't." He sniffles.

"If I would have lost you…I would have died" he whispers. I turn around to face him.

"Vince…I'm sorry." I touch his tear stained face.

"What do you have to be sorry for?"

"I'm sorry for putting up a wall…I just never believed that anyone would love me as much as you do."

"Oh, baby…"

"I should have never let my past keep us from having a future, Vince. I love you. I love you so much, and I want you to move in with me." His eyes light up in surprise.

"Really, baby?"

"Really. I want to move forward." He hugs me tightly.

"I love you too, baby, and I'm looking forward to spending the rest of my life with you." He kisses me deeply, and whatever was left of my emotional wall of pain comes crashing down.

Chapter 30 *Looking Forward*

"Is this the one, Sir?" The jeweler brings out a platinum princess cut diamond engagement ring.

"That's the one." He nods and gives it to me so that I can get a closer look.

"This is perfect, no flaws" I admire the diamond's beauty.

"None at all. Should I *ring* it up?" He laughs at his corny humor and I raise my eyebrows.

"Well, I'll put down a deposit to reserve it. I need to talk to her father first."

"Of course, Mr. Marks." I give him my credit card and he hands me a receipt which I put in my wallet.

"Thank you, Francis."

"My pleasure. See you soon." I walk out of the jewelry store and take a deep breath as I prepare to have lunch with Madeline's father. She has no idea he's in town, and I want to keep it that way. I want this to be one of the biggest surprises she's ever had.

I drive to the restaurant and see Mr. Davis' SUV parked in the front. Suddenly, I grow extremely nervous. I never thought I would be doing this, and now, it scares me a little. I give myself a pep talk and repeat that everything is going to be fine as I jump out of my car. I walk into the restaurant and see her dad sitting in a booth drinking a glass of iced tea.

"Mr. Davis, how are you?" I say, as I approach him.

"Fine, thanks, Vince." I slide into the booth.

"Can I get you anything to drink, sir?" A waitress approaches me.

"Yeah, a glass of chardonnay please." She scribbles the order in her pad and says she'll be right back.

"So, do you want to go ahead and tell me why I'm here or should I wait until you get some liquid courage?" He smiles.

"Well, Mr. Davis, I…" my breath gets caught in my throat.

"Go on, son" he coaxes.

"I've been with Madeline for three months, and I know that is not a long time…" The waitress brings my wine and I take a sip.

"No, it's not" he replies. I feel the nervousness creeping back.

"But, sir, I want you to know that I love her very much. I'm thirty-five and I have never had what I have with her. That is why I'm asking for your daughter's hand in marriage." He clears his throat and eyes me seriously.

"Vince, I am honored that you respected me enough to ask. I haven't seen Madeline as happy as she is since you came into the picture, and on top of that, you saved her life."

"She means the world to me. I only hope that you've seen that for yourself."

"I see that, but, I'm worried. Nothing would make me want to grab my gun quick enough than a man who breaks my daughter's heart. Before I say yes, I need you to promise me a few things."

"Anything."

"I know that you will protect her, you have proven that to me. But I need to know, when the children come, when the makeup comes off and…the good times in the bedroom are not as frequent, will you still see in her what you see now?"

"Absolutely. I could never see myself loving her any less than I do now. With children and age comes more love, Mr. Davis. After all, hasn't that been what has happened for you?" He smiles.

"Yes, I suppose so. Will you continue to support her in her career? None of this stay at home business?"

"Of course I will support her. She's an excellent executive, I'd never want to take that away from her." He sighs and sips his iced tea.

"Then you have my blessing. As long as you take care of her in every way possible, you'll hear no resistance from me."

"Thank you, sir. I promise that Madeline will always be the most important in my life."

"I have no doubt. Now, look, I don't know about you but I'm hungry." I laugh with the relief that it's over. I'm going to ask her to marry me and couldn't be happier. After saying good-bye to Madeline's father, I go back to the jewelry store. Francis raises his eyebrows.

"Back so soon!" He exclaims.

"Yes, I have spoken with her father."

"And? Am I selling a ring today?" He asks.

"You are indeed selling a ring today." He smiles as he takes the ring and carefully places it in a black box. I hand him my credit card to pay off the balance.

"Good luck to you sir." He smiles genuinely as he hands me the box.

"Thank you." Taking the box, I give him a sincere good-bye and get into my car. I take a deep breath as I dial my mother's number.

"Hello, Vince, bambino!" My mother's voice rings out.

"Hey, Mom. How are you?"

"I'm great, how are you?"

"About to make the biggest move of my life..."

"You're not selling the company are you?" she asks with concern.

"Of course not! Mom, I'm going to ask Madeline to marry me." She is silent.

"Mom?"

"I'm sorry, I'm not sure I heard you right."

"I'm going to propose to Madeline."

"Oh my goodness..."she sniffles.

"Come on, Mom don't cry."

"I just…never thought I would hear you say that, honey." She sobs.

"Well, now you've heard it. How do you feel about it?"

"Well, I love Madeline and I think she's the one for you. She will take good care of you and help your company grow." She sniffles.

"I believe the same thing, Mom. Now, let's just hope she says yes."

"She will, any fool could see that girl loves you, and I know that you love her. I saw it in your face when we were in LA."

"Mom, I'm so excited to spend the rest of my life with her." I start to become overwhelmed at the thought.

"I'm so happy for you, darling. I love you very much." She continues to cry. Jeez, sometimes she can be overly emotional.

"I love you too, Mom. It'll be next weekend, do you think you can make it down here?"

"I'll be there."

"Do you need me to get Shira to book everything for you?"

"I can handle it."

"Talk to you soon." I hang up and relax for the first time since I decided to propose. I drive home, eager to celebrate my secret.

I walk into the condo and see Madeline sitting on the couch watching TV. She's in a t-shirt and shorts and I'm ready to devour her. She smiles at me.

"Finish your errands?" she asks. I say nothing as I move to the couch and kiss her deeply. She moans in surprise as I yank off her shorts. Thank God she's not wearing any underwear.

"Vince…"she whispers and I quiet her with a hungry kiss. A burning desire consumes me as I kiss her neck. She unbuttons my jeans and pulls out my cock which is painfully hard. I push myself all the way into her and she calls my name, her legs trembling.

"What's gotten into you?" she moans as I pound into her. I can't answer, I'm too lost in her. She squirms under me, whimpering until I feel her come, her body squeezing my dick.

"Fuck!" I groan thrusting into her with all of my strength.

"Vince!" she sobs, digging her nails into my back as she comes harder than she did before.

"Goddamn girl..." I grab her up and cover her mouth with mine. She whimpers, tears rolling down her cheeks. I keep going harder, not able to stop until I feel the rush I need so desperately. Dizziness overcomes me as I fill her, shaking from the hard release. I stare into her bright brown eyes and she reaches up to touch my face. I take her hand and kiss it tenderly before I lay my head on her breasts. She strokes my head as we both lay in silence.

"Vince!" Madeline calls out hoarsely as I make her come for what seems to be the hundredth time. Her body trembles violently, and I pour myself into her with an almost agonizing release, groaning loudly. I haven't stopped making love to her since I got back. We've been all over the house, and I can't get enough of her today. She playfully pushes me off her and I fall to the other side of the bed.

"Oh my God, you're a maniac!" she exclaims breathlessly. I laugh and kiss her swollen lips.

"You like it..."I tease.

"You've had me in bed all day!" she pouts looking at the clock.

"And? What plans did you have?" I ask. She chuckles.

"Well, I thought I was going to watch a couple of movies and share a bottle with you."

"We can still do that."

"Well now I'm tired." I pull her close to me.

"We can lay in bed and watch movies." She stares into my eyes and shakes her head.

"Oh, no...I've been in bed enough, and don't we have to eat at some point?"

"We'll order take out."

"Vince Marks, you are impossible..." she gets up, quickly covering herself with my button up shirt which makes her look even sexier. I get up, put on some shorts and follow her into the kitchen. She takes out two flat iron steaks, red potatoes and bag of spinach.

"You don't have to cook you know..." I say smacking her behind. She yelps and turns around.

"Behave..." she scolds.

"Okay, fine, cook dinner. I probably need to check my email anyway." She laughs as I retreat to the living room and get my laptop. Scanning through a bunch of unnecessary emails, I see one marked "URGENT" from Gus. Cocking my head curiously, I open it.

*Vince, I did a comprehensive check on Dina's communications: emails, text messages, browser history and I found some things you would be interested in. I only selected the ones that might be useful to you. Check Alistair's report below:*

*SUBJECT: DINA ANDREWS*

*MARCH 30, 2013: Text message from GIOVANNI LUCIANO*

*DINA: Talked to Vince Marks about the business deal today. Don't think he's gonna go for it.*

*GIOVANNI: Why not?*

*DINA: He doesn't think you're legit*

*GIOVANNI: What does he know?*

*DINA: I'm not sure*

*GIOVANNI: Keep trying*

*APRIL 2, 2013: DINA ANDREWS receives text from JOSEPH DENT*

*JOSEPH: Just got word a promotion might be available*

*DINA: Yes*

*JOSEPH: Might go for it*

DINA: You should
JOSEPH: I will email Marks
DINA: If you do as I say, you will get the job
JOSEPH: Like the sound of that

What the fuck? Joseph and Dina were already conspiring before everything went down? I can't believe this. I continue reading:

AUGUST 15, 2013: DINA ANDREWS receives text message from JOSEPH DENT
JOSEPH: Marks requested for the CFO to come to New York. Know anything about that?
DINA: Only chief that works outside of New York.
JOSEPH: Don't let him fuck her, I know how he is
DINA: You don't have anything to worry about, he's mine
JOSEPH: Yeah right
DINA: Asshole

Yeah, he was an asshole. Like he had a claim on Madeline. This shit is going to be damning in court. Trying to contain my anger, I read on:

September 5, 2013: DINA ANDREWS sends text message to JOSEPH DENT
DINA: What the hell is your CFO doing?!
JOSEPH: I have no clue what you're talking about
DINA: She's fucking him!
JOSEPH: I doubt that
DINA: She spent the night at his apartment
JOSEPH: Are you stalking him?
DINA: I have my ways. Tell her to back off!
JOSEPH: I'll have to see it to believe it
DINA: (picture message)
DINA: (picture message)
DINA: (picture message)

I almost hyperventilate when I see the pictures. Madeline getting out of the car in my parking deck, Lou typing in my passcode for her, and her going inside my apartment. That bitch!

*JOSEPH: I will handle it.*
*DINA: You better!*
*JOSEPH: I will!*

I think back to that time and remember Madeline confronting me about my flirtatious interview a year ago. He must have put that bug in her ear thinking she would break it off. Bastard!

*SEPTEMBER 12th: TEXT MESSAGE FROM JOSEPH DENT*
*JOSEPH: What the hell did you do?*
*DINA: What?*
*JOSEPH: You've got Marks hiring security. What did you do?*
*DINA: I had to confront that bitch.*
*JOSEPH: You are a jealous woman.*
*DINA: And you are a jealous man.*
*JOSEPH: Where are you?*
*DINA: Bitch called the cops. They tried to get me to go back to New York but I snuck off the plane.*
*JOSEPH: Maybe we can convince her that Marks is in on this. Let's watch her for a few days.*
*DINA: I'm way ahead of you. Can you meet me?*
*JOSEPH: Where?*
*DINA: There's a warehouse near McDonough Blvd. Gio gave me the keys. I'll text you the address.*
*JOSEPH: Give me twenty.*
*SEPTEMBER 13th: TEXT MESSAGE TO JOSEPH DENT*
*DINA: They're going to California.*
*JOSEPH: How are you finding this stuff out?*
*DINA: Like I said I have my ways. Let's send Gio and his brother to get her. She's gonna slip up at some point and go somewhere without Vince.*
*JOSEPH: Marks is a smart man. He's not gonna let her out of his sight.*
*DINA: We'll see.*
*JOSEPH: You need to make sure you keep Lacy alive. We don't need a murder charge.*
*DINA: She's not the one I want to hurt.*

I close out the document, unable to read anymore. Trying to compose myself, I type an email to Gus.

*Gus,*

*This should all go to the district attorney. Thank you for telling me first.*

Almost immediately, I hear the ping of an instant message. I should have known we would be online at the same time.

*I'll take care of it, Vince. How is everything going in the south?*

*It's going well. I was wondering if you and Emily had time to come down next weekend.*

*What for?* I look up and see Madeline busying herself in the kitchen.

*I'm going to propose.*

*Wow. I'm happy for you, man. Wouldn't miss it for the world.*

*You also need to meet our new CCO Rosalyn Bianchi. She's a beast, you'll like her.*

*Perfect. I'm going to send you a few things. We need to have a videoconference on Monday.*

*Sure thing. Email Shira with the details.*

*See you Monday, Emily's distracting me.* I chuckle.

*I bet she is. Turn the computer off and give her some attention.*
*Oh shut up.*

On Monday, I sit with Rosalyn in my office after a videoconference with Gus and his ad team. She takes a sip of mineral water and completes her notes.

"So…Rosalyn, I need your help." I look into her sharp blue eyes.

"Anything, Mr. Marks."

"Nothing leaves this office" I warn.

"You have my word."

"I'm planning to surprise Madeline next Saturday, but event planning is…not my forte." She raises her eyebrows.

"What kind of surprise if I may ask?"

"There's one part of it I won't reveal, but I'm planning to propose. I want her family and close friends there as well as mine." She squeals.

"Oh, I'd love to help!" I hand her a list of everything I need.

"I trust you'll make it happen?"

"Leave everything to me." She puts the list in her portfolio and stands up.

"I'll get on it right away." She smiles and steps out of my office as Shira, my secretary walks in.

"Mr. Marks, you have a few messages and schedule updates. Is now a good time?"

"Of course, Shira." She sits down and takes out her tablet.

"Your mother called asking if you could have lunch with her and your father Friday."

"Put it on my schedule." She nods and expertly taps her tablet with a stylus. As she continues running down a lengthy list of things to do and people to call, Madeline taps on the office door. I signal for her to come in. She looks like she's seen a ghost.

"What's wrong, Madeline?" I ask. She looks over at Shira then back at me.

"Julia Dent is here."

"For what?"

"I don't know, but I don't want to face her alone."

"Shira, direct Mrs. Dent to my office." She gets up and hesitates in the doorframe.

"Shira?"

"I'm sorry, Mr. Marks, I have to compose myself before seeing her again." She takes a breath and steps out. Julia Dent walks into my office, pausing as if she's trying to erase a horrible memory. I really don't understand her husband's need to go after other women. The former model still had her toned body and smooth olive skin almost reminding me of my mother's youngest sister.

"Julia..."Madeline gets up and shakes her hand.

"Madeline" she regards her with a freezing stare, those big blue eyes shining with a hint of sadness, "can I speak with you please?"

"Not without me" I say, returning her stare.

"Very well." I gesture for her to sit in the chair opposite my desk. Madeline pulls a chair beside me, grabbing my hand.

"What can we do for you Mrs. Dent?" I ask.

"Rizolli please, I don't want to be associated with that asshole." Her face hardens.

"Fine, what do you want?" She turns her attention to Madeline.

"Madeline, I'm not going to pretend that this whole situation didn't happen, what I'm more concerned with is the well-being of my children and myself."

"Well, if you're fearing retaliation, it's unfounded. No one blames you or the children for what your husband did" I reply.

"No, I don't fear retaliation. I fear poverty."

"What the hell are you talking about, Julia?" Madeline asks.

"Madeline, though my soon-to-be ex-husband harmed you, I was generous enough to accept you into our family. I was hoping that you would think about that and….do us a favor." Madeline freezes as if she is having flashbacks.

"Well? What do you want?" I inquire. She looks at me in surprise as if she thought I'd leave this to Madeline.

"I need Joseph's retirement and the remainder of his yearly salary. I know that officially he's been terminated, but I'm never going to be able to afford to keep the kids up." I sigh with a bit of annoyance at her assumption that she is entitled to anything after what her crazy husband did.

"Don't you have your own account?" Madeline asks.

"I did, but our joint account will be frozen until Joseph either gets convicted or takes a plea deal. I can't wait that long, and honestly, it's going to take some time for me to find work again." Madeline looks at me with pleading eyes.

Regardless of Joseph's offenses, I knew that Madeline was close to his family, and if helping his family will help her heal, I'll put myself on the line.

"Alright, Julia. I know that you and the children have been put in a less than stellar position, but if I do this for your family, you must sign a contract" I pull up the company's payroll schedule on my computer.

"A contract?" She looks confused. If she thinks she's going to get money from me without a legally binding agreement, she's lost her mind.

"I need to be assured that you will not impose any further legal action. I don't need a greedy woman bleeding this company dry."

"Well, how much are you planning to give me?" I look at the computer screen and make a decision. I'll have to give her what he would have gotten had he retired in his current position.

"Five thousand a month for the next ten years is the best I can do considering that your husband won't be generating any profit for me."

"Five thousand is the mortgage on my house." I huff in frustration.

"Then you will need to find a smaller mortgage, Ms. Rizolli."

"At least let me cash out his retirement account." Sensing my annoyance, Madeline squeezes my hand.

"Fine. You can cash out his retirement which has two-hundred fifty thousand, and you will get the five thousand a month." She adjusts her glasses pensively.

"I can live with that."

"James Livingston will draw up the contract, and you can come back later today to sign it. You will get your semi-monthly payments starting on the fifteenth." I type a quick email to payroll scheduling an emergency meeting. Julia gets up and shakes my hand. Her eyes fill with tears as she looks at Madeline.

"I am...truly sorry for everything, Madeline." She stifles a sob.

"It's not your fault, Julia." Madeline walks over to her and takes her hand.

"Twenty years under the same roof, I should have known something was up and I ignored it. I can't help feeling I could have prevented it." Madeline shakes her head.

"It's okay, Julia. I'm a better woman because of it." Suddenly, Julia pulls Madeline into a hug before she begins to cry. Despite my aggressive hatred towards Joseph, I never stopped to think about his wife and three children who would never be the same. Madeline returns the hug and begins to sniffle. I decide to step out and give them some privacy.

Later that night, Madeline and I retreat into her condo, both of us exhausted. She immediately goes to her refrigerator and pulls out a bottle of chardonnay. Her silence is worrying for me. She hasn't said much since Julia left the office.

"Wine?" she asks quietly as she retrieves two glasses from the cabinet.

"Sure." I sit at the breakfast bar watching carefully as she corks the bottle and pours wine into the glasses. She hands me my glass and takes a long sip from hers.

"You want to talk about it?" I ask. She sighs.

"I probably should, but I don't want to." She sits down next to me and runs her finger around the rim of her glass.

"Baby…you've had a rough ordeal. I know that seeing Julia probably threw you for a loop." She looks at me, her eyes brimming with tears.

"I…felt so bad for her!" She starts to cry and I pull her in between my legs.

"Shhh…she'll be fine. I'll do whatever I can if she needs more help. Will that make you feel better?" She sniffles and it is absolutely killing me that she is feeling sad.

"Thank-you…that helps, baby." She pulls away from me and takes my face in her hands.

"I'm glad you're here to help me through this." Her hands move down to my chest and I take them in mine.

"I'll be here for you no matter what" I whisper.

"I know…" she smiles and loosens my tie.

"I love you, Madeline."

"I love you, Vince." She kisses me passionately.

"Mmm, careful there…you're starting a fire" I warn as she rubs her hands up and down my thighs.

"I know you don't mind…" she laughs softly as she takes my hand, leading me to the bedroom. She pushes me on the bed and kisses me again.

Chapter 31 *Many Surprises*

"Madeline! I've got something for you!" yells Vince as he comes in the door.

"What is it?" I call from the kitchen. I smooth out my gray maxi skirt and put down my cup of tea.

"Come here!" he shouts from the door excitedly. I rush to see what this big surprise is. Vince smiles as he hauls in a few shopping bags.

"What have you got here?" I inquire suspiciously.

"I'm going to cook for you tonight; one of my many surprises for the evening."

"Mmmm, I like the sound of that. What else do you have in there?" I ask, noticing that not all of the bags are from the same place.

"Patience, darling. All in due time" he whispers, flashing that gorgeous smile of his. He takes the other bags to the bedroom.

"No peeking..." he says. Now, I'm really suspicious. What does he have up his sleeve? Vince gets started in the kitchen and I sit at the breakfast bar watching him. The spicy aroma of jerk chicken fills the condo. We sip chilled glasses of Pinot Grigio as we talk lightly. Soon, dinner is ready and Vince sits down two steaming plates on the dining table. Jerk chicken, yellow rice and steamed veggies. The man can cook.

"So...Madeline," he looks at me, "what do you think about going to Connecticut for Christmas? My family can't wait to see you again."

"I'd love to." I smile lovingly.

"Get your coat. We're going out" Vince says as he clears the table. I'm intrigued, but don't question him. I hurry to the bedroom and get my coat while eyeing the suspicious bags on the bed...maybe just one peek.

"I know you're not thinking of doing what I think you are" Vince growls from the doorway with a smirk. I give him a sweet, innocent smile.

"Of course not, darling" I say harmlessly and grab his hand as we head towards the elevator.

When we get downstairs, the valet is waiting with Vince's new Porsche Cayenne. Vince opens the door for me and eyes me with heat. I return his gaze with equal desire. As we drive through downtown Atlanta, I see party and dinner crowds walking the sidewalks. Vince finally pulls up to the tavern at Piedmont Park. I wonder what we're doing here, we can drink at home.

"I thought maybe we could have a couple of drinks" Vince says as he leads me inside the tavern. As we walk in I hear "Surprise!" and see all of my friends, family and co-workers. I laugh as I receive hugs from everyone. Lacy comes up to me.

"Oh, Madeline, I'm so glad to see you!" she says with happiness.

"You too, Lacy. When are you coming back to work?" I ask.

"I'll be back after the holidays. I've gotta get used to being a married woman, you know?" she winks at me and she takes her new husband's hand. They wave to me and I see Nathan barreling towards me. He pulls me up into a bear hug.

"Madeline!"

"What is this all about?" I ask him curiously.

"Well, you were never congratulated on your…um… survival!" I know he's lying. I wonder what Vince is up to? Suddenly Vince stands up and the crowd becomes quiet.

"First, I want to thank all of you for coming tonight, Madeline deserves every ounce of congratulations as she takes on the position of Chief Business Development Officer of PharmaCO." My eyes light up as our friends and family cheer. I run to Vince and give him a hug and kiss.

"And also…" Vince takes a deep breath and looks at me, "Madeline, you have impacted my life in a way no one has, and have allowed me to feel things I never thought I would." My breathing becomes shallow as he reaches in his coat pocket and gets down on one knee. He pulls out a gorgeous platinum ring with a large princess-cut diamond.

"Madeline Davis, I know that no woman will ever compare to you. You would make me the happiest man alive if you would be my wife. Will you marry me?" Tears well up in my eyes and I fall down to my knees in front of him.

"Nothing, absolutely nothing will give me more pleasure than being your wife." I whisper, tears falling. The whole room erupts in cheers as Vince and I kiss passionately. He helps me up and I am dizzy with happiness. As we are caught in our moment of fervor, Vince holds me close and whispers in my ear.

"Don't drink too much, Madame, you'll need your energy tonight" he growls seductively.

"Yes, Master" I say. Through some…well a lot of coaxing, I decided to sub for Vince. Though my experience with Joseph put me off BDSM for a while, Vince brought me back into it in the wonderful way he first awakened me. I'm not into it as much as I used to be, but sometimes we like to play. I look at him and stroke his face lovingly.

After a couple drinks, many congratulations and consistent promises to my mom that we would go shopping tomorrow, the crowd starts to thin out. Luis and his wife, Rosalyn come up to me. I can tell she's a little tipsy.

"Congrats, Madeline and Vince. We are so happy for you! We'll work on the announcement next week." Rosalyn says as she embraces me. Luis shakes Vince's hand and gives me a quick hug. We wave at them as Luis helps a giggling, stumbling Rosalyn out the door and to their car. They stop and he gives her a slow kiss which prompts her to stumble even more. Soon, everyone is gone and we head outside. I see that Vince has called Jack to drive us home.

"I figured a DUI would put a dent in our plans" says Vince with a laugh. Jack opens the door and gives us his congratulations. Vince whispers something to Jack and he nods. When we get into the car, Jack turns on the engine, blasting Reggae music. On the way home, Vince and I are engaged in an intense make-out session. He explores my body with his hands, teasing me. He finally finds my panties under my skirt and looks up at me as he rips them off and slides two fingers inside me. I moan as he twists his fingers around inside of me.

"Wait, what about Jack?" I pant.

"Don't worry about him…" Vince gives me that naughty grin of his. He kisses me to muffle my moans. My body starts to climb and he reaches up to release one of my breasts and thumb my nipple. I can't take anymore. He caresses the sensitive nub below my waist with his thumb and I explode, shaking around his hand. He moans through his kiss and strokes my neck. I look at him, anticipating what else he has planned for the evening. We arrive at my condo and I can't keep the silly grin off my face.

Vince goes into the bedroom and retrieves the shopping bags he had earlier. Eyeing me, he pulls out a beautiful silver bustier with matching panties. This man is unbelievable. He hands them to me, not saying anything.

"Wait…before we do this, I have something for you too" I interrupt him and lead him to the bedroom. I hand him a small box and he looks at me curiously. He opens it and there is the key to my "closet". I figured this would be the ultimate gift in my compromise with him. He takes a breath as he looks at it.

"I wanted to let you know that I am officially yours…Master."

"You're entrusting me with your closet?" he asks.

"Yes, darling." But I'm not done yet. I lead him over to the closet and open it. I bring out a brand new black riding crop.

"For when Master desires to have his way with me" I say. He takes it and gazes at me.

"Madeline, this means so much to me. I know it was hard for you to give up some of your authority, but I promise you won't be disappointed."

"I haven't been so far" I smile, thinking of the first time I let him dominate me completely.

"Get dressed, and pull your hair up. I'll meet you in the bedroom." Vince goes into the bathroom and I slip on the bustier, matching underwear and the mask. I pull my hair into that familiar lustrous ponytail. I turn back the sheets on my bed and dim the lights

He is dressed in leather pants. The muscles in his abs are mouthwatering. I feel my panties moisten and tremble at the sight of him. He takes my hand, leading me to the bed. He binds my hands with the handcuffs, chaining me to the bedpost. I'm standing with my back to him. He kisses my back and removes my panties. My breathing quickens in anticipation. He runs the riding crop up and down my back before slapping it against my ass. I moan at the pleasurable pain. He hits me again and I start to shake with anticipation. He puts a cool hand on the warm spot and kisses my neck savagely. The riding crop clatters to the floor and I feel him untie the corset.

"Mmm, you look delicious. Maybe I'll have some dessert now" he whispers in my ear. I feel his tongue on my sex and he devours me, making my legs wobble. His expert tongue runs circles around me and I feel my body heighten. My breaths quicken.

"No, no, not yet" he scolds. I shake so badly that the handcuffs rattle against the bedpost. He unlocks the handcuffs and turns me around. He lifts up my chin and kisses me with fervor. He leads me to the bed gently places me on it looking at me, eyes wild. He hovers over me and slides into me slowly letting me feel every inch of him.

"Oh! Vince" I moan as his tempo quickens.

"Oh, fuck…Madeline…" he moans. I look into his eyes with affection as he continues his hot slide into me.

"Come for me" he says, trembling. As if on cue, I come, my body embracing his.

"Vince! Vince! Vince! Ah God!" I wail as my orgasm rips through me. My body goes into spasms as I come again and again. I writhe on the bed clutching him as he continues pounding into me.

"Oh…shit…Jesus…" his breathing escalates. He roars and the whole bed shakes as he comes, his hot seed flowing into me. He pulls me into a deep kiss.

"I'm not done with you" he says as he gently turns me on my belly, my body still wilted from our intense lovemaking. I'm almost too weak to say anything. He reaches over to retrieve something from the nightstand. I feel warm oil on my back as Vince's hands knead my back. His hands feel so good, and I moan in pleasure to his expert hands. My body starts to come back alive with arousal and my breathing becomes erratic. He plants a kiss on my shoulder blades and I feel him slide into me again with a groan. He pulls me up on my hands and knees and starts a gentle, rocking rhythm.

"Vince" I sigh. He continues to rock me as his breathing increases. He finds the sweet spot below my waist and strokes it softly. I start to whimper.

"Please, Vince, harder" I whisper. He honors my request and speeds up his tempo.

"Ah…" he groans going even faster. He turns me over.

"I want to see your face when you come" he says, speeding up more.

"I don't know…how much… more…. I can….take" I say with every thrust, shaking weakly. Another orgasm might do me in.

"I want to feel you come…" he says softly, sinking deeper inside me. It's all my body needs to let go.

"Oh, Jesus! Vince!" I scream arching off the bed, as the orgasm tears through me again. I wrap my legs around him, crying as the almost painful convulsions take over my body.

"God...Madeline...God!" he yells as pushes into me one more time before coming forcefully. Tremors take over his body and he fills me up yet again. He collapses on top of me, shuddering. He strokes my hair and I look at him, this man that tore down my walls and made me love again.

"You brought me back to life..." I whisper as I kiss him deeply.

Early the next morning, I wake up to Vince holding me tightly. I plant a kiss on his head and he moans softly. His eyes open slowly and he smiles at me.

"I'm going for a run, want to come?" I ask. He nods and we both jump out of bed.

After a four mile run, we stop at a coffee shop for water and coffee. As we sit amongst the bustling Saturday crowd, I take Vince's hand in mine.

"I can't wait to spend the rest of my life with you." I tell him, and he smiles, squeezing my hand.

"And I can't wait to spend the rest of mine with you." Once we get to the condo, Vince eyes me with lust and kisses me passionately.

"Let's take a shower" he suggests.

"Sounds great to me." We both go to the bedroom and shed our clothes.

"You are so fucking beautiful..." he says as pulls me into another steamy kiss, leading me to the shower. He turns on the water and helps me step in before hoisting me against the wall. He rubs his hard cock on my wet, swollen opening before pushing into me.

"Ah!" I cry out as he fills me. He kisses me greedily as he claims me with his long, slow strokes. I wrap my legs around his waist as he pushes deeper.

"God, you feel so damn good..." he growls as he speeds up. My body climbs as I feel the multiple sensations of the hot water, Vince's solid wet body and his hot kisses on my neck.

"Oh! Vince!" I holler as I climax, my voice echoing through the bathroom. He moans shakily as my body embraces him. We both get lost into each other, the steam of the shower surrounding us as though we were in a hazy dream. Vince's moans raise an octave and he bursts inside of me, cursing loudly. I kiss him softly as he comes down from his high and we hold each other silently.

Later that afternoon, I busy myself cleaning up and Vince is on the phone with his realtor. After I toss the sheets in the washer, I go into the living room and notice Vince is off the phone. He looks up from his laptop and smiles pointing to an envelope on the counter. I eye him questioningly.

"What's this?" He laughs and comes over to the counter, pouring me a glass of wine.

"Shhh. Just open it." I take a breath and open the envelope. At the top of a very thick document it says Livingston Law Firm LLC. I cock my head to the side and sit down to read the letter as I take a gulp of wine. Is he making me sign a prenup?

*Dear Ms. Davis,*

*We are pleased to inform you that Mr. Vincent Marks, CEO of PharmaCo has offered you ownership of the Atlanta branch. The details are outlined in the contracts attached to this letter. Congratulations on your promotion. Livingston Law Firm is always here to assist you with your acquisition.*

I nearly choke on my wine and drop the letter on the table. My coughs turn to laughter of disbelief. I look at Vince.

"This is a joke, right?" I say.

"It's no joke, Madeline. I want you to take ownership of the branch in Atlanta."

"I'm...not...I mean I can't..."

"Yes, you can." I sigh and look back at the letter.

"What does this mean?"

"Well, I'm relinquishing my ownership of the Atlanta branch. I will remain CEO, but the branch itself is yours. My partners and I all agree that you are the best advocate for the Atlanta office. A share of every profit turned from the Atlanta office will be yours."

"What about when we get married?"

"When we get married you will be co-owner of the New York and Los Angeles Branch. Everything I have will be yours."

"Oh, Jesus." I say nervously.

"Madeline, when I said I wanted to share my life with you, I meant it. Our children will never want for anything…you will never want for anything." Tears start to well up in my eyes.

"It's too much.." he grabs me and covers my mouth with his.

"I love you, Madeline…Christ, I love you so much woman" he kisses me again before I can respond and picks me up leading me to the bedroom. He gently lays me down and undresses me. My body shivers as he unbuttons his pants and pulls his shirt over his head. He leans over me for a second and looks into my eyes before slowly sliding inside of me. I gasp and call out his name as he begins a slow, seductive rhythm. He kisses my neck and takes my hands holding them behind my head. My body trembles as he speeds up.

"Oh! Vince!" I cry as he claims every part of me.

"Ah!" he groans as he looks deeply into my eyes. I feel a strong release brewing below my waist and come loudly as I squeeze his hands.

"Vince!" I arch off the bed as tears roll down my cheeks. He yells hoarsely and slams into me repeatedly. Before I know it, another release shatters me into pieces and I writhe on the bed.

"Oh, Madeline!" He roars as he pours himself into me. He covers my mouth with his once again and collapses on top of me. Throughout the evening, he and I explore new heights of ecstasy as we make love like never before.

The next morning, I know I have to get out of my love coma and do some work. I leave Vince sleeping soundly on the rumpled sheets and grab my laptop secretly regretting that I didn't check my email this weekend. Sure enough, I have about a hundred new emails in my inbox. Suddenly, a chat box appears. It's Rosalyn. I swear that woman is a work-a-holic.

*Taking a break from work?* I laugh.

*I'm sorry Rosalyn, Vince and I have been celebrating our engagement. Is anything urgent?*

*Oh, I see…enough said…nothing really pressing but…uh…there's some rumors going around.*

*About what?*

*Word is you're the new owner of PharmaCo ATL.* I roll my eyes. The lawyers at Livingston can never keep anything from her. I swear she either bribes or threatens them sometimes.

*Well…it's not official yet…but yes, the proposal has come to me.*

*Take it! You deserve it!*

*I think I will; look, just don't confirm anything yet until everything is ironed out.*

*My lips are sealed. I'll talk to you later. Enjoy your man!* I laugh again.

*See you later, Rosalyn.*

I continue to work through my emails, most of which contain questions about holiday off days and group messages asking about accommodations for kids on holiday break. As I finish answering questions, I hear Vince's heavy footsteps.

"What are you doing up?" he asks as he leans down to kiss my head.

"Work…something you've kept me from this weekend." I laugh. He comes around and sits next to me.

"Please, you'll be fine." He kisses my nose. I look at him seriously.

"How do you think they are going to take it that you gave me the branch?"

"What do you mean? You deserve it!" He scoffs at me.

"Vince, you know how people are." He takes my hand and leans in closer.

"Who the fuck cares what people think? You're going to be my wife and own everything I have anyway. They might as well get used to it." My heart lurches in my chest and I caress his face.

"You always know what to say" I whisper.

"Damn right, I do. I love you, Madeline, and no gossip, dirty looks or whatever will ever change that." He graces my lips with a gentle peck and gives my hand a reassuring squeeze.

"I love you too, Vince." I give him a huge grin.

"Now, let's get some breakfast and catch up on our work…" he says, heading to the kitchen.

The next day, after some coaxing from Vince, my signature is on the ownership papers and he is addressing the head executive board.

"I'm pleased to announce that Madeline Davis will be taking ownership of the Atlanta branch" Vince says to a long table of board members and trustees. The whole crowd, looks at me as I stand beside Vince.

"Well, Marks…" Jay Newton takes a breath, "I think that is the right decision." I let out a huge sigh of relief. Jay Newton is one of Vince's mentors, a man he fully trusts to help with decisions, I am surprised he agreed so quickly and glance at Vince who probably told him before Livingston could draw up the contract.

"I thought you would say that, Jay." Vince flashes a grin while the others murmur in agreement.

"Welcome to the trustee board, Madeline" A younger guy, I think his name is Benjamin, gets up to shake my hand. I give him a big smile and grab his hand with executive strength. He raises his eyebrows in surprise at my grip but looks entertained by my display of familiarity with the big boys.

"This calls for celebration! Madeline, would you like to join us for dinner this evening?" Jay asks.

"Of course I would!" I beam at him and he seems pleased with my answer.

"I will announce it immediately" Rosalyn says gathering up her notes. Before she ventures out of the room, she gives me a tight hug.

"I'm really happy for you, honey." She smiles genuinely and exits quickly, probably dying to finally let out the secret. As the rest of the board members file out, Vince gives me a passionate kiss.

"Well, you now own the Atlanta branch. How does it feel?" he asks.

"It feels amazing…"I smile grandly.

"Well…you'll feel even more amazing when I give you my private congratulations." He gives me that seductive grin.

"I have no doubt…"I kiss him again.

After shaking off the nervousness I'd been feeling since the night before, I go to my office to find some peace. Knowing that I'll probably get a swarm of questions, I email Lacy to tell her to take my calls. She comes over my intercom almost instantly after I hit send.

"Is there anything I can help you with?" she asks.

"No, I just need some time to breathe. I don't think we have anything pressing today."

"We don't. I'll put a do not disturb on your email."

"Thanks."

As I try to immerse myself in work, I hear a hard knock on my office door. Looking up, I see Vince's face staring back at me. I gesture for him to come in and give him a smile as he sits down across from my desk.

"Something I can help you with, Mr. Marks?" I ask with an endearing look.

"You can help me with a whole lot, but I only have one favor to ask of you right now..."

"Oh?" He gets up and turns my chair around so that I'm facing the wide windows overlooking the city. He kneels in front of me, pulls up my skirt, slides my panties down my legs and begins to devour me.

"Vince..." I scold.

"Mmm-mmm..." he warns, his licks becoming more urgent. I place my hands on his damp head and push him towards me, loving the hot sensation of his talented tongue. My legs tremble as he slips his tongue inside of me, his moans of pleasure vibrating on my clit.

"Vince...I can't..." I pant, my breaths coming quicker. He pulls me closer to him, his fingers brushing my thighs.

"Oh...God..." I whimper as I feel the waves of pleasure radiating through me. My body jerks as I grip the arms of my office chair, willing myself not to cry out. Vince stays in between my legs, continuing his oral assault.

"Stop...stop..." I moan, twisting in my chair. He locks his arms around my legs, trapping me. I climax again and I can't help but to let out a shout. He kisses my thigh softly and looks up at me, his hazel eyes reflecting satisfaction. I eye him in disbelief as I lay my head back on my chair, too exhausted to speak.

"One day...I'll fuck you in this office...but I'm going to take it step by step."

"This is so inappropriate" I complain.

"You are the owner of this company...and I am the boss...if I want to fuck you in the office, I will." I cut my eyes at him.

"You are so..." He puts a finger to my lips.

"Get used to it." He smiles deviously.

Chapter 32 *The Prenup*

The next day, I sit in my office and gape at the papers placed on my desk by James Livingston, our company's head attorney.

"Jim, you don't really think I'm going to do this." I look at the title of the document that reads *Prenuptial Agreement*.

"Madeline, I would think that someone as educated with you could see the necessity. You will be co-owner of one of the largest medical supply companies in the country. You don't want to lose that." I scoff.

"Jim…what makes you think that I'm not entitled to the obligatory fifty percent?"

"You are not just entitled to fifty percent, Madeline…. You are entitled to seventy-five percent." I snap my head up to look at him.

"Excuse me?"

"Seventy-five percent given your stock in all three branches as well as your job position." This is unbelievable.

"I won't do that."

"Why the hell not?" He leans back in frustration.

"Vince owns this company, not me. Furthermore, I trust him enough not to sign one. Who brought this up?" His lips form a line.

"It wasn't Vince?" He clears his throat.

"You have thirty seconds, Jim. Who suggested a fucking prenup?" His face reflects anxiety.

"Gustavo Cruz" he says quietly.

"Oh is that so? Tell me something, do he and Emily have one?" I ask knowing he represents them as well.

"Yes." I can't believe what I'm hearing and close my eyes.

"But…in his defense, it's more protective of her than him. Just like this one is more protective of you."

"I don't care. You might as well put that in the shredder. Look, Jim, I've known you for years and you know what I am capable of. Even if something happened...I could still take care of myself. I don't expect that to be the case."

"You don't want to just think about it?" He asks.

"Why don't you show it to Vince and tell me what he thinks? I'm almost sure he would tell you the same thing; although, I'm not sure he would be as nice about it." He sighs, his stormy blue eyes darkening.

"I'm only looking out for you, Madeline..."

"And I appreciate that, Jim. I really appreciate it; however, it would be in your best interest to tell Gustavo to mind his own fucking business. I'm not even married yet and other people are assuming that we need contractual agreements. If you want to take this to Vince and have him deal with Cruz then so be it."

"Madeline, at least think about it..." I stand up.

"This meeting is over." He huffs and takes the papers off my desk. Once he gets to the door, he turns around and looks at me.

"Not doing this would be a huge mistake..." He leaves out and I have seething desire to call Gus and curse him to hell and back. Who did he think he was? Just because he married her when she was in her early twenties doesn't give him any right to dictate my personal or business relationship with Vince. I sit down trying to cool my temper and remind myself that maybe he was just trying to protect me, but it is no one else's concern.

"Well, Madeline maybe it is in your best interest..."says Nathan as we sit at the bar. I was so upset about Jim's proposal that I told Vince I needed to see my best friend.

"Whose side are you on?" I ask, annoyed that he doesn't see it from my point of view.

"Look, I'm not saying that you won't spend the rest of your life in wedded bliss. But this is also a business thing. You don't want to be left high and dry if something goes wrong.

I'm speaking to you as a lawyer and a friend; if you need to change anything in the agreement that you don't like, I will take it on personally." I take a sip of the chilled Pinot Grigio.

"You're asking me to assume that I'll get divorced when I'm not even married yet..." I say sadly.

"No, I'm asking you to protect yourself and your stake in the company. Vince is a reasonable businessman; he already gave you ownership of your branch because he trusts your instincts and knows that you will handle it well." I say nothing as I drain my glass.

"Maddie, you know that this is necessary. It would be different if you had no job and were marrying this guy, but you own a company with him. You have to consider your future, the future of your children. Do you really want to take a risk?" Just as I'm thinking, I feel chills on the back of my neck and glance towards the door. Sure enough, Vince walks in. Armed with a manila folder, he approaches Nathan and me.

"Nathan, how are you?" He shakes Vince's hand firmly.

"I'm alright, how about yourself?" Nathan replies cautiously.

"Look...Madeline...I talked to Jim and then I talked to Gus. I know you are dead set on not signing this, but I figured if you talked it over with Nathan you might reconsider." I scoff.

"Oh, so now you want me to sign a prenup as well?" I start to grow angry.

"Hear me out, the only concern in this agreement is you." Nathan holds out his hand for the envelope which Vince hands him willingly.

"Look, you two can sit here and have a discussion about my life. Maybe you can conference call Jim and Gus while you're at it." I get up.

"Madeline..." Vince pleads.

"No, it's fine! It's fucking fine! I'll see you at work tomorrow." I jerk my coat off the back of the chair and leave out as Vince hopelessly calls my name. I tell the valet that I need my car quickly and he honors my command. I speed off, not knowing where to go. I find myself taking a familiar route and pull up to the townhome I used to live in. Inhaling sharply, I get out of my car and knock on the door. The familiar slender figure dressed in dark jeans and an oversized sweater opens the door and looks at me with surprise.

"Madeline…" My distant friend, Megan greets me with surprise. I haven't seen her in months; our friendship was somewhat strained from a disagreement. I always knew that if I really needed her, she would come through. We survived college and grad school together, and as much as I hated to admit it, she had sometimes been my only friend before I met Nathan.

"Megan…I know we haven't spoken much, but I need you."

"Of course, honey. Come on in." She holds the door open for me and I walk in, feeling lethargic from my constant swirling emotions.

"I'm sorry, I didn't mean to barge in." I eye her apologetically.

"It's perfectly fine. Do you want anything?"

"A drink." She chuckles and goes into her kitchen and emerges a few minutes later with two glasses of red wine, one of which I take gratefully.

"I'm honestly surprised to see you, Madeline. I heard you were engaged now…" her dark brown eyes burn into mine.

"I should have told you."

"Yes, you should have. That's water under the bridge now. Everything is." She puts a hand on my arm.

"Well, I'm…a little confused."

"About what?"

"He…wants me to sign a prenup." She clears her throat and runs a hand through her thick, black hair.

"Did he say why?" I explain to her that he had given me ownership of the Atlanta branch, and that the prenup guarantees seventy-five percent of my stake in the company. She listens intently before responding.

"Let me ask you something, Madeline. Do you love him?"

"Of course I do!"

"Then why are you afraid?" She takes a long sip of her wine before hearing my answer.

"Because I feel like that would be an easy out for him! I want him to fight, knowing that if he ever gave up, he would lose everything."

"But isn't that what this agreement says? That he would only have twenty five percent of his stake left if he ever decided to desert you?" I look down in shame.

"Yes, I…didn't think of it that way." I really didn't consider that if he were to leave, I'd be more of an owner of PharmaCo than him.

"Madeline, for Christ's sake, you are so headstrong. If you think that you will truly make it, this is your insurance policy. You can't fault him for trying to protect you, and letting you know that if he fucks up, you will own most of what he's built. That's not distrust, honey. That's love." I sniffle.

"I just find it so hard to believe…years and years of broken hearts and disappointments have damaged me." Megan puts down her glass.

"If you truly believe that this man loves you, and I have no doubt he does, then you have to stop with this insecurity, Madeline. You're never going to be happy if you constantly feel like someone is trying to fuck you over." I start to realize that even though I assumed my emotional walls were torn down, they really weren't. Megan puts her arms around me.

"It's okay, sweetie. You've been through a lot of bad relationships. I don't blame you for being cautious, but not everyone is out to get you." I take a tissue that she hands me and wipe my eyes.

"Oh, everything just happened so fast!"

"Well, wait awhile to get married if that's how you feel."

"I don't doubt our love, I'm just overwhelmed."

"Overwhelmed by what?"

"The promotion, the proposal, the ownership of the company..."

"Okay, first of all, you need to stop overthinking it. That does nothing but stress you out."

"I know...I stormed off on Vince and Nathan." She raises her eyebrows.

"Nathan agreed with him?" I nod.

"Well, he would know, he's a lawyer."

"I guess I overreacted." She cocks her head and gives me a smirk.

"Still the same drama queen you were in college..." She laughs and drinks the rest of her wine. I scoff and shove her playfully.

"It's good to see you." I look into her eyes.

"You too. I'm glad you came to me. So...are you gonna tell me about this guy?"

"You gonna get yourself a refill?"

"Oh, it's like that?"

"Most definitely." She gets up, taking both of our glasses to the kitchen for a refill. When she comes back, I've finally pulled myself together.

"So.." she says handing me my glass, "tell me about Vincent Marks."

On Friday afternoon, Vince and I brave the harsh Atlanta traffic in our trek to the mountains. After our talk about the prenup, I'm glad that we decided that some time alone might be good for us. I have to admit I'm excited about having him all to myself in a secluded paradise.

At around seven, we pull up to the large cabin. I'm assuming it is normally meant for a large group of people. We walk in and survey the glossy hardwood floors, black leather furniture, and huge modern kitchen.

"Very nice! Good choice, baby." I give him a kiss as he sits our bags on the floor. I take our groceries and put them away in the kitchen. Vince comes up behind me, putting his arms around my waist.

"What do you say we go check out the bed?" He whispers seductively before kissing my neck. I laugh.

"Vince…so eager to jump into bed." He picks me up and takes me upstairs to the bedroom which has a huge king sized bed. He puts me down before loosening his tie with a smile.

"Oh, I think I'm going to love this weekend" He growls pushing me gently down on the bed. Kissing me passionately, he runs his hand up my skirt stroking the slick area with his thumb.

"Naughty girl, you didn't have underwear on today?" I laugh.

"I took them off before we got on the road." He growls and hikes up my skirt. I unzip his pants and eagerly pull out his growing erection. He groans with pleasure as he sinks into me.

"Vince…" I moan as we begin a slow rhythm, losing ourselves in each other.

The next day, we decide to explore the hiking trail. As we walk hand in hand, we come to a small cabin and hear the happy yipping of puppies.

"Come on…" Vince leads me to the cabin and knocks on the door. A middle aged woman with short black hair opens the door with a smile.

"Mr. Marks?" she looks at Vince.

"Ms. Carter...this is Madeline Davis." She shakes my hand.

"Come on in! She's ready for you." I give Vince a quizzical look as we walk inside the house.

"Have a seat, I'll be right back..." She disappears into the back of the house.

"What are you up to?" I ask him as I settle on the couch.

"You'll see." I narrow my eyes at him in suspicion. The lady comes out holding a beautiful Golden Retriever puppy, and smiles at me.

"Would you like to hold her?" I tremble, reminded of Pricilla when she was just a puppy. Swallowing back tears, I nod slowly. She hands me the ball of fluff who seems quite happy to see someone new.

"She's yours..." Vince says softly as I run my hands through her thick fur.

"She is?" I ask.

"Do you like her?"

"She's beautiful..." a tear slides down my cheek. Ms. Carter retrieves a stack of papers from a nearby table.

"She is bred from champions. I understand you've owned a Golden before, Ms. Davis." She hands Vince the stack of papers.

"I did...I'm sorry...I lost her a few months ago. It still stings."

"Oh, yes, they are lovely companions. This one is very friendly; I think you two will get along well."

"What do you want to name her?" Vince smiles. I look at the sweet face and endearing eyes.

"Faith..."

"That's a beautiful name" Ms. Carter says.

After thanking Ms. Carter and retrieving a black leather collar with a leash for our new family member, Vince and I head back to the cabin. Faith bounds happily in front of us, occasionally turning her attention to squirrels scurrying across our path. I laugh at her endless energy, and look forward to a new playful spirit in the house. It has been terribly quiet without Pricilla. Once we get back to the cabin, I release Faith to explore the cabin and give Vince a thankful kiss.

"You're amazing…" I smile.

"I try." He kisses my forehead tenderly.

That night, Vince and I decide to take it easy and toss a frozen pizza in the oven. Faith has become my shadow and follows me every time I make the slightest move. Vince laughs as she slides on the hardwood floor in an effort to keep up with me.

"I love her." I tell Vince.

"She most definitely seems to love you. I know it doesn't make up for Pricilla, but I hope that you will find a new companion in her." He takes my hand.

"I already have a companion." He scoffs.

"Oh, so I'm just a companion?"

"You know what I mean!" His smile fades and he looks into my eyes.

"Madeline…the smile that I've seen today…I haven't seen since I first met you." I sigh.

"It has been a rough couple of months…" He squeezes my hand harder.

"I know, and it kills me that I responsible for most of it." I shake my head and squeeze his hand back.

"I don't blame you…never have and never will. Think about it. Joseph would have eventually snapped sooner or later. He was obsessed with me before I even met you."

"He specifically said…"

"He said it was because of you, but Joseph was no angel. Now that I know how he really is, some of the things in the past make sense to me now."

"Like what?"

"Like at events he would get drunk and say inappropriate things to me, or make comments that were…strange when we would be alone. I thought he was a flirt, but now that I think about it, he was never that way with the other women in the office. Look at Shira, his secretary. He never treated her unprofessionally." Shira was a beautiful woman and one of the youngest in our office. Her dark brown skin and cropped curly hair were a part of the many traits that gave her a unique beauty. Many men at our office eyed her curves and Joseph was never one of them. He treated her with the upmost respect.

"I never thought about it that way. This is the first time you have really talked with me about it."

"That's why I'm glad we are here. I feel like we haven't had time to really be since everything happened…you went back to work and I stayed home for a while."

"You can always talk to me, Madeline."

"I know, but with both of us working we barely have time to spend with each other."

"Then that will change" he declares. I smile.

"Maybe we can do this once a month? Go away somewhere?"

"Baby, we can go wherever, whenever. You just say the word."

"I was thinking that on those weekends, we could take that Friday and Monday…" he exhales.

"Just that week! Once a month! We can do that, right?"

"We can, but you have to take into consideration that we have a wedding coming up in June."

"So…maybe after we get married we can take one four day weekend a month?" He smiles.

"That sounds doable. The middle of the month is the least busy. We will put it on the calendars after we come back from our honeymoon."

"Our honeymoon..." I sigh dreamily thinking of spending time on the white beaches of the Caribbean with my new husband.

"Yes, our honeymoon. It will be nice to have two weeks alone with you in a secluded villa on the beach." His eyes stare at me seductively.

"Are you sure you're ready to spend two weeks in seclusion with me?" He grins.

"Oh, baby, the things that you're going to experience with me...you will never want to leave that place."

"Oh my..." I bite my lip in anticipation.

"You will come back to work glowing like you never did before." I start to laugh.

"Let's just make sure that glow is not because we have a new addition coming." He shakes his head obviously not wanting to touch that subject.

"You have to think about it. It's always possible, and as often as we...are intimate, we up our chances."

"Well, isn't that why you got on birth control?" I cock my head to the side.

"I said possibility" I reiterate.

"I know it's possible, Madeline. That's why we need to keep up with your fertility calendar." In that moment we are both relieved from the uncertain conversation by the beeping of the oven. I get up and place the pizza on the cooling rack. Vince picks Faith up and gently places her in the living room, closing the sliding doors.

After dinner, Vince and I lay in bed together our bodies close, his arms around my waist. A part of me feels sadness that it is our last night here. The weekend seemed so short, and I loved every moment alone with him. I was glad that he decided to go along with my idea of spending one long weekend a month together. It was nice to feel close to him, have intimate conversations and make love endlessly. God, I can't wait until our honeymoon. Two weeks of beautiful scenery, quality time and intimacy. I hear Vince sigh and feel him pull me closer. I stroke his hands feeling exhaustion from our session in which we took time pleasuring each other. My eyelids grow heavy and I drift off to sleep, dreaming about my future with Vince.

Chapter 33 *Publicity*

I rush into the condo, frantic about an upcoming dinner in which Gustavo and Emily are going to show Vince and me the feature article that I took photographs for in New York. That seems so long ago now and almost like a dream. Trying to quiet my thoughts, I step into the bedroom, where I see Vince waiting for me on the bed. He walks towards me, planting a gentle kiss on my lips.

"We have a little time..." he whispers as he picks me up and places me on the bed. I look up at him, my eyes gleaming with excitement. He caresses my shoulders before sliding off my top. I bite my lip in anticipation as he unbuttons his slacks and slides them down just enough for me to see his undeniably thick erection. My lips curve into a smile and I pull him down to me. He lifts up my skirt and shreds my panties before pushing into me.

"Vince!" I moan. He pushes all the way inside, stretching me to fit his rigid cock.

"Damn, girl...you're always ready for me" he growls as he starts a torturing rhythm.

"Yes...faster..." I beg. He honors my command and speeds up his tempo, groaning with intense passion. My body climbs higher and my whimpers grow louder until everything inside of me clutches to him.

"Jesus!" He hollers, gripping the sheets, pausing as the space between my legs squeeze him tightly. I twist on the bed, moaning loudly as the pleasure moves through my body. He thrusts harder through my pulsing flesh. My body trembles violently and I clutch him harder as the sheer force of his relentless, harsh rhythm stirs a sea of emotions inside of me.

"Oh...Vince!" I yell as I come again, tears streaming down my cheeks. He pulls me closer to him and slows his rhythm.

"Baby..."his voice rises. He holds me tightly, shuddering as I feel him swell inside of me.

"God! Ah! Madeline!" He cries as I feel the hot spurts of his release. He lets out a shaky breath, coming down from his high. I grab his face, devouring him with a hungry kiss. An hour later, Vince and I walk into *Cantina*, a small Mexican restaurant on the West side of town. We sit down and wait for the couple. Both of them walk in, looking as fabulous as ever. Gustavo is donned in a perfectly tailored black Armani suit and Emily in a fitted turquoise blouse with a brown skirt.

"Vince! Madeline!" Emily squeals enthusiastically as she pulls me into a hug and places two light kisses on both of my cheeks. Gustavo and Vince firmly shake hands and Vince kisses Emily on the cheek.

"Well, sit down you two..." Vince gestures at the two chairs opposite ours. Gustavo pulls out Emily's chair and she sits down gratefully as she pulls out a huge photo portfolio book.

"Emily, dear, always straight to business. Put that away. Let's have a drink first." Gustavo regards her with teasing eyes. She scoffs and touches his nose.

"And you are always straight to drinking." She laughs with affection.

"You got that right" Vince says with a smile. Emily sits the portfolio in an empty chair beside her and Gustavo signals for the waiter. He says something in Spanish and the waiter nods with understanding.

"I've ordered their finest tequila" he says.

"Gustavo, tequila! We have to drive!" Emily scolds to which he shushes with a kiss. She blushes and settles down. Emily is a feisty one, but Gustavo seems to love every minute of it.

After two rounds of tequila in which we were told to sip and not gulp down, Emily finally brings out the portfolio. She opens it to a gray and white glossy photo of me donned in a black suit sitting at Vince's desk in the New York office. The elegant skyscrapers make a perfect background.

"Oh, Emily!" I gush at the photo which has been so delightfully airbrushed.

"Now, Madeline, we know that the recent events are still…simmering. But the magazine would like for you to talk about bravery and courage as a woman who has been through so much, yet triumphed to become one of the most powerful businesswomen…" Gustavo says.

"Gustavo, stop it…many women go through the same stuff…" I start.

"Oh, Madeline, come off it! Not many people can say they were kidnapped!" Emily looks at me.

"How much….do I have to share?" I ask them nervously. They both look at each other and of course Emily has an answer.

"We'd never ask you to recount those horrible details…all we want is for you to talk about your experience has taught you."

"Okay…I think I can do that…" I glance at Vince who smiles at me.

"Of course she can…"he says.

"Excellent! We'll get the columnist to meet you next week" Emily says.

"Now, are we gonna celebrate or what?" Gustavo asks with a gleam in his eye. He calls for another round of tequila. A few hours later, as our significant others are engaged in a heavy business conversation, Emily looks at me.

"So…how's the wedding planning going?" I give her a shy smile.

"I haven't had time to think about it." She sips her tequila ruefully.

"You know, these whirlwind romances…phew! What energy they take!" she says.

"Oh? Did you and Gustavo have one of those?" she laughs.

"Did we?! Gustavo and I ran away to be married after three months; although, that is a detail that no one knows." My eyebrows rise.

"But...I saw your wedding all over..." She leans over to me.

"Honey, we were married six months before that. We just had to keep it from our families."

"Really?" I'm intrigued. She cocks her head to the side thoughtfully.

"Gus was just...everything I'd ever needed. He met me at a time when I wasn't in the best place in my life. I was young...twenty-four and he was twenty-eight."

"That's not so bad..."

"Madeline...Gus is a force to be reckoned with; he and Vince are not so different. You and I are not so different either." She puts down her drink.

"Emily, I'm not sure what you're getting at here." I start to grow uncomfortable as she takes a long, skinny cigarette out of her purse.

"We can smoke here, right?" I nod as she lights it up. For a minute, I contemplate asking her for one. She takes a light puff and blows the smoke away from the table.

"I'm not getting at anything. Consider it trading information. We are both involved with powerful men, and you've experienced a rather traumatic experience already."

"Emily...I really don't like where this conversation is going." She takes another puff, the smoke lingering beside me. She picks up her drink again and gulps it down.

"Madeline, with this article coming out, you've gotta know that not everyone is going to be happy...hell, I remember when Gus made me partner at the ad company. The dirty looks, the inane gossip, and the complete lack of faith in my abilities almost drove me insane. You, my dear, are not only a partner but an owner now. The crazy bitch he was fucking might be locked up, but don't think there aren't a million more behind her." I take a deep breath and grab my drink. She's probably the first one I've talked to that knows how I feel.

"Emily...don't you think I worry about that every single day?" I look into her somber gray eyes. She takes another puff of her cigarette and pauses pensively. She then digs into her purse and hands me a cigarette.

"Oh, I'm trying to quit..." I shake my head.

"Honey, take it. You've been through so much in the past three months. Humor me." I surrender and take the cigarette and a fancy engraved lighter from her. The buzz from the first puff compliments the one from the alcohol.

"I didn't think anyone would ever understand..."I blow out a thick cloud of smoke.

"There's not many that would, but I do. That's why I brought it up. I could see the nervousness when we brought up the subject of the interview. It's scary, but you have a hell of a track record. No one can ever say that you manipulated yourself to the top. You did it on your own. I don't think you hear that enough." Tears roll down my cheeks.

"Actually I do...but never believe it." I laugh and wipe my tears.

"Then start believing it. Vince Marks didn't make you anymore than Gustavo Cruz made me. They just...enhance us." She laughs at her own joke and I smile.

"Listen, here is my card. Anytime you need to talk..."she hands me a business card.

"Thank-you, Emily." She grins and Gustavo turns his attention to us.

"Ladies, you feeling it yet? I see the cigs have come out." He and Vince laugh heartily.

"Only as much as you, baby." She caresses his face before kissing him gently.

"Okay, enough mush you two." Vince feigns disgust.

"Oh, somebody's jealous. Go ahead, Madeline, give him a kiss before he turns green" Emily tells me. I turn my head, looking at Vince and he plants a soft kiss on my lips. After saying good-bye to Emily and Gus, and figuring that neither one of us are sober enough to drive, Vince calls Jack to drive us home.

Once we are safely inside Jack's car, we spend a few minutes in silence.

"What's on your mind?" Vince finally breaks the quiet.

"Nothing, really. Whatever Gus had us drinking has me a little tipsy." I laugh.

"Well, the man always had a head for quality alcohol if nothing else." He smiles fondly.

"Vince..." I look over at him.

"Yes?" he heeds me with question.

"Do you know how much I love you?" His grin is a mile wide.

"Oh, baby, I know." He pulls me into his lap, branding me with the sweetest kisses and confirming that he loves me just as much.

A few days later, I sit across from the magazine columnist at the wine bar down the street from our office. Kim Hudson seems to be nice, a fairly attractive young woman who is all about business.

"Well, first Ms. Davis, let me just say that this is an honor. I admire your work." I smile and sip a glass of Merlot.

"Call me Madeline, please."

"As you wish. Now, I'll ask some questions, but you can steer the conversation in any direction you like." I nod.

"Madeline, what keeps you going? I mean, you have done an excellent job and are fairly young. You have to have some kind of inspiration."

"Truthfully, I'm a perfectionist. My mother can tell you that I was super competitive in school. I had to be the best at everything" I laugh fondly.

"When did you decide you wanted to be in the corporate world?"

"I was in college, in the pre-nursing program and I…just found out that it wasn't for me. When I took an accounting class my sophomore year, my professor convinced me to change my major."

"Really? Why?" She stares at me through a pair of sharp emerald eyes.

"I had done so well in the class and even taught him a few things."

"As you have taught all of us. After your ordeal with the kidnapping and harassment, how has that changed you? Does it scare you? Or does it make you more determined to rise to the top?"

"That is a loaded question…" I laugh.

"Take your time."

"When all of this started happening, I still had control. I was spiraling but wasn't there yet. When they finally abducted me, I had to gather strength from places I never thought I would. That's how I realized I have a lot of fight in me. Does it scare me? Of course. Does it make me even more determined? Absolutely." She nods.

"And…now you are the owner of the Atlanta branch…how do you feel about that?"

"I'm still not comfortable with it, honestly. I know many may think that I haven't quite earned it…"

"Why would they think that? You have an excellent track record."

"Well, because I'm engaged to the CEO."

"But before you two were even in a relationship, you were making your mark, girl." She laughs and takes another sip of wine. I chuckle.

"Or at least attempting to."

"How does it feel to be engaged to the CEO of your company? Have you thought about how your colleagues are handling it?"

"He's the love of my life, but I have to admit that it will be an adjustment for some. I'm still the same person and absolutely nothing will change about my work ethic. I will still do what's necessary to keep the company running smoothly."

"I have no doubt about that." She scribbles something on her notepad.

"Well, thank you for believing in me."

"I hope, Ms. Davis that you believe in yourself just as much."

"I'm getting there."

"Well, thank you so much for the interview. The magazine will be printed next month, and you will receive the first copy." She drains her glass and gets up, tossing a twenty on the bar.

"It's been a pleasure." I shake her hand and she gathers her notes before leaving. Just as I dig in my purse to pay my tab, my phone rings. I answer without looking at the caller ID.

"Ms. Davis, it's Detective Sommers." My heart pounds.

"Hi, Detective, how are you?"

"As good as can be expected. I'm calling to let you know that Joseph and Dina have been indicted. We're still hoping that they will take a plea deal, so that you don't have to go through a trial." I sigh.

"What do you think will happen?"

"I think it would be in their best interest to take it, but Joseph's lawyer is a dirty bastard and will drive a hard bargain. If they don't, you'll have to get on the stand."

"I sincerely hope I don't have to do that."

"I hope you don't either, but look for a call if they decide to go to trial. The DA's name is Adam Griffin. He's a beast and I have no doubt he'll go hard for a conviction."

"What does he expect me to do?"

"All you have to do is tell the truth, but just be prepared for some tough questions...especially about your relationship with Mr. Marks. Joseph's whole thing is that he was infatuated with you and lost it when you started seeing Mr. Marks." Really? He's blaming me for his craziness?

"It's going to be difficult to face him again."

"We'll cross that bridge when we get there. For now just be prepared."

"I'll try my best."

"We'll keep you updated, but I want you to know that I will be there every step of the way." I smile.

"I appreciate that, Detective." I suddenly hear a female voice asking him what he's doing.

"I'll be off the phone in a minute, baby...I'm sorry, the wife is glad to have me home before dark" he says.

"It's perfectly fine. Go spend time with your family. I know you don't get to spend much time with them." He chuckles and I assume the faint female voice's owner has probably come next to him. His laugh sounds happy and relaxed.

"Take care, Ms. Davis."

"You do the same." I hang up, pay my bar tab and walk to my car, eager to see Vince and feel his arms around me. I hope to God I don't have to testify. I thought I would never have to see Joseph's face again...now I might have to and it scares the hell out of me.

Chapter 34 *Do What?*

The next weekend, Vince and I sit across from my mother and father at a small barbecue restaurant south of city. Earlier in the week, they called and ask if they could speak with the both of us. I'm a little nervous as I don't know what they could possibly want to talk to us about. Vince seems a little tense as well which I find amusing since he's usually so put together. As the waitress sets down glasses of their famous sweet tea, my mother and father look at each other.

"So, Mom and Dad, what did you want to talk to us about?"

"Well, we've been thinking about all that you've been through and the quickness of your engagement..." My mom starts. My heart begins to pound. Are they having second thoughts about approving our relationship? I grab Vince's hand under the table.

"And?" I ask.

"Well, we think that it would be best if you two did pre-marriage counseling with the minister." The minister I had selected to marry us was a good friend of our family and I trusted no one else.

"We just want to make sure that you two really know what marriage entails..." My dad adds.

"I don't see any issue with that, Mr. and Mrs. Davis" Vince says with a smile. My mother relaxes and sips her sweet tea.

"He wants to have a session with you next week. If he feels like you need more, he'll let you know." My dad eyes me seriously and I nod.

"What day works for you?" I look at Vince.

"Next Saturday works, will we need to go down there?" Vince asks.

"No, he'll be up here for a conference, so I'm sure he won't mind staying an extra day." My mother grins at us.

"And...there's also the issue of cost..." My dad says.

"Oh...Mr. Davis you have nothing to worry about..."Vince starts.

"Well, I do want to help. It's tradition, Vince." Vince glances at me. I never really expected my parents to pay for my wedding. They were both retired, so I automatically assumed I would always have to pay for it.

"Dad...don't pressure yourself. Vince and I can take care of everything." He shakes his head.

"No, I want to contribute." So stubborn, just like me.

"Okay, Dad. I'm meeting with the wedding planner later this week. I'll let you know what the estimate is." He nods, satisfied at my concession.

"Well, how many people are we talking about?" Mom asks.

"Honestly, it'll be in the hundreds. Vince and I have business associates...then there's friends and family" I say thoughtfully.

"What do you want?" Vince asks me.

"I don't mind having a big wedding, but I don't want it to be a circus." My parents nod in agreement.

"Well, we'll most definitely have to hire security. There's the problem of the press..." Vince says. My parents gape at us.

"It's that serious?" Mom asks.

"Unfortunately, yes. We've been a big news story since Madeline's...situation." Vince's hazel eyes reflect seriousness. The waitress brings our food and I am thankful we can be quiet for a minute. It has hit me that I'm getting married, and I need time to process it.

The next Saturday, I hand Reverend Lockhart a cup of coffee as he settles in a chair adjacent to the couch. His warm smile comforts me as it always did when I was younger.

"Well…" He sits his cup on the coaster and pulls out a legal pad, "where should we begin? Maybe I should I get to know you better, Vincent." Vince looks nervous.

"What do you want to know?" He asks.

"Well, let's start with your family life…" Vince takes a deep breath.

"I grew up with my parents…they've been married forty years. I have a younger sister…Chloe who's in college." Reverend Lockhart smiles.

"Are you close to your parents?"

"Yes, I am. I never make a life decision without asking them for advice. My father is a little more opinionated than my mother, but I value his input."

"Now, both of you, that's where we can start. We all love our parents, but in marriage sometimes parents are not your best point of contact." Vince and I look at each other.

"Elaborate…"I reply

"Well, I'm sure you have seen the cliché "evil in-laws" which of course is not always the case. But I advise you not to involve them in your marital issues…especially if there is a disagreement between the two of you."

"I agree…" Vince says.

"Vincent…what is your relationship history?" Reverend Lockhart eyes him seriously.

"I…."he huffs, "don't have much of one."

"Meaning? Be honest."

"I was never really a monogamous man before I met Madeline. I dated, but didn't have a serious relationship."

"And what made Madeline different?"

"Everything made her different…"

"Like?"

"She wasn't superficial. She was real with me from the first day, and I never had that before. I've always been…attractive, I guess, and I come from a wealthy family. Most of the women I came into contact with were just there for the money or because I was nice to look at. She tried to get to know me and was interested in my feelings, hopes and dreams." Reverend Lockhart looks at me.

"Madeline...what about you?"

"Well, my life has been a series of failed relationships...it took me a very long time to recover from the last one."

"Why was that?"

"I don't know...I assumed I was going to marry him. When he dumped me...I started to feel worthless, like no one would ever want to be with me."

"Madeline..."Vince whispers softly as he grabs my hand.

"Do you know now that your relationship status has nothing to do with your self-worth?" I nod.

"Even though Vince makes me feel loved and desired, I know that I still have to work through my insecurities."

"And you're going to have to do that on your own. Vincent can't make you love yourself. He can love you as much as he wants, but that does no good if you don't love yourself first." Tears well up in my eyes and I look down.

"I'm getting there. Every time I think I've achieved it, a conflict reminds me that I haven't yet."

"Give me a recent event that made you realize that."

"A couple of weeks ago, our lawyer approached me with a prenuptial agreement." Reverend Lockhart raises his eyebrows.

"And what are the conditions of that?" He looks at Vince.

"If I were to ever divorce her, she would have more stake in our company than I" Vince says.

"So, Madeline, what is the problem with that?"

"I just felt that a prenup indicated that one day we would get divorced. I overreacted."

"I am no businessman, but I do know that when there is a lot of money involved, steps must be taken to ensure that no one loses their shirt in the event of a divorce. You shouldn't see that as a doorway to divorce."

"I know that now."

"You two knew each other only three months before getting engaged, correct?" We both nod.

"What's the rush?"

"It took a week to fall in love with this woman, Reverend. I knew that I would never find anyone like her again" Vince answers.

"And were you afraid that if you didn't propose she would leave?"

"No, that wasn't it. I wanted her to know that I was ready to commit to her, and after she was kidnapped...I..."Vince's voice breaks and I squeeze his hand.

"Take your time." He sniffles.

"I went through hell when she was kidnapped. My whole life would have fallen apart if I had lost her. I never felt that way in my life...ever. Never needed a woman as much as I need her."

"Why do you need her, Vincent?"

"She makes me feel whole. I always knew something was missing, but I filled that void with possessions, work and sexual encounters."

"So, I'm assuming then, you two have engaged in a sexual relationship." My cheeks grow hot with embarrassment.

"Why does that matter?" Vince asks.

"Because you've said yourself that you used sex to fill your emotional void. No one changes overnight." Vince looks down.

"You're right."

"And when did you two first engage in that?" I blush even more.

"The day after we met…" I say quietly. He puts down his pen. "Madeline Davis, I'm surprised at you. Were you that emotionally traumatized that you had sex with a man the day after you met him?"

"I know it speaks everything against my upbringing…"

"It most certainly does. Now, I'm not here to preach to you but it seems to me that you two have a lot of work to do if you're going to get married. You cannot let sex be the only defining point in your relationship…"

"It's not!" Vince says, exasperated.

"But it is a big part. Lust is a huge monster, and if you two slept with each other the day after you met, that means both of you thought with your loins before your heart. Look, I have no doubt that you two are in love, but both of you have emotional issues that you need to deal with."

"I know…" I say.

"I have a challenge for you both. For two weeks, I want you to abstain. If you need to sleep separately in order to do that, so be it. Work on yourselves and getting to know each other inside out." Vince and I look at each other.

"If you two can do that, I will sign off on your marriage."

"I guess it is a good time for me to go back to New York and finish my move here" Vince says. Reverend Lockhart nods in agreement.

"Madeline, I suggest that you use this time to see a therapist about your confidence issues. I will be back Saturday after next. Work on yourselves, work on your relationship and we'll see where we are." He gets up and I hug him tightly. He shakes Vince's hand and we walk him out to the elevator.

Chapter 35 *Time Apart*

"Sir..." The stewardess interrupts my thoughts.

"Yes?" I answer.

"We're about to land. Buckle your safety belt please." I nod and snap the belt across my waist. I can't believe that Madeline's minister suggested that we abstain from sex. I guess he's right, though. We spent the first two weeks of our relationship making love all over the place. Maybe we do need to make sure that we can survive without it.

I exit the airport and see Lou waiting for me with a big smile on his face. I sure have missed this guy.

"Mr. Marks!" He says happily as we shake hands.

"How's it going Lou?" I ask with a grin.

"Great now that you're back. I've been bored" He laughs.

"I'll bet it was a nice vacation from me though..."

"Never." He opens the door and I slide into the back of my Porsche.

A few hours later, I'm back in the New York office and am pounded with friendly greetings. I didn't realize how much they missed me, or how much I missed them. I know that this transition will be hard for everyone. I go to my window and look out at the city which is bustling as always. I will miss the fast paced life of the city, but I know that it is time for me to settle down. Home will be where my girl is.

I sit at my desk and call Alexis in. She steps in, her long brown hair swinging at her waist.

"You called, Mr. Marks?"

"Yes...have a seat." I gesture to the chair and she sits.

"Alexis...I'm sure you've already heard that I am transferring to Atlanta." She nods.

"I'm going to miss you..."

"As I you, but just know that you will remain head executive assistant no matter what. Your family is here, but if you ever want a change, there will always be an office in Atlanta with your name on it." She smiles.

"I think that I would be better off here, Mr. Marks. These past two years have been amazing. You've been the best boss I've ever had, and I hope that I receive a wedding invitation."

"Of course you will. You keep everything running here, and I'm glad you're staying. I will be giving control of this office to Ryan Lowe, my partner. Take good care of him."

"You know I will."

After several conversations, some of which ended in an agreement to transfer with me, I am exhausted. I take in the quiet of my office and realize that I miss Madeline. Looking at my phone to check the time, I decide to call her.

"Davis" She answers.

"Madeline..."

"Hey! How is New York?"

"Same as always...busy." She laughs.

"Well, I have some news for you."

"Oh?"

"We have gotten a proposition to build an office in London." My eyebrows raise.

"Really? How did you pull that off?"

"Well, our merger with MedInc has the pharmaceutical companies' attention, and I received a call from the CEO of Valley Pharmaceuticals. They want a partnership with us which would include a branch in London as well as exclusive rights to their medical technology."

"Who is this guy?"

"His name is Jacob Benjamin." God, my rival in college. I didn't realize he was a CEO now.

"Small world. I graduated with him."

"You did?"

"Yes, and we did not like each other. I'll arrange a meeting with him later this week."

"Vince this could be very big for us. Our technicians could work better if they were given access to that technology."

"I know. I'll talk to him casually and we'll all meet when I get back to Atlanta. All business aside, though, how are you doing with this…abstaining thing?" She giggles.

"I miss you being here, but I can see why Reverend Lockhart felt it was necessary. Do you feel the same way?"

"In a sense, yes, but nothing will prove to me that you're not the one, baby, even blue balls." She sighs.

"Same here. I love you very much."

"I love you too, baby. I'll call you later tonight unless you have plans…"

"Actually, I need you to be on speaker tonight. I'm meeting with the wedding planner."

"You don't want to wait until we finish this experiment?"

"Well, we're not going to dishonor it since you decided to go to New York for two weeks." She laughs.

"I guess you're right, okay, what time?"

"Seven-thirty."

"I will call in." she giggles with happiness. I love it when she laughs, it always comforts me.

"I'll talk to you then…" she says.

"Can't wait…" we hang up and I get ready to leave the office. Suddenly, I have an idea as I pass Alexis' desk.

"Alexis…forward all calls to my cell. I'm going out of town for a few days."

"Already?!" she looks shocked.

"Not back to Atlanta yet, calm down. I'm going to see my family." She smiles.

"Would you like me to arrange your travel?"

"Yes, I'm going to Ithaca first to see my sister for the day and then to Connecticut to see the rest of my family. Arrange a flight for first thing in the morning." She nods.

"And...how long will you be staying in Connecticut?"

"Until Sunday. We'll videoconference every morning."

"Got it."

"Thank you, Alexis."

"You're welcome, Mr. Marks, have a good night and safe trip."

"Good night." I head out and decide that if I'm going to spend time apart from Madeline, then I might as well catch up with family and friends. I also need to get my groomsmen together since Madeline has gone ahead and hired a wedding planner. As I get into the back of the car, I call Gus.

"Muchacho!" He answers.

"Hey Gus, guess who's back in New York?"

"You're here? I thought you already made Atlanta your permanent home" he laughs.

"Well, I have to take care of some business here. I know it's short notice, but do you think you can get the crew together say about nine?"

"Hell yeah! We can do it at my place."

"Perfect. I'll see you then."

"Adios." He hangs up and I call my sister to let her know I'm coming for a visit. She squeals and tells me she'll take the day off from her classes to spend time with me. I refrain from telling my parents as I would like it to be a surprise.

Getting out of the car into the bitter January cold, I rush into my building so that I will be ready to speak with this wedding planner. I turn my key in the lock and see Mrs. Lovett standing there with a big smile.

"Mr. Marks!" She hugs me tightly.

"Mrs. L..." I hug her back.

"I stayed a little late to cook you dinner, I hope you don't mind."

"Not at all." I smile.

"I made stuffed peppers for you and there's some if you want lunch tomorrow."

"Sadly, I won't be here for long. I'm going to see my family." She nods.

"How is Ms. Davis?" She asks as she sits my plate on the kitchen island.

"She's well. We are getting married in June." She nearly drops the wine glass in her hand and sets it down carefully.

"Oh my God! I'm so....speechless!" She pulls me in an aggressive hug which knocks the air out of my lungs.

"Thank you..." I gasp after she lets me go.

"So this means that you are moving to Atlanta?" she asks as she pours me a glass of wine.

"Yes...but I assure you that you will not lose your job. I intend to keep this place."

"I had no worry about that, Mr. Marks, but I'm going to miss you."

"No need, I'll be up here frequently..." She serves me the plate and glass of wine. I eat, relishing in the fact that the woman is a damn good cook. She sits down on the other side of the table.

"Have some?" I offer. She shakes her head.

"I had one before you came, but I wanted to talk to you. You have several messages from a woman named Charlene Hendricks." I drop my fork in surprise. Yet another ghost from my past: a scary ghost.

"Did she say what she wanted?" Mrs. Lovett shakes her head.

"I'll call her...eventually." I'm secretly wondering what she wants. We haven't talked in years. Charlene was my so-called girlfriend in college. I wasn't really invested in it, but loved fucking her. When we graduated, she pressured me to propose and I said no. She got angry and I never saw her again. I'm shocked she found me.

"Do me a favor. If she calls again...give her my cell number." Mrs. Lovett looks up in surprise.

"Are you sure?"

"I'm sure."

After a painful call with the wedding coordinator and Madeline's frustration at me for putting all of the decisions on her, I'm thankful to have a couple of drinks with my crew. I take the elevator to Gus and Emily's apartment, hoping I won't get ribbed too much for my recent engagement. Emily opens the door after I knock, looking like she and Gus have been busy in the bedroom. Donned in an old t-shirt and a pair of Gus' shorts, she blushes when she sees me.

"Vince..." She gives me a hug and I idly notice the smell of Gus' signature cologne all over her. That man is a machine; though, that was one of our commonalities. We practically had to time share our apartment because we spent so much time getting laid.

"Hey Emily, am I the first one here?"

"You are...Gus got a little...preoccupied." Preoccupied my ass. She should definitely know I don't believe that because they've been caught more than a few times in throes of passion.

"I know how it goes, Emily." She blushes even more. Gus comes out shirtless. Jeez that's the last thing I need to see.

"Do I...uh...need to come back later?" I say as Emily goes into the kitchen.

"Nonsense...we were just in the shower...er...I mean I was just in the shower" says Gus gesturing me to sit down. As he turns to head to the laundry room, I notice that his back is covered in red scratches. He comes out with a t-shirt on and Emily hands him two glasses of scotch.

"You guys have fun..." she says as she retreats to the back of their apartment. Gus gives me the glass and sits down.

"Man, your back looks like you had a fight with a cat." I laugh.

"I did." He grins and I shake my head.

"Nice, real nice, man." I roll my eyes and take a sip of scotch as I hear pounding on the door. Gus gets up to answer it and is almost tackled by five of our best friends. They look over at me and call my name in unison as they come over. I get up and greet each of them: Kendall, Ray, Ryan, Charles and Brandon.

"Where's the alcohol, man?!" Kendall asks Gus giving him a hard hit on the back. Gus winces.

"Keep your shirt on…" Gus says as he heads to the kitchen.

"Yeah, I wish you would have done that when I got here…" I tease.

"Fuck you!" he laughs as everyone sits down. Ray brings out a bottle of Remy Martin and hands it to me.

"For you, man. Congratulations on your engagement."

"Thanks!" I take the bottle as Gus comes out with a case of beer and bottle of scotch. Everyone digs in and selects their poison.

"So, when's the wedding, man? You know I need stuff years in advance" Charles asks. Charles is head pediatrician at one of the largest children's hospitals in the state.

"June 26th, and I would like all of you to be by my side."

"Of course, Vince, we'll be there" says Ryan.

"And we're going to throw you a hell of a bachelor party!" Kendall exclaims. I roll my eyes.

"No strippers…" I warn. They all look at me, dumbfounded.

"You're joking, right?" Brandon says.

"I promised Madeline. We can get drunk and go to the club or whatever, but no strippers."

"It'll still be a hell of a bachelor party!" Kendall declares. Of course I know this, Kendall owns several nightclubs in New York, Atlanta and Miami. If nothing else, he knows how to throw a party.

"So, tell us about the girl…" Brandon inquires.

"What can I say? She's the woman that made your boy turn to a one woman man" I reply.

"Beautiful girl. You did well my friend" Ryan says.

"She must have fucked you good!" Kendall laughs.

"Not that it's any of your business, but let me say this: if I could do it all day long I would." They all break out into laughter.

"You better get ready to kiss that goodbye after your honeymoon" Charles says. Everyone looks his way.

"Who says?" Gus asks.

"You're a freak of nature Gus. Just because you and Emily fuck everywhere doesn't mean everyone will." Charles glares at him.

"Yes, I am, and Emily loves it so much it makes her scream…loudly." I narrow my eyes.

"Gus!" Emily warns from the bedroom.

"You know it's true, baby!" he yells back with a stupid grin on his face. We all hear her scoff.

I look at my friend, and imagine Madeline and me sharing our lives together. I could picture it. Her laughing with her friends, sipping wine in the living room of the house I'm looking at. Me, maybe bringing the guys down for a visit. Children, family and love. It seems like it would be a great life.

"TMI…" says Brandon as we all laugh.

"Oh, get off your high horses. Charles, you're telling me with that hot model you have in your bed every night, you don't hit that?" Charles shrugs at Kendall's question.

"Not every night…"

"Why the hell not?!" Gus' tone reeking of disbelief.

"We get busy...she travels...when she comes home she's not in the mood. Besides, that's not why I married her." We all gape at him.

"Why did you then?" Ray asks, taking a long swig out of his beer bottle.

"Because I love her, man, why else?" Charles was always modest about his sex life. His whole thing was all romance, flowers and jewelry. I always wondered if that was a front.

"Don't worry about that, Vince. I'm sure Madeline will keep you satisfied for the rest of your life." Gus looks at me.

"And you...don't give him cold feet, brother." Ryan looks at Charles who shakes his head and drinks the amber liquid in his glass.

"I don't think this one is gonna get cold feet. It took forever for him to find the one." Ryan nudges me.

"I didn't think there would be one for me, but she is a perfect fit...in every way" I smile grandly knowing Gus will get a kick out of my inappropriate statement.

"That's what I'm talking about!" Gus slaps my back.

"Aw man, not you too. Hey listen, dude, you guys keep talking like that and Emily is gonna close up on Gus" Charles turns his attention towards Gus.

"She wouldn't be able to go without it..." Gus jokes. At that moment we hear footsteps and Emily comes into the living room with her hands on her hips. Dressed in dark jeans and a fitted maroon sweater, she looks more put together than when I first came in.

"Uh-oh!" Kendall warns.

"I know that you guys find our sex lives interesting but can you please not get him going?" She looks at us with laughter in her eyes.

"Oh, come on, baby..." In one move, he pulls her into his lap, kissing her with an audible smooch.

"Well…uh I think maybe we should let these two be alone…"Ray says. Emily gives Gus a pat on his cheek and hastily slides off his lap.

"Nonsense, Ray. I wouldn't dream of interrupting your boy talk." She smiles.

"Hang out with us…" I request. No one would know it, but Emily and I are pretty close. When Gus was going through hell with his family and distanced himself from everyone, we teamed up to get him straight again. I look at her now in admiration, he struggled so hard and she stuck by him. Only I had been aware of their plans to elope, and never spoke of it, not even after seven years. I make a mental note to tell Madeline that story; she'd be fascinated by it.

"Ha! Gus needs his guy time and I…well need my girl time." She grabs her purse off the breakfast bar and blows a kiss at us as Gus' security guy, Thomas walks in the door. Hey surveys us carefully.

"Evening, gentlemen." He says in that stiff manner of his. We all respond with murmurs of greetings.

"Hey!" Gus gets up and grabs Emily's hand.

"Can't wait until you get home…" She laughs.

"You are such a…"she shakes her head and kisses him tenderly before waving to us as she follows Thomas out of the door.

"So…I have something to tell you all…when I got home, I had a few phone messages from Charlene…" They all pause and look at me.

"Charlene? Like, *the* Charlene?" Gus asks. I nod.

"What does she want?" Ray asks.

"I have no idea. You guys didn't give her my number did you?"

"Hell no! I'm trying to marry you off, man!" Gus says.

"I haven't heard from her in years…" Ryan muses.

"Well, I talk to her every once in a while…"Brandon says. We all turn our heads towards him.

"What? I didn't give out your number…but I did tell her where you were working."

"For what?" I demand.

"She asked! Besides, man. Have you seen yourself in the tabloids lately?"

"You could have said no."

"Man, don't you think that's a skeleton in the closet that you need to bring out before you get married?"

"No, Brandon I don't!" Gus refills my glass begging me to take a sip so that I will calm down. I take a long sip, realizing that Brandon is not at fault here.

"Well, she's called now, so just call her back. You don't want any trouble, and you definitely don't want her finding Madeline" He says.

"What does she want, Brandon?" I give him an icy stare.

"She wants to bury the hatchet."

"There is no hatchet! She tried to make me marry her by pretending she was pregnant!"

"I'm assuming she wants forgiveness. Just call her man, maybe she needs it to move on." I scoff.

"Unbelievable, it's been over fourteen years since that happened." I shake my head and finish my drink.

Feeling a little drunk a few hours later, I turn my key in the lock of my apartment. Maybe this is a good time to purge my demons. I pick up the phone and call Madeline.

"Hello?" she answers sleepily.

"Madeline…" I slur.

"Vince? Are you drunk?" She seems amused.

"A little bit."

"What's wrong?"

"I have something to tell you." Her breathing becomes shaky.

"Well, out with it."

"I…have a ghost from my past that I thought was long gone, but it has popped up again."

"A ghost." She repeats, her voice more alert.

"Her name is Charlene. We dated in college, and she's been calling my apartment."

"You're telling me that you seriously dated someone and you didn't tell me?!"

"It was not serious to me…."

"Vince…I have heard you say this twice. You need to evaluate how you deal with women" her stone cold tone reflects that of Reverend Lockhart.

"I know."

"So, what is the story with this one?"

"We messed around in college…when we graduated, she wanted me to marry her and I wouldn't…so she faked a pregnancy."

"And?" her tone is demanding, hard. It almost reminds me of how she handles herself at the office.

"And it was a big mess…our parents got involved and she was dragged to the doctor's office where they confirmed it was not true. I never spoke to her again, but now she's been calling the house in New York." She sighs.

"Vincent Marks, I'm going to say this once and hope I never have to tell you this again. While you are in New York, you need to confront every skeleton and every ghost in your life. I refuse to marry you until you do so. The whole shit with Dina fucked me up! I will not go through that again! I will take over your duties at work while you do it, but you need to fix whatever it is you did to whatever woman you did it to." I never expected to hear that from her.

"Madeline…" I start.

"This is something I will not compromise on, Vince. You fail to realize that women are emotional creatures. Sex is not a game! It's intimate! Haven't you learned that with me? Haven't you felt the emotional connection when we make love? Vince, every time you make love to me, it's so intense…don't you feel it?"

"I do…" I admit. The truth was that I never felt the way I do when Madeline and I are intimate. I lose myself every time I'm inside of her. The others were just nights of absent fucking.

"So, how do you think these women felt when you were fucking them for months and then suddenly decide to find another toy to play with? If it takes me holding back on you until we get married for you to understand that, I will gladly do it." Her statement shocks me sober, God help me if this woman refuses to fuck me.

"Madeline…I never meant to deceive you. I just wanted a new beginning. I didn't think it would come back and bite me on the ass."

"Why did you think it wouldn't? There are consequences to everything! God!" she huffs in frustration.

"I never thought…" I start to tremble.

"That's right, you never thought. You were mindlessly fucking up the lives of the women you were involved with. I'm telling you now, fix this and don't call me until you do!" she snaps before hanging up. I lean back on the couch, the haze of the liquor coming back. I am in big trouble, but I know she's right. If I don't want to have a repeat of what Dina and Joseph did to Madeline, I am going to have put my pride aside. I look at the phone and notice it's just after eleven. Staring at the many messages Mrs. Lovett placed on the table, I pick up the one with Charlene's number. I take a deep breath and dial it.

"Hello?" I hear the familiar voice and a flood of memories come back to me.

"Charlene?"

"Yes? Who is this?"

"It's Vince…" she's shocked into silence.

"I've been calling you…"she sounds tearful.

"I know, I've been out of town for a while."

"Your housekeeper told me. Are you...coming to Connecticut any time soon?"

"I will be there the day after tomorrow."

"Listen, I know there is some bad blood between us" she starts. I shush her.

"Fourteen years ago...what's in the past is in the past."

"Still...if you will see me, I need to talk to you."

"I will call you when I get to Connecticut." I hear her take in a shaky breath.

"Thank you. I will see you then." She hangs up and I wonder what she wants. Could there have possibly been a child? Did her parents lie to us? I do not need this now. I get up and shed my clothes, tossing them in a nearby laundry basket. Looking at my bed, I notice how lonely it looks. I've spent four months sleeping beside my beautiful fiancée, and now, it will be a long two weeks without her. I hope she will know that every effort I make on this trip is for her, to show her that I've changed. I wanted her trust, needed it and I would gain it.

Chapter 36 *The Mask Comes Off*

Dr. Lisa Wilder is a very attractive woman: her mocha face is framed by a wild mane of natural hair and her brown eyes shine through a pair of Chanel glasses.

"Hello, Madeline!" she greets me cheerfully.

"Hello, Dr. Wilder..." I smile at her.

"Have a seat." She gestures toward the big red leather couch and I sit, nervous about sharing my life with a complete stranger.

"So, tell me why you're here..." she gets out a tablet and stylus.

"Well...I'm about to get married..."

"I read, Congratulations!" she grins.

"Thank you...and well...I have some insecurities that I need to work through."

"Okay...so tell me about the things that started this insecurity."

"I...haven't been the best at relationships."

"Why do you say that?"

"Every relationship I've had ends without me knowing why they dumped me. It just seems like all of a sudden, I'm no longer relevant. Then they go on and marry someone or get into this relationship that is just great and I'm left alone..."my voice breaks.

"Do you think that something is wrong with you?" she asks.

"Sometimes..."

"Did you ever stop to think that maybe you're not the problem?"

"What do you mean?"

"I mean that you have been a strong, independent woman who knows what she wants. You own a company, correct?" I nod.

"A lot of men are not at the emotional maturity necessary to handle that unless they are truly in love with you…tell me about your fiancé."

"He's the CEO of our company. Young, successful…and I know he loves me."

"But?"

"But, his past is coming back to haunt him."

"How so?"

"He has a history of being promiscuous and using women." She looks up.

"And you're okay with this?"

"He completely changed when I met him. I was kidnapped by his ex and he came through in ways no one has ever come through for me." She nods with understanding.

"So why are you still insecure? He's asked you to marry him. What more do you need?"

"I honestly believe that I am going to wake up and he will be gone." She cocks her head.

"Has he given you any indication that will be the case?"

"No…"

"When you first met, how did it go?"

"He invited me to a benefit and we had a great time. The next day he was in my hotel room and we…"

"Yes?"

"We made love for the first time."

"You let your guard down quick." She observes.

"I was filled with so much need and want. It was a driving force."

"At any time did you feel like you were forced to have sex with him?"

"No, never."

"So sex aside, what is the appeal?"

"He is the only man who has shown me that he is fully committed. There's nothing I can't tell him and vice versa. Of course, being engaged so quickly we have to learn to be together."

"What do you call 'quickly'?

"Three months…" I look down.

"Why are you ashamed of that?"

"I'm not, it's just I get raised eyebrows every time I say it."

"Madeline, when are you going to admit to yourself that you care too much about what people think?" I look up.

"How can I not care? All eyes are on me…"

"Of course, but you cannot make decisions based on what everyone thinks. Tell me something, when you make an executive decision, does everyone like it?"

"No…"

"But you do it anyway because that is what's best for your company. You need to stop trying to please everyone and do what's best for you. So what if you slept with your boss? So what if you're marrying him? It is your life and you make choices as you see fit. No one: not your parents, not your fiancé, not your friends or co-workers have a right to tell you what you are doing wrong." Tears sting my eyes and she takes my hand.

"I think a big part of your insecurity is that you have lived life worrying about everyone else. It is your life. If you want to marry this man, marry him and live the rest of your life in marital bliss. Run your company like you want to run it. Be the woman you want to be."

"How do I even begin to break that cycle? I've been doing it my whole life."

"You break it today. Yes, you have a past. He has a past. But part of marriage is beginning a new life together, a clean slate. You will never move forward if you keep taking steps backwards." She makes a lot of sense.

"You are worthy of having the life you want…until you believe that, you will continue to be insecure." I start to sob, knowing that she's right. She hands me a tissue and I take it gratefully.

"I guess I just always thought I was meant to be alone, unhappy…"

"And this man is proving you wrong. What do you have with him that you love the most?"

"I love the fact that he believes in me, that he would do anything to protect me."

"There it is. The fact that this man changed his ways because he had feelings for you proves so much. It is hard to change a man who plays games with women. He wouldn't risk asking you to marry him unless he was being serious. Believe that he loves you and whatever he does is for your benefit. I read in your referral that you are taking a two week break. I would love to see both of you after that break." I nod.

"We'll do that."

"Well, Madeline, it was nice to meet you. I'm looking forward to working with you both." She gets up and shakes my hand.

"Of course you care too much about what people think! I could have told you that for half the money…" Nathan says over drinks that night.

"I'm already paying you enough to handle my premarital affairs…" I tease. He scoffs.

"Baby, I didn't charge you half what I would charge some gold digging slut." We both laugh.

"So, how are you doing with the abstinence?" I sigh.

"It's…been hard…"

"I bet he's been hard too" he interrupts.

"Nathan!" I scold playfully.

"What? You left that one wide open!" I shake my head.

"Well, it's the only way my pastor will marry us. It's easier with him being in New York. I don't think we would make it otherwise."

"Oh, so it's like that?" He stares at me.

"None of your business…"I take a sip and wink at him as he laughs heartily.

Later that night, I start to miss Vince and am reeling with regret at my outburst. I wasn't wrong, though. He needs to deal with his past actions, and I…well I need to figure out how to start loving myself. It's been a long time coming, I guess. I toss and turn, missing the heat of Vince's body next to mine. Morally and biblically wrong or not, I missed him making love to me. The thought of his strong thrusts as he looked lovingly into my eyes makes my body hot with desire. It wasn't just a sexual act to me, it was amazingly intimate, and I love it.

The next morning, after a sleepless night, I sit in my office willing myself to stay awake. Lacy knocks on my door gently and I signal for her to come in. Her face twists into a curious look when she sees me.

"Are you okay, Madeline?" She asks.

"I'm fine, I just…need sleep."

"Why don't you telecommute today?"

"I can't…"

"Why can't you?"

"There's so much to do."

"Nonsense!" She narrows her eyes at me.

"Lacy…I just can't…with Vince being out of the office I can't be." She huffs.

"Well, you need to start sleeping then." I put my head in my hands and Lacy sits down in the chair across from me.

"You want to talk about it?" she asks gently.

"Not really."

"Well, whatever is going on, it'll be fine" she says. I want to believe her, but a part of me wonders if Vince is going to fix his issues. It worries me that he hasn't reached out to me. I hope he's just honoring my wishes.

"I hope so, Lacy…" She gets up.

"Why don't I go pick us up a couple of mochas?"

314

"That sounds great..." I manage a small smile. She leaves out of my office swiftly as my phone rings.

"Madeline Davis..." I answer.

"Madeline..."Vince's voice sounds husky.

"Vince..."

"Don't talk...I just want you to listen."

"Okay. I'm listening."

"I went to see Charlene in Connecticut. It wasn't what you think...she seems to think she's suffering from a bit of karma from our situation fourteen years ago. She and her husband have been unable to have a baby. She felt the need to apologize and clear the air."

"Vince..."

"Shh...you were right. I do need to work through my shit and I intend to do that. But I need you to know something: I fucking love you. If it takes the rest of my life to prove that to you, I will." He grows silent.

"I love you too, Vince." It seems to be the only thing I can say in response to his overwhelming declaration.

"I'm spending the rest of the week in Connecticut with my family...so that I can work through my past, but I can't do that if I'm not able to talk to you."

"You don't have to...just showing me that you're putting in the effort is enough." He breathes a sigh of relief and I close my eyes feeling better than I have these past two days.

The next Saturday morning, I'm busy tidying up the condo in preparation for Reverend Lockhart's return as well as Vince's. I have missed him so much, and am looking forward to spending time with him again. Faith happily follows me around, turning her head in curiosity as I run the vacuum across the area rugs and toss laundry in the dryer. As I'm turning on the dishwasher, I hear keys turn in the lock and my heart leaps. Vince walks in with a grand smile that reaches those beautiful hazel eyes. It takes everything I have not to jump into his arms. Instead, I walk over and give him a passionate kiss. He wraps his arms around me, deepening his kiss, his tongue massaging mine.

"I missed you" I whisper, breathing in the delicious scent of him as I hug him tightly.

"Oh, you have no idea how much I missed you" he replies. For a moment, time seems to stop and I close my eyes, thankful that he is back home. Just as our hands start to explore each other, the intercom lights up.

"Ms. Davis, there is a Reverend Lockhart here to see you?" a deep male voice says. I go over and push the button.

"Send him up, please" I answer. We attempt to get ourselves together as a soft knock graces my door. I open it and Reverend Lockhart walks in with that warm smile as Vince takes Faith to the bedroom.

"Madeline!" he hugs me.

"Reverend Lockhart. It's good to see you" I coo as I gesture for him to sit down.

"Would you like something to drink?" I ask.

"Water would be good, Madeline." I scurry to the kitchen and retrieve a bottle of water from the refrigerator. After handing him the bottle, Vince and I sit hand in hand on the couch.

"Well, tell me about the past two weeks" he asks after taking a seat.

"I think we've both done some growing" Vince says taking my hand.

"Really?"

"I dealt with some past demons in New York…and Connecticut."

"What compelled you to do that?"

"Well, Madeline got upset with me after another old flame popped up…" Reverend Lockhart looks at me.

"Madeline, why did you get upset?"

"Because I didn't want a repeat of what happened four months ago." He nods with understanding.

"And what did you learn?"

"I finally understand that I haven't been the best when it comes to my relationships with women, so I spent time apologizing to those I've hurt."

"Did they accept your apologies?"

"Most of them did, some said it wasn't necessary."

"Madeline? How did your session with Dr. Wilder go?"

"It was eye opening to say the least. She was honest with me about my issues and we're going to take steps to change that." He smiles again.

"So, once we took the sexual relationship with you two out of the equation, how do you feel about each other?"

"I...know now that this is real" Vince says.

"How did you determine that?"

"It was a couple of days after I left, and Madeline told me not to call her until I fixed my issue. I quickly found out that I couldn't go a day without hearing her voice."

"Interesting...Madeline, what do you think about that?"

"I felt the same way. I missed him so much." Rev. Lockhart closes his notepad.

"Well, for these next six months, I want you both to continue working with each other. Get the rest of your affairs in order. Tell me, what is a general plan for your future?"

"Well, we're looking for a house. That's the first step" Vince says.

"What do you both see in ...say the next five years?" Vince looks over at me.

"I see a home, maybe some children, travel, and the growth of our company" I say.

"Vince?"

"Honestly? I see the same things, but I'm...a little nervous about children."

"Why do you say that?"

"It just wasn't anything I ever considered until I met Madeline, but I fear my son will be a jerk like me or my daughter will be hurt by a jerk like me." Reverend Lockhart chuckles.

"Vince, I think you have redeemed yourself enough that you will be able to teach your son or daughter how a woman should be treated. It is obvious that you love Madeline very much…and that love will be what conceives your children, raises your family, and grows your business." I smile grandly and hook my arm through Vince's.

"So, Reverend, are we good enough for you to marry us?" I ask.

"I will be more than happy to marry you two. June 26th correct?" We both nod.

"It is now officially on my calendar. I look forward to helping you two start your journey together as a married couple." He finishes his water and gets up to throw it in the trash. I unlink myself from Vince and give Reverend Lockhart a tight hug, thanking him for what he's done for us.

Chapter 37 *Settling the Score*

On Monday, I sit at my desk, humming with nervous energy as I try to go over the expense reports with Vince.

"You're off today. What's on your mind?" He asks.

"His trial is coming up..." I say quietly. Vince pulls up a chair next to mine and takes my hand.

"I know, but, actually I'm glad that it is so that we can put it behind us before we get married." Maybe he's right. I was secretly hoping the bastard would plead guilty. After all, he was caught red handed. However, he found a lawyer who thinks he can get away with an insanity plea. Yeah, he's insane alright, but his ass needs to stay in prison. Now Lacy and I will have to testify.

"Why don't you take next week off? You don't know how long you'll have to testify."

"Oh, Vince, I'm already taking time off for our honeymoon..."

"When are you going to get used to the idea that you are the boss, here?" He scoffs.

"Never." He scoots closer to me.

"You have to. Besides, had it not been for you he could have taken this company under. You deserve all the time off that you need." I shake my head.

"Hey..." he caresses my face and kisses me with tenderness. I smile at his attempt to cheer me up.

"Okay, get out of here. I have work to do." He gets up.

"I'll see you in a bit. I have a surprise for you." I laugh. What could he possibly do now?

A few hours later, I get into the passenger side of Vince's car, exhausted and terribly stressed.

"Relax, baby..." he says observing the look on my face.

"I'll be fine." I force a grin as he cranks up the car. We head up the highway but I notice he's going further than the condo.

"Where are we going?" I ask.

"You'll see." He frustrates me when he says this. After a few more minutes of driving, Vince pulls into a small neighborhood. I look around curiously as he pulls up to a huge house.

"Come on…" he turns off the car and gets out. I step down on the concrete and look around.

"Well? What do you think?" he takes my hand.

"It's beautiful…"

"It's ours." I gasp.

"It's ours?!" He nods.

"Come on." He leads me inside. The house is absolutely gorgeous with new hardwood floors, full dining room, luxurious kitchen and five bedrooms upstairs. I look around in wonder.

"I'm speechless…" I laugh imagining Vince and I living here as a family.

"Well!" a female voice comes out of nowhere as a petite lady with caramel skin and wildly curly hair walks inside the house. Vince smiles and shakes her hand.

"Carol. This is my fiancée, Madeline."

"It's nice to finally meet you! How do you like the house?" she asks with a grin.

"I love it."

"Perfect! Mr. Marks, the inspection came back today and we're ready to close this week. You can probably move soon. Whoa. This is going so fast.

"I'm sorry…I'm just a little shocked" I explain my silence.

"That's perfectly fine. It is a lovely house. Why don't we sign the paperwork soon? Do you need to work on getting a mortgage?"

"Are you crazy? My accountant will draw up a check for you once the paperwork is signed." Vince eyes her seriously. Now it is her time to be shocked.

"You're paying cash?"

"Of course. Here's her card if you want to verify our finances." She takes it from him, dazed by his confidence.

"Well...I'll leave you two to explore your new home. Mr. Marks, I'll be in touch." She smiles and disappears as quickly as she came.

"Oh Vince!" I jump into his arms. He laughs and looks at me.

"There's that smile I love..." he kisses me deeply. The next week, I sit nervously in the courthouse as I wait to be called in to testify. Detective Sommers sits with me, and I'm glad he's there to comfort me.

"All you have to do is tell the truth, Madeline. Don't let his lawyer sway you." I nod nervously as a police officer comes out of the door.

"Ms. Davis?" He gestures for me to come in. I walk slowly in the crowded courtroom and am blinded by the flash of cameras aimed at me. I take my place on the stand, my anxiety leaving me breathless. The prosecutor, Adam Griffin, steps close to the stand.

"Ms. Davis, what do you remember about September 15th?" I clear my throat.

"I was in Los Angeles at my fiancée's home, and had gone outside to smoke a cigarette. I felt a hard blow to my head..." I try my best not to look at the hard face staring me down from the defendant's table. Adam paces as he continues.

"What is the next thing you remember?"

"I remember being in some sort of vehicle, but I kept feeling drowsy..."

"Did you feel an injection in your arm?"

"Yes, a few times."

"Did you see your assailants at this time?"

"No, they were masked, but...I could hear their voices."

"Did you recognize them?"

"No."

"What happened once the van stopped, Ms. Davis?"

"I woke up in a warehouse of some sorts. At first I was blindfolded..." my voice breaks.

"Take your time..." the judge says gently.

"The blindfold was taken off and a man in a mask approached me."

"Now, Ms. Davis, did he reveal himself to you?" I nod.

"He did..."

"And who was it under that mask?"

"Joseph Dent..." the courtroom erupts in murmurs and the judge bangs his gavel.

"And what did he do to you?"

"He...hit me with a leather belt, called me names, and insulted me." I swallow hard.

"Ms. Davis, were you wearing clothing?"

"I...was wearing underwear at first."

"At first?"

"After he got done hitting me the first time, he stripped off my bra and panties." The courtroom murmurs again.

"Ms. Davis, to your knowledge did he sexually assault you?"

"He tried..."

"Explain what happened."

"He...got on top of me and tried to..."

"Tried to what?"

"He tried to rape me...I kept fighting as hard as I could until the police came."

"What was Dina Andrews' involvement in this process?" he asks.

"She was just egging him on. She never really touched me besides throwing her shoe at me."

"No further questions, your Honor. Thank you Ms. Davis." The judge looks to Joseph's lawyer: a short, fat balding man with a scowl. He gets up from the table.

"Ms. Davis, have you ever lusted for someone?"

"Objection!" Adam yells.

"Your honor, if I am to prove that this man had a moment of temporary insanity because of his feelings for Ms. Davis, then she must answer the question" the lawyer says.

"Overruled..." the judge says.

"Yes, I suppose I have."

"And have you ever found yourself doing unusual things because of your lust for that person?"

"Who hasn't?" He approaches the stand.

"Things like participating in BDSM?" I gasp.

"Objection!" Adam yells again.

"Sustained. Move on, counselor!" The judge glares at him.

"I'll remove that question. Ms. Davis, did you know that Mr. Dent had feelings for you?"

"Well, he always flirted...but..."

"Yes or no?"

"No." Where is he going with this?

"Even after the incident last Christmas?" He must be talking about when Joseph groped me at our company Christmas party.

"He was drunk, so...no I didn't know even then."

"Ms. Davis, did you engage in an illicit affair with Vincent Marks, the CEO of your company?"

"Objection! Your Honor, what does this have to do with the case?!" Adam yells, exasperated.

"Again, his temporary insanity stemmed from the fact Vincent Marks outbid him when the company was up for sale and, if he had feelings for Ms. Davis, her relationship with Mr. Marks would be his breaking point."

"I'll allow it, but you better go somewhere with this" The judge warns.

"I...started dating him, yes."

"Just dating him or did you have a sexual relationship with him?" I start to breathe heavily and see Joseph's cruel smile.

"Yes, I had a sexual relationship with Vincent Marks. Why does that matter?"

"And when was it made public?"

"It was never made public until now. No one knows what I do in the privacy of my own place." He seems to get frustrated with me and walks to his table to pick up a paper. He slams it down on the stand. It is a picture of Vince and me in my hotel room having one of our most intimate moments. I start to get dizzy.

"Where did you get this?" I ask.

"Ms. Davis, Mr. Dent was so infatuated with you that he installed a feed from your company laptop camera." I start to hyperventilate. This guy was spying on me? Oh my God.

"Ms. Davis before it was made public that you and Mr. Marks were dating, Mr. Dent already knew. You weren't aware of that?"

"No! I wasn't aware of this!" The courtroom murmurs again. His eyes grow wide in surprise.

"You mean to tell me that you never had any suspicion—"His voice grows soft, he must have suspected that I already knew.

"How in the hell was I supposed to know he was spying on me?! Is a person required to assume that in a normal situation?" I shoot back.

"How did you think you were being tracked?" I feel defeated.

"I don't know...I...thought maybe he tracked my phone..." The room spins around me and the lawyer's face begins to grow distorted.

"Ms. Davis?" The judge stands up. I feel dizzy and hold on to the rail before I pass out.

I wake up on a leather couch surrounded by concerned faces.

"Madeline! You okay?" Adam takes my hand and helps me up. The bailiff hands me a glass of water.

"Why? Why didn't anyone tell me?" I gasp.

"We actually assumed you knew. I should have asked, and I'm sorry." He looks regretful.

"Do you know, how fucked up this is? How long was he spying on me?!"

"Madeline..."Detective Sommers looks at me worriedly.

"I want to see..." Everyone looks at each other.

"I don't know if that's a good..." the judge starts.

"I want to see! This man violated my life...my home...let me see, damnit!" I scream. Adam looks at the judge and Detective Sommers.

"Well, you heard the woman" Sommers says. I am handed two thick envelopes.

"This is all of them?"

"We..uh have the video as well..."Adam looks at me nervously. I open the first envelope and see pictures of me in my condo. Totally unaware that a sicko was watching me. On the couch watching TV, eating dinner, undressing in my bedroom. There are even pictures from when I was on different business trips. Most importantly, there are pictures of Vince and I that first time in the hotel room. This guy was sick!

"How long?" I look up at the gentlemen.

"This was over a period of two years, Ms. Davis" the prosecutor says. I shake my head in disbelief.

"Ms. Davis, if you like, we can delay until tomorrow" The judge suggests.

"No..." I get up.

"Let's get this over with today." I shove the photos in Sommers' hands and walk out. The courtroom is still pretty crowded. I give Joseph a scowl as I pass his table. Once the bailiff calls the court to order, Joseph's lawyer approaches me again.

"Ms. Davis, I hope you're okay." I nod silently.

"Ms. Davis, when you were kidnapped, had you ever seen Mr. Dent involved in the behavior you observed that week?"

"No…" I say quietly.

"Did he ever exhibit threatening behavior towards you before that incident?"

"No."

"No more questions, your Honor." He goes to sit down.

"Thank you, Ms. Davis. You may step down" the judge eyes me. I leave the courtroom go outside. I haven't smoked in months but right now I need a cigarette. I fumble around for one but can't find a lighter.

"Need a light?" I see Luis coming toward me.

"Luis! What are you doing here?"

"Vince asked me to come here and make sure you were okay." He takes a lighter and lights my cigarette as well as one for himself. I blow out a thick plume of smoke.

"Luis, he had been spying on me for years. I never thought that my work laptop would be his weapon…"

"He is a sick individual, Madeline. I've dealt with his type more times than I'd like to think about." I sigh.

"I'm ready for this to be over."

"Listen, Madeline. As a victim, there will always be that feeling of uncertainty, but you must move on with your life. You're getting married in a few months and you have so much to look forward to. Don't let this asshole ruin it."

"Has anyone ever told you how wise you are?" I smile at him.

"Eh, I hit one out of the park every once and awhile" he laughs. I put out my cigarette.

"Well, I'm going to go home. Thank you for looking out for me."

"No thanks necessary. Come. I'll walk you to your car." Once I get home, I notice that Vince is still out, probably working late. Hell, I need to do some work myself. I sit down on the couch with my laptop and my cell phone rings. I look at the caller ID and notice that it's Detective Sommers. I wonder what he wants. I answer the phone as I pet the big ball of fluff that has joined me on the couch.

"Hello?" I answer.

"Hey, Madeline, I was calling to check on you."

"I'm fine, Detective, although it was nice of you to check on me."

"Well, it's not just a curtesy call. I have something to tell you."

"I'm listening..."

"Joseph took a plea deal. Your testimony was damning and your reaction to the pictures made it worse. He knew he had no shot in hell."

"What's the deal?" I ask nervously.

"Fifteen years...I know it's not enough."

"Fifteen years..." I whisper. I'd have children by then, maybe I wouldn't even be living in Atlanta at that time.

"You will have a permanent protection order against him. If he comes near you or Lacy, his ass will have to go back to jail for an additional ten years."

"It's not a win, but I will take that over an acquittal."

"I will do everything in my power to make sure he's not paroled any earlier than that."

"I know you will, thank you Detective.

Vince comes through the door just as I hang up. Faith immediately jumps of the couch to greet him as he walks towards me.

"Hey babe..." He brands my forehead with a soft kiss.

"Hey..."

"How did it go?"

"He took a plea deal." Vince loosens his tie and sits next to me.

"Are you okay with that?" I shrug my shoulders.

"Vince, he had been spying on me for two years through my work laptop. How will I ever feel secure again?" Vince wraps his arms around me.

"Knowing that bastard is behind bars, and that I'll be here to protect you...as long as I live." He smiles at me.

"You promise?" I ask.

"Madeline...I love you more than anything. You're about to be my wife goddamnit. I would move the Earth for you."

"Oh yeah?" I chuckle.

"Yeah..." he whispers, kissing me softly.

"Baby, spending the rest of my life with you...growing a family with you...I couldn't ask for more. I can't wait to see what the future holds for us."

"I can't either Vince...I love you so much." He leans in close to me.

"Race you to the bedroom..." I raise my eyebrows at him as he gets up and makes a surprise dart around the other side of the couch. Faith yips excitedly, happy to see us involved in our little game. Once we reach the bedroom, he pulls me into his arms and picks me up, covering my mouth with his.

After a steamy session that leaves both of us wilted, I lean on my side and look at the beautiful specimen staring at me with a smile.

"Come here..." Vince pulls me on top of him and wraps his arms around me, stroking my back. I lay on his chest, finally feeling the effects from my lack of slumber. Vince's breathing becomes even and I follow his lead, closing my eyes and drifting into a deep sleep. Despite everything I've been through, it feels so good to be out of the mask, with no walls around me. It's not as much about having the love of my life as it is finding my true self, following my dreams, and achieving the ultimate measure of happiness. Once I discovered what kind of woman I truly am and what strength I had, it was so easy to love again, and for that I will always be grateful.

"Paris..." Watson looks at the lady donned in dark jeans and a black sweater.

"I'm ready, you stand back. You don't want anyone to recognize you" she says as she puts a mask on her face cursing Vincent Marks. She had been a hit woman for the rival family of the Luciano's, the Moretti's. It was such a rarity that she was almost undetectable when she did her work. As a gift, Papa Giuseppe Moretti blessed her with a job at his record company and told her she would no longer have to kill for money. She balked at the idea that she was doing this for a man who screwed her during a one night stand.

The two men, identified as John and Gio Luciano pay their tab at the raggedy pub and stagger out.

"Maybe we should call a cab..." John looks at his older brother.

"Bullshit, I ain't leaving my car here to get towed" Gio growls, clicking the remote to unlock the car. This is her chance.

"Well, let me smoke first, eh?" John says. Poor fool, he was handsome and seemed to be the more intelligent one. Paris couldn't imagine sharing a space with these two as Vince's fiancée had. That must have been torture.

Paris slips into the backseat with Rob, her accomplice. Taking a deep breath, she watches as the two men get into the car. As the doors close, she and Rob both throw rope around the men's necks. They both struggle wildly, their hands waving frantically.

"Shhh..." Paris whispers to John as he grows weaker. Both men finally become still and Paris uses two gloved fingers to check for a pulse. She nods to Rob indicating that he is dead. They make sure to take whatever evidence and exit the car, disappearing into the night.

"You okay?" Rob asks as they drive to the Hamptons. She nods.

"This is the last time I'm doing this shit."

"Why did you want to do it in the first place?" Paris looks over at him.

"You know, when I first met Vincent Marks, there was an emptiness in his eyes. He just...took me to the hotel and fucked me. No emotion, no passion."

"So? Not like you wanted him in that way...did you?"

"No, but usually I get men to show a little passion. That was scary. Then I remember seeing some pictures of him and his girl, Madeline." She laughs with remembrance.

"And?" Rob coaxes.

"I saw this light in his eyes...then I heard she'd been kidnapped and...I worried about him. I knew it would do him in. She was something he never had."

"I'm curious. How did he know to come to you?"

"He didn't. That bitch Dina stalked me the day after Vince and I had our little one night stand. I started doing research on her and found out she was associated with your dad's rival family." Rob smiles and looks over at her.

"You know Papa Moretti was more than willing to take care of those bastards."

"Yeah, but I didn't mind doing it one last time. You guys helped me get to where I was with the record company. I didn't want your name attached to this." Rob shrugs as her phone rings.

"The bodies have been dumped in the Hudson..."a voice says quickly before hanging up.

"It's finished..." she says as they approach the sprawling mansion.

"Come on, let's burn these clothes..." Rob hops out of the car.

After all of the evidence is destroyed, Paris nestles on a plush brown leather couch with a glass of wine and her phone. It's eleven, hopefully he isn't gone to bed yet.

"Hello..."A hoarse voice answers after she dials.

"It's done." The other end grows silent.

"I...didn't think you'd go through with it."

"Then you don't know me, Mr. Marks. Hopefully, once the news of their disappearance comes out, your lady can rest easy." He sighs.

"How will I ever repay you?" He asks quietly.

"This time only...it's on the house."

"No...I'd like to pay you. Let me at least send you on vacation or something." Paris laughs loudly.

"How about an invitation to your wedding and a first class flight to Atlanta then?" He chuckles softly.

"That I can do. I'll see you in June...Paris? Thank you."

"Only for you..."she hangs up with a smile and Rob comes into the living room to join her.

"Did you tell him?" She nods.

"How'd he take it?"

"He was shocked, but grateful." Rob takes her hand, pulling her to him.

"Well...now he's got his love, and I've got mine..."he whispers in a low voice, taking her mouth to his.

## Author's Note

*Madeline and Vince are not finished with their adventures as a couple. We know that with both of their brains, survival skills and business sense, they will endure more challenges as well as victories. I wrote this book as a response to heartbreak a few years ago, my first intention was to make up a fantasy man that I would never encounter, who would give me everything I ever wanted and more. However, as the pages grew, I fell in love with Madeline: a strong woman, who could stand alone. Her thought process became more intricate, her sensibility not swayed by a smooth talking handsome man with money. Yes, she loves Vince, but he had to prove himself to her. He had to suffer with his own growing pains, throwing away his careless dating habits. This story became a commentary on maturity when it comes to matters of the heart. Anyone can visualize a girl who stumbles into a rich man and lives out her dreams, but it takes more for an independent, intelligent woman to give herself to a man when fear of a broken heart has ruled her life. I hope that you have enjoyed this first installment in the 'Mask' series and will feel compelled to follow Vince and Madeline through their future endeavors.*

*Nicolette*

## Acknowledgements

When I first tested this novel on some of my friends, I reminded them that this may be my first novel but not my first story. I have been writing for a long time: it is my therapy and passion. I never thought I would ever make this story public, but I had many who encouraged me to try.

I am so incredibly grateful to my co-workers: Dawana and Yolanda. Both of them are amazing women in their own right and fell in love with the characters as much as I did.

I am also filled with gratitude for the brave male friends who were my test audience: Max, Uday, Oscar and Justin. You were all amazingly open to reading out of your comfort zone and gave me great suggestions moving forward.

To the other amazing women in my life Jamie, Christina and Tracy: you all may live far away, but always have a special place in my heart. Thank you for believing in this novel and me. An extra portion of gratitude goes out to my friend, Tracie, who read the draft and created a beautiful painting that is now my cover.

A special thanks goes out to my brother, "V". Without him, I would have never known what steps to take to get the process started.

I'd like to extend eternal hugs to my mother, Kathy: who passed on her love of reading to me and was my very first "book critic". Without her, my characters would have never seen any page of this book.

Last but not least, I'd like to thank my readers who took a chance on a new novelist. I hope that it was worth your time and that you enjoyed being in the world of Madeline Davis and Vincent Marks.

52965910R00187

Made in the USA
Lexington, KY
16 June 2016